SEA SMOKE

BY

BETTIE HAMILTON

ISBN: 1-4140-2384-7 (e-book)
ISBN: 1-4140-2383-9 (Paperback)

Library of Congress Control Number: 2003098503

This book is printed on acid free paper.

Printed in the United States of America
Bloomington, IN

1stBooks - rev. 11/21/03

Dedicated to Jack, the apple of my eye.

Psalm 17: 1-9

"Keep me as the apple of your eye;

hide me under the shadow of your wings."

For Lissi,
with best wishes,
♡ Bettis (Hamilton)

iv

CHAPTER 1.

Sea smoke was rising in vaporous clouds on Marblehead Harbor. This occurred rarely when the ocean temperature was warmer than the air. As a rule the Atlantic ocean was exhilaratingly icy cold. Great roiling, rolling strings and clouds of undulating steam danced across the heaving water in a beautiful ballet. One could almost envision Degas' ethereal ballerinas.

Enthralled, Leanora Lantana watched for an hour from her studio on the harbor first sticking her paint brushes in an old coffee tin of turpentine. Out front the incoming tide sucked sibilantly against the rocks which resembled enormous chunks of marble, thus the fishing town's name, originally called Marble Harbor later Marblehead.

Seagulls; the common gray, brownish spotted yearlings, and Great Northern black backs swooped past the window, sailing and soaring high on a Northeast tail wind. A lobster boat sputtered down harbor with a full contingent of gulls following as the lobster man jettisoned old bait.

1

Lea read the name "Dolly's Sugar Daddy" on the rusty side of the less than pristine once white lobster boat. Another, "The Happy Hooker" followed. Boats like race horses were given strange and provocative names. She laughed aloud speculating whether Dolly's Daddy had much sugar to give her? Lea was aware few fishermen earned a great deal in Marblehead, Massachusetts, this three hundred fifty year old town on the North Shore about eighteen miles from Boston and halfway to Gloucester. Wryly she reflected many local painters rarely did, as well. Artists and photographers were attracted by the rocky coastline, a plethora of sail and lobster boats and the crooked, narrow streets that once were cow paths.

At one time she'd precariously climbed a ladder and painted a sign for the local Elks Club. She needed the money for art supplies and she still considered it "painting".

Framing and art supply stores were where the profit really existed but for bone deep fishermen and painters the bottom line remained firmly fixed; it was process not product that mattered. It was time to pack it in and quit in either profession if one did not passionately, even maniacally, love what one did for its own sake. Not that either calling was at all averse to being paid well for their efforts, indeed both lusted after seed money in order to continue to do what they liked best.

In good or bad weather or good or bad times both felt compelled to pursue their work from an inner conviction that for them this was the only way to live. Many 'headers however would purchase fish and lobster long before dreaming of purchasing a painting which was looked upon as an unnecessary luxury. Yet the public did turn out in goodly numbers when an art auction was held for a charity benefit or scholarship. The hope was to bid as low as possible and acquire a bargain; a piece of art done by a local artist whom they thought charged too much anyway. Some often derisively laughed, "My five year old could do better."

Artists were solicited to give their work free and of course nicely framed in return for their five minutes of publicity and be gratified to contribute to a worthy cause. Most were pleased to donate money instead of an expensive piece of art; as a group they were mostly generous, sensitive and caring. A few cynically remarked, "Why will anyone buy the cow if the milk is free?" and refused to give their work away but often gave money to the cause.

While Lea mused on the parallels between her late fisherman father and her own vocation a loud explosion came from the dirt cellar, a clattering, crashing noise. Alarmed, she raced barefoot to the door to the cellar in the kitchen, opened it and flew down the rickety wooden steps with the yellow Lab, Lucy at her heels. Lea was always a little fearful some of the paints and solvents stored in the cellar might implode. This was a worry to all painters and printmakers most of whom were extremely careful. She looked around and all appeared in order other than some debris around a tipped over rubbish barrel of oily rags she'd planned to burn that day. Since she could see no obvious damage she placed the barrel upright again and turned around to collect the rags. She heard a spitting, snarling sound. Under the bottom step fierce, malevolent eyes were glaring at her. A large raccoon had somehow dug his way into the dirt cellar and tipped the barrel over rummaging for food.

Lea and Lucy fled up the stairs with the coon spitting at their heels. With her heart pounding and breathing hard, she bolted the door. Lucy, a card carrying pacifist and tremendous coward felt safe now and self-righteously barked vociferously at the door.

Some raccoons were found to be rabid and were becoming bolder and seemingly fearless of humans as they tripled and quadrupled in numbers. They'd been driven from what little wooded land there was left when developments had mushroomed. A few naive friends of animals actually (Lea thought stupidly) put food out for them because the masked babies were so "cute" thus helping to insure the out-of-bounds population explosion that had hit Marblehead and many suburban towns on the East coast.

Some home owners trapped the raccoons in a Have-A-Heart trap baited with moldy vegetables or peanut butter only to release them illegally in the twenty-five acres of conservation land adjoining an estuary of brackish water (Forest River) between Marblehead and Salem. One man was reported and fined for inhumanely trying to drown one, trap and all, in the ocean off Devereux Beach.

The slightly insane, ecological logic which forbade destroying the animals, advocating their removal to some other area solved nothing. Protected, the coons flourished. They were spotted swimming at night in back yard swimming pools and in broad daylight marching down the center of the streets; a surreal, masked raccoon parade.

When Lea found one in her trap, with little remorse or compunction she asked her current friend, Tony, to shoot it. Although illegal, it was a quick and merciful death. Many were destined to starve as they outgrew the food supply. Tony Amberetti seemed to enjoy offing them a bit more than Lea felt he should but since she enjoyed partaking of his many delightful other attributes she said nothing. She was much enamored of his sea color, blue-green eyes, blond hair and cleft chin. Lea had a strong desire to paint his portrait (he was beautiful, she thought) but he kept refusing to permit her to do so.

"Never, Cara Lea, do I wish my puss hanging in any la-di-dah gallery exhibit!"

He seemed rather scornful of the local art scene and its devotees yet he possessed an excellent eye for color, form and design. Tony enthusiastically praised Lea's work saying.

"Why you don't always win every ribbon in those effing shows you enter is a shit-faced mystery."

Stubbornly Lea continued to enter art exhibits all over New England and each year she mounted a one-woman show. Antonio was a skilled framer and cheerful transporter of heavy pictures as well as her handy, willing raccoon assassin. This kept Lea from asking the many questions from the secret reservations she harbored.

Lea's meager income was augmented by teaching painting in the Art association at King Hooper Mansion on Hooper street and in watercolor workshops.

Where had he come from? What was his background? Who was Antonio Amberetti (if that were his real name?) Was it a put on, a send up? Tony had floated into her life like a stormy petrel one Spring day when she was painting outdoors at Fort Sewall. Instantly attracted they became friends and in time, lovers. Her friend, Sarah, thought they looked remarkably alike with an abundance of strawberry blonde curly hair on Lea's part and ash blonde on his. Lea had yet to notice this as his eyes were fascinatingly like the color of the ocean she loved and she thought her own a mundane, pedestrian green.

Tony worked off and on as a carpenter for a boat builder in town yet he always had sufficient ready cash to take Lea out for dinner at Maddie's Sail Loft (she adored their fried shrimp), the Landing Pub on the wharf or the Barnacle on Front Street near the Fort. Occasionally he took her to opera, concerts and plays in Boston. Tony drove his second-hand red Volkswagen beetle to Boston, as old as it was he loved it.

They dined at Anthony's Pier Four on the Boston waterfront. Michael, the proprietor, was a friend of Lea's. He was impressed with Tony's savoir faire which struck him as an anomaly for a boat builder. Michael was curious how Lea had met him but politely didn't ask. Obviously Tony was knowledgeable, conversant and fond of the arts. St. Lucia, Tony's shy, oversized and loving yellow Labrador Retriever he'd found at the local pound adored Lea and spent many ecstatic hours peacefully dozing in her studio when Tony was at the boat yard. This was a happy excuse for Lea to talk out loud when working alone.

"Lucy, do you think Winsor yellow or Gamboge for this passage?"

When spoken to Lucy always thumped her tail in the affirmative.

"Dammit, Loos, this is a bomb, I hate it!" Agreeably saint-like Lucy wagged her tail, "yes, no, whatever you say." She was the perfect critic.

At this moment volatile Lea was annoyed both by Tony's absence and the raccoon's unwelcome invasion. In the same irrational way she felt annoyed when her nickname for Leanora was pronounced Leah instead of Lee, she was irritated now.

"Where the hell is Tony when I need him?" Early that morning he'd left saying only, "Arriverdici, lovely Leanora, watch St Lucia for me? See you in a couple days."

He kissed her and was off in his dilapidated red bug roaring and smoking down Front Street.

Lea had no right nor desire to question his actions or how or where he spent his time. By unspoken mutual agreement he had not moved in with her and kept his own small apartment in the shipyard section of town. In truth she preferred her own space and carefully avoided urging Tony to share her home. This arrangement worked well for two stubborn, independent people. When they occasionally quarreled Tony would stomp off, eyes blazing like St. Elmo's fire, to sulk and bang things around in his own small flat. Most of the time Lea reveled in her solitude after an early disastrous marriage in her teens to a machismo, controlling and insensitive boy. She could paint when and what she wished without his jealous yelling, "Give up that arty stuff, you stink! Have some

7

babies, do some cooking and cleaning as you're supposed to, like Ma does, this place is filthy."

Lea retorted, "I know I'm not the greatest housekeeper, Ray, but this place is never filthy and I'm a pretty good cook." She hated living free in his nosy, patronizing parents' apartment in their basement. Ray desultorily worked for the town. His father had advised him to take it because it offered a low salary but a good pension. Ray had started college on an athletic scholarship when Lea became pregnant and he quit school, resenting her for it. His grades were poor and he probably wouldn't have been able to continue anyway. They married, both still in their teens.

The distance of even a few miles from Ray Larson and his family solaced and nurtured Lea's soul and spirit. She avoided the Larson tribe. They were hardly art aficionados and rarely did she run into them. If she saw any Larson shopping at Crosby's Market she was usually able to duck behind a tower of canned goods or display of vegetables and make a hasty exit. These days apparently Ray was also busy siring several year apart children with his much younger, timid and passive wife, Claire. Their paths seldom crossed. Lea fervently prayed it would remain that way. Small towns had rather strait jacket circles moving parallel in different interests and not often overlapping.

Their youthful marriage had grown out of a torrid high school romance. Lea and Ray had little in common other than the raging hormones of teenagers which resulted in an unsought pregnancy and produced their daughter, Nora, the apple of Lea's eye, who was now living in Sydney, Australia with a handsome Aborigine.

Lea called the police and the Animal Control Officer and waited impatiently for either or both to arrive and help. She hoped for the blessed woman in charge of animal control who sternly fined all dog owners who left dog poop in the parks or streets.

Wincing, she could hear the probably rabid raccoon trashing her cellar and Lucy barking her yellow head off at the bolted door in the kitchen. Lea desperately needed someone to allay the racket and destruction which now sounded as though all her extra supplies and boxes of difficult to find and expensive Fabriano water color paper, hand made in Italy, were being knocked viciously off the shelves.

She glanced out the window for distraction and to see any remnants of sea smoke. Surf and white caps were stronger now, the ocean had returned to its usual colder than air temperature of the Atlantic. Looking out, she suddenly saw a figure clinging to her rocks and staring in at her. He or she wore a hooded sweatshirt and she couldn't make out the face. Startled and more than a little spooked Lea quickly pulled her inside Indian shutters closed and latched them. She was now completely in the dark, the coon running noisily amok beneath her and Lucy barking in a furious uproar periodically jumping and hurling herself at the cellar door.

"Oh, please God, don't let Lucy break through!"

As Tony would have put it, Lea was really pissed off by the stranger. She muttered, "Who is that

9

weirdo, why is he or she climbing on my rocks to look into my studio?" She was indignant as well as uneasily disturbed by the peeping Tom but her other uninvited guest had to be dealt with first. In the dark and unable to concentrate to work anyway, she went into her galley kitchen, she'd painted a raspberry which usually cheered her up, and made a cup of coffee. She waited stoically for help and tried to stop Lucy's barking, growling and attacks on the cellar door.

Finally, a young policeman arrived simultaneously with the Animal Control woman. Together they expertly entrapped and removed the animal to the police car cage while Lucy, snarling bravely, kept a safe distance. Lea did not ask or care what they would do with it, she vehemently hated it.

She opened her blinds to let in some light. The policeman curiously examined the large partially done abstract oil on her easel. Politely he asked, "What's that all about?"

Like most people he was suspicious of abstract painting and couldn't relate to it.

Just as politely (after all he had come to her rescue) Lea responded.

"It's about a mythical country I invented, named Zulazandia," (mischievously she added) "It's run by women, each has two men, one for work and one for making love."

He blushed and blinked and then grinned. "If you say so, Lady."

At least Lea thought, he hadn't said, "I don't know much about art but I know what I like," All

10

artists had heard this refrain ad infinitum and ad nauseam.

To him it was obvious she was one of those freaky, freakin' art nuts, his town had too many to suit him. He and the business-like Control officer left with their prey to Lea's enormous relief. She had forgotten to point out to the young officer, the sinister seeming stranger on her terrace. Shrugging, she decided it probably was nothing of importance, most likely just another nosy tourist and in any case the rocks were empty now.

Once again there was a knock on the door. Nervously Lea kept the chain fastened and Lucy by her side and cautiously peered out. A young woman with stringy unwashed hair and a colorful black eye stood there. Four small children were clinging to her sweater and an infant was on her hip.

"I'm Claire Larson, Ray's wife." She announced with tears in her eyes. Tremulously she quavered, "I came to ask you if Ray ever hit you, too? I want to leave him, he beats on me and the kids when he's drunk. I don't know what to do."

She began to sob as though her heart would break, Lea saw with a great stab of empathy and pity.

"I need someone to help me and back me up. Ray says if I try to leave he'll kill me and keep the kids. His mother says I'm a slut and she can prove I am an unfit mother and Ray will get the children." She sobbed louder, "I can't leave my babies with them, he'll hurt them. What shall I do? Will you help me, could we stay with you? I took all the abuse and beatings but now he's hitting on the little kids, too. He's mean, I think he's crazy. He used to just slap me

11

a little, now he punches me so hard. It hurts so bad, I'm afraid of him." She wailed and wept.

Cannily she added, "You should be, too. He hates you! When he's drunk he yells, "I hate artsy-fartsy Leanora, I'm going to fix her wagon!"

The only good thing Lea had ever received from Ray was their beautiful and talented daughter, Nora, who was now twenty-three. She breathed a prayer of thanks that Nora was out of his grasp living in Australia. Lea had walked out with Nora leaving Ray forever the day she got out of Salem Hospital after the baby's birth. Nora was just a few days old when she took a taxi to Siri, Lea's mother's house.

She opened the door wider and drew Claire and brood into the one large room that served as studio, dining and living room. At one end a spiral ladder led to the loft bedroom she'd painted an eggplant purple. There was a small window on the ocean side and a large skylight. Kitchen and bathroom adjoining the living room were partitioned off by oiled and waxed teak panels she'd acquired from a boatyard in exchange for a large painting of it. The bathroom was painted a Derby gold (like the hall of the Derby house in Salem) and held a small sink, toilet and shower; no room for a bath tub.

Lea had redone her Dad's old fishing shack into a studio on a shoestring using a lot of paint.

The main "keeping" room had teak walls which were covered from ceiling to floor with her vivid, colorful paintings. A large rough hewn beam ran across the wooden ceiling painted a creamy white. She'd kept his pot bellied stove for her source of heat. The old shack had been converted into an all purpose, live-in studio. Lea loved it. Her private "Fiord" in America. She named it "The Fisherman's Fiord" after Einar, her father.

She seated Claire and the children at the old, enormous, scarred pine table and poured Claire coffee. She gave the children orange juice and graham crackers.

"Claire," she began somberly, "You have to understand I can't get involved with Ray, I must protect my child, Nora. I'm sorry. If you stayed here Ray would soon find you. But I will give you the name and telephone number of a fine lawyer, my close friend, Sarah Gross, who handled my divorce. This is the most I can do, Claire. Sarah can really help you, she did me, trust her and do what she says."

Looking disappointed Claire left in a little clutching tightly the paper with Sarah's telephone number at the Salem office of Queen, Pedersen and Gross. Lea immediately went to her phone to call Sarah, explain the situation and beg her to help poor Claire as she had once helped Lea. Ray was poison for every woman who fell for him, Lea was convinced. She shuddered. She was overwhelmingly grateful she'd gotten away from under his spell. It had been hard raising Nora alone (and being pretty much as celibate as a nun) but it was worth the freedom and the joy she received from painting and seeing Nora successfully through college. Best of all Nora was a happy, productive girl without any neuroses she might have had if Ray had been in her life. He made a lousy father as well as husband, Lea thought, *Poor Claire, I hope Sarah can help set her and the children free.*

CHAPTER 2.

Tony had caught a shuttle from Logan Airport in Boston. He was now entering the elegantly furnished office of his lawyer, John Randall on Park Avenue in New York City. The lawyer stood up from his hand tooled leather desk chair to shake hands. Strains of Vivaldi's "Four Seasons", playing softly in the background added to the ambience of rare paintings and sculpture everywhere in the room.

"Tony! Greetings, man, aren't you a little late?"

"A bit, I'm sorry. I stopped first at the Guggenheim to catch the Leonard Bacon retrospective show on my way here. I'm afraid I got so mesmerized by the lumps and bumps of tortured flesh I stayed longer than I intended to."

"How did you like it, what did you think of it?"

"Sad, for the most part. Bacon was a fine painter, there are many virtuoso passages. His agony or pride in his homosexuality seemed to take over the work until that is all you see instead or before you can appreciate the marvelous sensuous color and forms of the intertwined figures."

"You enjoyed it, then?"

"No, I appreciated it. Sometimes joy has little to do with good painting. My taste is catholic and I suppose eclectic."

"I see. Well, are you enjoying your sabbatical off in the boondocks of that fishing town you said you were living in? What's its name again?"

Tony inwardly smiled and did not offer the name. He thought if John could see the posh estates on Marblehead Neck and Peach's Point and all the yachts, ketches, yawls, sloops, motor and sail boats not to mention the $400,000 picnic boats celebrities loved moored in the harbor, he would change his patronizing tone and move there post-haste, at least for the summer. John was a total snob.

"Yes," he replied quietly, "I really am."

Fishing for more information John asked, "Ah! Then you must have met a beautiful native?" He was consumed with curiosity.

Tony merely smiled again, thinking with amusement, "Lea is not only a lovely looking 'native' but she is interesting, talented and warm as well."

At Tony's lack of response and failure to enlarge further John said, "More power to you, Big Guy! Let's get down to work. How much more money do you wish deposited in the Cayman Island bank? Have you found those elusive Sicilian cousins you've been hunting? Isn't it unlikely they would settle in a small, out-of-the-way village in Massachusetts?" He laughed, "More likely they've sold the marble and gone off to Capri or Iberia to enjoy the profits. Mafiosa are said to love those places."

"Not to worry, John. I'll find them sooner or later." Tony frowned darkly. "When I do, I'll retrieve my grandmother's statue they stole from me and see them in prison. It's an original Bellini and I want it back."

His Italian temper flaring, he pounded his fist on John's desk. "I want all the money you can bank out of their reach, too."

In a calmer tone he asked, "Where are the reports from the private detective you hired for me, Donald Bell?"

"It's odd, there's been nothing lately on fax, e-mail or by courier. Bell's almost dropped out of sight. The last I heard he had flown from either Rome or Heathrow to Boston, why, I don't know. He sent a note he'd attended the opera at La Scala in Milan as you urged him to do through me. He said to tell you it was super boring and although he speaks Italian he said he could not follow the screaming arias, in short he loathed it."

"That figures," Tony laughed, "Just where is this Bell?"

"I guess we'll just have to wait for him to surface, he will soon for money. Has he contacted you at all? I told him you didn't wish to see him personally and would contact him through me. Of course, he could have left Boston by now."

"Give him another week. Then if you don't hear from Bell put another private investigator on the case and when you do hear from Bell, fire him. Try to choose someone a little more civilized this time."

Now John was amused, "The nature of the beast in that profession is rarely an artistic taste. That's definitely not part of the job description. However, I want to warn you, Tony, no matter how large your fee I won't tolerate any blood shed or the statue stolen back for you." He said this piously. "When the marble is found we'll sue legitimately in court for its return to you, the rightful owner. Understood?"

"Understand, John." Tony's fingers were crossed in his tweed jacket pocket. He stuck out his tongue. "See? Not a lie on it and my nose hasn't grown an inch, either."

"Okay, I have to trust you, I guess." John frowned.

"And I, you?" Tony said softly, wondering if he could or should. He'd had an instinctive feeling of distrust for the lawyer from the beginning.

"How about lunch, Tony? If you care to we can go to MOMA, there's a Matisse exhibit showing."

Smiling back at John, Tony gracefully refused not really wanting Randall's company or listening to his fatuous comments on art which in truth he knew little about.

"I'd love to but I have a plane to catch in less than an hour from Newark on Continental. First, give me another look at Bell's picture and I.D.?"

He examined the papers carefully noting a scar on Bell's right cheek, otherwise he was a handsome man. They again shook hands and Tony left to hail a taxi out front for the airport. He got the last seat on the shuttle from Newark to Logan where he picked up his car to drive to Marblehead. He drove through East

Boston, past the Don Orione shrine, Chelsea, Revere, Lynn and Swampscott along the shore road. He thought of stopping in Lynn at the Porthole Pub for lunch but decided to hurry back to Lea and Lucy.

At his tiny apartment Tony changed from his New York clothes to blue jeans and an old sweater. He went to Lea's studio. He found her door locked, unusual for her, and a note on the door which read "Gone for groceries and to the bank with Lucy. Have a lot to tell you, Tony my boy!"

He wallked to the Driftwood Diner on State Street Wharf for a fish chowder lunch. It was only served on Fridays and Tony liked it a lot. It was filled with large pieces of haddock, onion, potatoes in an unthickened thin milk broth. He preferred his own Mediterranean fish chowder with tomatoes but he had admitted to Lea this New England style was also delicioso when cooked right and not thick and paste-like.

Downtown with Lucy by her side Lea had popped into the Eastern Bank where dog biscuits were given out to the client's pets. Lucy was not only familiar with this routine but quite smitten. A line of people was in front of the teller's window. Quietly Lucy took her place at the end of the line and waited patiently for her turn. With no bank business to transact today other than dog biscuits, Lea stood by the door. Raising his eyebrows the next man who entered politely got in line behind Lucy. Lea dearly loved his reaction. When it was Lucy's turn at the window, the young buxom teller, Deirdre, with great abandon tossed cookie after cookie to Lucy who leaped to catch them in her mouth while the customers applauded, transfixed.

Finally Lea signaled, "It's time to go, say thank you, Loos." The dog wagged her tail. Nonchalantly they walked decorously out of the bank to more applause. Next Lea tied Lucy up outside Crosby's market as they were not eager fans of dogs inside near all the mounds of open bins of fruits and vegetables.

Lea shopped for a special meal for Tony hoping he would be back by dinner time. She loved to cook and Tony was impressed by her culinary ability as creative as her painting. He also liked to cook, another thing they had in common. Lea decided on stuffing the gorgeous big red, green and yellow fresh peppers, it would go for two meals. She bought the top grade chopped sirloin, fresh garlic cloves, a Bermuda onion, a package of croutons and some pine nuts. Mixed together with parsley, oregano and an egg, salt and pepper; this would be the stuffing for the parboiled peppers she would bake in her homemade tomato sauce. She bought brown rice and Parmesan cheese.

An unassuming even simple meal yet a favorite of Tony's. In Italy he'd had peppers prepared many ways but none like Lea's. She added some fresh mushrooms for the tomato sauce and a bottle of red wine, Merlot, to complement the dish. Outside again, she untied Lucy who was looking mournful and abandoned. She greeted Lea with a leap of joy. Together they walked home to the studio past the boatyards on Front Street. Lea and Lucy were bosom buddies, happy to be together.

CHAPTER 3.

Antonio Amberetti-Scola had spent his first twelve years in Manchester-by-the-sea on the North Shore. His father the seventh Antonio, (Tony the eighth) had been sent from Rome to the National Gallery in Washington, D.C. as a curator consultant of Italian Art and Antiquities. Later he was offered a position at the Museum of Fine Arts in Boston as an expert on Roman religious artifacts. There he met Tony's mother, Elizabeth Hawthorne, an archivist in the museum library and fell inextricably in love with the gentle, beautiful girl. He accepted the post in order to stay near her and except for visits he never returned to Italy.

Elizabeth was an only child. Her father, Stephen Andrew Hawthorne died when she was small. Anna Elizabeth, her mother, was in frail health and had been an invalid for some years. She could not accept her daughter leaving her to live in Europe so when they married they moved into "Sunny Top", the Hawthorne family estate in Manchester-by-the-Sea. There Tony was born and until he was twelve lived quite happily. It was a tragedy both his parents were killed in a horrendous automobile accident returning on Route I-95 from a consultation at the Portland Museum in Maine. Anna was devastated by her beloved daughter's death and became increasingly incompetent and withdrawn. She died a year after her daughter, Elizabeth.

At the time of his parent's untimely death, Nonna, Angela Amberetti-Scola, his other grandmother, asked Anna Ellizabeth to send Tony to live with her in Rome and on her summer estate in Lake Como. Now widowed, she was lonely. Reluctantly, grandmother Hawthorne who also loved young Tony agreed Tony should go to her to live. She knew she was not able to raise him adequately and that the servants were mostly caring for him. Anna was wasting away and felt she was dying.

Starved for affection Tony immediately adored Nonna. He worshiped her. Once again he had someone who lavished love and attention on him as his mother had done all his twelve years and grandmother Hawthorne had become too ill and weak to do.

For several years when they went to Lake Como in the summertime Nonna imported his father's sister's sons, his cousins, to be his companions for horse back riding, sailing, swimming and playing. His aunts, Isabella, Gina and Sophia had married beneath them (Angela thought) to Sicilians whom she did not like or approve of. Her daughters liked their summers free for their own amusement; gossip and shopping, and were hopeful of currying favor with Angela. They sent Roberto, Georgio and Andreas to be Tony's friends and playmates.

Naively, Tony liked them at first. His cousins were 15, 13 and 11. Soon they became rough and bullying, envious of his status with Nonna, when out of her sight. Loyally and stoically Tony never told on them. The oldest, Roberto, was the ringleader.

Georgio followed him and Andreas, the youngest and weakest obeyed his cousins as he feared their cruel retaliations.

One night they locked Tony in an old abandoned boat house. Andreas cried nervously as Roberto and Georgio tied Tony tightly but went along with the plan, afraid not to. They hoped their favored cousin would never be discovered and would starve to death. Each summer as their jealousy grew their bullying had increased. It became almost unbearable and now had reached a crescendo as in the most passionate of Italian operas.

Nonna was frantic at Tony's disappearance and directed the servants to search every inch of the large wooded estate on the lake and all the outbuildings. Searching vigilantly at last Vito, the elderly gardener, found Tony in the old boat house tied up and weeping tears of despair. Each cousin vehemently denied having anything to do with this and blamed each other while protesting their innocence.

Nonna was infuriated and enraged and forbade these grandsons to ever return to Lake Como. Family meant a great deal to her but she held an Italian sense of justice. Now the boys' mothers were hysterical and angry and Tony was marked for retaliation for usurping their spoiled sons with Nonna. Vito went to his church and made a novena of thanksgiving for the cousins banishment. He believed them to be evil, "bad seeds" with the devil in them. Vito also detested Sicilians except for Nonna's cook, Fat Maria, whom he much admired. He liked large and voluptuous women and she was a good cook, too.

Nonna was tiny and elegant, her once blonde hair now platinum. She was bejeweled at ears, throat, bodice, fingers and wrists with priceless gems. Tony thought she looked like a senior Madonna and would have given his life for her. By the time of her death at ninety-two, her lands, vineyards and estates had dwindled and deteriorated. Her daughters' husbands had borrowed heavily against these leaving them to crumble and much of Angela's fortune disappear. They assured the lenders under oath that eventually they would inherit all the remaining assets. Nonna confided in Tony that she'd permitted them to borrow from her as well.

"They are still my girls and dear to me although they married louzisimo men!"

She thought she was using American slang that Tony would know. "It is not my daughters fault. They are stupido. My favorite, your father, got all the brains. You, Antonio are to have the most precious inheritance of all, the Bellini St. Theresa because I love you and you are intelligent, learned and educated like your father. You will always get along in the world but this will be your nest egg if you run into hard times."

He could not bear to tell Nonna the full extent of the perfidy of his aunts' "louzy" men, the cheating, selling off tracts of vineyards and outdoor sculpture from the Rome villa and Lake Como estate. They were able to hide this from Angela because in her later years she rarely walked very far and did not see well thus she did not notice the missing artifacts. Tony worked hard to transfer her assets to the United States and establish a separate bank account for her his Aunts could not touch. He was a curator at the Tate Gallery in London. Nonna had seen to it he had a fine education, majoring in Art History at Eton and Oxford to follow in his father's footsteps.

Tony had consulted and met with many lenders and bankers in an attempt to straighten out and salvage her fast dwindling income. "I vow they are not going to rob her of any more!"

He wanted help from professionals to stop the thieving; many of these turned out to be relatives of the Sicilian uncles or had a connection to them. It Italy the "family" was often intertwined, bribes, advantages, a fierce and perverted kind of loyalty influenced the lawyers and bankers he'd contacted. Because he had been born in the United States he was not true "Italiano" and was looked upon with suspicion.

Nonna's once grand, extensive properties were heavily mortgaged. Tony was bitter toward his Italian relatives but he didn't wish to further sadden or burden his beloved Nonna with the details of her daughters' and their husbands' betrayal. He knew this would completely break her heart as losing his father had years ago. Tony's presence these past years had partially made up for her son's death.

Bellini's marble study for his large statue of St. Theresa was kept in a triple locked glass case in the villa in Rome where the family gathered after Angela's death for the reading of the will. Since Tony was the last of the male Ambertti-Scola line she left the nine inch statue to him, worth millions. It had been in the family for centuries, a gift to an early bride. It was a study for the large St. Theresa Gian Bellini sculpted for the Carmelite church of St. Maria della Vittoria in Rome in 1658 and with a fountain he designed and to which he may have added turtles, Bellini restored Rome's beauty. It was thought the original design by Giacomo della Porta called for dolphins to match the base.

Four young boy dancers stand on dolphins, each lifting a turtle into the vase of the fountain. There are local legends that claim Bellini was the original designer but curators attribute it to Giacomo and the later restoration to Bellini.

This fountain is in the heart of the city and considered the most beautiful fountain of many in Rome. The "Turtle Fountain" was described by the famous Italian poet, D'Annunzio, as "serenity with a voice of rock and words of quietness like a magic fountain of the days of chivalry." Bellini's marble statue of St. Theresa in the Carmelite church in Rome was an acclaimed and moving example of his genius.

On Tony's last visit from London to Nonna before she died she told him.

"Tonio, my prayer and wish for you is someday to have a son to carry on your father and grandfather's name and heritage. My husband was a gentil homme, an aristocrat but blood lines weaken over centuries and need an infusion of strong, even peasant blood every hundred years! Perhaps you should marry a Nordic woman who could add the genetic Viking energy to our blood? We need this to survive and continue on proudly. This kind of union is necessary for you and a sacred trust."

Although rapidly tiring, Nonna continued to speak. "It was good you had an American Yankee mother. Much of Europe is decadent. You are doubly endowed. I approved of your father's marriage to the gentle Elizabeth. I saw her several times. Your father was my adored son and my only son. Your father's sisters were indignant and angry influenced by the greedy paisanos they married. Most Italian women follow their husbands in every opinion. Your aunts said when your father married your mother.

"We are Italian forever and American, never!"

"You have been good to me, Antonio and I love you with all my heart. These past years with you have been a little heaven for me." She kissed him on both cheeks. "I pray you will soon marry and have a son, the ninth Antonio Ambertti-Scola!"

A solemn, high funeral mass was celebrated. All Nonna's faithful servants attended along with family and friends. She had made loyal friends of her servants who wept copiously beside her casket crossing themselves. She had remembered each one in her will. A few days letter the will was read by her lawyer and executor of her estate. The cousins were visibly incensed when they learned Tony had been left the Bellini. His aunts screamed and shouted this was unfair and even spit at him. The next day when the lawyer accompanied Tony to retrieve the statue they found the case smashed open, fragments of glass all over the parquet tiled floor and the Bellini missing.

Long ago Nonna had given Tony the keys to each of the triple locked cases within a case.

When the theft was reported in the press all of Italy was indignant and outraged calling the Bellini statue a national treasure. The finger of suspicion was soon pointed at the American grandson even though it had been willed to him. The public either did not know this nor believe it. Tony felt certain it had been stolen by one or all three of his cousins. Standing by Angela's grave he vowed to find, punish and send them all to prison.

If they were acting as a team he surmised they would eventually fall out amongst themselves as thieves so often did and would be easier to track down. They were elusive and leads and tips on their whereabouts yielded little.

Tony remarked to Nonna's Roman lawyer, "My gut feeling is that somehow through their shady underworld connections, they plan to either ransom off the statue to the Vatican or museum or an unscrupulous private dealer for thousands possibly millions of lira."

The lawyer was shocked. "Members of her family would do such a reprehensible hing? If you retrieve it what are your plans for the marble?" He looked suspiciously at Tony with a sidelong glance.

"I'm not certain. For centuries it has been loved and revered and kept in our family. I could donate it to a museum or to the Roman Catholic Church or perhaps place it in the church that holds the large statue of St. Theresa. I don't know right now. But," his temper flared, "I am determined my cousins will neither own nor profit from it.!"

27

Tony decided to take a leave of absence from his position at the Tate in London and travel to the United States. He expected to find and hire more experienced lawyers and detectives than he had been able to it Italy.

He told Nonna at another graveside visit before he left, "You will always be in my heart, Nonna, I'm not leaving you. I want to stay out of reach of the cousins and undercover until I apprehend them. I'm going back temporarily to a small, seacoast town a few miles from where I was born. The cousins were never interested in my first twelve years and they know nothing about Massachusetts or much about the States, either. I doubt they could find me in Marblehead or have even heard of Massachusetts. I love you, Nonna."

Tony rented a small flat in Marblehead and signed on with a local boat builder as a carpenter. During summer vacations at Lake Como he had apprenticed to a boat builder which had amused his Italian relatives. It was beneath his cousins to work at anything.

One could not drive through the peninsula of Marblehead which stuck out into the ocean. Tony was careful not to overtly spend a lot of money on clothing, housing or an expensive car. He bought a second hand Volkswagen beetle. Lea was concerned he was spending too much of his small salary taking her out frequently to dinner and the theater. Because of his inheritance from his parents and both grandmothers there were more than sufficient funds to institute a search.

Tony adopted what he naively thought was a down-to-earth working man's vocabulary which struck a false note with Lea. It never occurred to him that his tastes were still rather aristocratic and not those of most working men.

In New York he hired his grandmother's stateside lawyer, John Randall, to find a reputable private investigator to track down his thieving cousins. He periodically made secret trips to the city to check on the P.I.'s progress, trips he never explained to Lea.

In a short time Andreas surfaced in Italy. Always somewhat unbalanced and full of envy and resentment he was now the darling of the paparazzi giving hysterical interviews to the press. He accused his American cousin, Antonio Scola, of stealing his and all of Italy's inheritance. Emotions were whipped up to a national frenzy. Politicians and some members of the Vatican hierarchy became involved demanding Italy cut off all imports from the United States as well as their own exports. This wild idea did not fly since they exported many plaster statues, rosary beads and other religious artifacts that were profitable.

When the climate cooled down and interest waned Andreas would once again rant and rave to further inflame a nationalistic fervor. He basked in the limelight. Andreas saw himself as a noble, charismatic orator and leader. Never had he even approached such a status when cowed and dominated by Georgio and Roberto. He was giddy with self-aggrandizement and drooling with delight. He wanted badly to get even with and outshine all his cousins. Andreas made at least a hundred inflammatory speeches to the public through the press who exploited him for his sensational value.

Roberto and Georgio were less volatile, shrewder and cannier and remained hidden. Doubtless they were protected by the network of Sicilian relatives where everyone was either a fifth cousin or in some way related. Bribes were prevalent and a useful tool to employ to help their continued silence and non-appearance. Widespread corruption as well as cruel retaliations for betrayal made them feel safe from discovery. They also had the power to put punishments into effect.

Tony said to John Randall, "They might still be together? I think each will sit it out patiently biding his time until one or all can in the future realize an enormous fortune.

Ambition, greed and expediency has always motivated them all."

"Andreas, too?"

"Andreas was a fragile, unstable child always whining and rather scorned by his older cousins. He's more greedy for recognition and fame than wealth. In his teen years, even though he could not sing a note or carry a tune, Andreas tried his luck as a rock star. He was booed, hissed and laughed off the stage which was accompanied by many rude gestures. Poor Andreas wept bitterly over it and always resented the humiliation."

He continued. "You know? Italian audiences are rarely shy of voicing either approval or disapproval at public events such as concerts, theater, prize fights or political speeches. In Milan at the opera at La Scala the noise from bravos or boos is extremely loud."

The vast majority of Italians, Sicilians in particular, were sincerely family oriented. They were hard working and deeply religious people. The minority embraced at the core a more primitive and darker side. This spread a pervasive giant spider web throughout the country which was difficult and almost impossible to circumvent. Because Tony recognized these facts to be true he felt he had a better chance to outwit his Italian cousins by utilizing the American side of his heritage, personality and psyche by basing himself in the United States.

John Randall had hired P. I. Donald Bell for Tony. Bell was a former FBI agent who hinted he had worked as a mole and double agent in Russia. He proclaimed his expertise lay in finding wanted criminals and felons. "Search and Find." Tony preferred not to meet him personally, he thought it best to keep a low profile and accept his lawyer's recommendations. He'd also squirreled funds away from Angela's holdings she had signed over to him a few years back in order to keep some of her money from her daughters' scheming husbands. He had a sizable amount of money for the search. Nonna's St. Theresa was his Holy Grail to be found no matter what the cost. Nonna had taught him to value beauty, integrity and truth over material things. He sincerely did.

CHAPTER 4.

After Bell and Roberto checked into the Ritz Carlton Hotel in Boston, the latter was paying for, they entered the Ritz Bar. Bell ordered a Dewar's and owned it quickly. He left to go to their suite eaving Roberto drinking his third peach brandy aperitif, ironically named a 'Bellini'. He sat at the desk in a straight chair to clean his Biretta. He'd pretended not to notice Roberto also carried a gun strapped to his leg. Bell liked Search and Find assignments and was excellent and cunning. When Randall hired him to find and follow Roberto Daniro and Georgio del Piano it was almost too easy given the detective's Sicilian mafioso contacts and his smattering of Italian.

Eight years before he'd been pensioned off by the FBI for what was deemed "unethical conduct." Donald Bell had been involved in a vicious shoot-out where his wife Bianca and baby son Beau were being held hostage. They were instantly killed. At that precise moment he lost all his faith and idealism in the government. No one had listened to his advice on how to proceed to free them giving his wife and child a chance to escape unharmed from the clutches of the kidnappers. The FBI had gone in with guns blazing. After a few questionable affairs the FBI let him go.

He cared little and was now a cold, bitter man who only lived for money and revenge. In a perverse way he enjoyed the hit murders on contract he was hired to do. Bell was an intelligent man. He relished the intricate game of making several plans pay off simultaneously which he achieved by a certain rakish charm and believability. Blackmail was now a favored tool as well.

With his animal intuition, Bell sensed the lawyer, Randall, had cultivated tastes and affectations and might possibly be turned with the Bellini marble to salivate for. Or, he thought, for the promise and prospect of a large cash payment Randall could be used against his client, Antonio Amberetti-Scola. Bell suspected it could be Randall, not one of the cousins who forged Tony's name and removed large sums from his accounts.

Donald Bell had changed sides from crime fighter to criminal. He took the precaution of having an acid treatment done on his fingertips as he well knew how expert his former employer was on tracing fingerprints from an enormous, computerized file. DNA evidence was now more widely utilized, too.

When the P. I. ran down Roberto Daniro in Italy he subtly suggested they fly together to Boston. He had learned from a Continental pilot contact where Tony had fled and was sure he could track his base in the Northeast. He proposed to Roberto they secrete the statue near Tony to be retrieved later and sold to an art dealer in South America that Daniro had lined up. He had already received a healthy down payment for the exchange to come after there was enough obfuscatory time and space elapsed between Roberto and the South American agent.

"If the statue is discovered, which is most unlikely as Scola would never suspect it being close to him, he would receive all the blame for the theft and you plead innocent," He told Roberto convincingly.

"Donald, I want the whereabouts of the St. Theresa as convoluted as possible and if it becomes necessary involve the United States and my cousin," Roberto chortled, "and unbeknownst to the great Antonio, he will be keeping the statue safe and hidden for me!"

The challenge for Bell was getting the statue out of Roberto's hands and pocket as he intended to sell it himself. Roberto kept St. Theresa wrapped in a silk handkerchief and on his person at all times, even in bed. At this moment Roberto was in the elegant Ritz bar enjoying the Bellini cocktails with another Bellini in his pocket. He smiled affably at the bartender and ordered another.

From the window of the reserved suite the P. I. could see the famous swan boats in the Public Gardens. He watched for awhile tamping down the emotion he felt seeing small children with their parents or Nannies laughing in the park. Had he lived Beau would be almost nine. Bell shrugged and muttered, "My son didn't live nor did his mother."

Angrily he threw some clothes into a carry-on bag and paged Roberto to settle up their bill and come to their rooms. They wouldn't stay the night, he decided. He telephoned a taxi. They would drive to

Marblehead, the town to which Bell had easily tracked Tony thanks to his talent for Search and Find. Once there he had little doubt he could discover where Scola lived. Usually local bars were a fertile source of information.

Roberto didn't know Bell had already been to Marblehead before he flew to Rome to find Daniro. He knew exactly where Lea lived and that Tony was often with her. He'd scouted out a hiding place for St. Theresa to be kept temporarily until the art collector in Brazil was ready to complete the transaction and receive it. The P.I. didn't take the time to find Tony's apartment, he figured Tony probably slept at Lea's place most of the time.

Bell had found out much about Tony on his first visit to the Tidal Rip barroom. He had struck up a conversation with a drunken man who'd said.

"Yeah, I know who the bastard is." With a maudlin sob he added, "I hope you're going to take care of him? He's trying to ruin my life and take my kids away from me. I'll pay you plenty to do a couple hits for me." Somehow he'd pegged Bell for a hit man.

It could mean some extra cash but Bell didn't trust drunks. He'd have to carefully check it out first and be paid in advance. Each time he killed he was killing those who had killed Bianca and Beau. It amused Bell there was always someone wanting to kill another person and eager to hire him to do it for them. He refused the offer and left the barroom.

He felt John Randall would be easy to turn with his greed and affected pretensions. While with the company he'd turned many. Bell was good at it, a little flattery, enough money and they eagerly fell into your pocket. Aesop had said it best: "Honeyed words and a bribe in hand precede villainy." Few could resist the persuasion of a great deal of cash.

Every murder was his revenge on both the system and the rotten, criminal low-lives he loathed and despised. After losing his much loved wife and son and being ousted from the FBI he rarely smiled but now he broke into a broad grin gloating over how cleverly and slowly he was able to manipulate both Roberto and John Randall. Bell loved the chase and the denouements; each time he was always the winner and richer. He suspected Roberto had plans for his demise after he was finished with his usefulness. Bell also had plans for Roberto and the Bellini sculpture.

In a short while they boarded the taxi waiting out front and took off down Commonwealth Avenue weaving their way through the dense traffic. Neither man spoke on the forty minute drive nor did the cab driver who was new to the United States.

CHAPTER 5.

Lea stood in front of the mirror in the tiny bathroom she'd painted a Salem Derby House gold and hung the walls with her life drawings of nudes. She chopped at her hair recklessly with a small manicure scissors.

She murmured, "I should get a decent haircut." She rarely did and never had a manicure because she disliked taking time away from whatever her current painting project was. Now it was her mythical country, "Zulazandia" and since her hands were her tools used for both clay work and painting an expensive professional manicure would last only a day. Besides, long nails annoyed her and she kept hers short.

She continued to hack away at her hair and ignored a knock on her door. Then came a louder one accompanied by Lucy's (the wannabe-watch-dog) barking. There was an insistent louder knocking. Lea sighed in exasperation and with scissors still in her hand went to answer the door. A dark, obese, heavy-set man stood there. He started and stared askance at her scissors pointing at him. Lea realized to him it was a weapon.

Good, if you think I can defend myself you won't try anything stupid.

Swarthy, fat Georgio smiling ingratiatingly said in broken English, "Please scusi me? I'm looking for a dear cousin of mine, Antonio Amberetti-Scola. I was told you are his friend and he lives here?"

"He is my friend if you are referring to Tony Amberetti but he doesn't live here.   Try his apartment." She answered coldly, suspicious of him on sight. "Why do you want him?"

"I have such sad news to give him. Our grandmother died in Rome and left him some artifacts in her will and I am kind enough to bring them to Antonio. I am Roberto Daniro, his cousin."

He walked curiously around her studio. He stopped in front of a large photograph of Nora with the Sydney Opera House in the background.

"You've been to Australia?

"My daughter lives there near Sydney."

Your work is very nice. Are you represented by a New York or European Gallery?"

"No!" Lea snapped. "I just paint for my own amusement, it's called 'Leanora's Folly." She disliked this oily man and thought to get rid of him with a little rude sarcasm.

Ever a traitor, (Lea thought) Lucy went over to Georgio and licked his hand. He roughly pushed her away. Her feelings hurt she stood close to Lea. She appeared uneasy.

Georgio hated dogs.

One summer when they were children he and Roberto and Andreas (sniveling as usual) drowned Alonzo, Nonna's much loved large, white cat. Their grandmother was too fond of him and they instinctively knew she liked the cat better than she liked them. Tony and Alonzo were her favorites. She was always petting the cat while often curt with them especially when she caught them teasing Alonzo which they did as often as possible out of their jealousy. They pulled his tail, emptied his food from his dish before he could eat, stepped on his toes and made the cat's life as miserable as they could.

One night when Nonna and Tony were both asleep, they sneaked Alonzo out of Nonna's bedroom. They tied him up tightly in a burlap bag while Alonzo scratched and hissed and fought valiantly for his life. They threw the bag containing a howling Alonzo over the end of the pier into the lake. For days Angela had everyone searching for her missing and beloved pet. Vito, the gardener, eyed the many scratches on the boy's arms but said nothing to his mistress. A loyal and gentle old man he felt she'd been hurt enough by Alonzo having gone missing. Why make it any worse?

After that, however, he watched the cousins closely. He had seen them hanging around the abandoned boathouse for several days longer than the falling down structure should have been of interest. When later he was searching for missing Tony Vito remembered this. If he had not discovered Tony tied up in the old shack, Tony would have surely died from hunger and thirst and dehydration. Vito loved Tony and tried often to intervene when the boys bullied and harassed him. This only made them more resentful and angrier at him, Tony and Nonna.

They set many traps for Vito and Tony on the large estate hoping one or both would fall into the brush-covered deep holes with steel animal traps inside and be hurt or die. Knowing every inch of the grounds well Vito was careful to skirt any place that looked artificial, man-made or out of place and warned Tony to do so. When finally Angela banished the cousins Vito went to his church and made his novena of thanks the bad seeds with the devil in them were gone.

Georgio continued to walk around her studio to Lea's annoyance. At this moment she had almost an uncontrollable desire to push him out the door bodily. She restrained herself but it amused her to keep her scissors pointed at his large belly.

"I'm sorry but I have work to do," she said brandishing the scissors and thinking of her half completed hair cut. Georgio seemed alarmed and backed off making a hasty retreat.

Lea heard the dump truck rattling down the street. Earlier that morning in a fit of impulsive disgust she had put two large canvasses out to be thrown away. Realizing now she could gesso them over and reuse them she changed her mind and raced out to the barrels in front of the house.

The rubbish man seemed puzzled by her inquiry. "There weren't any paintings out here, Miss." (Where had they gone? Fretted Lea) but said only, "Thank you, I changed my mind and I wanted them back."

It wasn't until a few months later that was one mystery that was cleared up. Lea attended a luncheon at Tedesco Country Club after the funeral of an elderly friend, Louise who was ninety-six and had made provisions for this luncheon with her lawyer before she died. She wanted all her friends, neighbors and service people invited. Louise had been childless and widowed for many years.

Lea was chatting pleasantly with Louise's neighbors and caretakers when a man came over and introduced himself as the deceased Louise's hairdresser as well as an antique dealer. (Louise had laughed and mentioned in the past, "His antiques are mostly garage sale items he sells at a big commercial flea market."

"How kind of you to come to Louise's house each week to shampoo and set her hair. I know how much she appreciated it and how it cheered her up to have her hair look good."

"She paid me well. Ms. Lantana, I was driving around town a while back and a white van pulled up to your place and a man took two big paintings you'd thrown out that were out front. Did you see him?"

"No. Do you know who it was, I'd really like to have them back, perhaps I can, I never should have thrown them away, I'm willing to pay to have them back again."

With a smarmy smirk he said, "That man was me."

Taken aback but still courteous Lea responded, albeit coolly, "I hope you've enjoyed them."

"Oh, I didn't keep them, I sold them at a Flea Market."

Now Lea stared coldly at him, saying sarcastically, "Then I hope you got a good price for them." (thinking she wished she hadn't signed them.)

"Not too bad, probably not as much as you usually get."

All the rest of the day Lea fumed at his nerve. She thought it colossal brass not only taking her paintings and not even asking her if she were *really* throwing them out but to tell her he'd sold them at a flea market was so gross and demeaning it hurt. Her compulsive impulsiveness frequently got her into trouble. She made another vow for the umpteenth time to correct this trait and think before she leapt! She never could keep this resolution. Angry at herself she muttered, "I got what I deserved, damn it all anyway!"

The next morning Tony left on another unexplained trip she supposed to get in touch with this relative but she'd be damned, even drawn and quartered, before she'd ask. Lea was not only impulsive she was proud.

Around 10 a.m. Lea stopped working on Zulazandia, put down her palette knife and took a break for a cup of coffee. Mug in hand she strolled out to her terrace she'd made on the flat rocks and set it down on an old lobster trap of her father's that served as a table. Pots of multi-colored impatiens, scarlet and yellow hibiscus, red and pink geraniums; all the hardy plants that liked and thrived on salt air were blooming riotously.

A thick gray velvet curtain of fog was descending smelling pleasantly salty while the fog horn on Baker's Island mournfully blasted its warning to boats that rocks were close by.

She looked up and screamed when she saw the dead raccoon nailed to the seaside door. Then she screamed louder and longer when she saw the dead body sprawled on the rocks by the lobster pot table. Ray had always told her she was a great screamer before he intimidated her so much she stopped arguing with him. They had fights that went nowhere except for bruises to her. Now she was in full voice and could not seem to stop. This brought a street full of neighbors who called the police.

When the police arrived they asked so many questions she couldn't answer, it made her head ache. She repeated over and over, "No! I don't know who he is, I've never seen him before." She'd taken only one quick look before the body caught in a crevice was removed. Finally they and the neighbors left to her relief and she was alone.

Tony met a pale, shaken and angry Lea when he returned that evening who demanded, "Who is your relative who came to my studio looking for you? What does he want with me? What is it he wants to give you? He was a fat, smarmy pig and I disliked him!"

While hugging and comforting her, Tony gently kept on asking for a better description and to describe the dead man in more detail. "Do you think it was the same guy who said he was my cousin?"

"Of course not!" she yelled. "The police said the man was probably shot last night in the dark. I never went out there until the middle of the morning. You must have left by the street door this morning so you didn't see him either? Someone must have nailed the raccoon on the door after your cousin left or I would have noticed it earlier. My kayak was stolen, too, what the hell is going on, Tony? I'm really upset!"

Tony nuzzled her neck and patted her back in soothing circles until she calmed down a little. He was disturbed. Perhaps it was time for him to leave Marblehead if the cousins were getting close to him? He wanted to find them and St. Theresa first before they menaced Lea or him. Tony was reluctant to leave Lea now he had found the love of his life yet he didn't want to place her in danger nor did he wish to hurt her by dropping too abruptly out of her life and incidentally her bed. He acknowledged this was going to take some sensitive and serious thought. Tony didn't want to leave Lea.

The previous night Lea had slept soundly as apparently had Lucy. At a dead low tide nearly midnight, two visitors in oilskins scaled the rocks in front of the studio. When the tide was in this would not be possible. They carried a thickly wrapped package tied with heavy twine and weighted with a heavy piece of wood. Silently they removed the plants and bric-a-brac from the lobster pot table and inserted the package, piling the old seaweed always in the trap on top, then closed the cover again. Lea never opened the trap, she sentimentally used it as a table in memory of her father. She'd had a piece of heavy plastic cut at the hardware store to use for the top instead of glass that could easily break in a stormy wind.

One of the men pulled out a gun and whispered hoarsely, "I don't think I need you any more!" The other man was quicker and already had his gun out.

They scuffled on the slippery rocks each trying to grab the other's gun. One fired and the man shot in the head fell against the lobster trap. The victor tried to drag the body to push into the incoming tide below but it was tightly wedged in a crevice. He reached for Lea's kayak which was upright resting against the studio wall. He removed the paddle, hanging on to it, he slid the kayak down the seaweed covered slippery rocks to the water below. Holding the paddle he then skidded on his rear into the ocean after it. The incoming tide made it too difficult to leave on foot the way they'd come. Silently he inserted himself into Katie, Lea's kayak and made his escape. Lea and Lucy had heard nothing. The gun was equipped with a silencer. Lucy was a lover but an abysmal failure as a watch dog.

Two days later Tony, high on a ladder at the boat yard sanding a boat looked down to see Officer Robert Orne looking up and yelling to him.

"Would you come down for a minute, Mr. Amberetti?" (Tony had dropped the Scola in Marblehead.) Tony climbed down.

"Does the name Roberto Daniro or Donald Bell mean anything to you? We've traced some bar tabs found in the victim's pocket to the Ritz Carlton Hotel in Boston. Both men were registered there but did not spend a night. They only had drinks in the bar and a cabby said they hired him to drive them to Marblehead. The fare was fifty bucks. He dropped them off at the yellow Town House in the center of town."

Impressed by the local detective, Tony said, "Amazing! Good work!"

Without changing expression the officer continued. "A corpse was found at your girl friend's house, that old fishing shack she uses for an art studio."

No secrets in old Marblehead, Tony thought ruefully. *I hope Lea likes being identified as my girl friend!*

"We think the body is probably that of a Donald Bell. The face was so destroyed by the bullet wound, identifying marks from the FBI photo files such as a facial scar he had are not present. Fingerprints were hard to get and are being processed. He did have an FBI badge in his pocket. What little we got seems not to be on file anywhere. We still need to check in Italy. We should have the identity of the victim in a few days after the Medical Examiner completes the autopsy."

"Thanks. Daniro is my cousin."

"Do you have any idea why he was with Bell? Were they perhaps coming to see you or Ms. Lantana?"

"None. I've not seen my cousin in a year. (To himself, *not since they stole my statue and ran away.*) I don't know why these two were together. I'd like to know."

Officer Orne thanked him and added, "By the way stick around town until the investigation is finished." That solved the problem of leaving Lea, for a while at least.

Tony puzzled over Roberto's, or was it Georgio's? connection to Donald Bell, the P. I. "Do they have a plot against me? Why did they involve Lea? I still believe either Georgio or Roberto has the statue stashed away somewhere. For some reason Roberto came here to kill me?"

Recently he'd been informed that Andreas' delusions which incited people to violence had led to his confinement in a mental hospital. Andreas if he had been, was no longer a part of the equation leaving Roberto, Georgio and perhaps Bell and John Randall to deal with?

CHAPTER 6.

Sarah Gross, at the law offices of Queen, Pedersen and Gross on Federal Street in Salem, smiled sympathetically at Claire who was seated across from Sarah's desk in the midst of five small waif-like children she confided she was afraid to leave with anyone, especially her mother-in-law who was not at all fond of her or the children.

"I don't know what to do. I'm twenty-four and I never even finished high school when I married Ray. He was handsome and he wanted me and I was flattered. It feels like I've been pregnant the whole seven years and I'm a little scared I might be now."

Sarah reached across the desk and squeezed Claire's hand. She thought it was truly a pitiful case but she couldn't turn her back on the girl when her best friend, Lea had asked her to give what help she could to Claire. Briskly she said.

"Claire, first things first. I know a safe house that you and the children can stay in out of town where Ray can't find you. We'll file today for a restraining order against him and next for a divorce. Then we'll arrange job training skill for you. You WILL be okay, Claire, believe it. Fortunately you have a small nest egg in the bank from your mother, you told me, to start with. Since it is in a joint account with Ray, when you leave here today immediately go the National Grand bank and withdraw it, it belongs to you. Ask for a cashier's check, bring it to me and I'll deposit it for you in a new account in a Lynn bank where Ray can't touch it."

Although dejected and still frightened Claire looked at Sarah with a glimmer of hope and a growing adoration. "I'm not smart or strong like you and Lea. I'm awfully scared. Maybe I should put up with Ray and stay?"

"What about the children, Claire? Can you allow them to continue to be abused?"

Claire broke down, crying and pointing wordlessly to four year old Tommy's arm in a cast. His big blue eyes, like his mother's, stared at Sarah appealingly.

Sarah gazed at Claire steadily. *Poor little rabbit,* she thought and waited.

Firmly she said, "You have more inner strength than you realize, Claire. We all do. You'll be a new and much happier and better woman and mother. For that you have to have self-respect, self-esteem and determination. It won't be easy, we'll take one step at a time."

She continued, "You're also very pretty. When you leave here, after the bank go to the Silver Shears Shop in the Village Mall and have your hair shampooed and cut. You'll feel better. Ask for Eleni to do it. Here's an advance, you can repay me later."

As a lawyer and a woman Sarah knew this would do much toward giving Claire some self-confidence. Looking good always helped she'd discovered in her practice, a lot of which consisted of dealing with abused, downtrodden young women overwhelmed by their early disastrous choices in their lives and now willing to give up.

She knew only too much about this syndrome as she had been there once herself. Her salvation and rebirth had been summoning up the courage to walk away from an abusive, bad marriage. She had worked as a waitress at Glover Inn for six long years. In her free time she attended Suffolk Law School. Sarah knew from experience what steps she must painfully take Claire through. Grateful for the successful life and career she'd wrested from God and man she had vowed to help other women, pro bono if necessary, and never forget her own horrible mental and physical abuse in the past.

Claire said sadly, "Maybe it's my fault I can't please Ray?"

"No, Claire, it's not your fault! Only if you remain in a destructive relationship."

"Victims often feel they are at fault when involved with an alcohol or drug addict even when their partner is a mentally disturbed personality or a verbal or physical abuser. You are NOT to blame. People like you must learn what I call the three C's-cause, control, cure. You did not cause it, you cannot control it and you cannot cure it. Victims must love themselves and their children, if they have any, and remove themselves from the offender to save their own physical and mental health and stability."

Claire stared at Sarah, "It's not my fault?"

"Of course not! Bless you and stay strong," She said softly, dismissing Claire.

When Claire returned the next day she had both the bank check and a new, flattering hair-do. Her demeanor already showed a change, occasionally she even smiled revealing deep dimples.

"She's really a beautiful girl with those violet eyes and dimples! If she could act or sing she'd be a winner." On a hunch Sarah asked, "What are your talents? You'll need a job to support yourself and the children. What do you do well? What do you love to do, Claire."

"Nothing, really. I'm not a very good cook, Ray tells me. I don't know how to sew. My grades in school weren't awfully good, but the boys liked me a lot," she added shyly.

Exasperated, Sarah burst out, "Claire you must have done something other than sleep with high school boys!"

"Well, I used to sing in the Baptist Church choir and I sang solos before Ray got jealous and he made me quit even going to church. I like to sing. I sing a lot to my kids."

Sarah thought, "Could it be there's some talent here? Perhaps some vocal lessons would be in order?"

"Sing for me, Claire."

Wobbly at first Claire obediently started to sing. With her eyes fixed on Sarah's encouraging gaze she gained in volume as she went on.

"Amazing grace, how sweet thou art, to save a wretch like me. I once was lost but now I'm found, was blind but now I see."

51

Her voice was heartbreakingly sad but sweet and true in pitch. The stenographers, paralegals and clerks in the outer offices came to the doorway and listened. A young lawyer, Abe came, too. They all applauded when she finished and Claire blushed happily. Sarah was elated. Claire's voice might be the key to a steady, paying job? This gifted child could make her life and her children's lives better and she would, Sarah felt sure.

She knew there was a long road ahead for Claire and what road blocks Ray Larson might be able to throw in her way they didn't now know. Sarah felt a great deal of empathy for Claire and resolved to help her latest Galatea. Sarah was the most fortunate of wretches to have been led to compassionate Sarah who completely believed in and dedicated her life to the law and justice for women.

Even before she passed the bar Sarah had encouraged her friend, Lea, to attend Montserrat College of Art in nearby Beverly, Massachusetts. With Nora to raise and a small amount of money earned as a waitress at the Glover Inn where she met Sarah, Lea attended part time. Siri's generous baby-sitting Nora and Sarah's encouragement had kept Lea at her art school studies. Lea's instinct to send Claire to Sarah was right on the mark. Lea had an artist's sensitive intuition she almost always paid heed to. Sarah sensed Lea had some doubts about Tony she was denying to herself and brushed off Sarah's gentle warnings and questions. There was something mysterious and withheld about him and his past. Tony's warmth, charm and affectionate ways had made Lea feel cared for and wanted, she had been alone for a long time. Lea tamped down any uneasiness because she was clearly infatuated and ignored both her own inner voice and her friend, Sarah's.

Sarah was troubled and anxious for her friend but had nothing concrete on which to base her feeling. Lea was so obviously enjoying everything about Tony, Sarah tried not to bring up the subject of his past too frequently. When she did Lea would fake a lascivious leer and joke, "Admit it, Sarah, he is a hunk!"

"And you admit it, Lea, you're besotted with the man, there's no other word to describe it."

"I'm afraid I am, Sarah my love, I go all foolish when he touches me, damn it!"

CHAPTER 7.

Tony divulged July 14 would be his 43rd birthday. They'd had little recreation lately, both working long hours-Tony at the boatyard and Lea trying to complete her series of oils on "Zulazandia." They had skipped attending the Culinary exhibit on Fort Sewall, part of the Arts Festival Fourth of July events. (Privately, Lea along with some of the other artists called it the "Pig's Festival." and rarely attended but of course were pleased more money was raised this way for the Arts Festival.)

For the most part it consisted of female Yuppies dressed up in flowered hats and long dresses usually escorted by men in pink pants. After the judging of the local restaurant's food tables was completed, all rushed greedily toward the delicious foods and more champagne. This was truly not an edifying sight.

Since it had been a while since Lea and Tony had really relaxed she decided on a birthday celebration with a sail and picnic on Misery Island off Manchester-by-the-Sea. Lea borrowed a town Class sailboat from her high school best friend, Emily. Emily was a good old girl, generous, pretty and extremely loyal. She'd married well and took a lot of pleasure in her present status. Lea understood her and loved her and forgave Emily's occasional, childlike oneupsmanship, Emily was unaware she did this probably out of her former insecurity growing up without a great deal of money or material things although she'd had a loving family who were close to one another.

Emily generously arranged for Lea to pick up the "Emmy Lou" at the Corinthian Yacht Club on the Neck where the boat was moored. Years before Ray and Lea had sailed and raced on his old, wooden, second-hand Townie, "Mermaid", so it was an easy, familiar boat for her to handle. Since Tony had mentioned he had sailed as a boy on Lake Como in Italy, she figured he would be an adequate crew and she would skipper.

Lea prepared an elegant picnic to take with them. Usually she cooked her own lobster but this time she bought lobster meat already cooked (and expensive) at the Barnegat fish market, "the Lobster Company", to save time boiling, cracking open and retrieving the lobster meat. She lined frankfurter rolls with Bibb lettuce and piled large pieces of lobster mixed with a little chopped celery and her homemade mayonnaise in each.

She'd poached chicken breasts in white wine, lemon juice, fresh chopped basil, dill, rosemary, parsley, garlic and a bay leaf, poured off the poaching liquid before chilling it and then cut it up in chunks for salad. Lea added some slivers of ripe olives, capers and toasted pecans to the chicken and again mixed it with her mayonnaise. She spread this on lettuce lined whole wheat bread for another sandwich.

"Are we going for a month?" Tony teased. She had one left to make as his surprise. On Italian bread she placed fresh figs, thin slices of smoked Prosciutto ham, a dribble of olive oil and some watercress. Lea hadn't ever had these but Tony had spoken of them as a favorite. There were two of each kind of sandwich for the picnic hamper.

A birthday pie instead of cake had been a Lantana family tradition growing up, each child had a favorite Siri made on their birthdays. Lea baked Nora's choice for Tony, a brownie pie with cashews. She smiled recalling one time John Peder, blowing out his birthday candles on his lemon meringue pie had plastered the meringue all over the dining room wall, he blew so enthusiastically. Embarrassed when the family cheered and booed, he then changed his birthday pie choice to strawberry. A bottle of Bolla Soave, two ripe peaches, paper plates, cups, napkins and plastic forks were added to the now stuffed full cooler and hamper. Lea looked it all over and was happily pleased with her birthday lunch for Tony.

It was a fine day with a fair breeze and a mackerel sky looking like the square chunks of a Georgia O'Keeffe cloud painting. They started out about 9 a.m. and on a steady reach sailed into Cocktail Cove on Misery island close to quarter of 10. The island was presently owned and operated by the Trustees of Reservations and kept clean and manicured by a permanent Park Ranger who lived there all summer until Labor Day in September. They tied up

"Emmy Lou" onto a mooring in the cove and took a swim, cavorting, trying to duck each other and playing in the crystal clear water. They'd worn their bathing suits under their shorts and t-shirts which they quickly shed to leap into the ocean. When they finally came out on the sandy beach, Lea breathed happily, saying, "Oh, poetic, magical day!" Tony smiled at her and bent down to kiss her.

They walked the trails where the remains of the long ago old Misery Island Club and nine hole golf course could still be seen amongst the undergrowth. In the 'twenties there had been many cottages for wealthy summer residents, all gone now, but the old photographs posted on a glassed in bulletin board showed what splendor it had possessed in its heyday. Lea and Tony were the only people on the island this weekday and they made love in total privacy on a grassy knoll enclosed by trees. Then Lea spread a cloth and opened the hamper removing all the goodies she'd packed, to Tony's awe.

Tony was poised to take a joyous big bite from his fig and ham sandwich when Lea exclaimed, "Wait, wait, stop! We have to say the birthday grace first."

"Jeez, Louise," He muttered, a new phrase he'd picked up from Will, one he liked better than Lea's "Oh, fishcakes!"

Lea smiled at him sweetly, reciting, "Today is my birthday, Lord, come be my guest. Of all I've invited I love Thee the best."

"That's a lie, I'll have to go to confession now. I love you the best! Lea, you're more Catholic than I am." Yet he was touched by a special birthday grace for him. "Your mother must have spent most of her time saying grace."

"Yup. Siri was a great Mom."

"Mine, too," Tony murmured wistfully. "I only had her until I was twelve but then I had Nonna who was wonderful, too. Such mysterious ways God works?"

Reluctant to end a perfect day they set sail late around 7 p.m. The wind was freshening and the sun would soon set. Smoothly sailing on a reach again just off Cat island suddenly an ominous roar of loud thunder claps and flashes of lightning indicated a freak squall was rapidly approaching. Lea was explaining to Tony, "Cat Island was often called Children's Island because the YMCA holds a summer sailing day camp on it and the kids are transported from the town wharf by the Hannah Glover-" when the squall hit and the small Townie tossed and turned and heeled way over into the white-capped heaving ocean. Alarmed Lea shouted, "I'll steer into the wind, you reef the mainsail!"

Tony shouted back, "No! I'll take down the mainsail, we'll sail on the jib!"

He proceeded to haul down the mainsail as Lea handled the tiller steering as best she could into the wind so as not to capsize. Huge sheets of drenching rain enveloped them but doughty little "Emmy Lou" gamely rode the waves as though the ocean were a bucking bronco. Tony grinned at her, exhilarated, his white teeth shining in his tanned face. At last he took the tiller from Lea who took over the jib and he ably brought the boat about, at last rounding the Fort and heading into the harbor. The squall was over almost as fast as it had begun.

Lea realized Tony had a lot more sailing experience than he'd revealed. Still sailing with just the jib Tony brought "Emmy Lou" to her mooring off the club. Lea leaned over and picked up the mooring and blew a whistle for the club launch to pick them up. As they waited for the launch boy they cleaned up the boat and tied the sails down. Walking up the Corinthian ramp to Tony's car he kissed Lea's salt-soaked, drenched face and laughed exultantly.

"Best birthday I ever had and an excellent gourmet lunch, too!"

He'd loved the fig sandwiches Lea had never made before and had looked up in an Italian cook book. She really enjoyed reading cook books for pleasure. On Misery, Tony had smiled with delight and announced, "Nonna used to make these for my birthday picnics when I was young," so Lea gave him hers, too. (Nonna rarely cooked, it was Maria, the cook, directed by Angela who made his fig sandwiches.)

Squall and all it had been a nearly perfect day. Both were totally water soaked, sneakers squishing as they walked into the studio, yet euphoric. Lea felt completely happy. She'd made Tony a lovely, memorable birthday and one he volubly appreciated. She had not been as alive and attuned in a long time, attuned with Tony and her beloved sea. She repeated her mantra silently, (no one should know another's private and personal mantra; "Alizarin crimson, cerulean blue, and thank you, God.") Lucy's reproachful looks at being left behind didn't even make her feel guilty. Lucy usually could lay guilt trips when not included on an outing.

The next morning Lea and Tony awoke early to the sounds of the screeching gulls as he had to be at work at the yard by 7 a.m. and first he wanted to stop in at the police station to see if there were any new information. The night before he'd thanked Lea with abundant caresses for his beautiful birthday. Teasing, Lea whispered, "Might you be able to have a birthday every month? It seems to do great things for you."

"I don't think so, Carissima, but I can find *something* to celebrate with you this way every night! Tomorrow night will be the new moon, is it a date?"

Tony had stayed the night, Lea teased, "What do you think this is, your birthday?"

They carried their breakfast of Scandinavian Spinach pancakes, lingonberry jam, coffee and juice out to the rock terrace and watched the remains of the splendid, surrealistic Van Gogh sunrise over Cat Island, long fingers of shimmering sun on the water reaching to the terrace on the ocean. It was a serene and beautiful morning which always followed after a storm with the gulls soaring overhead and the water sparkling. It was virtually impossible to believe a murder had taken place here.

Lea said grace as she did before every mealtime since her childhood. Siri had taught her five children many different ones and encouraged them to compose their own. Patting Lucy, lying beside her with a piece of pancake dangling from her mouth, she chose a favorite.

"In the early morning with the sun's first rays, all God's little children, thank and pray and praise. We, too, thanks would offer, Jesus Savior dear, for thy loving pasture and thy tender care." Tony crossed himself automatically and smiled fondly at Lea with an amused expression, she was really into saying grace, he mused, shaking his head.

Growing up, Lea's family had filled a pew at the Lutheran church. All five children on pain of death from their father, Einar, were quiet as little church mice. Wherever Finns, Germans, Swedes, Norwegians, Icelanders or Danes had settled in the new world a Lutheran church sprang up.

Leanora was the baby, named for her grandmother Eleanora. Twins, Lars and Erik were the oldest. After them came Maria Patrice and then John Peder who was two years older than Lea. Siri had said indignantly to Einar when the twins were born first.

"If your babies are going to come double I'm not sure I want any more!" This became part of the family history, Einar telling each child, "You're lucky you're here." This puzzled them until they were old enough to know this was a kind of private joke their parents shared.

The twins had been their sibling's mentors, ever protective. They had divided up the world between them. Lars was the practical scientist, Erik the artist musician. Sister Pat had sung minor parts with the San Francisco, California Opera Company where she met and married Dan Stevens, its manager-director. They lived outside of San Francisco in a town similar to Marblehead, Sausalito, with three daughters, Tina Marie, Kristin Siri and Lizzie Lea.

Sister Pat, along with Sarah was Lea's other best friend.

Dan had taken them sailing when she and sixteen year old Nora visited. Lea spotted a racing boat named "Down Bucket." Delighted, she called over.

"Whip! Up for Air!" Laughing the crew in unison caroled back, "Rock 'em round the corner!" Marblehead greetings in the Pacific Ocean. By these words a 'header could be identified anywhere in the world. They stemmed from the early 1500's when "thunder jugs" were emptied from the windows with the warning "Down bucket!" "Rock 'em" was a warning to "furriners" to go back where they came from by pelting them with rocks. What the derivation of the popular Marblehead greeting "Whip!" was nobody seemed to be sure.

John Peder with a humorous, sunny disposition and kind and thoughtful ways was Lea's favorite brother. When he was small he would importune Siri, "Am I your favor?"

Lea often told him he was *her* "favor."

He'd been a bush pilot in Alaska and later flew for a small airline in Bar Harbor, Maine. Now married to a Danish Maine girl, Gerda, he flew some charter flights for private owners and raised antique apple varieties, there were literally hundreds, whose nostalgia value made them sell well. Einar had always had a few fruit trees in their yard. Each time a family pet passed on it was buried in the orchard under a new tree planted on its grave. Parakeets, rabbits, several dogs, cats, tropical fish and Lea's pet white rat, Matthew enriched the soil. Matthew would only let

Lea approach his cage, snarling and showing his ugly yellow teeth to anyone else. Inexplicably she loved Matthew. John Peder pronounced him 'gross' to Lea's indignant denials.

With the help of his wife and their strapping, huge teenagers, Erik and David, John Peder raised apples and sold them from a farm stand in front of their farmhouse.

They grew Baldwin, Blaze, Cortland, Criterion, Elstar, Empire, Fameuse (snow apple) Gala, Golden and Red Delicious, Gravenstein, Idared, Jonagold (a cross between Golden Delicious and Jonathan), Jonamac (Jonathan-Macintosh cross), Jonathan, Liberty (Macoun-Purdue cross), Macintosh, Macoun, Milton, Monroe, Mother, Northern Spy, Pound (or Pumpkin) Sweet, Russet, Rhode Island Greening, Rome Beauty, Spigold (red Spy and Golden Delicious cross), Splendor, Winesap, Tomkins King, Twenty Ounce. Also a Russian apple, Lubsk Queen, a Japanese apple, Mutsu (renamed Crispin in the United States) an English apple, Cox Orange Pippin and the family favorite, a Scandinavian apple, Ingrid Marie.

Now Siri and Einar were gone the siblings had a reunion once a year taking turns hosting and planning a trip together. Spouses enjoyed this as well as there were wonderful times in San Antonio, Texas; Seattle, and salmon fishing on April Point in British Columbia; St. Augustine, Florida; Washington, D.C.; Williamsburg, Virginia; Boothbay Harbor and Bath, Maine and in Marblehead and Boston and New Brunswick, Canada.

Theirs' had been a close loving family mostly because of Siri's influence with Einar's strong support.

She set up birthday hunts for each child, writing a rhyming clue to lead to each spot until the final one with the gift was discovered. Siri invented a Christmas elf "Brownie Jingle", who left a little present under their pillows even before they opened their stockings. Sometimes it was walnuts she'd placed a quarter and a penny in, glued the shell halves back together and painted them gold. (Lea still had one she'd saved for at least thirty years.)

The three boys sailed, fished, hunted with Jess and Benny, the pointers, and clammed for quahogs with their father. Siri would not permit the two girls to hunt because of the killing of the pheasants and use of guns (she vigorously disapproved) but they did everything else Einar and their brothers did. He was pretty much in charge of the boys. Finally Siri persuaded him and Einar substituted a camera for a gun. The boys' shooting days were over and all became excellent photographers instead. They had to earn money for their film and all had paper routes.

Lea's customers loved to see her efficiently going door to door at ten years old, her pony tail bobbing up and down. Not all were amused to wait for John Peder dawdling along his route with a long trail of dogs following. He led them around trees and lampposts eventually remembering to deliver the newspapers. Once he was so jealous of Lea and her chum busily collecting grasshoppers in jars, he quickly grabbed a jar from the array on the back steps. Lea indignantly yelled for her mother. Before Siri could intervene he swallowed them! The girls screaming, "He ate them, he ate them!"

The twins were golden boys, capable, handsome and well-liked especially by girls. Their many awards helped them attain college scholarships. When he married Lars seemed to grow away from his twin and his family, he'd been especially close to Erik, his double. Lea noticed he often said and did odd things completely unlike the loyal Lantana he'd been in the past. With wife Rebecca he had four children; Margo, Dan and Nick in their teens and a late baby, Elizabeth Siri, Lars apparently liked his mother's name.

Lars' family now saw him only a few times a year on special occasions although he didn't live far away. Siri tried to hide her hurt. One day Lea found her weeping at her kitchen table, head down amongst the strewn brown paper wrappings. Lea begged her to tell her what was wrong. Wordlessly, Siri held up a child's beautifully illustrated book of Peter Rabbit Lars had returned in the mail with a curt note. Among other things it read, "That baby was not named for you." On the first page she had inscribed the book, "to Elizabeth from grandmother Siri Elizabeth on your first birthday."

Lea knew they'd refused his mother's offer to baby-sit saying, "Grandparents are disruptive." This was particularly odd as he had particularly loved his grandmother, Eleanora, and spent a lot of time at her house? Some of the incidents were downright cruel and Lea was indignant, Lars was breaking his mother's heart. She couldn't understand it. The actions were irrational and unlike the Lars they'd all loved in the past. She consulted her older psychologist friend, Dr. Lois Garr once again.

Dr. Garr explained and outlined all the possible explanations. She started out with the most extreme, "Folie A Deux", in which the dominant person in a relationship of two controlled the weaker one who parroted all he or she was told. "The Stockholm Syndrome" was another manifestation where prisoners of war so identified with their captors after brainwashing they would do and say almost anything in order to please and receive a kind word.

"Do you recall the kidnapping of Patty Hearst? Those in control alternately punish and reward. Of course these cases are the bizarre extreme and I'm pretty sure do not apply to your brother except possibly in a much milder form. Soft-hearted people who want to please are easily manipulated and suggestible to propaganda."

"How often do you see your brother and his family?"

"Only a few times a year, mostly duty visits or invitations on a holiday like Christmas or an event such as a child's baptism or graduation. I promise you, Lois, I swear we've all reached out to and been kind to Rebecca, Lars' wife who showed animosity to our family from the beginning, constantly making excuses why they couldn't come to see Siri and turning down our invitations. Its hurt my mother deeply."

"You feel, Lea, you've lost Lars as he once was?"

"Oh yes! Does he gain something by this behavior, Lois?"

"Perhaps Lea, even if it is only surcease from nagging and emotional abuse and harangues? It's hard for me to believe that Lars would think his first family

66

is unworthy of his trust and affection! Could his wife feel you have somehow offended her and he is her protector? You told me he was over protective of you younger children growing up."

"And then, Lea, and I'm reluctant to say it, his wife may possibly have a borderline personality disorder which is more common than people realize. These are people who must control, who interpret everything as intended to insult or offend and in order to keep close control over their spouses and children beat off anyone who gets too close as everything and everyone is some kind of a threat to this personality."

"An extreme example is the behavior and mind set of a paranoid-schizophrenic but I think it 's more likely this is an insecure person who twists and invents things to convince her partner everyone is out to hurt her and she needs his protection and exclusive attention with no sharing allowed!"

"Don't take it too seriously, avoid confrontations where you will be possibly deliberately misunderstood and pray for them. Their children are also missing out on the warmth and love an extended family can give. Try to feel compassion for both your brother and this poor insecure and probably jealous woman, if you can manage it, Lea."

"There's nothing we can do, Lois? Can't love heal everything?"

"No. Unless Lars wishes to take some remedial steps there's little you can do but accept the situation and love what you have left even more. Lars apparently permits the unhappy situation to continue? Erik and Patrice and John Peder and their spouses and all their kids are still close, aren't they? Enjoy them.

Don't let yourself be embittered or you'll take on the very traits you deplore."

To Lea this seemed a Finnish family tragedy akin to the Greek ones she'd read about in high school English classes. Couldn't love overcome anything? Family was so important.

Lois hugged her. "Dear friend, you might never solve the coolness. Lars is used to the pattern now and unless he wants to get into a big argument he must think he has to go along with the myth his birth family is the enemy and to be kept at arms length at all costs."

"Perhaps he is in self-denial and can't admit even to himself how bizarre it truly is? Eventually he'll be back, I think I know it's very painful for you in the meantime. Another thing, Lea, from what I know of your almost story book family growing up you are a prime target to be shot down by an envious person who feels deprived. Jealousy is usually at the root of animosity." She laughed, "Lea, I was a little jealous of you all myself when I was younger."

Lea stared at her. "But you had so much—that beautiful house on Peach's Point, private school and college!"

"Believe it, Lea, the family you had was worth a lot more. I was an only child with an alcoholic mother and without siblings to share and have fun with. It helped make you caring and sensitive. And many envied you and still do for your talent."

Lea thanked her good friend and advisor Lois, and left for home to ponder what she'd said. Life often deals heart aching blows but you had to get up on your feet again and again. The antidote was grace, courage as well as keeping a certain means of escape.

For Lea this lay in her passionate love of color and painting, sublimating all evils into good as in her much beloved fairy tales and fables by Hans Christian Andersen, Aesop and the Brothers Grimm. In their world ogres and evils surely existed yet were always overcome by the good. The archetype heroes kissing a frog into a prince, changing an ugly duckling into a swan, or as in The Red Shoes, literally dancing your feet off!

Like life itself the tales always contained an element of the ugly as well as the beautiful and sometimes the ugly duckling became transformed. Jung had taught, "The whole is a gestalt, made up of both light and dark and man must always try to balance it."

Lea had received a grant from the Massachusetts Arts Council to mount a large exhibit on "Fairy Tales And Fables" in a public building, (she chose Abbot Public Library). This came after her personal struggle with what appeared to be on the surface the destruction of Lars' bond with his birth family. She prayed he'd come around and also prayed, "Please God, don't ever let me be envious or resentful of anyone. I do have so much for which I am truly glad and grateful."

Their mother had told each child when reading them bedtime stories.

"All of you have your own special guardian angel watching over you all the time, especially when you are asleep."

Lea had hope and faith Lars' guardian angel was watching out for him and would guide him safely home so they could love and help him and his children and also his wife if she would permit it. Lars did try to remember birthdays and often came alone to see them, only God knew how difficult it was for him to do that much?

CHAPTER 8.

Although Nora was geographically distant she remained emotionally close to Lea and wrote her long, full confiding letters her mother loved. She missed her more than Nora would ever know.

Dear Mom:

Aunt Pat telephoned me she and Uncle Dan are coming to Sydney next month, hooray! Dan has to attend a conference at the Sydney Opera House and San Francisco is paying for Pat, too. The Opera House is gorgeous architecture, it looks like giant sails in the harbor. They'll love it. They haven't decided yet whether to bring the little girls along on such a long trip.

Did I tell you Rod is an adopted Aborigine? I worried a little bit about telling you but then I realized who my Mom is. He was adopted by an Australian couple, the McFinches, when he was four at a time when there were mass adoptions of Aborigines. The government thought this would help the children to be educated. (I guess they did not consider all the history

71

and lore of nature and knowledge the Aborigines possessed was equivalent to the white man's book learning? One thing I have learned, they were fantastic artists.)

Should I tell Aunt Pat ahead of time? I know like you she is probably not prejudiced in any respect but Rod is pretty black! (His skin is like black satin.) He's a wonderful guy, Mom, intelligent, sensitive, open and friendly with everyone, almost too naive and trusting that way. We're not ready yet for marriage but we bought the little house on Grantly Beach I wrote you about. This was Rod's first choice as it's only a thirty minute commute by ferry to Sydney. He's a CPA with many bookkeeping and tax accounts in the city. Grantly is great for surfing which we both love although Rod is far better than I. Also it has a "nudie" beach Rod approves of because of his ancestors, he says! (I don't, I find it shocking and embarrassing and I'm too chubby.)

I'll also commute to Sydney and drive to the Waritah School where I teach Eurythmy, art and music to the mentally challenged children.

I'm not giving up raising, breeding, showing and selling my Persian cats. I admit it is hard for me to sell them as I fall madly in love with each new kitten and I hate to let any go! I do a thorough inspection of each prospective owner's home to be sure they will get the proper care, attention and affection. Once I had twenty-nine at once! I never told you as I knew you'd probably have a cow, (read kitten)! To tease me Rod pretends he is allergic to Persians, he really isn't. He loves them and plays with them as much as I do. He's an awful tease and I fall for his bait every time.

Why didn't you tell me you were showing in a New York gallery? That's marvelous! Rod met a Robert Daniro at the Aborigine Gallery in Sydney, one of his accounts. He was chatting with this guy about my American relatives and Daniro said he'd heard of your work in New York. He asked Rod if he could come to our house and see more. I guess Rod had told him our place was full of your things. He was especially interested in any sculpture I might have to show him. Mostly I have paintings, the only ones I have are the two ceramic doves, called "Pax Paloma". He can see them but not buy them.

I still laugh when I recall the misprint typo in the Festival Sculpture show program one year that listed them as "Pay Paloma" and Uncle John Peder said he was going to put a tin cup in front of them on the pedestal for donations because it sounded like a demand from the Mafia!

You asked about my birthday? Could you, would you, part with "Poppies in October", part of your poetry series, done from a Sylvia Plath poem? My favorite, I hope it's not sold? Sea mail is cheapest, take it out of the glass and frame and Rod will have it framed at the gallery IF it's to be my very best birthday present!

Also I would like a ton of your recipes. I'm cooking now, believe it or not. Please send Baked Stuffed Shrimp (prawns here), New England Fish and Clam chowders with the thin milk broth, (I hate the floury, thick kind.) And I want my birthday Brownie Cashew Pie, and the Strawberry Pie recipes. Don't forget the baked Finnish chicken with Havarti cheese, grapes and almonds. I want a lot more but that's

73

enough to start with! When I get through cooking all your great stuff Rod is going to love me twice as much as he seems to now which is a lot! I love him, too, Mom.

And please if not too much trouble, could you send via sea mail some Devereux Beach rocks and some blue mussel shells from Fort Beach for my small rock garden to remind me of home? I do miss you.

All my love, forever,
Nora

XXXXXXXXXXXXXXXXXXXXXXX00000000000000

Oh, Mom, this is ten days later, I haven't mailed the first letter yet, we were so busy.

Continued. P. S.

My God, Mom this is awful!
Mr. Daniro came out to Grantly and seemed very disappointed I didn't have more of your pottery and sculpture to show? He kept asking me if I were keeping a special piece safely hidden! Friendly Rod decided we should be hospitable and give him a tour of Sydney, the zoo, galleries, museums and so on. We met him outside the Opera House a few days later and took the hydrofoil across the harbor to the zoo. This man (later his wallet showed his name was a Georgio del Piana (not the name he told us) is grossly obese. What happened was terrible, Mom! Getting out of the boat at the zoo pier, he slipped and fell into the harbor

and nearly drowned. They said later he'd had a massive stroke. He's in a coma in the hospital.

I feel like the kiss of death! We were only trying to be nice to him. Frankly, he was smarmy and I disliked him. Rod likes everyone although this guy was not at all likeable. In fact, I thought him a bit sinister looking with a thick Italian accent and he seemed suspicious but I certainly never meant to drown him, honest! More later, then I'll mail this.

Love again, Nora

She added a postscript.

P.S. It was quite a scene! After they fished him out of the water Rod gave him CPR. There were sirens, police, police boats and crowds of people waiting by the ambulance when we reached the dock at the Opera House. I feel bad for him and I suppose I'll have to visit him in the hospital although to be honest I'd prefer not to. (OKAY, Mom, I will.)

Nora

"I wish I were seen in New York,." murmured Lea. "I must ask Tony what he thinks of this guy seeking my daughter? How does he know me, I'm not famous in New York, or anywhere else, either! What did he want he thought Nora had?" It was baffling and made Lea feel uneasy.

She was touched Nora wanted some rocks from Devereux Beach where she'd spent many of her summers in her college years. On her days off from serving as a waitress at the Boston Yacht Club on the other end of Front street, Nora and her friends usually headed for the beach to work on their tans. Lea wished her to be as free, productive and happy as she seemed to be in Australia. Nora went as an exchange student her junior year at Wheaton College in Norton, Massachusetts and became enchanted with the wide spread educational system and philosophy known throughout the world as the Waldorf School system and stayed for what was going to be another year. When she met Rod and began to write glowing letters about him, in her heart Lea knew Nora would never permanently return to her home town. Her time kept being extended.

For every sadness, hurt or blow Lea turned to her art and became absorbed in a watercolor, oil or collage. She made collages from her torn up failed watercolors. She started now on a collage of twenty-nine cats to send Nora as an extra birthday gift. As she cut, tore and pasted she felt more lighthearted. It was evolving into an amusing piece with cats on chairs, tables, hanging from curtains; cats everywhere! She could almost hear Nora's delighted laugh when she unwrapped it. It pleased Lea to please the daughter she dearly adored.

CHAPTER 9.

Waves were pounding on the rocks and the fog descended like a great blanket of gray velvet. Lea could only see about a foot outside as though the studio were enclosed in a thick curtain. However, the salt aroma intensified by the fog was pleasant and the mournful sound of Baker's Light fog horn was eerie and yet heartening. While waiting for Sarah to pick her up for Tai Chi she played some of Robert Schumann's "Scenes From Childhood" on her beat up, second hand piano, again this had been a swap for a painting of the antique store where she'd found it. Sarah was coming by to take her to their once a week Tai Chi and Chi Gong class. Sarah came in the unlocked door.

"Hi Sarah, you're early. We have time for a cup of coffee before we try to find our way in this pea soup fog. Why don't we walk? You can leave your car here."

"I brought you some hot popovers I just took out of the oven, Luv, I know you like them a lot. I think the fog might lift soon, Lea. Did you rehearse every day? Did you do "repulse the monkey" or "crane cooling its wings"? They both always promised Mr. Lee Sah they would faithfully go through the forms every day between classes but rarely did.

Lea slathered a hot popover with sweet butter, no one made them like Sarah- brown and crisp on the outside and soft and lovely on the inside. "Oh, Sarah, yum! Please tell me your secret, your popovers are the best!"

Sitting at her old pine table after pouring fresh coffee for them both and laying out some Finnish coffee cake beside the popovers, Lea said hesitantly, "Sarah, I think I'm becoming a little paranoid. I keep having this feeling that I'm being watched, I sense eyes on me. I know it's crazy!"

"Paranoid? Of course not, Luv! Perhaps you *are* being watched. How about that elderly semi-senile neighbor who was starkers on your patio a while back? Maybe he wants to give you another peek at his delicious family jewels," Sarah chortled.

"Oh please!" Lea groaned, "I saw them once and that was enough. Such a pathetic, shriveled up bag of paste gems, you can't imagine. He looked like a painting by Egon Schiele. Besides, Bernice, the neighborhood gossip, said he's gone into a nursing home. He kept running around naked until he was taken away, poor soul. This feeling is really different. I did see someone once looking into my studio windows from the terrace but we get so many nosy tourists I pretty much ignored it. Someone being funny nailed a dead raccoon to my door," she shuddered "and then, too, there's the man who was shot out front, that was real, Sarah."

"Seriously, Lea, if you feel this strongly about it report it to the police."

"How can I report a feeling?" Lea logically responded. "the way the police log is written up in the "Reporter", they seem to ridicule every telephone call. Last week it said, 'Woman reported intruder. It was found to be a bag of clothing." Then when they were called by another neighbor about our bare bag of bones, it read 'Naked man reported on Front Street. Caller said it isn't funny.'

"I heard the "Village Voice" in New York prints our police reports verbatim for laughs and now the dispatchers seem to vie to be the most clever and amusing. I don't think I am imagining it but perhaps-" Her voice trailed off.

"Be careful Lea, I do believe you and I know you don't always lock everything up tight even at night. It's probably a teenager or a wandering tourist." Sarah tried to reassure her. "Neither seem to have any limits or know the difference between public and private property. I've caught sweet old ladies picking the lilacs right out of my front yard, apparently they think anything seaside is 'quaint' and fair game for souvenirs. They can be real pains in the patoot," She frowned, "Sometimes rude but usually harmless."

Lea nodded, "That must be it." But stubbornly she thought, *Why sneak around and not show themselves? Who nailed that dead raccoon to my door? Someone shot that man on my patio.*

She got up from her chair saying firmly, "I refuse to let it get to me. It's ridiculous and I'm obsessing. Another month or so and the B&B's will be mostly empty. There'll be fewer day-trippers and

Marblehead will be our dull, quiet, small town again where nothing much exciting happens." (*Except, they both thought, a dead man.*)

"Amen! That's the way I like it. You have Tony's dog for protection, too." Here they both laughed knowing the oversized and fierce looking Lucy was in truth a sincere card holding wuss and pussycat. Hearing her name Lucy thumped her tail in agreement.

Sarah went on, "The population in the summer often triples with sixteen B&B's, the day trippers, Race Week, the Arts Festival, visiting boatmen, and seasonal yacht clubs open for their members many who live out of town in the winter."

Lea added, "The traffic on our narrow mostly one-way streets which were never intended for automobiles is horrendous, absolutely fender bending and trying to park anywhere down town, the tourists call "OLDE TOWNE" as taught by the Realtors, while the natives laugh. We're fortunate to be able to walk to most of the shops and fish market and grocery store."

Some 'headers even left the greatest place on earth to be in the summertime and escaped to Maine, New Hampshire and Vermont to lakeside cottages or to Nova Scotia for their vacations charging hefty rents for summer rentals. To their dismay they often found similar situations except now they were the interlopers to those natives who also were into soaking the summer renter.

New England had too much sparkling waters of ocean and lakes, green gold mountains and meadows, too brazenly beautiful for people not to descend upon it like locusts in the summer and for the spectacular blaze of autumn color. Winter snow brought skiers to the mountains. In season nothing could beat sweet, wild blueberries, corn on the cob, fresh dug clams, cold water fish and lobster. The native vine-ripened tomatoes were another fatal attraction. Many natives survived financially only because of these treasures. They were philosophic about it and willing to share and welcomed all visitors and tourists.

The icy cold water bred good, firm fish and lobster and the semi-rocky soil grew the delicious berries and vegetables to which the effete, warmer climate's produce could never compare in a million years, so said the Yankees!

One old timer drawled, "Florida lobsta? It's crawfish and it makes you puke."

Indeed, haddock and cod and halibut were firmer and tastier than pompano, red snapper or any of the softer, warm water fish, Tony's fishing buddy Will, loyally maintained.

The fog lifting, Sarah and Lea drove off to the Tai Chi class they'd been taking for several years and admitted shamefaced to each other they were still barely proficient at the forms. Secretly they followed a couple other students, Paula and the lone man, Marvin, who obviously did practice at home.

On the way, careful to stay within the bounds of lawyer-client confidentiality, Lea asked, "How's Claire coming along? You are a saint to take her on, Sarah, thanks."

Enthusiastically Sarah responded, "Claire is going places! Did you know she can sing like an angel and under that messy, bedraggled exterior she is absolutely gorgeous? I placed her and the kids in a safe house where Ray cannot find them. I filed for a restraining order against him and this week am filing for divorce. I'm afraid he is quite angry. The bank told me when Ray went to withdraw Claire's money and found it gone he had a large screaming tantrum in their lobby! It was Claire's inheritance from her mother, not a lot but enough to give her a start away from Ray. But of course, he thought he owned it just as he did Claire."

Lea was surprised yet felt a wave of happiness for Claire and love for Sarah who was unfailingly kind. It seemed Ray might not win this one after all? Another victory for their side!

For Hanukah and Christmas combined Sarah had given Lea a gift of an amaryllis bulb planted in a pot. When it burst into glorious pink bloom Lea painted a small oil on canvas of it for Sarah's birthday. She intended to give it to her today.

After class she urged Sarah to stay for supper with her and Tony. Cautiously Sarah asked, "What is it?" Once she had been stuck with Lea's specialty of fried eel. She had pronounced it frankly nauseas but Lea was not offended. Few people other than Scandinavians and Italians liked eel.

"Your favorite baked stuffed shrimp."

"Well then of course I'll stay, I love it!"

While Lea assembled the casserole, layering the shrimp with cracker crumbs mixed with melted butter and lobster tomalley, Sarah made a salad. She tossed some avocado slices with lemon juice so they would not discolor, then added leftover crumbled breakfast bacon from the counter, shallots and tinned mandarin orange segments. A dressing made from balsamic vinegar, garlic, olive oil and lemon juice and spices was poured over all. She lined a bowl with leaf lettuce as they both disliked iceberg. "La Salade!" she crowed.

They began to giggle like school girls as they worked companionably. Sarah, who rarely swore said, "Where's Tony? You know I've always wanted to say to someone, 'get your ass over here!' I never dared. Shall I call him and say it? I hear the guys in my office using this expression all the time and there are times I envy them!"

Both rather looked down upon women who used bad or dirty language but tucked into their repertoire were pretty racy phrases, sometimes wistfully they wished they dared say aloud. Thinking they were alone they indulged their desire to "talk dirty."

Sarah repeated, "Get your ass over here!"

Emboldened, then from Lea, "How's your macaroni, Tony?" With a sly glance at Sarah who was dating a lawyer, Richard Rubin, she dared, "How's your prick, Dick? Or vice versa."

"Go blow it out your leggings," Sarah said, "A sailor told me that once. I think he was in the Coast Guard, who else wears leggings?"

Lea: "Leggings suck."

Sarah: "He sucks, she sucks, everything sucks." Laughing they tried to top one another.

Lea: "Shit sucks."

Sarah: "Fucks suck."

They dissolved into childish uncontrollable spasms of laughter like naughty school girls yet felt better for their private catharsis. Tony, standing in the doorway listening was vastly amused. If aware they'd been overheard both girls would have blushed beet red. Grinning, he ducked out and made a noisy reentrance with loud foot steps and whistling nonchalantly.

Sarah whispered, "It's that damn Ray who makes me want to curse."

Lea whispered back, blushing, "Ray's a bona fide fucking bastard! I win!"

Tony sniffed appreciatively, "Am I invited?" He joined them at the table before they could answer in the affirmative or negative. He uncorked a bottle of new Beaujolais he had saved since it came in December and poured it into three jelly glasses. Lea only owned two wine glasses. (He made a mental note to buy her half a dozen if she would let him.) While they ate Tony told them the fellow he'd met at the boat yard, Will Bartlett, with whom he had gone fishing, had invited him out on his lobster boat "Mandy" to fish again tomorrow.

"I'll bring back a cod or a striper or a bluefish for sure, Lea. You can dickey it up with all the basil, dill, tarragon, garlic and crumbs your little heart desires and we can bake, broil or grill it. And Sarah, my dear, you can come for dinner, too," He offered generously.

"Better bring a can of tuna," Lea teased. "He usually catches hake or old rubber boots."

Tony put on a hurt look and mock punched her on her shoulder. "You wait, Caramia, you'll have fish swimming out of the house. We'll have to make an announcement on the steps of Abbot Hall to give it all away!"

"There's always the Fish Market, Sarah."

Tony gave Lea an accusing glare pretending he was greatly offended. Demurely Sarah said, "I'd love lobster too, can you manage that, Tony?"

"Anything for the birthday girl," he said magnanimously. "You shall have it."

"And I want you to have your birthday present right now," added Lea.

The telephone rang and she went to the kitchen to answer. She called to Sarah.

"It was some sort of message for you, Sarah. A man said you're wanted back at your office right now and then he hung up before I could ask him who was calling."

She dialed Sarah's office for her but got a busy signal. "Want me to try it again?'

"No, don't bother. Who wants me and why at eight o'clock I wonder? Which lawyer was it, Lea? Did it sound like Dick Rubin? I'd better run over and see what's up. I'll be back for my present, Lea, never fear, this shouldn't take long."

She kissed Lea on the cheek and left hurriedly. Lea and Tony washed up the dishes, Lea washed and he dried with a towel wrapped around his middle. Lea thought he looked so cute but didn't say so. She had few appliances other than an old refrigerator and stove. Tony was eager to remedy the lack and at least buy a dishwasher for her but Lea did not accept gifts easily and put him off whenever he mentioned shopping for new kitchen appliances. "I get along fine with what I have," she'd almost bristle.

After the dishes were done Tony said, "Let's have dessert," kissing her soft, vulnerable neck and whispering in her ear, "How dolce you are," they climbed up to the loft.

At 10:30 they realized how late it had become while they made love (Lea had opened like a flower after a long drought), she rushed to the telephone and called Sarah's office. All she heard was a taped message giving the office hours and the partners' names.

"I've got to go over there and see if something's wrong, Sarah's not answering the phone, I'm a little worried but I suppose she could be on her way here but so late?"

Sensing her anxiety Tony said, "I'll drive you to Salem right now. Let's go."

When they arrived at the law offices on Federal Street they found the front door ajar. Apprehensively Lea walked up the dimly lit stairway to Sarah's office with Tony close behind her. Calling, "Sarah? Sarah?" She walked into the office. Sarah was sitting in her desk chair with her face down on her desk. Blood was all over her sabra dark hair. Lea screamed. "She's dead, oh God, Sarah's dead!"

Tony gently pushed Lea aside and examined Sarah for a pulse or heart beat but there was none. Cradling sobbing Lea in his arms he covered one hand with a handkerchief careful of possible fingerprints and dialed 911. Lea was keening, crying over and over, "Why? Why Sarah? My wonderful friend I love so much, she's so good, who could do this terrible thing, kill my lovely Sarah?" She was hysterical with grief and shock. Irrationally she sobbed, "And I never got to give her the painting for her birthday."

After the police arrived and Sarah's body was removed they questioned them both extensively. Finally Tony held up his hand and stopped them, "Can't you see she's distraught?" He said angrily, his eyes flashing, "This woman was her best friend. I'm going to take her home, please move."

With his arms around Lea he pushed through the policemen and led her to the car. She wept all the way home. Tony's heart ached for her. He brought her in and helped undress her for bed. He gave her a sleeping pill he found in her medicine cabinet in the bathroom left over from a recent root canal. Tenderly Tony tucked Lea in bed while tears were still running down her face and piteous moans were coming from her mouth.

He prayed desperately this wasn't connected to his cousins or the St. Theresa. Superstitiously he was beginning to feel the sculpture had a curse on it. Tony imagined Gian Bellini writhing in his crypt and St. Theresa weeping tears of blood, as an old legend related.

How could a beautiful piece of art be a catalyst for so much evil and death? Art imitates life as life often imitates art and was never innately corrupt itself. Only those around it could be. He tried to think logically. There had to be some good come from the sculpture. All art was a gift given by the creator so that artists could also create. Surely it was intended to be healing and spiritually renewing, wasn't it?

"I vow if I ever reclaim the statue I'll sell it to a museum and give all the proceeds to the "Little Sisters Of The Poor Innocents.""

They ran an orphanage in Rome and in grace and faith accomplished miraculous good works for those little one without an advocate. Their patron saint and role model was St. Theresa. Tony whispered, "I know Nonna, you will approve this use of the marble and bless the intention."

CHAPTER 10.

Lea was determined not to cry openly at Sarah's memorial service held at the Hebrew Reform Temple Emmanuel on Atlantic Avenue in the Clifton section of Marblehead. Sarah had been proud and brave, Lea's role model. Lea wanted not to break down at Sarah's service but remain as proud and as brave as her friend had always been. Her eyes were red and puffy and her handkerchief a sodden ball in her hand.

Sylvia Sherman, Sarah's assistant, sat beside her holding her hand. Although a Jewish Princess with a substantial independent income, Sylvia had graduated from law school and passed the bar with flying colors. She had worshiped Sarah, her employer as well as friend and mentor.

An intense, colorful, pretty young woman, she was dressed today in a scarlet caftan, size four. Sylvia seemed to almost vibrate with the palpable anger under her genuine grief. She had taken over most of Sarah's cases and was determined to continue with the rehabilitation of Claire and safely see her through her divorce. Emotionally shattered and frightened by Sarah's brutal death, Claire wanted to withdraw from the bitter divorce suit. Comforted and cajoled by Sylvia she'd been convinced Sarah would want Claire to carry on to a good resolution for her and her children's lives.

Sylvia was tiny and slender, black hair swept into a chignon and eyes like jumbo black olives. Extremely pretty, she honeyed over her razor sharp intelligence with a great deal of charm. She'd passed the bar recently and the other attorneys in the practice respected her for the number of cases she'd already won. At the moment her love life was at a standstill. She was in love with a young detective, Skip O'Halloran. They'd broken up because of religious differences. Stubborn Sylvia wouldn't give up her Judaism for his Roman Catholicism and they remained at an impasse.

The other lawyers respected her abilities and took her seriously once they got beyond dismissing her because of her flashy, almost frivolous appearance. Amongst themselves they called her "the little Jewish bombshell" but were extremely careful not to say this where she might overhear, although of course she had. They thought she would be capable of suing on Anti-Semitic grounds!

She as well as they knew the sobriquet meant little except profound awe for her talent and a lot of admiration for her beauty. Sylvia never let on she was wise to her nickname, indeed she took a secret, flattered delight in it, proud to be a Jewess and pleased to be considered a bombshell!

Tony sat on Lea's other side, also holding a hand. Lea put on a stony, stoical expression yet when the Rabbi read from the Old Testament, "Sarah was a woman beyond jewels, true, steadfast and loving." she swallowed painfully and hard. She knew absolutely just how true and loving Sarah had been to everyone. The children's Bell Choir was ringing in her honor. Sarah would be delighted, she loved children and was their advocate. Sadly all Lea could think was, *my sister, my friend, my Sarah is gone! May angels fly her to her rest. (*Do Jews believe in angels? She wondered forlornly.)

Recently they'd helped plan an annual interfaith service; Sarah represented the Temple and Lea the Lutheran congregation. It had been well attended and a success, a testament to the solidarity of the various faiths as all the churches and temples took part and took turns hosting the service. The covenant was passed each year to another church, or temple stating the promise of ecumenicity and brotherhood. This was sponsored by the Marblehead Ministerial Association made up of Rabbi's, Roman Catholic Priests and Protestant Ministers, Anglican Rectors, other Pastors and denominations such as the Sufi and B'hai. Twenty years before a temple had been defaced and vandalized. Outraged, the Christian clergy and lay people resolved this could and would never again happen and the Ministerial Association was formed.

Sarah had been the past year's convener for the monthly luncheon meetings arranging for outside speakers and the current issues to be discussed.

The clergy processed in together and filled a front row in the temple. One at a time each went to the podium and spoke a few words during the eulogy of glowing tributes to Sarah's sterling character and especially her good work for abused women.

Lea softly wept murmuring, *Oh, Sarah, I've lost you forever.*

Tony and Sylvia could only each hold one of her hands and grieve as well for lovely Sarah. Sylvia's caftan was sewn all over with tiny silver bells. Dabbing at her eyes, Lea sneaked a peek down at Sylvia's red shoes. Yes, each had a silver bell on its toe.

Lea had to smile, longing for Sarah to laugh fondly with her at this Oz creation. Whenever Sylvia even slightly shifted, myriad bells tinkled softly giving an aura of a Buddhist rather than a Hebrew temple. Sarah would have definitely approved, Lea was sure and been deliciously amused. She'd been tickled by Sylvia's new lavender Porsche and had laughed and cheered when Sylvia drove it to her house to show it off. Lea felt an epiphany moment-perhaps loyal Sylvia is my heritage from Sarah?

Sarah's beloved Bach, Brahms, Beethoven, Chopin and Debussy were being played, some of the usual funeral rules were bent for Sarah. As the congregation rose to leave for the funeral meats in the large hall prepared by Hadassah the closing hymn was a Christian one for ecumenical Sarah she'd often played on her flute for Lea: "Jesu, Joy of Man's Desiring" by Bach.

Emotionally drained, Lea shook her head "no," to refreshments and passively allowed Tony to take her home in silence. There she sat on the rock terrace, patting Lucy and staring out to sea. She had stopped crying, she imagined she heard Sarah saying, "Enough already, Lea!" It was painful to lose a friend, however. How could she ever get over it?

Tony stopped at the Police Station on Atlantic Avenue the following morning. The officer on duty at the front desk told him when queried, "We've not yet got a match from the victim's prints or DNA results and we're still waiting to hear from the Italian Central Intelligence Bureau. This whole thing turned out to be more complex than we at first thought. There are no records for either one at the FBI headquarters so far, but we have a partial identification of Donald Bell, a former agent."

"With his face demolished by the bullet wound, it ain't been easy! His picture shows he had a long scar on one cheek. The weight, height, and build is similar."

"That's all the information I'm authorized to give out at this time," He added a bit pompously, quite self-important. "Don't leave town, we want to interview both you and Lea Lantana again."

Tony thanked him. Who the hell had been shot? Cousin Roberto or the P.I. Bell whom Randall had hired for him in New York? Or could it be someone else entirely? And why? What was the motive? He worried the nagging questions in his mind.

Tony thought of an old Italian proverb, "If you want to find the runaway horse, first you must think like a horse." He laughed, "Okay, Nonna, I'll try."

CHAPTER 11.

Lea was running sad. Sarah's death left a big hole in her heart, she grieved for her and for her own loss. Life was drab without her buddy to talk and laugh with and confide in. To distract her and since now he was unable to leave Marblehead (he was glad about that) Tony suggested they drive into the Museum of Fine Arts to see the Sargent Exhibit and have lunch in the charming cafe I. M. Pei had designed. He had done an outstanding architectural feat of the whole wing, sort of a miniature of the one he'd designed for the National Gallery in Washington, D.C. Boston Lutherans were proud of the new church Pei had designed for them, too.

"Lea, you have two free tickets to the exhibit, anyway, as a member? I really think you can use the diversion."

After driving into Boston they parked Tony's red Volkswagen in the last open spot on the roof of the parking garage. They took the elevator down and crossed the street to the museum and then mounted the escalator upstairs to the Sargent show held in the

Graham Gund Galleries. Carefully they viewed the blockbuster show in attentive silence each going at his own pace. Lea liked this, not being hurried by a fellow viewer. They met in the gift shop then descended to the cafe for lunch.

"We should have made reservations for the dining room upstairs. Here it's la-di-dah lady's food," Tony complained looking over the menu. "At least we can get a glass of vino."

Enjoying her Caesar Salad and Chardonnay wine (to her satisfaction the salad actually had anchovies in it not just a hint in the dressing) Lea asked quizzically.

"Well, what did you think of the show?"

Smiling ruefully Tony answered decisively and bluntly, "A crashing bore! Like the Monet and Mary Cassatt exhibits before this one."

Tony continued coolly. "They seem to recycle old paintings from the archives most of us have seen a hundred times in other exhibits or art books. I didn't realize the MFA had become such a fusty old lady!" Nostalgically he thought of his early years going in with his Dad and Mother who worked there when all had seemed fresh and new to him.

Lea said defensively, "The MFA mounts some innovative and excellent shows in their smaller galleries from time to time. Last month, Nora's Cuban friend from college, Abe Morell, had a wonderful photography exhibit. They have to raise money to do that from these huge blockbusters the public will attend because they've heard of the artist and haven't heard of, for the most part, an unknown like Abe who thanks to his exposure here is getting more acclaim."

95

"Yes, I agree it's pretty blatant and embarrassing to make money on T-shirts, mugs and posters in the gift shops, "She laughed, "But is there anything really wrong with that?"

Tony gave Lea one of his eyebrow raised looks. "The best part of this exhibit was Sargent's murals they restored and cleaned and placed in the rotunda of the Grand Staircase. That was a fine effort."

"Mostly it seems to me rather patronizing to exploit the largely non art-educated public into thinking they are gaining instant culture and status by attending a famous name show. Yes, Lea, you are correct, the museum does raise a lot of money this way. I suppose if it helps newer and younger painters, of course I'm all for it."

"Sargent was a virtuoso painter although poor at drawing hands! I like his watercolors which are spontaneous, lovely and moving. Why did the curator give such a prominent place to his black male model? Are we supposed to be titillated and assume they were lovers because Sargent never married? What's that got to do with painting?"

"Actually I found that portrait the most exciting piece there with genuine emotion and a painterly impact. Perhaps I malign those who planned the exhibit? Anyway, Caralea, we had a nice day?" His spirits were improved and he was glad to see Lea's were, too.

"It's always a nice day for me, Tony love, when looking at paintings no matter whose, the known and the unknown. Next will you take me to the Addison Gallery at Phillips Andover Academy? They are doing a large retrospective of Alice Neel's work.

She was way ahead of her time, born one hundred years ago. I'm told the centerpiece is a nude self-portrait she painted at age eighty! A "here I am, warts and all"! I'm really eager to see that, I love that kind of spunk." Her eyes sparkled.

Tony smiled at her. "That sounds more promising, I like daring and innovative work even if it were done twenty years ago. Yes Cara, let's drive to Andover soon and have a nice lunch at the Inn, too."

Unaware Tony's first twelve years were spent on the North Shore Lea was surprised he knew of Andover, a prominent prep school and also the noted Andover Inn.

Lea's spirit was very slowly healing when she received another gut-wrenching blow. For a year Elissa Craig had been a private pupil. She was in her early twenty's and an old school friend of Nora's. Elissa had attended an exhibit of Lea's and shortly afterward telephoned to ask if she would give her some private lessons. Not knowing from whence it came on an impulse Lea agreed. Private lessons were not usually profitable and were time consuming to have only one student to demonstrate for and teach rather than a class format of six to eight. However, Nora had spoken highly of Elissa and Lea had liked her immediately and felt drawn to the forthright and attractive girl.

She wondered how Elissa would be able to come in the mornings which she'd requested as she had recently graduated from Middlebury College in Vermont and presumably should have a job?

Elissa was a vibrant, thin, sweet and charming girl who after the third session announced matter of factly she was suffering from Hodgkins Lymphoma, a type of cancer.

"Can't you tell I'm wearing a wig? I lost all my hair in chemo."

Lea was impressed with Elissa's talent for watercolor and with the sensitive cheerful girl she seemed to be. She made elaborate, color related set-ups of still lifes of fruit, bottles, flowers, and vases for Elissa to paint from at her old pine table. Lea became fond of her and felt anxious the days Elissa would telephone to cancel when she had more chemotherapy and was too ill and weak to come to class.

Nora was delighted her mother was teaching an old grade school friend of hers and wrote to Elissa. In a great burst of flowering creativity Elissa painted lovely, truly beautiful watercolors with only a little instruction and tutelage the days she felt strong enough to come to Lea's studio. When the weather permitted they painted outdoors, plein air painting.

Their last session before Elissa was to go into Dana Farber Caancer Hospital in Cambridge for a bone marrow washing Lea drove them to Redd's Pond. Lately Elissa had seemed more frail. Lea worried about her sitting in the sun for so long but Elissa refused to stop until she'd finished the painting.

"Elissa! This is your masterpiece! It's a moving watercolor of the pond and the willow tree reflections, and it's quite beautiful. It's perfect!"

Lea sincerely and extravagantly praised and congratulated Elissa, they hugged one another. They'd never talked about her illness much; Lea sensed Elissa needed and wanted their time together to be happy and absorbed in color and painting. Her mother said when she concentrated on that for an hour or two it was a brief surcease from her illness. One day Elissa told Lea she had given up her therapist a few weeks before whom she'd been sent to for emotional and psychological support.

"She's a nice person and kind but I told her I didn't need to come any more because I had Lea Lantana for my therapy! Painting helps so much."

Lea was touched and humbled she could help Elissa through what turned out to be the last year of her young life.

Elissa was to stay isolated for a month in a completely sterile environment in the hospital after the procedure. She could have no visitors other than her parents who had to be robed and masked to see her. Lea talked on the telephone to her and wrote encouraging letters. Learning a nurse had to hold the phone for her, Elissa was so weak, Lea knew the progress was not going as well as everyone had prayed.

When the call came that Elissa had died that morning Lea took a long walk on the beach. At the studio she painted a spontaneous watercolor without preliminary drawing, including the vases, pears and flowers she'd used for Elissa's set-ups. It was an extraordinary gift Lea felt she had been given by God to share Elissa's last year and perhaps helping a person to die on almost a joyous note? She wrote a poem to Elissa.

For the memorial service at the Unitarian-Universalist Church on Mugford Street, Elissa's stalwart mother placed many of her daughter's paintings in the front of the church near the pulpit.

The last picture of the pond Elissa had given to the hospital telling her mother it was because all the doctors and nurses had been so kind to her. Maybe she had some foreknowledge? A nurse who loved her drove the painting from Cambridge to Marblehead to lend for the funeral.

Elissa had helped plan her service with the woman minister who told the congregation, "Today is Elissa's first birthday in eternity."

She said "Elissa said, I will be giving a party!"

Elissa had chosen a whimsical tale to be read of faith and hope, a favorite of hers. The song she'd chosen for all her friends and family to sing, Cat Steven's "Morning Has Broken," just about broke Lea's heart. As Elissa had requested for her "party" there was much festive food, laughing and visiting after the service in the church hall which was crowded.

Lea met the therapist Elissa had told her about. Generously she told Lea how much the painting lessons had meant and were spiritually so important to her Elissa felt she needed no further therapy sessions. "I was happy for her because it made her so happy. I felt you resonated with each other."

And so yet another memorial service of much loved people in her life. Lea felt depressed and emotionally, mentally and physically devoid of strength. Without Tony's love she felt she could have given up painting and perhaps even living. He was an enormous emotional support whom Lea now loved without reservations. He was kind, patient and gentle. When she sometimes cried Lucy's sympathetic devotion touched her too and gave her a measure of strength. Hugging the dog, she whispered, "We resonate, Lucy." Lucy licked Lea's hand and thumped her tail in assent.

ON THE SIDE OF THE ANGELS
(Sonnet for Elissa)

You left in autumn, the day of the golden leaves
Life bursting before the death of life.
The breath of angels like gossamer sheaves
Breathed on you after that brave and gallant strife
To fly you into the golden light, somewhere a rebirth.
All whom you magic-touched grew in love
And life and caring, left behind on earth.
Each day was new to you, a great feast of love
And life a celebration! Elissa, who only knew
How to live and love, and scattered rainbows
everywhere
With the inborn wisdom of what is good and true,
Laughed and made of life a grand affair. We who
Cared, sweet girl, know you always chose to be
On the side of the angels, joyously.

CHAPTER 12.

Lea and Tony were lingering on her rock terrace after dinner with their coffee as the night descended. She had prepared a Finnish chicken dinner with Havarti cheese, grapes and slivered almonds and invited Sylvia to join them. First Tony brought out his antipasto to nibble on with bread sticks and the Soave wine. Dessert had been Siri's old fashioned Pineapple Upside Down cake and Sylvia's Raspberry Cheese cake.

Tony had never had an upside down cake and declared it Lea's best cake yet so she decided not to tell him it was her easiest, made with a cake mix, brown sugar and a can of pineapple rings.

Sylvia had brought her one "claim to fame" dessert her mother had taught her to make-a raspberry cheese cake with a subtle bit of crumbled fresh lavender in it. Tony obligingly sampled each cake and lavishly complimented both cooks. Generously, Lea kissed Sylvia and told her sincerely hers was the best. Sylvia left for her Swampscott home, roaring off in her lilac color Porsche.

Suddenly a miracle! A huge, bright-orange full moon appeared on the horizon popping up in front of their eyes. As it rose in the sky it cast a silver path on the ocean, its orange turning to a silvery moon color. The green light on top of the lighthouse on the neck cast its wiggly green reflection on the water as well. Tony and Lea sat in awed silence for a while absorbing how breathtakingly beautiful a full moon-rise was on the ocean and in the sky. They were quiet as they drank in its spell-binding magic.

After a while Lea said, "Tony, I really have to know what is going on. I'm vulnerable where Nora is concerned and it alarms me a strange Italian man came here and then approached my daughter in Australia. Where is all the death coming from? Why here, why close to me? I want an explanation! I desperately need to know and feel Nora is safe," She pleaded.

Just then the telephone rang and she ran inside to get it. It was Nora. A sixteen hour time difference meant it was only 1 a.m. in Sydney and this further upset Lea.

Nora, in a subdued tone said, "Mom? That man died. He'd been brain dead for two weeks. Rod and I were the only people who went in every day to see him. He never regained consciousness. They could find no relatives or friends, at least not in Sydney. The doctors at the hospital asked us to sign permission to remove the life supports as it stayed a flat line for so long. Maybe we shouldn't have? Rod felt it was the most merciful thing to do and insisted on taking care of the expenses. He's a compassionate guy. They said we could sign "in loco parentis" as we were his only known contact. I just wanted you to know, Mom. Love you, 'bye."

The usually bubbling Nora sounded sad and troubled. She'd always been a sensitive girl and taken things to heart despite her jolly manner.

Lea went back outside to the patio and repeated Nora's news to Tony who hugged her close and kissed the top of her head.

"Lea, I'll tell you everything I know. It all began with a nine-inch marble statue of St. Theresa sculpted in Italy in 1658 as a kind of template by Gian Bellini. It has been in the Amberetti-Scola family for centuries, a wedding gift to an early bride. My grandmother, Angela, willed it to me. When she died it was stolen. I've been trying to recover it with the help of a lawyer and a private detective, a former FBI agent."

Tony continued, "I feel sure my cousins stole it and want to get rid of me and sell the statue for millions of dollars." He groaned, "I'm afraid I've put you and Nora in jeopardy and danger by falling in love with you, Carissima, I'm full of remorse. Please, can you forgive me?"

He went on relating more details, holding nothing back, anxious to tell Lea everything, telling her also about his childhood not many miles away.

She listened attentively. "But why Sarah?"

"I don't know. Perhaps to hurt you because I love you or to scare us both off? It makes no sense. However I'm more determined than ever to see my cousins in prison for theft and murder. If you want me to I'll leave Marblehead today. Perhaps that will draw them away from you."

"Tony, no! It's best we carry on as normally as possible and we need each other- at least I need you, badly."

"And I, you," he whispered as he bent to kiss her. "Especially," He teased, "your cooking."

Lea felt happier the next day relieved of the mystery and lurking doubts she'd had about Tony. She wished she could tell Sarah. Humming, she went out into her small kitchen garden where she grew herbs and a few tomatoes, planning to pick the very first ripe tomato she'd noticed from her window. Lea wanted to surprise Tony with a BLT for lunch.

She knew it was absurd to be so excited about a tomato but Lea gave almost equal emphasis to all natural events in her life from sun and moon rises to the first tomato of the season. It was an Early Girl, her favorite variety, at that.

In her kitchen garden she found Bernice, her least favorite neighbor AKA "the voice of ultimate authority." In Bernice's hand was Lea's first gorgeous large, red ripe tomato. Startled, Bernice said defensively, "You have so many about to ripen, I didn't think you'd mind if I took one for my friend Irene? She loves home grown tomatoes."

As usual Lea thought, she'd think of the perfect retort later, probably in the middle of the night. Nervously, Bernice chattered on. "I really came here to tell you, even though you are living in your father's old fishing shack this is a zoned, historic residential area after all. Some people don't like you conducting a business here."

Puzzled, Lea said, "A business?"

"Selling paintings from your house!" Bernice snapped triumphantly.

Lea had to smile a little. She'd sold about six the whole year showing them at a small local cooperative gallery, "The Art Guild" on Washington Street. Although irate, she was too upset to do more than turn on her heel and go back inside. With a sudden inspiration she drawled over her shoulder, "I don't know anyone I'd rather have steal from me than you, Bernice," closing her door with a slight bang.

Angry from her head to her toes she gripped the kitchen counter top counting to ten. Bernice had this effect on everyone. Then Lea laughed out loud and muttered.

"Right, Bernice. You are the bitchiest neighbor anyone could be blessed to have!"

Lea was miffed she'd missed her first tomato of the season, one she had watched ripen and so looked forward to picking to surprise Tony with a delicious BLT.

"So? I'll make tuna sandwiches with celery, scallion, cucumber, olives and pecans mixed with my homemade mayonnaise instead. I'm being childish, there'll be many more tomatoes. I'll be damned if I'll offer Bernice any again, she'll have to steal them!"

Bernice was the same neighbor who when invited to view Lea's renovations to the studio, formerly a fishing shack, had laughed scornfully, saying.

"Purple? Purple in a bedroom? I guess we all have different taste."

Lea knew she meant inferior and murmured, "It's eggplant." If anyone did not paint his or her walls the same boring off-white Bernice did, their taste was execrable. She had also complained to the Post Office about Lea's return stickers because they read "Lea Lantana's Studio." The mail carrier said she was told it was none of her business and as long as street, number, town, state and ZIP code were on the bottom two lines you could call your place anything you wished. Flippantly he said, "You can call your place the Good Ship Lollypop if you want to." Under his breath he muttered, "Or Bernice's Brothel." Bernice definitely was not popular.

Like most people Lea avoided her. She could just barely stand her rudeness and nosiness. Still she reluctantly felt sorry for her. Intuitively she guessed something sad in this woman's past must have shaped her vitriolic, sharp-tongued and critical personality? Lea was correct. Bernice's daughter confided the facts to her one day.

"My grandmother died in childbirth when my mother was born. My grandfather hired an overly strict, unaffectionate German housekeeper, Elsa Smitt. She was a live-in Nanny and housekeeper until mother was nine and grandfather married Elsa. My mother said Elsa told him she was pregnant but she wasn't. He probably had slept with her all those years after his wife died? My mother said Elsa constantly criticized her and made her cry. Mother didn't seem to see she'd taken on the same traits she had despised in her step-mother and almost made me hate my own mother! My father died young and my mother was bitter about that, too. My childhood was not a happy one."

The stern, unloving archetype of the wicked stepmother had shaped Bernice's persona, Lea surmised. Why do so many people do this? They either take on and repeat the same behavior they hated in their parents or pell-mell went racing to the complete opposite extreme.

When Bernice's daughter, who rarely came from Oregon to visit her mother, told Lea her mother's history, she said to herself feeling ashamed.

"How can I stay angry with what really is a manifestation of a nine-year old child's pain?" She shouldn't she knew, it was just the woman was so maddeningly irritating and frequently abrasive it was difficult if not impossible to refrain from resenting her. "I resolve I'll turn the other cheek and give dear Bernice a huge bag of tomatoes when they ripen." Wickedly she added, "Then again I might shove them in her face!"

She felt sympathy for the hurt little girl Bernice must have been. Actually she was quite pretty but her habitual scowl and whining nasal voice obscured her good looks. Lea hoped she'd be able to be more patient with her but patience was not her long suit and Bernice, in truth, was a real witch however she'd come by it.

CHAPTER 13.

Tony was reveling in the beautiful blue-green ocean (Lea said matched his eyes) and the cobalt blue sky from Will Bartlett's lobster boat, "Mandy." Early morning was always the best time to fish. During the past year he'd developed a strong friendship with the fisherman-carpenter he met at the boatyard. Now they were close buddies. Loyally, Will supported Tony through the many interrogations he and Lea had been forced to undergo and Will filled in for him when this made Tony late for work. He also ferociously put down any rumors he heard in town or at the State Street Wharf purporting that Tony had killed Lea Lantana's lover.

"Hey Tony," Will said as they headed out to fish for striped bass off Tinker's Island, "If you need any kind of an alibi, buddy, you can count on me. I'm your man."

"Alibi? I didn't kill anyone, for God's sake!"

"I'm just sayin', paisan, I don't give a shit if you did, I'll back you all the way."

"I'm grateful for your vote of confidence," Tony retorted sarcastically, "But I'm not the one who needs an alibi. What can you tell me about that guy, Ray Larson?"

"Cripes, Larson's a bad lot. He's a sore loser and a drunk but he's a handsome devil. Don't cross him! We heard the young girl he married after Lea left him is getting a divorce, too. I knew Claire way back in high school, she was pretty then. She should leave him, he's a brutal bastard to her and his own kids. I hope she's safely hidden someplace because Ray's apt to kill her if he finds her."

Will gave Tony a searching glance, "I don't wanna know nothin' I might spill after a few beers at the Tidal Rip or at Maddie's." Turning serious, "Watch your back son, and make very sure Lea stays out of his way."

Will was only a few years older than Tony but he loved to give him advice.

"Ray always was a jealous son of a bitch. Nobody dared ask Lea for a date when he was going with her. By the way who's the skinny little wop in town looking for an Antonio Scola? That wouldn't be you, would it? I told him I never heard of the guy. Hey, hey! There's a bunch of schoolies, let's get fishin'."

Tony loved fishing with Will on the Mandy, he also loved Will. Soon he gaffed and pulled in a large striper, perhaps thirty-two pounds, well over legal size. Will guffawed and pounded Tony on the back saying.

"For a wop, you're a helluva fisherman!"

Tony grinned as he took this for the compliment it was meant to be, a "guy thing". Will himself was half Italian on his mother's side. She had married a fifth generation Marbleheader. They caught a lot more stripers and cleaned and filleted them on the boat. When they pulled into the wharf Tony left his for Will to sell. He brought home to Lea a choice white, firm filet of cold water bass. They were best fresh caught and didn't freeze well. He was sure she would cook it to its best advantage. She did.

That evening they feasted on grilled striped bass that had been herbed, lightly crumbed and basted with Chardonnay, lemon juice and melted sweet butter. Tony revered Lea's cooking skills. He praised her lavishly and frequently to insure she wouldn't quit.

"Amorata, whatever you cook is equal to or surpasses the finest Roman cuisine!"

Her secret was the enthusiastic, creative joy she took in cooking. Tony was an amateur chef as well and he taught Lea how to do many Northern Italian dishes. They ate their fish with a Caesar salad loaded with anchovies, Parmesan and croutons while Lea related the terrible accident she'd seen in the harbor when the Mandy was far out at sea.

Interested, Tony said, "When Will and I got in at State Street, people were talking about a boat fire, you saw it happen? I thought you were going to paint." He looked at her accusingly.

That afternoon she had been enthusiastically painting with palette knife on a very large canvas using oil paints. This was to be the "Butterfly Festival" for her upcoming Zulazandia exhibit. She had tersely informed Tony, "Leave me alone, don't come near me, I have to finish this today!" He had good-naturedly gone off early to fish with Will. Lea stationed her easel where she could look out at the Saturday races. Boats were sailing out to the starting line which was off a committee boat. She saw Ray's "Mermaid" amidst a large group of "Townies." The Town Class was a popular, relatively inexpensive boat and almost all purpose. They were 16' long, beamy with a centerboard, mainsail and jib. One could race it or just sail for pleasure unlike some of the larger racing machines built solely for speed and rather uncomfortable They were good looking as well, resembling a small schooner. Lea watched the class going out. She saw them again at the mouth of the harbor, apparently they'd been given a twice around course. She paused to watch for a moment putting her palette knife down after cleaning it off with a rag.

She recalled when she had raced with Ray in his second-hand wooden lap-strake Townie when they were kids in high school. Of course, he was always the skipper and she the crew to be berated and yelled at for every false move. But there had been some good times with black haired, boisterous Ray before everything turned sour and he became an alcoholic Genetically Nora had inherited his good looks, dark hair and eyes. Fortunately she had Lea's attractive personality, character and value system she'd acquired from her environment growing up.

Suddenly a fireball enveloped one of the Townies. In front of the lighthouse it burst into flame and the harbor became pandemonium. Police boats, sirens screeching; the Harbor Master's boat, five Yacht Clubs' launches, motor and sail boats milled about in chaotic confusion converging close as possible to the fiery sailboat trying to rescue the sailors aboard.

Lea completely stopped painting now. What was going on? Whose boat was it? Was it Ray's that was going up in flames? What made it catch on fire or explode? Ray was not stupid enough to have a propane gas grill aboard especially when racing and every ounce of extra weight was removed. He used to even make her sail with just a t-shirt and shorts so her sweat shirt or oilskins couldn't add any extra weight.

She was anxious to know the cause, if it were the "Mermaid" and if there were any survivors. To find out she'd have to walk all the way up Front Street to State Street wharf. "Don't I have to finish this huge canvas of the 'Zulazandian Butterfly Festival?'"

Lea was reluctant to take time out but she admitted to herself she was also a coward. She couldn't bear to discover her first love and Nora's father had perhaps burnt to death. Once Ray had been a beautiful boy with so much promise whom Lea had completely loved. Their "song" was an old one, "Crazy." They liked both Patsy Cline and Willie Nelson's versions that were old even in their day. Dancing to it at an outdoor ballroom in summertime at "Kimball's Starlite" was a cheap and romantic date for kids. Lea often thought later she had been crazy! She sure had been crazy about Ray.

Tony slept at his place that night. He said he'd be late getting in as he wanted to see someone. Lea lay awake with the 3 a.m. blues and thought about Ray. Was he dead? The waves were lapping against the rocks which usually soothed her and put her to sleep. Lea felt a measure of guilt she'd kept Nora away from her father. When she was a baby Ray would telephone and beg to see her and the baby. Occasionally Lea permitted him a brief visit with Nora with only Siri, her grandmother, present without Lea.

Lea was not interested in falling under his spell ever again. Ray had always had charm and a certain charisma. His descent into alcoholism started when he was a star athlete in high school and became a slow, steady decline. It changed his outgoing, gregarious personality to one with no limits at all. He had been persuasive and charming, now he'd become overbearing and a loud drunk.

When Lea had only a few weeks left in her pregnancy, a drunken Ray pushed her to the floor and grabbing her by her hair he rocked her back and forth. She didn't know what he was angry about this time. He was further infuriated she wouldn't cry or plead but lay there protecting her stomach with her hands. Later, as he was after every such incident, he was remorseful. Kneeling on the floor with his arms around her legs as she sat in a chair he would cry, beg for forgiveness and make extravagant promises that were never kept.

Lea secretly went to see an old friend of her older twin brothers, Dr. Lois Garr, now a psychologist, for advice.

"Sometimes Lea, Alcoholism is not the primary disease but a symptom of another one, Manic-depression. His wide mood swings suggest this except you tell me he drinks not only when he is feeling low or depressed but also when he is up and euphoric?"

At Lea's nod she continued. "Lea, you're still young. The future could be a disaster for you and your child if you remain in this marriage. Selfish, self-destructive, narcissistic alcoholics can bring down everyone around them. Usually their abuse escalates as they blame their spouses for all their troubles turning them and their children into scapegoats. As their self-esteem declines an alcoholic gets worse. Rarely do they change nor can you cure the person any more than you caused it."

"It has to be the person himself who desires to change his life. Listen to me, as long as you are under Ray Larson's domination neither you or any children you may have will ever be able to realize your or their full potential. Your spirit will be crushed right out of you. Already you are not the same vivacious girl you were when I dated your brother, Erik."

"Honey, as a doctor I am against advising my clients to divorce and I cannot, but as your friend I can urge you to do so for your salvation and the coming baby's. I know what I'm talking about, Lea, my mother was an alcoholic. My father separated from her and brought me up alone which was the best though hardest thing he could do for me."

Lea felt Lois was right. She resolved she would leave Ray as soon as the baby was born and never return. She kept a meek demeanor and a low profile around him which saved her from more physical abuse. She ignored completely his verbal abuse and put-downs. He sneered, "You look just like a big, fat sow, Lea. How did I ever think you were pretty? God, you're a mess. Never mind, you don't have to answer, there's plenty of women out there who like to talk to me and that ain't all they like, either."

Lea knew he was fooling around with other women from tell-tale traces on his clothes. She didn't care. Freedom from Ray was all she dreamed about in the last stages of her pregnancy. *She and her baby were going to have a life!* This belief sustained her. Lea told her mother her plans. Fearing for her safety, Siri urged her to come home before the baby came but Lea needed to save every bit of extra money she could from what Ray tossed in her lap for groceries each week. He still liked her cooking. Lea knew Siri would have to help support her and the baby and she wanted all she could get out of Ray first.

She concocted cheap but good tasting meals for him so that he was not aware the lion's share of the grocery money was hidden under a pile of bras and panties in her dresser drawer. She didn't know yet exactly what she was going to do but she vowed she'd be on her way as soon as her baby arrived to a life a lot better than the last few years had been. Lea had lost all affection for Ray and couldn't bear to have him touch her or feel his boozy breath on her. Fortunately he didn't find her sexually attractive now and rarely approached her.

It amused Lea that the cheapest meal she prepared was Ray's favorite so she made it a lot. She bought the very cheapest hamburger and mixed it with day old bread, also inexpensive, and soaked it in milk. She loaded the mixture with Worcestershire Sauce, garlic and nutmeg to form a meat loaf. A can of a store brand tomato soup poured over it just before it came out of the oven and dear old Ray was in heaven.

She swore that after she left Ray's house (actually all they had was a two room apartment in his mother's basement.) she would never make that kind of meat loaf again and she never did. Instead she made the Scandinavian Friccadeller with equal parts of ground beef, pork and veal which was a family favorite and delicious.

Worn out reliving old, sad memories Lea finally dropped off to sleep.

On Thursday Lea read the weekly newspaper, "The Reporter", old timers still called "The Messenger" which was its name years before. Ray Larson's "Mermaid" had been totaled in a tragic fire due to a propane gas explosion. There were two severely burned survivors. These young men were part of a group of engineers from Cambridge who had leased Ray's boat to race for the season. Taking turns, two or three would drive down for twilight races Tuesday and Thursday evenings and also for weekend races on Saturdays and Sundays. They were enthusiastic about racing although not experienced.

They told the police from their hospital beds at Shriner's Burn Center they were always pressed for time to make the starting line especially as they had to work on Saturday mornings. They would cook and eat their lunches and suppers aboard while sailing during the races! Thus the group had installed a propane gas grill when they tired of eating cold sandwiches. They would live to sail another day after lengthy treatment at the excellent burn center but the "Mermaid" was gone.

Lea hoped for Ray's sake he had insurance. He never had in the past when she raced with him and she doubted he did now. She was greatly relieved he hadn't burnt to death but she still despised him. All the many bizarre, embarrassing when in public, outrageously cruel and abusive incidents had shamed, offended and hurt Lea so deeply it was not difficult to make the sad decision to leave him. Billy-be-damned!

She was not going to permit him to make her life and their child's life a shambles as he had his own and she swore he was not going to drive her away from her home town and ocean she loved, either. When Lea got her back up she could be a fighter.

CHAPTER 14.

Tony was informed through his lawyer, John Randall, the International Crime Center bureau reported Andreas had been released from the mental hospital in Milan six weeks earlier. Both the bureau and the lawyer had moved slowly with the news. They were told there were no further legal means to keep him confined. Tony called Rome and talked to the Chief of Criminal Affairs who warned him that Andreas had made threats against all his cousins to both his doctor and fellow patients. He was reported to have repeated over and over, "I shall get rid of them all, one by one, the bastardo!"

"We thought you should be alerted because he may have traveled to the United States. He's not been seen in Sicily or Rome nor have the other two, Daniro and Del Piana. He is delusional but the psychiatrist who treated him and signed his release stated he is not dangerous so they had to let him out."

In rapid fire street Italian he said what sounded like "Dottores are as stupido and crazy as their patients!" He gave a scornful short bark of a laugh,

"I'm sorry, Signore, there's nothing more I can do except to urge you to be watchful and on guard."

Tony thanked him and rang off. Apparently Andreas was still to be reckoned with?

When he was discharged, Andreas first went to see his mother, Sophia, who told him all his cousins including Antonio had disappeared. Next he visited Aunt Gina who was voluble and excitable and only too pleased to tell him her brave, heroic son Georgio had followed Roberto and a companion named Bell to America. Georgio had telephoned her from a remote town somewhere she thought was named something like Marblerocks. He said next he would travel to Sydney, Australia to recover the statue Antonio had stolen from the family and sent to a woman in Sydney. "Georgio will soon have it back and we will all be wealthy!" She crowed triumphantly.

Andreas didn't bother to visit his other aunt, Roberto's mother. He'd learned all he needed to know. He sold some drugs he'd stolen from the mental hospital and booked a flight to La Guardia in New York. There he contacted his grandmother's lawyer, John Randall. He told him it was Antonio who had stolen the statue and much of their grandmother's money. He piously proclaimed himself to be the "savior of the Bellini!"

The lawyer was impressed by Andreas' Armani Italian-made suit and his oratory and gave him all the information he asked for about Tony and also revealed that he'd hired the P. I. Donald Bell to find the cousins and St. Theresa for Tony. He got out a map and deduced the town of "Marblerocks" Aunt Gina had given him must be Marblehead, in Massachusetts.

Andreas borrowed the map to study and rented a car in New York. Although it frightened him to drive in another country he was used to the daredevil Roman drivers and managed to get safely to Boston and then to Marblehead. After making inquiries he found Roberto and Bell. He dogged every step they took although Roberto threatened him with mayhem if he didn't take the next flight back to Italy. Andreas looked for Tony everywhere, calling him Antonio Scola and asking strangers on the street if they knew him or where he lived. Most, if they did know Tony knew him as Amberetti. No one had heard of a Scola and Andreas' broken English was hard to decipher.

Andreas pestered Bell continually when Roberto was not with him and bombarded him with whining questions. This aroused Bell's quick temper even though he considered Andreas an ineffectual, certifiable raving lunatic. He anonymously reported him to the FBI as an illegal alien using and selling drugs which was partially true in order to be rid of him. That was easier now than going to the trouble of killing him which could bring unwelcome attention to the former FBI agent if caught.

Andreas was picked up and interrogated shortly after the murder on Lea's terrace. He stuck out like an Italian sore thumb in the small fishing town. Until they could receive a dossier on him from Rome he was kept in the two-celled police station on Atlantic Avenue near Seaside Park and the Star of the Sea Catholic church.

Andreas asked to see a priest. An Italian speaking priest, Father Joe, visited him and conversed with him in Italian. When Father Joe came from

Andreas' cell, Police Detective Blaney asked, "Did you learn anything? The orders are this guy is to be deported to Italy but not before he is cleared of the murder of the yet unknown victim. His fingerprints have also been sent to the FBI for checking and cuz he's a dago, oops, sorry Father!, to the Central Crime Bureau, too. What did you find out?"

"This man is clearly a nut but he swears on his mother's grave and the Virgin Mary he did not kill that man. I doubt his mother is even dead from other things he babbled on about. He is a classic pathological liar, I think."

"No, he did not confess to anything and if he had I couldn't tell you but he didn't. He claims he is one hundred percent innocent of murder, drug use or drug sales although he certainly seems high on something! I am supposed to tell you and the whole world he is incensed and indignant at such accusations and that he is unjustly being held in this sty of a jail. You are to know he's a famous and respected statesman in all of Italy and his government will soon retaliate to the pig Americans."

Father Joe grinned. "There's more, do you want me to go on?" He was young and friendly, apparently enjoying a novel twist to his day.

"Please don't! I've heard all the hysterical invective I can cope with from this Andreas ever since he was brought in. I'd like to bat him one on the side of the head to shut him up. Unfortunately, that is strictly forbidden," he muttered sourly.

The broken English interspersed with Italian in Andreas' high pitched whine made his head ache badly. He tossed down some more aspirin. "I hope we'll be rid of this weirdo soon, like yesterday," He muttered gloomily.

"Bless you, my son.," said the priest to the officer twenty years his senior and left the station.

Tony was heartily sick of his Sicilian cousins so lacking in grace, and as devious, mean-spirited and bumbling as they ever were in their childhood. All he passionately desired in addition to Lea, was to find Nonna's Bellini to do good with it for her sake and to keep it out of the cousins' greedy, thieving hands. This was a priority. And of course he wanted to keep Lea safe from them. He regretted that both she and Nora had been drawn in and possibly endangered. Sarah's murderer had not been found. One detective thought there were a few earmarks of a professional, hired killer as her office had been wiped clean of any evidence. *Jeez, I better think like a horse,* thought Tony.

Lea had cried out in agony, "Why Sarah? What could be the motive?" The police had gone over all the more recent cases she'd handled. None seemed to warrant a murder. The most recent and unfinished divorce suit of Claire Larson led them to look closely at her husband, Ray. He had an ironclad alibi which was verified by his buddies and the bartender at the Tidal Rip. He'd been drinking there the whole evening through the crucial hours.

"God knows," said the bartender, "I hate to testify for that bastard but he was here and I kept wishing he'd get out. He was maudlin as usual and crying in his beer."

Stubbornly Sylvia still suspected Ray. She had uncovered a tape to Sarah with a voice saying, "Cancel the divorce or you'll be sorry." It was uncertain and unproven who had made the threat or which pending divorce was meant. A voice print proved little. Sylvia said to Lea, "Who else hated Sarah that much? It had to be Ray."

CHAPTER 15.

Lea knew she and Tony desperately needed some just plain lighthearted fun. She telephoned her sister-in-law whom she loved, Laura, Erik's wife.

"Laura, honey, can I borrow your darlings, Suzie, Jay and Libi for a day? Tony and I would love to take them to the Topsfield Fair if it's all right with you and Erik?"

Enthusiastically Laura agreed. The three red-headed and freckled children, Suzie, 8, Jay, 6, and Libi, 4 were a second family for Laura and Erik. Their older two sons, Erik, Jr. and Leif were in college. They had had some problems with the boys but apparently learning from the mistakes made with them were doing an admirable job of raising the younger three. The boys had been undisciplined and thoroughly spoiled and it was a relief to Laura to have them away at school. Their talent for arguing and wheedling her into all they wished to do and have was phenomenal. Erik had to travel a great deal when they were growing up and alone, Laura couldn't cope with their strong personalities.

With the younger ones Erik was home every night. He told Laura, "Kids are like dogs. You have to establish at the very start who is Alpha Dog!" Laura knew she'd never been able to do this with her strong minded sons who did seem to be easier to deal with now they'd been forced to learn how to get along with their peers and teachers or be left out of all the fun and games at college, and also had to study to stay there.

The three youngest were sunny-tempered and generous. They shared without sulking and were well-behaved. They obeyed Lea and Tony, indeed all adults, without question. Best of all their exuberance was catching. Tony and Lea were uplifted just seeing the children's joy when they picked them up. They bundled the children in with Lucy who licked their faces while they giggled., "Lucy, Lucy!" and drove to Topsfield.

There they took them on every single ride; the Dodge-ems, Merry Go Round, a miniature Roller Coaster and the adult sized Ferris Wheel. Two were in a seat with Tony between them, and one with Lea. Some rides they did more than once, delighted with the children's squeals of joy. Their laughter was infectious. Tony bought them hot dogs, sno-cones, cotton candy and out and out junk food. (Lea had asked Laura who said.

"Don't worry about that, they have a good diet and iron stomachs, once in a blue moon isn't going to hurt them."

They went through every single exhibit of cows, goats, pigs, sheep, fancy rabbits and cavies, exotic birds and chickens. The kids loved them all and petted all who would let them. Finally they entered

Lucy in the "Mutt Derby". She was shy and loathe to start racing when she was unleashed. Urged on by the screaming children who loudly cheered her along the course with shouts of "Go Lucy, Go!' she came in second after an adopted greyhound. Lucy was awarded a huge, garish purple ribbon pinned on her collar.

The children cheered loudly and lustily and patted and kissed her for her second place. Proud Lucy, tail wagging furiously, preened and panted. Jay got a man at the popcorn stand to give him a bowl of water for Lucy who lapped it up to the last drop.

By late afternoon Jay, Suzie and Libi were still energetic and appeared to be indefatigable while Lea and Tony were exhausted. "I am so pooped," laughed Lea.

They decided to call it quits and piled the kids and dog into Tony's red bug returning them to Laura with many thanks for letting them borrow the children. It had been almost a spiritual renewal for Lea and Tony. Lea said seriously, "Only small children and animals who are innocent, vulnerable, trusting and truly happy can heal souls? It's because they have so recently been in touch with their guardian angels, I believe."

Tony smiled at her, Lea was ever a romantic idealist and he loved her for it. Tired as she was Lea felt blessed and a sense of peace, even joy, for the first time in many days of suffering anguish and pain. Tony felt satisfied that this day had been good for her although he was ready to drop. He was not only astonished but impressed little children and a dog could possess so much unflagging vitality and good will and so effortlessly restore adult's spirits with their energy. They were wonderful kids filled with pure love of life and everyone and everything in it. He whispered to Lea, "Let's get married and have a batch of kids!" Lea raised her eyebrows. "I don't think you'd like it so much on a daily basis, signore."

It would not, could not be Saturday night in New England without baked beans, franks and brown bread. Lea had soaked three kinds of dried beans overnight; pea beans, kidney beans and soldier beans. She had left them in a covered bean pot on the back of her potbellied stove all day with plenty of liquid to absorb, a mixture of molasses, cider and water. A chunk of scored salt pork was placed in the bottom of the pot along with a whole yellow onion. She had stirred in salt and pepper, brown sugar, mustard and Worcestershire Sauce. The beans had simmered all day. When they returned to the studio, Lea uncovered the bean pot, turned her oven to 350 and poured a generous dollop of real maple syrup on top to glaze for about 10 minutes. Served with Maple Leaf frankfurters, boiled just until the skins burst, warmed canned brown bread, her pepper relish and Gulden's yellow mustard, it was a satisfactory and pleasant ending to a heartwarming day.

Since this was not a well-known dish or staple in Europe Tony approached the meal warily but politely not wanting to hurt Lea's feelings. When he refilled his plate two more times Lea laughed out loud.

She decided she wouldn't tell him of some of the after effects of home baked beans recalling how the twins would make Siri frown and scold at the ditty they recited every Saturday night: "Beans, beans, the musical fruit, the more you eat the more you toot. The more you toot the better you feel and then you're ready for another meal."

Einar never failed to laugh, he loved to see the twins tease their mother until she blushed like a school girl. He would add, "Siri, it's healthy to toot, I toot and so do you," and Siri would blush even more. "Einar, stop it! Not in front of the children!"

CHAPTER 16.

Tony had now seen two harbor illuminations with flares outlining the harbor on the Fourth of July followed by spectacular fireworks launched at Riverhead Beach.

"This is a grand thing for this town to do," he told Lea enthusiastically. He also visited the Glover Regiment encampment and artillery group at Fort Sewall which was complete with cannons roaring and a reenactment of General John Glover's regiment rowing Washington across the Delaware.

"His eyes twinkling, "Lea, I'm impressed with the patriotic fervor in your town!"

On this Saturday Tony had made a date with Will to go clamming at Devereux Beach on an early dead low tide. He brought Lucy who dearly loved to clam with him. She ran up and down the beach barking 'hello' to everyone. She would run into the water for a swim, come out shaking her yellow fur and resume racing up and down the sand. Lucy poked her nose into every clam digger's bucket. They were good natured about it and liked the friendly large dog. She would even unearth a clam or two with her paws. St. Lucia thoroughly and deliciously enjoyed clamming with Tony.

"Lea," Tony had asked, "May I have Will and his wife Julia for dinner at your place if I get enough clams? You know my place is virtually a bed-sit, a tiny kitchen and bath. I promise I'll do all the cooking." Lea cheerfully agreed.

He cleaned and chopped the quahog sea clams all afternoon. Will and Tony had an ongoing running argument about the merits of Will's New England milk-based clam chowder versus Tony's Italian tomato-based clam chowder. Tony was determined to prove to Will how good a Mediterranean chowder could be although Will remained skeptical. Lea set the big old scarred table and placed a large heavy pot of red geraniums and some candles on it. Anxiously Tony was busily stirring and cooking. When Will and Julia arrived, Julia warmly admired Lea's paintings on the walls. She confessed she had gone to the MFA art school in Boston and always wanted to continue painting.

Shyly she asked, "Would you give me some lessons?"

"Of course I will, and free too, for all the fish Tony catches on Will's boat. But I doubt if you need lessons if you went to the Museum school."

Lea liked this pretty, quiet woman and she could see that earthy Will adored her down to his very toenails. Tony brought out a bottle of Valpolicella red wine. He cut and spread with garlic butter a long loaf of Italian bread he wrapped in foil to warm in the oven. When he took the bread out and placed it in a napkin lined basket he ladled the soup into Lea's large, mismatched bowls. Tony grated a generous amount of mozarella cheese on top of each and ran them under the broiler to melt and be stringy. On the table he had already put a bottle of hot Tabasco sauce, an open bottle of rum and one of sherry for extra flavor to be added according to each diner's taste.

For hours Tony had chopped celery, onions, parsley, potatoes and the clams diligently adding these ingredients one at a time to the wine, chicken broth, tomato and clam juice mixture. The clams and ripe olives went in last as all delicate seafood must or it will toughen. Will watched him looking amused as Tony at last took off his apron and sat down. He looked a bit frazzled and housewifely and Will had to grin. Tony asked Lea to say grace, knowing she would anyway.

"In the early evening with the sun's last rays, all God's little children thank and pray and praise. We, too, thanks would offer, Jesus, Savior dear, for thy tender pasture and Thy loving care."

Tony muttered under his breath, "Jesus, I didn't mean that long."

Will laughed. "I dunno if I should be so disloyal as to even try your red soup, Tony." Julia frowned at him, "Hush, Will! All this trouble Lea and Tony have gone to for us."

Modestly Tony said, "It was mostly me," and winked at Will. He nervously watched Will's every mouthful for his reaction. Finally, Will said, "Dammit, Tony, I gotta say this is freakin' good. It's a lot like the conch chowder Julia and I had in Florida, not of course as good as our Marblehead chowder but we liked it, especially with the rum in it. Why didn't you tell me you meant conch chowder instead of calling it that asshole name all the time, Mediterranean chowder?"

Lea and Julia smiled at each other; they were amused at the men and tickled by their obvious fondness for one another. For dessert Lea had made a light Akvavit sorbet in refrigerator ice cube trays she served with Gerda's apple cider sugar cookies.

"Hey Tony, you can really cook, Buddy!"

"I bet Lea made the dessert," Julia said loyally.

They played some games of Canasta with more wine. After that Will and Julia left to walk home and Lea and Tony washed up the dishes. Lea praised Tony extravagantly, reassuring him over and over, "Yes! Will really loved it." She was touched Tony looked so pleased. He went to take Lucy for her nightly walk. She had not liked his chowder as much as she did Lea's franks and beans but she loved having her supper put down for her to eat while they did making her part of the family.

Tony had sternly instructed Lea, "Lucy is not to have three meals a day, she's getting much too heavy."

Retorted Lea, "How would you like to have only supper every day like some poor dogs do and wait all night and all day for another meal?" She made Lucy's three meals relatively small knowing it was eating when they did that Lucy really liked.

Tony and Lucy planned to walk all the way up Franklin Street, then Orne, then Norman past Redd's Pond and home again. While they were gone Lea showered and prepared for bed. Only owning a shower she had not had a bath in so long and wondered what a good soak in a tub would feel like- with bubble bath?

She heard a loud noise at the kitchen garden door and then it was roughly pushed open. Ray stood there glaring at her.

"Lea, you're a bitch!" His eyes were red and bloodshot, the alcohol odor emanating from him was strong and fetid. "You put Claire up to a divorce, didn't you?" I know it was you and that dike lawyer you're pals with. You took my baby, Nora, away from me," he whined in a maudlin, self-pitying tone, "And now you're trying to take my other kids away. I'm not taking this shit, Lea!" He reached out and shoved her hard on her shoulder. Lea shrank away from him, praying for Tony to come back.

"Don't look for your wop boyfriend, he and his goddam dog will be out of it for a long time."

He lunged toward her again, his fists upraised and his eyes wild. One hand was bloody from what looked like a dog bite. Lea looked desperately around for a weapon to defend herself. Grabbing the pot of geraniums off the table she slammed it as hard as she could at his face. Drunk and slipping on the floor Ray went down heavily, hitting his head on the clam bucket Tony had left on the floor near the kitchen. He literally knocked himself out.

Lea was hysterically half laughing, half sobbing when a policeman burst in the open door with Lucy snarling and jumping at Ray. Lea was glad to see it was Dog Mcdougal.

"Your friend is in the hospital but he's going to be all right. He asked me to bring his dog to you. Mr. Amberetti was attacked and when I found him the dog was standing guard over him and crying. This happened near Redd's Pond. I was out walking my dog, too. This guy, Larson, who jumped him from the back ran off when your dog bit him. I'll have to call 911 and have this gentleman removed. Would you like a ride to the hospital, Lea?"

Lea knelt down and hugged a whimpering Lucy. After the patrol car arrived and Ray was taken off in handcuffs (Lea was pleased to see) she was driven to Salem Hospital to see Tony. Ray had shouted curses at them all as they shoved him into the police car.

Tony was in a hospital bed in a ward, his arm was bandaged and one leg was in a cast with pulleys. He was groggy from pain killers but he managed to whisper, "Hi, Belissima, tell Will I can't go fishing with him tomorrow."

Lea patted his good hand, kissed his cheek and left him to drift back to sleep. Dog, the officer, had waited patiently to drive her home. She was touched Tony was concerned about Will and a fishing date when he'd been so brutally beaten up. Knowing he would also worry about his dog she'd whispered, "Lucy's fine, you are both my heroes."

Tony slowly mended, he had been badly beaten. When able to leave Shaughnessy Rehabilitation facility he convalesced at Lea's studio. On her last visit to the hospital she had shyly said to him.

"Tony, come live with me and be my love, and we will all the pleasures prove."

Puzzled, he looked at her, his eyebrows raised quizzically and wearing a big smile.

135

"That's a Christopher Marlow poem, stupid! But I mean it, at least until you can walk again." He still needed to use a cane.

Ray was being held in jail pending a trial on aggravated assault with intent to kill. Lea had filed and pressed the charges with Sylvia's help. Tony was ambivalent and reluctant to do so. He could not help feeling some empathy and sorrow for a man who had been given so many of life's gifts, including Lea, yet who had deliberately taken every wrong turn and recklessly threw all away.

One early morning Lea received a call from Sylvia. "Lea, I hate to have to tell you this, Ray committed suicide in his cell last night. He hung himself with strips of his clothing he tore up. I'm so sorry, Lea!"

Lea wept for Ray's wasted life and tragic ending and for Nora's father. She was still able to conjure up a picture of the Ray she'd loved at sixteen. He had been a handsome and superb athlete with a flamboyant personality whom she, only a child herself at the time, had completely worshiped and adored as did most of her fellow cheer- leaders. Siri had attempted to dissuade her from this high school infatuation but like all teenagers, Lea knew better than her mother and was in love. The Ray he was then was her God, her idol. Nothing could change her mind. Eventually it was Ray, himself who turned her off with his drinking and abuse and her infatuation became disgust and loathing.

Later, Lea was profoundly grateful her innate intellect and proud Viking genes had socked in and helped her realize in time life with Ray Larson would be no life at all and she and her baby had to escape.

Tony and Lea were weary of the questioning and investigation that continued to slowly drag on without any apparent resolution. They put as much as they could out of their minds. Lucy adjusted herself to Tony's hesitant and limping walk holding a cane on his other side from her leash. She paused for him to rest, wagging her tail which spoke volumes. Her patience was a lesson in unconditional love and loyalty few humans manifest as well. Animals, bonded to a master were capable of such love.

Sylvia brought Claire over to see them now she did not have to hide any more or continue with the stressful divorce suit. Claire was well-groomed and even prettier and seemed more mature and self-confident.

"Claire, you look wonderful! I'm so glad to see you."

Claire handed Lea a CD. "What's this?"

"It's a present for you and Tony," Claire dimpled.

"You know, because of the suicide there's no insurance money from Ray?" Sylvia broke in. "I found a top rated music agent for Claire. This is the first album she recorded!" Sylvia went on excitedly. "It's called, 'Claire Croons'. I didn't make up the title." She disclaimed wincing, a little embarrassed at the hokeyness.

"It opens with a lullaby Claire has always sung to her five children, "Tender shepherd, tender shepherd, let me help you count your sheep. One in

137

the meadow, one in the garden, three in the nursery, fast asleep." Sylvia warbled off key.

"She has some hymns on it, 'Amazing Grace' and "How Great Thou Art". The agent wanted some blues and jazz, too. Claire chose, "Good morning, Heartache", "Cry Me A River," and Billy Holiday's "I'm Having Myself A Time."

"It's really great!" Sylvia enthused with obvious pride in her protegee.

"While she was living in the safe house, Claire even wrote a song for herself, called "Claire's Song." Sylvia sang a few bars of a lively pop tune, again quite off key, which amused Tony, Lea and Claire as well.

"Hey baby, baby, I'm awfully sorry, but maybe, maybe I ain't ever goin' your way again, no way again, no way."

For her birthday Tony had given Lea a CD player saying, "I wish I could take you sailing instead." She liked classical or jazz music playing softly in the background when she painted. Lucy liked it too. "Lady Day" with her tremulous sad voice was a favorite. Lea had once painted a portrait of her while listening to her tapes.

After Sylvia and Claire left, both with busy appointments to keep and rush to, Tony played Claire's CD. Her voice, pure, plaintive and quite beautiful made Lea want to cry; the album was so much an autobiography of Claire's life. The final cut was a rousing rendition of "When the Saints go Marching in." Lucy hid under the table. She was not fond of loud noises, music or thunder. Lea's music was usually softer. In deference to her Tony turned down the volume.

"Claire's on her way. This CD will hit the top of the charts for sure, "Tony exclaimed, "What a voice!"

They were both thrilled and happy for Claire who had gotten by "with a little help from my friends" which was also on the album. She had pulled far out of the dark, seemingly hopeless tunnel she'd been in for so long and could now sing for joy. Her friends, Lea, Sarah and Sylvia were partially responsible for Claire's reclaimed and reinvented life.

With all her heart Lea believed, "Sarah knows and is pleased for Claire."

CHAPTER 17.

As Lea's Zulazandia exhibit drew closer Tony prevailed upon her to let him read the script that accompanied the non-objective oil paintings on canvas. She had always firmly refused, aware she was a half-way decent painter but unsure of her writing ability. Tony persisted and teased until she said, "All right! All right! Read the bloody thing!"

Tony chuckled as he read. When he finished he put the story down and gave Lea a big, smacky wet kiss on her forehead. "Caramia, it is wonderful! It's droll and amusing and I like the satire on the extreme women libbers. Since most of them have no sense of humor, they won't."

"I can be funny, then?" Lea asked, awed yet pleased and gratified by Tony's approval. "You actually got it as a send-up. Do you think anyone else will?"

"Perhaps not, but it doesn't matter, Lea. What does is that you created your own country and painted it superbly and not illustratively. Did you know most famous writers invented mythological countries? C. S.

Lewis for one with his "Narnia" series. Swift with "Gulliver's Travels", Charles Dodson's "Alice in Wonderland" and even Dante with his "Inferno." This is something geniuses do."

Lea was flushed at his praise but made a face and drawled "not hardly" at the word genius. She now had some hope her "country" might strike a chord in and be both appreciated and enjoyed by other people. She'd had serious doubts any or many would understand or like it and the abstract paintings that went with it. Her morale was instantly improved. *Tony is so good for me,* she thought. *Such a jewel of a man I've found!*

For the opening at the DeCordova Museum in Concord she asked Tony to choose the wines. Lea added a whole wheel of cheddar cheese and crackers, grapes, strawberries, clam and crab dips, smoked salmon with sour cream, chopped onions and capers and rounds of sweet buttered pumpernickel bread. She topped it all off with a huge bowl of shrimp on ice accompanied by her own hot sauce. This put her bank account considerably in the hole. Tony insisted on providing the wine as his offering. He bought bottle after bottle of Bolla Soave, Riesling, Merlot, and Pinot Noir. Since Lea had not the vaguest idea of the cost she did not demur except to say, "A lot of people really like that white Zinfadel, I hate that pink stuff! They also like the tried and true Chablis, too."

Obligingly Tony added these as well as Moet et Chandon and Asti Spumonte champagne. There were wines aplenty, he knew from experience at the Tate Gallery in London people were more appreciative of the art after several glasses of free wine.

141

The exhibit had mixed reviews and few sales. The public either hailed it with enthusiasm or deemed it weird and disdained it. Lea and Tony overheard some saying, "I just don't get it" in petulant tones of voice. They grinned at each other. Nevertheless, Lea was content. The exhibit was not solely for sales or acclaim but to express her own unique emotions and to paint her invented country.

Lea was happy she had completed a project and brought to fruition what she had worked on and thought about for two long years. Her paintings were an explosion of color on the wall and looked splendid. Copies of the script were on a nearby table to read. if desired. Few guests read them. As at most openings, people milled about, visited with friends and voraciously devoured the refreshments.

Some really appreciated Tony's excellent choice of wines. A few seriously studied the work and a few were sold. Belinda and Jackie, artisan friends, purchased a large oil of the "Butterfly Festival." They both had been highly amused and admired Lea's work they never failed to praise. They were gay friends of Lea's-Jackie was an innovative potter, Belinda crafted stained glass pieces that were whimsical and colorful. Both were highly amused by the concept of "Zulazandia."

They had always admired Lea's painting which buoyed up her spirits when she was discouraged. Since Belinda and Jackie were vegetarians, Lea enjoyed composing special dishes for them. The girls particularly liked Lea's ratatouille and artichokes stuffed with blue cheese. As often as they could afford they purchased Lea's paintings which made a stunning assemblage in their apartment with their glass and pottery. Lea loved them, they were loyal artisan friends.

Sylvia was present with her whole office contingent of lawyers and paralegals, except one young lawyer, Abe Goldstein, Claire's new beau. Sylvia had introduced them and after dating several times he volunteered to baby sit Claire's children so she might attend Lea's opening. Abe honestly liked children. Claire thought him noble to do so and he won brownie points with her which was his aim. She looked lovely in a long peach dress. Sylvia was wearing a short, knee length burnt orange shift encrusted with beads and pearls and shoes to match. No bells.

She brought Tony a bouquet of violets and bells she fastened to his cane so that he jingled when he walked. Sotto voce to Lea he said, "I feel like an idiot and I look like a damned elf!" which made Lea grin widely yet both were disinclined to hurt the feelings of their much loved Jewish bombshell with the heart of gold.

Lea wore a simple, severely tailored white silk pant suit and looked dashing, quite unlike her usual barefoot, casual self To her shoulder Sylvia pinned Lea's favorite of corsages from long ago high school proms; a pinky orange camellia. An expensive designer scarf in a pale apricot matching her hair was Tony's gift. Her only jewelry was tiny stud diamond earrings bequeathed to Lea by her mother, Siri.

As in painting, less is more, thought Tony. *A lot more!* he almost said aloud admiring this soignee Lea who was charming, excited and vibrant. He thought her green eyes and apricot hair were a painting itself. She was beautiful and looked stunning.

Lea had received many awards and had had more than a dozen one person shows so she was used to exhibiting and how openings went. The hope always was to reach at least one person with your work, soul speaking to soul. That made all the expense of framing, transporting paintings and providing refreshments worthwhile. This yearning is what drives an artist or writer-the need to connect. Sometimes the connection was not made until long after the writer, painter or musician's death.

After the opening night of the exhibit they left the paintings on exhibit for a month and packed up the remaining food with special tidbits for Lucy who'd really resented being left at home. Julia and Will had offered to baby sit Lucy but Lea wanted them to come, even though Lucy would indubitably sulk it wouldn't hurt her to be alone for a few hours. Lucy, of course disagreed but Tony was firm when Lea suggested they bring her.

"Absolutely not! People will be shocked enough at some of your paintings, if they see a big galumph of a dog there, Lea honey, they'll be sure that you are a nut!"

Lea bristled, "Is that what you think, Tony? I'm some kind of a nut?"

He hugged her close, kissing her eyes, her cheeks, her mouth, "Of course I do, Caramia, you are my own darling, adorable nut, please don't ever change. I'm ape over nuts, "He teased and Lea's knees turned to jelly as she returned his caresses.

ZULAZANDIA—(Lea's Country)

A small country has recently been uncovered in Africa called Zulazandia. It is probably the sister country of the lost Atlantis. The earth is of various hues of alizarin crimson. The flowers are bright tone and shades of vermilion, cadmium yellow, Winsor purple and pinks and reds. The foliage is made up of glossy, shining greens and yellow ochers. The Zandia River that rocks the babies to sleep is a glorious cerulean blue with cobalt blue undertones. The mountains, perhaps made from volcanic ash as the country slowly rose again from the sea, are multicolored. The cattle are also of many colors.

The artists (the elite class in Zulazandia) paint the landscape in a style of empathetic sensory shape, form and color somewhat similar to a mixture of an El Greco, (flame like forms) Paul Klee and Joan Miro (much symbolism) and the abstractions of a Hans Hofmann. It could be termed a Primitive Abstract Expressionism.; a style and genre of painting which has been in existence a great deal longer than and indeed before, the Renaissance. Rarely do the artists paint in a boring, mundane or literal fashion. What is more all the people understand and appreciate their work, "the artists paint them, never have to explain them!" (Except sometimes to outside visitors from the Western world who, alas! are only able to perceive surface and shallow pictograms because they have been so corrupted by the camera, film, television and slavish renderings and reproductions of the obvious.) Zulazandians find this quite amusing and laugh behind their hand politely. As a people they are directly attuned to the real and the essence without encrusted artificial modes of thinking. For the most part the landscape is in a warm palate and high key in perpetual exciting movement of color. A lovely land!

The culture and mores are extremely interesting. The women are strong and beautiful as well as creative, sensitive, intuitive and compassionate. (It appears to be a form of a matriarchal society.) Men are sweet and considerate although they can be at times devious and capricious. Each woman takes two men. One is prized for his large genitalia, called zoobs, as a Stud Consort, another chosen to do menial chores and child care. The women will sleep with both but the Stud Consort most frequently as the Workers often complain of headaches. Children are universally loved; all adults love them equally. As infants they are placed in the river, like biblical Moses, in small hand woven baskets. The wind and the water gently rock them all day long filling the babies with bliss and contentment. Rarely do they cry but make soft, sibilant cooing sounds of delight. The reeds and rushes rock the little cradles while multicolored fish swim about amusing the ideal babies.

The tribe believes the body to be beautiful, a work of art, unadorned and unhampered by clothing. On occasion a heavily ornamented sash decorated with the native dyes is worn around their middles. These can easily be removed or dropped for the artists who constantly paint the population on bark canvas. The village is akin to a large Western Life Class. Zulazandians decorate only the face. The right cheek is painted with yellow and white stripes, with red around the eyes and green spots above. The left side is painted with a yellowish-green splotch. The remainder of the face is painted blue. Male faces are reversed in design. The Worker Males (wanting to establish some self-importance?) sometimes paint their right cheeks orange insssstead of green and add additional stripes of white and yellow over the left blue eye. The women are gently amused by this as it only draws attention to their status. There is a genetic inheritance, it seems, as all the women have a right true blue eye and a left brown eye. Males have a brown right eye and a blue left eye which is helpful to determine at birth the gender of some of the under-endowed baby boys.

Their banner, shields and flag have similar markings with the addition of The Good Blue Dragon.

The ruling Zulazandian women are much too intelligent to ever go to war or to battle with other tribes or countries. Instead when there is a contention they hold a large dance festival. One by one, they seduce each enemy until he is stupid and sated with love, sex, and the native wine and dreamily, willingly give up their quarrel.

The wine called "Zablee" is made from honey from the plethora of hives of multicolored bees and from the small white native grapes to which is added a narcotic nectar. Worker Males carefully milk this nectar drop by drop from the flocks of enormous multicolored butterflies. (The butterfly nectar when undiluted in wine is also used as a birth control device good for six full moons.)

Their language is based on vowels with a "z" inserted between them and a few consonants.

The men are encouraged to develop all their potential talents. Most prefer to tend to their babies in the river cradles and the small children playing nearby. They enjoy gathering by the river to gossip and to wash their sashes and painted bed coverings they spread out on the glossy green bushes to dry in the bright orange sun. The women enjoy drinking Zablee and smoking the native root, Zamel.

It was not difficult for the Anthropologist observer who had stumbled on the secret existence of this country to ascertain there appeared to be an elite group who are favored and looked up to with love and admiration. These are the artists, potters, poets, craftswomen and artisans, dancers and musicians. All are venerated and equally valued regardless of gender due to the generosity of the superior women artists and council. In Zulazandia all art is truly play, as it should be.

Artists usually enter into a serial, monogamous relationship based on twenty-two full moons. (There is no calendar as such in this country.) At the end of this period they amicably separate to form a new alliance. Sometimes after such an interim or sabbatical they return to an earlier one.

In the rest of the country when men come into the tribe or are chosen by a woman they sign over with a "Z" in blood taken from a small vein in the foot. All their cattle, Zinzers (dogs) and possessions and property are thus given over to the woman. If they are from the outside world they are required to bring with them some kind of offering or dowry. Only males with the right brown eye and left blue eye are permitted to become citizens. (The strain exists here and there outside Zulazandia from the adventurers who left many, many moons past and propagated.

When a Zulazandian woman tires of her Stud Consort or Worker Male or they grow too old to be useful in any capacity they are retired and put out to a large, grassy area similar to a pasture. The women never grow too old for anything. Here the men baby sit the collective grandchildren and often play games with one another.

One game is played with squares of colored bark with symbols painted on them. Four males sit around a large flat rock and exchange the bark cards. At intervals they bring out refreshments they make andserve with much Native White on the food. It's like a whipped cream or marshmallow fluff and is made from a root. The Senior Citizens happily play bark cards, gossip and baby sit. They call the game Zandia-zidge or Zilch for short.

Potters make all the unusual, handsome bowls, dishes, pots and urns for the tribe. These are heavily in demand by neighboring tribes and villages who travel many kilometers and moons to trade goods, cattle and food in exchange for this prized pottery. Since the clay found in Zulazandia is the color of alizarin crimson most of the articles are a vibrant red with yellow and green marks and decorations, signed on the bottom with either a butterfly by the apprentices or The Great Blue Dragon by the first class potters. Women, of course, handle all of the trade and business of Zulazandia.

By testing and the determination of the Council of Women it is clear at puberty which of the many unconditionally loved children will join the group of male and female artists and artisans. Surprisingly enough, many of the adolescent males prefer to become a Stud Consort or a Worker for one of the girl-women and eagerly go that route. Since there are no jealousies or frustrations amongst them it must be each chooses the role best suited to them (or their preference) to live out? Zulazandia has never had a rape since all have access to sex whenever they want. Nor is there homosexuality although being tolerant Zulazandians they would only shrug and say, "Not that there's anything wrong with it." There has never been a suicide or a need for a jail or crime or violence largely because women who are natural peace makers are in charge.

Because they operate as a large extended family there are no real in-laws as such. Every older woman acts as a mother, grandmother, aunt and sister to each child and the men are also father, grandfather, uncle and brother to all. (There are no funny uncles.)

These people are a happy, smiling people.

One of the chief industries is the large flock of cat-size butterflies. Male workers farm the butterflies through the stages of cocoon to emergence and milk them for their valued, rare narcotic nectar. The butterflies colors and markings range into the thousands of variations of breathtaking beauty and a few are even a solid, brilliant color As far as the anthropologist observer could discover Zulazandia is the only area for the exact correct, climatic conditions for raising these valuable and unusual butterflies.

Never have they been known to survive or be able to be propagated outside Zulazandia although others have tried and failed. The result is a brisk barter and trade for the nectar...

The women's big huts are handsomely adorned with the artists' work. Their two men live together in an adjoining annex called a Zarem and enjoy each other's company. This leaves the woman free to be alone when she wishes or to summon one of the men when she wants or needs to do so.

Some artists paint with the dyes and colors extracted from roots and vivid flowers and plants. They paint on a type of canvas made from slicing thin the Zandia tree bark which promptly grows a new covering. This canvas is then covered with their gesso, the Native White which is allowed to dry before painting on it. Print makers also are able to pull a kind of print by painting on flat rocks and pressing extra thin sheets of dampened bark over the painting, smoothing over this with a rounded rock or palms of their hands. The bark is then "pulled" (removed carefully) and allowed to dry. Rocks are excised with sharpened rock tool edges and prints, both relief and intaglio are pulled. A kind of early, primitive etching. Native White can e used as a masking out device and cleaned off with the butterfly nectar. Although the artists all regard their activities as creative play many of the other Zulazandians secretly consider this constant invention as hard work and would not themselves desire to be so engaged. The motto: 'to each his own' works well.

Any and all problems that may arise are handled by the Council of Women who meet once every twelve moons to go over the agenda of items and issues to be solved some of which have disappeared in the interim and no longer need addressing. The solutions invariably are creative and satisfactory.

A dissatisfied Worker Male is encouraged to try his hand (rather his zoobs) at either being a Stud Consort or joining the elite group of artisans. His talent or lack of same in either category is easily ascertained. (A Stud Consort must ALWAYS be erect and ready to meet his woman's every wish and desire and be good-natured about it, too.)

If, during his trial as an artist there is no demand for his work by the neighboring tribes who come to barter for the art works and if even in his own village no one chooses to use his pots or other art works in the huts or praises his singing or dancing, as a rule he cheerfully shrugs and happily returns to hut work, child care and butterfly tending.

Laughing, he will say a native expression which phonetically sounds like "zazelvit it." They joke and laugh a great deal, another favorite phrase is "zullszit." Occasionally the jokes made by the women are at the Worker Male's or Stud Consort's expense. This is accepted philosophically and they more or less say, "Well what the "zell," after all the women are supporting us."

Part of the artists' time is spent painting the faces of the people. The distinctive yellow and white stripes and green cheeks are unusually attractive. Their body color is similar to a Riviera tan acquired by Europeans on a nudie or topless beach. There are no ugly strap or bikini marks as one might see on those beaches, however. Free of clothing they receive an even, all over tan and the transparent nectar is useful as a sun block.

Except for formal occasions and festivals they seldom wear their sashes. It is always a perfect 70 degrees and like Camelot only receives rain or snow at night. Those who like to romp in this will nap during the day and stay up all night to go out in it to play.

They thoroughly believe in the beauty of the body whether tall, short, fat or thin and are willing to stop short whatever they are doing to drop their sashes, if wearing one, to pose for the artists. They do like to decorate their faces if not their bodies.

On our safari into this hidden country which was undiscovered for thousands of eons we were positively amazed at the huge number of friendly and affectionate animals who resemble dogs. Their markings are not only black and white but multicolored as well. In a way they resemble the English Springer Spaniel except each has one brown and one blue eye. They are called Zinzers. The curly coat is cut short in a Zinzer cut. Zinzers lick fingers and toes frequently to show they care and are devoted to the people. Their speech is a gentle, woof and the people and the children pat and pet them constantly.

The country obviously has a form of ceremony or religion. There is the Queen Earth Mother, the Daughter, and an older woman who is the Head Spirit Witch Doctoress. (A purely honorary title as Zulazandia has no physical or mental illness. When death or zassing comes it is peaceful and chosen. One goes to sleep lying on the soft grass by the river with the new generation, symbolically, happily cooing in their cradles. Each one decides for him or herself when it is time and announces, "I am ready for the final blissful sleep, today." There is much concern amongst us that expeditions such as ours might introduce germs, disease or violent death that mark other civilizations.

Zulazandians gather together for a ceremony with much joyful singing and dancing every full moon. ("Often enough for church going," one of our members remarked.)

Each drinks the wine from a red potter's vessel and chews a small white disc made from Native White. A hand woven basket made from riverside reeds is zassed (passed) around and each drops in a small artifact, a flower, or a piece of colored stone or shell.

The collection is dispersed equally to each hut, some getting their own contribution back again.

The Queen Earth Mother delivers a zermon. All sit quietly and with respect drink in her wise words to follow her kindly precepts for their daily behavior. She is distinguished from the others by the live butterfly crown she wears on her head for thee occasions. Like a kaleidoscope, the butterfly wings move and shimmer so the colors constantly change.

Our expedition found it surprisingly simple to acquire artifacts. The artists pressed pots, paintings, prints and poems on us generously and eagerly. When we demurred at such largess they laughed and told us they were free to make many, many more as others in the tribe did all the cooking, cleaning and child care leaving them totally free for their art work. (In some civilizations this was what wives were useful for.) We brought back some handsome paintings and lovely poetry One translates:

> "Ah, the butterflies and wine
> floating color, liquid color
> transport us to paradise
> where Woman is Queen."

Another very freely translated and rather humorous ditty reads:

> "How jolly, how lovely
> to have two men
> one to make love with
> the other for work!"

Now you will ask as we too, questioned, is there not some unrest amongst the Worker Males? None are slaves or required to stay in any way as there are always more available where they came from. Each is free to drop out, retire or leave the country. Few do. Their lives are pleasant and happy. Flowers and fruit and vegetables flourish with a minimum of tedious gardening and requiring only harvesting by the men and older children. Since the natives are vegetarian the colorful cattle are raised for barter only to others and are desired for their multi-colors. In addition to their pleasant sexual duties, Stud Consorts fish. The fish are cleaned and cooked for the evening meal at sunset. Because each man is so content and happy in what he does there's a long list of male applicants who wish to enter the tribe.

The Council of Women go over this list at the twenty-two moon meetings. There is also no necessity for any woman to nag, harangue or control any man or use them in any way the men do not desire as there are many pleading to be admitted to this benign society. Stud Consorts seem fulfilled and will even hide for a day or two to rest up. We learned at the very first sign of unrest, the intuitive, kind, beautiful, strong Zulazandian women free their men and say: "GO! You are free to fly your wings and be your best!"

(Silently adding, "There are plenty more where you came from.")

Part of the Stud Consort's duty is preparing the evening sunset meal. For this they wear large aprons and chef's hats painted with witty sayings, such as, "I'm a lover, not a cook."

They love to fish for the food and play in small boats with bark sails. In these they sail around and around in the nearby bay of the Zandia Ocean to see who can complete the circle first! For this the winner is awarded a pottery cup inscribed with The Good Blue Dragon sign at a solemn gathering. The women merrily laugh at these sailing games, they fish and sail for pleasure as they feel moved. In addition they conduct all the trading and bartering business once a full moon leaving them plenty of time to amuse and enjoy themselves.

Every twenty-two months a new Queen Earth Mother is chosen and instant wisdom is granted to her. This is simply done in rotation. Is there a better political system devised or recorded? If one should work out better than another, twenty-two moons is not too long to put up with a less able leader. However, because Zulazandian women are superior in every way they have had none but perfect Queen Earth Mothers.

The chief Festival among many is held every six moons, the "Festival of the Butterflies." Large banners with the symbol of The Good Blue Dragon and other banners are prepared by the artists. The Worker Males who farm the cat-size butterflies train them up to the festival opening and then turn them loose. Women are the lead dancers, leaping nearly to the sky and the chief musicians and organizers as well. The people wend their procession down by the riverside with hundreds of brightly colored butterflies fluttering over their heads and shoulders.

The Zinzers are amusing as they form a troupe who bring up the rear, woofing gently in unison in a staccato rhythm. This is the time the Worker Males and Stud Consorts get to shine as they are permitted to hand the handmade instruments to the musicians and also to collect the sashes that are dropped during the dancing.

The Butterfly Festival begins with extraordinary performances of beautiful music, dance and poetry readings. It ends with a large collation of Zablee and refreshments liberally covered with Native White prepared by the male cooks.

Everyone enjoys the Festival although the males too often over indulge which means they must sleep and rest up for several days and are good for little else. In their country their sense of humor is highly developed and the small children find these prone, snoring bodies hilarious. They play leap frog over the fast asleep adult men. The women are so strong and beautiful they never tire or over indulge (as the men do) but are kind and tolerant and laugh tenderly and merrily at the sight.

I, Dr. Lantana, hope to be a member of the next British-Canadian-Asian-Finnish Expedition to Zulazania if we can find our way back in again. We have a lot of fear and trepidation about that. There is a very tiny and narrow passage in the side of a striped mountain which once entered with dreadful squeezing, slipping and sliding reveals the whole panorama. One of us fell down this entrance by mistake and the rest of us followed. However, the artists are masters at camouflaging this entrance which is undoubtedly the reason for Zulazandia remaining a lost continent for so many a moon.

If we are successful at finding the opening again on our next trip we plan to gather up more of the artifacts and record the enchanting music played on their unusual instruments. If we can film their festival and dance it would indeed be a first as it seems to be a form of combined jungle rhythms and ballet. The women dancers are able to leap higher than Nijinsky ever did!

Ah, it is so! Zulandia is a wonderful and blessed country for women and artists.

NOTE: The Zulazandian collection of paintings and artifacts are kindly on loan by Leanora Lantana. They are for sale, preferably to women, the proceeds going to the Zulazandian Artists and Women and Children's Fund (and to Lea Lantana since the women and children need little and Lea definitely does!)

CHAPTER 18.

The identity of the murder victim and as well, the killer of Sarah and the murderer's identity apparently was not a top priority and yet to be determined. The investigation was also delayed and ham strung by total miscommunication between Italy and the United States.

A man wearing a long overcoat briskly entered the local police station. He nodded curtly to Chief Blaney who was on duty. To that officer's great relief he briefly flashed his badge, palmed it and said tersely, "I'm FBI. I have orders, (here he patted his pocket) to accompany the prisoner in custody to Logan Airport and then to Rome. He is being deported by our government."

"Thank the good Lord," The chief breathed under his breath. Aloud he said, laconically, "That's good news. This guy is a whining s.o.b. I hope you speak Italian?"

He went back and retrieved Andreas from his holding cell and walked him out to the larger room. When Andreas recognized the man awaiting him he began to shake and tremble and stutter in his high nasal voice in Italian. He shrank back in fear and tried to run back to his cell.

"Shut up!" He was told fiercely in both Italian and English. "I have no car here so the police will drive us to Salem. From there we'll go to Boston on the ferry moored at Derby Wharf. It will be a treat for you, "He added with a sly, leering smile. He grabbed Andreas roughly by the arm with a tight, vise like grip.

The man paid the fares and boarded the half empty ferry boat in Salem, The police car drove off to Marblehead with a wave from the driver. The man led Andreas who was shaking with fear to the bottom deck. There they were the only passengers as most preferred the fresh air and the view from the upper deck. Andreas could feel the gun under the man's heavy overcoat pressed hard into his side. Now Andreas was trembling uncontrollably and babbling incoherently. He had gone completely to pieces and his companion looked at him with utter contempt.

When they were halfway to Boston Andreas' "friend" ran to the Captain and reported his friend missing. Visibly agitated, crying and with sobs punctuated by moans he gasped, "I've looked for him all over the boat and I can't find my friend anywhere! He must have accidentally fallen overboard when I was in the men's room a while ago? He can't swim!"

The Captain paled, he was in shock. No one had ever been lost on his watch before, indeed his nick-name was Cautious Calvin and the ferry boat rides were noted for being safe and uneventful. Captain Cal had the boat thoroughly searched by the crew and radioed the Boston Harbor Police, the

Harbormaster and the Coast Guard to report in a shaky voice, "I have a missing passenger who possibly slipped overboard."

Soon helicopters were circling overhead. A police boat with the Harbormaster aboard hovered around the ferry boat making large circles in the area. A Coast Guard cutter joined the search. This continued for several hours after the other passengers were permitted to disembark. Andreas had disappeared. His friend left a false name and address with Captain Cal and the police, saying he would go directly to his friend's family and inform them of this tragic accident. He wept copiously and sobbed loudly, a truly Oscar winning performance. In between his tears and sobs he struggled to say, "My dear friend was on vacation visiting me in Salem from Italy."

Captain Cal was extremely upset and wanted to help this bereaved man. To show his sincere sympathy he refunded both the tickets the man had bought.

Andreas' body was not recovered for several months when scuba divers looking for lobster found him snagged on rocks at the bottom of Boston Harbor. The police, both in Boston and Salem were unsuccessful in their attempts to locate the "friend" to report their finding. The man had not been seen at all by anyone in Salem, he too, had disappeared.

About ten days after the body was recovered, Tony with Lucy by his side, cane on the other, limped to the police station where Will had told him he'd heard the "whiny wop" was being held for eventual deportation. Tony suspected it was Andreas and wanted to question and wring some answers out of him about the Bellini.

"He's, thank the Good Lord, not here anymore," said the Chief. "He's been missing ever since the day the FBI agent took him away to Boston to be deported back to Italy. That FBI guy is missing too. They suspect the Italian drowned off the ferry boat and no one knows anything about the agent who took him. The FBI says there was no authorization for an agent to take him."

He outlined all he had been told. "No body or bodies plural have been recovered yet. For all I care," he callously added, "maybe he swam to Italy."

Later, after Andreas body was recovered and an autopsy performed by the Medical Examiner, a report read: "This cadaver was shot in the heart through his left side. He did not drown, no water was found in his lungs."

Now looking at Tony apologetically, obviously embarrassed, the Chief said, "By the way, Ms. Lantana's kayak was found a few weeks ago dragged up on Riverhead Beach. A paddle was in it. It was placed in police storage and uh, "he stumbled, "it kind of got forgotten until she telephoned and asked about it yesterday. She can pick it up here later today or I can have an officer drop it off at her place," he added magnanimously. "Damn sorry about that."

Two of Tony's evil cousins had presumably drowned. Lea's beloved ocean, both the Atlantic and the Pacific, seemed stern and unforgiving making no distinctions between saint or sinner. The sea never ceased to be a powerful and sometimes avenging force of nature.

CHAPTER 19.

The next day with Lea's kayak, "Katie", safely home again Tony tried hard but could not fold his lame leg into it.

Trying to make light of their disappointment, Lea said, "Never mind, Tony Baloney, we'll go on a picnic to Brown's Island instead. At low tide we can walk over to it from Little Harbor. It's a dear little island, you'll love it."

Both wanted to be outdoors it was such a blue, blue sparkling sunny day with just a few puffy cumulous clouds. "We can eat and swim and relax and we can bring you, too Lucy." She wagged her tail vigorously and licked hands to show her eager desire to go.

Lea packed her WGBH tote bag, received for her generous donation to the station, with fruit and a plastic thermos of creamed and sugared iced coffee. Without much inspiration she made peanut butter and grape jelly sandwiches they had confessed to one another they both had loved as children. Lea made the local favorite a "fluffernutter" too. This peanut butter

163

and marshmallow fluff sandwich had been developed in Swampscott by the Durkee family who originated marshmallow fluff.

She smiled as she recalled Nora as a small child refusing to take anything but a jelly sandwich for her school lunch. Lea would say, "You are going to turn into a jelly sandwich, Nora!" She wrote Nora a story about a little girl who did turn into one and ducks and dogs and kittens followed her to lap up her drippings. It was called "Jessica Jellybread" and Nora loved it and the illustrations Lea painted in water color to go with it.

"Make enough," Tony joked, "In case the tide comes in fast and we get stranded on the island."

At dead low tide they slogged through the wet sand to Brown's with Lucy on her leash delighted to be included. After a swim which was good for Tony's mending leg they ate their lunch and stretched out on the sun-warmed rocks to take a nap. Lucy was extremely fond of napping and joined them lying between them.

Lea awoke in a half hour feeling water lapping on her knees. "We're stranded, Lucy, until the next low tide!"

Tony looked so peaceful she let him go on sleeping until he too, was getting wet and woke up. Without a boat to get off the island there was nothing to do but climb up higher on the rocks and grass and wait for the tide to turn. They reveled in their solitude and isolation.

"Me, Robinson Crusoe, you Friday," said Tony.

"No. Me Robinson Crusoe, Lucy is Friday and you are an obnoxious Italiano castaway." She grabbed both his ears and pulled his face close for a kiss. They chatted desultorily on various subjects as it got darker and the tide slowly turned and began to recede.

"Tony, what do you think of abortion?"

He winced. "Grazie Dio! You can't be pregnant?"

"Of course not. I'm upset at reading in the papers about doctors being murdered by people who make a big pretense of revering life."

"What do you think, Cara?"

"I believe in the sacredness of life but there are incidents of rape or incest when there seems no other choice for some women. Passing on a child for adoption with a genetic flaw of a mentally disturbed rapist or inbreeding seems no choice to me! Every woman must be permitted to make her own decisions. The court should not presume to make them for her." She added fiercely, "I'd cut off every abuser's ding-dong."

Tony laughed. "I believe that's been done already."

Seriously, Lea continued, "It seems to me killing a doctor is as violent an act as when hippie Vietnam protesters shoved roses in cannon's mouths, supposedly in the name of peace. Our soldiers did not cause the war! Doctors did not impregnate the women! How do supposedly intelligent people get a mind set of 'kill the messenger?'"

"Lea, I was brought up in the Roman church and I know what I'm supposed to think about abortion. In my opinion most people follow their own

conscience on sexual matters such as abortion and
birth control. Even so, perhaps they still suffer terrible
guilt for disobeying the church? I believe God does
not ask for blind obedience but a holy curiosity. I
think the Jesuits would agree."

Dryly Lea responded, "Martin Luther would,
he wasn't big on blind obedience."

Tony abruptly changed the subject. "I want to
apologize for all the swearing I subjected you to when
we first met. I didn't want anyone to know who I
really was before I found my cousins. I was trying to
act like a common, ordinary fisherman like Will."

"That was your first mistake. Will is far from
ordinary. My father was a fisherman and he never said
anything stronger than "Oh fishcakes!" when he was
upset or angry. He could get a lot of feeling into it.
Einar was an uncommon, common man and as
courteous and polite to everyone as a Roman
aristocrat," she needled.

"OH FISHCAKES! Look who's coming for
dinner, Lea!"

Swimming toward them in a couple feet of
water on the outgoing tide was a retinue of raccoons.

"We don't have any dinner left, Lucy ate the
last of it. I thought all these nasty creatures had been
deported and left town!"

"Come on, we can make it." Tony grabbed his
cane and Lucy's leash, she was staring in fear at the
horde of dark shapes heading toward them. Wading
through two feet of water Lea, Lucy and Tony went
right past the swimming raccoons going in the opposite
direction. They had set their sights on the island and
would not be easily deterred or deflected. Lea, Tony

and Lucy reached the shore at Little Harbor and squished in their wet sneakers all the way to the studio.

Safely home they washed off the sand and hosed down Lucy. They dried her with a fluffy towel. After changing her clothes Lea went to the kitchen to rustle up Tony's white clam sauce for supper. He and Lucy were contented lying on some cushions on the floor beside the blazing pot-bellied stove. Virgin olive oil, garlic, chopped fresh flat Italian parsley, capers, clams and Chablis wine went into the sauce. As usual the clams were added last to insure they would not turn rubbery but remain tender and succulent.

They enjoyed a bountiful supper feeling justified and virtuous because all they'd eaten all day were peanut butter sandwiches. Lucy was starved. Now they stuffed themselves with several helpings of linguini and clam sauce which was one of Lucy's favorites. She truly was a sea dog, gustily she ate clams, lobster and fish unlike most dogs. Lucy was unusual, special and a real Marbleheader.

Sitting at her old table Tony leered at Lea.

"Hey, you sure know how to throw a great picnic, each one is more exciting than the last. You are the mother of all picnics!"

Secretly amused, Lea tapped him on the side of the head with her spoon. The spoons had been set out for dessert which was Siri's Caramel Custard Lea had made the night before and refrigerated in individual glass cups. She'd been wanting to show Tony the dish Siri always made for her children when they were ill to coax their appetites back.

Tony and Lea took turns showing off their native cuisines, sharing their recipes and also trying to out cook one another. It was a friendly rivalry as both honestly admired the other's skill. They felt strongly cooking and eating well was an art more people should practice and enjoy as they did, and Lucy most certainly did.

CHAPTER 20.

Tony hired an accountant, a C.P.A. named Gitte Jensen from a Boston firm. The young Danish girl was the CEO. He wanted all his holdings, stocks, bonds and bank accounts checked and looked into. He had noticed alarming discrepancies in the papers and figures John Randall had given him. Tony had always felt slightly uneasy about John. He wondered now if he could be in league with Roberto or even Bell to acquire the Bellini? He knew John to be an avid and greedy art collector.

Gitte pointed out where the figures did not add up and how some entries had been cleverly doctored. Tony would not have noticed except he had a gut instinct making him suspicious of Randall. He decided to fly to New York and confront the lawyer.

He asked himself, sadly, "Is there anyone in the world I can trust besides Lea and Lucy?" His parents and Nonna and his other grandmother who all had been sincere and loving were now gone. His aunts, their husbands, their sons (his cousins) were far from honorable people. He added Will and Julia to his short list of reliable friends and Sylvia. It made him feel bad as he was basically a trusting person, however not naive and he knew one must temper idealism with realism.

In John's office in New York, Mahler's Fifth Symphony was playing in the background. Blandly Tony started in questioning John about some of his investments and the poor return on several? He had checked them out with Gitte and they were listed much higher on the Dow Jones and Nasdaq than John had on paper.

Unnerved by Tony's barrage of questions yet as suave as ever John made an attempt to go on the offensive. He drew himself up haughtily and said, "Are you suggesting I cheated you? I am very, very offended by this conversation and your apparent accusations, Tony!" He was pale and his forehead beaded with perspiration. The orchestra in the background reached a fitting crescendo.

"As a matter of fact that is just what I AM concerned about. Are you or have you been in touch with my cousins? Did you throw your hand in with one or all of them against me and incidentally betraying my grandmother who trusted and recommended you?" Tony said this in a quiet yet almost sinister tone of voice masking his fury.

John jumped up from his leather chair sputtering, "I want you to leave this office right now and take all your bloody business with you! I don't want to ever represent you again, get out!"

"Good bluff, John. I'm not leaving here until I have a check signed on your firm for every last cent you stole from both Angela Amberetti-Scola and from me. My accountant has all the necessary proof in a bank vault in Boston. She also has my power of attorney to start legal proceedings against you unless you cooperate. You're a rat, John as well as a snob. Call your secretary in here to get it all notarized and start writing. I want all the stocks you've been mishandling for me in my name listed in full. Get busy! I'll be back in two hours to get all the papers and my check."

"John, I'll have the District Attorney of New York, Jeremy Bradshaw with me. If you don't comply your law firm will be ruined and your personal reputation shot to hell. By the way, Jem Bradshaw was my roommate at Eton in England and we're still close friends."

Jeremy Bradshaw's mother was English and he'd been sent to Eton before he attended his American father's alma mater, Ohio State University, followed by Columbia Law School.

Tony left John sitting in his hand-tooled leather chair with a crumpled, defeated expression and pale and sweating. Tony almost felt sorry for him. He intended later with the D.A.'s presence to force out of John under a threat of conspiracy to defraud, his connection to any of his cousins and the theft of the sculpture and its whereabouts now.

When he returned with Bradshaw two hours later the door was open but John was not in his office. Wringing her hands the secretary entered saying, "Mr. Randall left all these papers for you on his desk. He said to tell you both everything is in order. He was terribly upset and looked ill and he told me he had to leave for Long Island right away. Mr. Randall said he would get in touch with you about a statue? Oh, I know there's something terribly wrong!"

"Tony, I think he has flown the coop. Take all this paperwork to your accountant and to an attorney. Have it all checked over before I start an investigation or a lawsuit by the state of New York. If you recover your assets you may not wish to pursue it further? Knowing you as I do, I doubt you will. I think Randall is already a broken man from the accusations and pretty much being discovered to be a thief and embezzler."

"I've no stomach for destroying the man or being vindictive, Jem. What I want to know is where those bastards, my cousins are, and what they've done to my grandmother's Bellini?"

"Ok. I'll send some people out to his Long Island Estate to question him under a subpoena. We'll lean on him a bit. I'll call you and let you know what information I uncover. Give me your telephone number again."

Tony thanked him and for his dinner invitation as well. "But," he told this burly, rusty-haired, former football half-back, "A beautiful woman is waiting for me in Boston for dinner and also a dog."

Jem laughed. Raising his eyebrows he drawled, "A dog? Is it human? Dinner with two women, one is beautiful, one is ugly?"

"Dio, no! One is honestly a beautiful woman and the other my beautiful, real dog, St. Lucia, a yellow lab. When you and Gwen visit us you'll be introduced to both my lovely girls."

Tony flew from Newark to Boston again and checked in with Gitte, updating her on all the developments and leaving the papers to be put in the safe.

He then returned to Marblehead in the red bug he cherished the way a teen-ager would. This time he was able to tell Lea everything that had happened. As they ate dinner she listened attentively.

Lea had prepared a meal of scalloped oysters ready to pop into the oven when he arrived. She would serve this with brown rice and garden ripe tomatoes she'd drizzled olive oil, virgin of course, ground black pepper and tucked torn basil leaves amongst them.

For dessert Lea brought out a covered jar of pistachio-apricot biscotti Tony had baked one afternoon when he was recovering from his hospital stay. He'd competed a little with Lea demonstrating he could also cook. Reluctantly, she finally admitted she liked his Lobster Tetrazzini quite a lot although at first she'd scoffed, "What a way to ruin good lobster." She also had to confess Tony's shrimp grilled with prosciutto was delicious. Generously she told Tony he was a marvelous cook. He allowed as she was too, "We're a perfect match, Carissima."

The telephone rang as they were having coffee with the biscotti. Tony went in from the terrace to answer it for Lea. She heard him say, "Oh no! I certainly did not want that! Jem, this is terrible news, I'm shocked. Why did he do that? What other felonies? He got all those beautiful objects and paintings by stealing his client's money? Thanks for calling. Yes, it is upsetting and it does make me feel bad."

From Tony's end of the conversation Lea guessed something had happened to the lawyer. He came back, looking shaken and sat down.

"Well?"

"John Randall shot himself."

Lea drew a ragged breath and whispered, "Death has become our brother, Tony." She shuddered. Tony gazed at her somberly. He couldn't think what to say to relieve her fear and anxiety. No longer hungry, he pushed his plate away.

CHAPTER 21.

Will and Julia invited Lea and Tony to their house in Barnegat for an authentic old-fashioned Marblehead salt cod dinner. "You're going to be surprised how great this is, Tony, especially the red flannel hash you make the next day for breakfast with the left-overs! Julia will be sure to cook plenty so there'll be enough to take home for the hash." He promised.

Tony questioned Lea about salt cod dinners but she preferred to be noncommittal surmising Will meant this as one great stunning surprise and she didn't want to spoil it for Will. Besides that she couldn't wait to see Tony's reaction.

Tony seriously doubted that stiff-as-a-board salted cod that had to be soaked overnight could possibly be as good as fresh caught. Originally, before refrigeration, all fish was preserved by salting it heavily. He had, as well, private reservations about the red flannel hash.

In their snug 16th-century house near Gracie Oliver's Beach, Will and Julia welcomed them with frosty mugs of ale, "Come on in, come in!"

Julia smiled shyly at Lea as she handed her a cold mug of Tuberg ale. Sipping from it, Lea walked around admiring some framed watercolors of Julia's that were delicate and nice. Julia blushed at Lea's enthusiastic praise. "Come to my watercolor class tomorrow morning at Crocker Park, Julia? You'll inspire the students with your work."

"I'd like to, yes, I will."

At the table Will winked at Tony in a conspirational manner and said, "I'll say grace." Holding up his mug to them in a toast, he intoned, "Thank God, good God, let's eat this treat."

Julia poked him with her elbow. "What Will meant to say is, "Oh let us give thanks unto the Lord, for He is good and his mercy endureth forever, Amen."

Will showed them, (Lea knew but pretended ignorance. Salt cod dinners had never been a favorite of hers as a child) how traditionally one ate the meal Julia had prepared of poached salt cod, boiled potatoes and boiled fresh beets with the "tried out" crisp pork rashers served on the side to sprinkle over all.

"You're supposed to mash everything together with your fork on the plate and top it off with the pork rashers," Will instructed seriously. Surreptitiously watching Tony Lea hid a grin. He was desperately trying to overcome his aversion to the mess on his plate, an awful red color, but determined to be courteous, enthusiastic and appreciative for Will's sake. Bravely he gulped down a mouthful. Raising his eyebrows and smacking his lips in feigned histrionic surprise, he exclaimed, "Dammit, Will, this is really good!"

Visibly pleased Will smugly said, "I told you so."

Lea helped Julia clear the table for dessert which were mammoth Joe Frogger cookies invented by Black Joe Brown and his wife some three hundred years ago. They ran a tavern beside a pond that came to be known as Gingerbread Hill. They were spicy with a lot of ginger, molasses and rum and especially good with coffee when dunked. Will encouraged them to dunk the cookies in the hot coffee as they were a bit hard.

Julia whispered to Lea in the kitchen, "I've always hated these salt cod dinners. Will loves them, for old time townies it's nostalgia, you're both so kind to be such good sports about it. Will's been dying to show Tony. I'll give you a doggie bag (emphasizing the doggie) to make the red flannel hash from. It's also yuk! You can toss it when you get home or perhaps Lucy might like it?"

"Lucy will be crazy about it if I know Lucy." She was.

The next morning Lea took her class of eight to Crocker Park off Front Street for some plein air painting. Softly and shyly Julia asked, "Did Lucy enjoy the red flannel hash ingredients?" "She sure did," Lea laughed, "She gobbled up every bit."

Some students would choose Herreshoff's Castle for their subject. He'd been a noted boat designer and a racing class boat was named for him. Other students would turn toward the town and the Boston Yacht Club and paint the myriad roof tops with

Abbot Hall looming over all. A few would face the harbor filled with boats. Both downtown Crocker Park and the Chandler Hovey Light House Park on the Neck embraced a plethora of painterly subjects, both sea and landscapes painters and teachers loved.

First Lea set up her French easel and quickly demonstrated a watercolor sketch of the castle, now part of it was a B&B. Pupils were usually itching to get started painting so she kept her demo short and took some questions they were eager to ask before beginning to paint.

"I love the loose, spontaneous way you paint Ms. Lantana. You don't ever seem to do any preliminary drawing as I was taught one must do. Why is that?"

"Please everyone. Call me Lea. If you draw everything first the tendency is to fill the drawing in with paint like a coloring book. The result is apt to be stiff and not very painterly looking. Draw with your paint brush, not a pencil."

"How do you achieve such bright, juicy color? My painting always seem washed out and pale. Yours look good enough to eat!"

"That's exactly what Georgia O'Keeffe said about mounds of oil pigments laid out on a palette. "They look good enough to eat!" But clean color is a very simple technique. Squeeze out a generous amount of paint from your watercolor tubes and place it on top of the old paint on your palette. Set your palette up like the spectrum, starting with warm and cool yellows and moving right around. Oranges, warm and cool, reds, purples, blues and greens. There are no browns. Burnt Sienna is a cool orange. Raw Sienna is a cool yellow. Never use black or white unless you are doing gouache.

At the end of each painting session don't do more than mop up what you have to, you'll lose a lot of expensive paint if you clean your palette when still very wet. When you begin a session wipe off the tops of the old paint gently and add fresh paint, drop on some water with your brush, then let it all meld together.

If you bring water with your brush to dry paint all you'll achieve is a tint off the top, giving a pale effect. You want to be able to really dig in and get the rich, juicy color from the melded pigments. Is everyone ready to paint, now?"

"Please, before we do, would you explain how you do those wet-into-wet watercolors you win so many prizes for?"

Lea laughed, "Not that many prizes! I'll be happy to, it's not a secret. Soak your paper in a bathtub, (if you have one, I don't) or sponge it three times on each side to open the pores. Allow the paper to dry until it is just moist. If it is too wet the paint will slide all over and make "curtains" at the edges. And conversely, if the paper is too dry the paint cannot spread or blossom or bloom as we wish it to. Test for the correct dampness in a corner with a stroke of paint, either re-sponge it if necessary of permit it to dry a little longer and test it again. After painting your subject matter, when the paper is bone dry apply your marks and delineations and so on. Not too many, just enough to separate a blossom for instance, or indicate an object. Please never outline! Draw in and out of register, not just around objects."

179

"And never be afraid to tear a stinker up and start over. For the sake of spontaneity I don't draw ahead so I often do a second painting to adjust the design and composition and discard the first. Many painters do some preliminary thumbnail sketches, it's thriftier but I don't enjoy that as I'm always too impatient to plunge in."

Another young man asked mournfully, "Why are all my watercolors muddy and gray? They're not clean and crisp like yours."

"Dirty water produces muddy or dirty paintings. That is another very simple trick. Always have two container of water; one is to act as your medium, the other to clean your brush off between applying colors. Bring plenty of clean water in a canteen or thermos and change the water frequently. Try using a small tuna fish can inside the water bucket that you clean your brushes in. Learn to bring just the right amount of water to the wet pigments with your brush as you paint. Shall I go on? I didn't intend to take up your time with a lecture."

The students nodded.

"Okay, then. I'll be happy to give you a mini-lecture if you really want it? Another very important principle is never to mix more than two colors together to achieve a shade you want. Why? Because three will always contain a tone of the three primaries,-red, blue and yellow, and make a gray. If you need a gray mix your own this way. I don't use pre-mixed Payne's Gray or Davie's Gray in the tubes. Three secondary colors-orange-which is red and yellow; green-which is blue and yellow: violet or purple- which is red and blue also contain the three primaries and will make a gray as well. For pure fresh color mix together two colors only or like Van Gogh use straight from your palette. Anyone else?" Lea glanced at her watch wanting her class to get the best of the light.

"Yes, me. I've been told over and over that water color is much more difficult than oils. I know you paint in oils, too. Is that true?"

"No, it is not!" Lea said emphatically. "Either is just as hard as you care to make it. Both need a ground to paint on; paper or canvas. Both use natural ground pigments made from stone, minerals and earth, not nasty, manmade in the lab, acrylics. (I have a prejudice here, I'll admit. Real watercolor and oil pigments will always mix the same. Acrylics do not.)"

"Beautiful, (it is really breathtaking) vermilion is made from South American cochina beetle shells and it is expensive."

"Both oils and watercolor follow the rules for form, design or composition and values and color. There are scientific rules to use for what is called Simultaneous Color Contrast. This is how the appearance of a color passage can change in warmth or coolness, brightness or darkness in value by the color that is placed next to it. To explain this would require another whole lecture. It is best for beginners to paint from the heart and learn rules so you can break them!"

"Of course, both oils and watercolors need a medium to mix with the pigment. In oils you use turpentine and linseed oil or liquitin. In watercolor the medium is pure water. Brushes need to be cleaned between each change of color. Water does this for watercolor, turps for oils. In oils one usually works from dark to light, putting highlights on last. In

181

watercolor one works from light to dark, saving white paper for your highest whites, never using opaque white paint. Passages in oil while still wet can be scraped off and redone. Watercolor is less forgiving but you can tamp a passage with wet tissue several times and when dry repaint. Paper towels will abrade the paper so use Kleenex. Don't you guys want to get painting, let's not lose this lovely morning light?"

The class seemed more interested in all the tips and information Lea was giving them and most of them took notes.

"Just one more question, I beg you!" An older woman spoke up. "I am strictly an amateur. Do you have a philosophy of painting or advice for new painters?"

"I'm going to answer this as it is important then we must get to work and take full advantage of the light and long shadows. The best advice I got was from Paul Scott, my mentor and teacher at Montserrat Art School. Paul had studied with the famous Hans Hofmann in his Provincetown school before it all got so cheap and commercial."

"He begged all his students to stay sensitive, be vulnerable, permit yourself to be hurt and to feel deeply. Don't try to wall your emotion off or seal it over."

Paul told us, "Good painting comes out of genuine feeling. Never copy another, express your own unique self and originality. It is the process not the product that counts. Painting must be your goal, your bliss, your joy."

The students scattered to paint, they were of mixed ages sex and ability. Lea helped when needed.

At the close of the session she critiqued each one's work, drawing out their opinions on their own painting, and finding the strengths and well handled passages in each to give the student something positive on which to build. Lea was known to be an excellent teacher who honestly enjoyed sharing all she knew and had learned. To her this was a sacred calling-to pass on to others all you could.

She was delighted to see Julia's painting of the harbor and boats was expertly drawn, (rigging on boats was notoriously difficult for amateurs) and quite lovely and lively. The other students generously admired Julia's painting who was gentle and kind in her response. Lea thought: *without trying to be, Julia is a naturally good person, one of God's angels on earth. Some of us have to work hard to be good, I know I do!*

Julia was shy and modest yet open to everyone and easy to love. Lea already felt a tenderness for her new friend and a little protective for her total lack of armor. Lea had had to learn the hard way to develop what little shell she had. She could well understand how Will virtually worshiped his Julia and from a checkered, carefree past had thrown himself into whole hearted monogamy with a passion.

CHAPTER 22.

As she was almost every morning, Lea was awakened by the screaming, squawking gulls. "Stupid birds! You'd think they had never known the sun to rise before they get so hysterical. (Are they frightened or rejoicing? Sometimes they sounded like a convention of meowing cats. When a storm was brewing they went into a frenzy, too.)

Soon all the yacht clubs would shoot off their morning cannon alert, never in unison but one at a time. There was such a raucous racket every daybreak no one on the harbor needed an alarm clock.

Regardless, Lea still loved living on the edge of the sea, gulls and all, it was lively in summertime, the harbor quiet and empty in winter. The tang of salt air and decaying seaweed was perfume to her, she could never live anywhere else.

Tony had gone to the boat yard early. Hungry Lucy was licking her face. Lea jumped out of bed, climbed down the spiral ladder, Lucy descending backwards after her, from the loft to the kitchen to be fed. Lucy was an old hand at going up and down the ladder.

Lea also had to prepare for a visit from her cousin Linnea, husband Paul, and their three teenaged children. They were traveling in their camper van from Kansas to Marblehead to show their children for the first time their parents' home town. The adults hated the Midwest compared to the Atlantic coast but Paul's job had taken them there.

On the telephone Linnea told Lea, "We want our kids to see Archibald Willard's painting at Abbot Hall, "The Spirit of '76", not just the print of it in a school book. We want to bring them to Old Burial Hill where General John Glover is buried and to read the memorial stone with all the names of fishermen and sailors lost at sea." This, the oldest cemetery in the country had been established in 1683.)

Linnea had an ambitious long list of historic spots for the kids to visit. One was Lighthouse Park on the Neck bought by Chandler Hovey, a noted yachtman, who gave it to the town for one dollar when it was decommissioned by the U.S. government. On Linnea's list was "Carcasonne", also on the Neck. It was a copy of a medieval castle built by Lydia Pinkham of patent medicine fame. ("A baby in every bottle" tonic.) It was situated beside Castle Rock where artists often painted the fabulous view of open sea.

"And," Linnea ran on, "they don't believe us when we tell them the Lafayette House on Lee Street had its corner cut off so Lafayette's carriage would have room to pass by on the narrow street."

On the agenda was the Jeremiah Lee Mansion, Generals Washington and Lafayette supposedly slept in (not simultaneously however) and the King Hooper Mansion nearby which was currently the home of the Marblehead Arts Association. Robert Hooper was fondly nicknamed "King" because he treated his slaves and crew so well and generously.

"Your daughter Trudy, would love the romantic story of Agnes Surriage, Linnea? Don't overlook Fountain Park and the well on Orne Street where Agnes, the poor fisherman's daughter, gave Sir Harry Frankland a dipper of cool water." Fountain Inn had stood there In 1742 Frankland came to Marblehead to oversee the building of Fort Sewall for protection from France. He fell in love with beautiful, teenaged Agnes at first sight and took her back to England as his mistress. Years later they were married after she rescued him in an earthquake in Lisbon thus proving her devotion! She then became Lady Frankland. They shared Tory sentiments during the Revolution, to the indignant disgust of her independent Marblehead relatives who felt Agnes had betrayed them.

"Paul wants young Paul to see Redd's Pond where he skated with your brothers, Lars and Erik, as a boy and sailed model boats. Oh dear, we have so much to cover in ten days!" After she hung up Lea thought, "They should include a visit to J. O. J. Frost Gallery on Washington Street." Frost's folk paintings which he'd sold for ten cents from a wheelbarrow were now worth millions, more for their historic than artistic depiction of Marblehead's past. A former fisherman he took up painting at age 70 after his wife, Annie's death.

Her cousins were vegetarians and Lea looked forward to devising good meals for them. She relished the challenge of vegetarian cooking and discovered early the secret was plenty of cheese for protein in place of red meat and mounds and mounds and mounds of mashed potatoes. All kinds of vegans seemed to love and eat great quantities of potato even without gravy. Lea planned a spinach pie, cauliflower Mornay, a vegetable lasagna and peppers stuffed with mushrooms, cheese and croutons. Tony gave her his recipe for Pasta e Fagioli, pasta and beans, Italy's version of Texas chili and offered to make it for Lea's cousins.

Singing and bustling about in her raspberry color galley kitchen Lea got busy.

"Lucy, want me to sing 'Little Brown Jug' to you?" She laughed as she fondly recalled her first dog friend, Ritz, at her favorite uncle's farm in Marlow, New Hampshire, where she and many cousins spent long, lazy summers. Uncle Bill's farm was on Gee Hill five miles from the village of six streets, a church and a general store close to the Bellows Falls, Vermont line. His dog was named Ritz because he thought this denoted class to the black and white Collie-shepherd mix who was far from good looking but had a saintly, patient disposition. Ritz would allow Lea to put bonnets on him when she was a little girl and sing to him. Over and over and over she would sing, "Ha ha ha, you and me, little brown jug, how I love thee, ha ha ha, you and me, little brown jug, how I love thee"-until her parents would beg her to stop.

Lea completely adored Uncle Bill, her mother's older brother who was childless. He and Aunt Mae

187

invited many nieces and nephews to spend vacations on the farm in the summer, supposedly to help with the chores but also to get them out of the hot city. Many of the older boys did help with the haying late in August and early September. Lea loved being perched high on the hay wagon Dottie the horse pulled to the barn.

She had taught herself to do a somersault in the air from a beam in the hay loft and was much admired by more timid girl cousins. It was easy in the beginning when the hay was high but as the summer wore on and the animals depleted the hay it became a much longer fall. She couldn't admit it scared her and courageously kept on performing when her brothers would urge her to show off for guests- "Do your somersault, Lea!"

Lea began to loathe the hay and the barn and strangely or perhaps psychosomatically developed an allergy they called hay fever. Hives, sneezes and a red, runny nose served to end her circus trick and to her secret relief she was ordered to stay out of the hay loft.

In the winter Aunt Mae knit mittens for each child in the rather poor village and Uncle Bill augmented his income by working in the saw mill. He was a huge, ruddy, jolly man everyone liked, full of jokes and teasing. Bill was always chosen to be Master of Ceremonies for Old Home Day in mid-summer. When Lea and her cousin Ruthie, won the three-legged potato race, (one leg of each in a coarse woven grain or potato bag) they were ecstatic. They had to hop in unison to win, holding up the bag and laughing hysterically all the way. Their prize was a newborn kitten donated by a resident anxious to find homes for this latest litter of barn cats. They named him "Billy Boy."

She suddenly remembered one of her favorite dishes on the farm was vegetarian! Aunt Mae's "thinnings." Never wasteful, when Aunt Mae thinned out her early vegetable garden she made a delectable dish from them. Baby carrots as big as Lea's little finger, tiny new potatoes the size of marbles dug from the side of a potato hill and the first new peas. They were scrubbed and boiled separately, drained, tossed together in a large mixing bowl with salt and pepper and a big dollop of home-made butter. Nothing since had ever tasted as good or as fresh.

To go with this meal Uncle Bill would race to the garden and pick ears of corn. He husked them on his way back to the farmhouse all ready to be plunged into the pot of sugared and salted boiling water Mae had waiting. Aunt Mae fried doughnuts and doughnut holes on top of the old wood stove and made blueberry and apple pies by the score in the oven.

Moments after a new calf was born her uncle would take Lea to the barn to see it trying to stand up on wobbly legs, blood and fluid still streaming from its mother. Aunt Mae disapproved of him showing Lea but he said, "Nonsense, Mamie, it's the miracle of birth, she'll remember it forever," and she did.

Once there were twin calves, each had what looked like a star on their foreheads. Uncle Bill told her she could name them. Every pig, cow, cat, dog and horse on his farm had a name, usually after a relative. Calling a large sow "Weewee" after an older sister, Louise, who was quite large, yet short and nick-named

Weewee did not fill her with enthusiasm. It obviously tickled him to do this.

Lea said, "I'll call this one "Star" and the other "Moonie," Bill found this most amusing as the children in the family all called their posteriors, "moonies."

After dear Ritz died of old age her uncle was given a pure bred Dashhound he named after his favorite sister, Siri. The Dashhound was a yippy, bad-tempered little thing but her mother knew this was meant to be a compliment as he loved the dog so she never told her brother she disliked her namesake.

The dog, Siri, slept under the covers at Uncle Bill's feet at night. Lea worried, "How can she breathe?" "She loves my smelly feet, it's like ambrosia to her, Lily."

He called her Lily, Uncle had a nickname for everyone, some were not flattering.

Many evenings Lea and her uncle sat on a stonewall in the pasture watching the sunset on the White Mountains in a companionable silence as he smoked his pipe. Invariably as the last visage faded and the blue twilight descended Uncle Bill would say, "You can't buy a sight like that, Lil." She'd learned from him to savor and almost become a palpable part of sunrises, sunsets and moonrises. Now she thought of this as a priceless legacy from her favorite uncle, more valuable than riches.

"Come on, Lil and Toodie, (cousin Ruthie) get your bathing suits on and jump in the truck and I'll take you to Sand Pond for a swim." Sand Pond, a few miles further up the mountain was spring fed, crystal clear and icy cold.

They also rode with him in the truck when he delivered milk to a Girl's Camp near the pond. His Holstein cow's milk was rich, flecked with butter and unpasteurized. His cows were inspected and tested regularly. Toodie was from South Boston and used to city life. Seriously she told Uncle Bill, "I'm sorry, I don't like your cow's milk. I like the kind of milk at home that comes in a bottle," never connecting the milk to cows.

He gave the girls an old, smelly, dirty unused hen house for a playhouse if they would clean it. They diligently scrubbed it and fit it out with their dolls, doll dishes and paper dolls. If they squeezed and pushed they could even get Ritz in.

On the open porch one day Lea was horrified to see gentle, beloved Ritz snap a chicken's neck who had tried to eat from his food dish. Hens and chickens ranged freely about. Her uncle removed the dead chicken (to be cooked and eaten later), "Never disturb an animal when he's eating, Lily." She never did although Lucy did not seem to mind an interruption of a pat or two while she was eating.

The pump to the well had been put in Aunt Mae's kitchen as a modern convenience. There was also a spring with a tin dipper for ice cold, wonderful water to drink several feet away.

Her Uncle Bill loved to tease and he loved practical jokes. When Lea was grown she gave him a gift certificate to a large junk yard, "Duane's" one Christmas. Bill loved junk and the farm had been filled with it. Old tires filled with manure and dirt grew platter-size nasturtiums in Aunt Mae's front yard. He thought Lea's junk yard gift was the grandest gift and told everyone about it. Lea had to persuade the owner to write it out. He said nobody had ever asked him to do that before! Uncle Bill really enjoyed poking around the huge junk yard and cashing in her gift for odds and ends.

When Lea had grown up and Nora was a baby Uncle Bill drove from New Hampshire in his old truck each year to bring her a perfect Christmas tree he'd cut from the many acres of his deep woods. Only a fraction of the land he owned was cleared for pasture.

They loved company or at least Bill did. They shared all they had. The big old farmhouse table would be extended with boards placed over sawhorses into the next room and on to the porch. Sheets for tablecloths were spread over them and twenty-five and often more guests would be fed at a jolly meal, old and young together. He had so many friends. "If you want good friends, Lily, you have to be one." Everyone liked Bill.

Jugs of cider, pitchers of buttermilk were set on the table. Heaping platters of corn on the cob, loins of pork, gravy boats, fried chicken, mashed potatoes, baked beans, biscuits, and home-made doughnuts and their holes, string beans cooked with salt pork, jams and jellies, corn bread, pickles, cucumbers, dandelion greens and sliced tomatoes were just a part of the gigantic feast. After that came all the pies.

For breakfast Uncle Bill always had baked beans, two or three fried eggs, slices of ham and a big piece of pie, wild blueberry or snow apple. Lea used to read his Wild West magazines lying in the hammock under the Snow Apple tree, chomping on the small green apples with pink flesh.

Uncle Bill had been a lovely man, a jewel of a man. Lea whispered, "God bless you, Uncle Bill, I still love you. I bet in heaven you're telling St. Peter corny jokes and giving all the angels and cherubim nicknamesand I KNOW Ritz is there, too. And you don't have to empty the honey cart any more," She smiled.

Uncle Bill used to shovel all the fecal stuff from the outhouse onto what he called the "honey cart" to bury in the woods. Teasing her he'd say, "Come on, Lil, I'm going to give you a ride on the honey cart," and Lea would run and hide.

While cousin Linnea was here they could celebrate a belated traditional Finnish May Day holiday with crullers and Sima to drink. Lea prepared the Sima to ferment with lemon, sugar, beer, yeast and some raisins and stored it in a cool place in the cellar. When the raisins rise to the surface the Sima is ready to be strained and chilled to drink. (Tony sampled the Sima for Lea and gasping said "WOW!) Lea had described Sima as "a kind of lusty lemonade."

"No wonder you Finns are so strong, if this is the kind of lemonade you drink! I never had anything like it, Lea. Lusty it is, lemonade it ain't! I can see why the May Day holiday is so raucous with people throwing their academic white caps in the air and dancing and singing. I'm crazy about the crullers too, please don't wait until next May First to make them again?"

"Will you help make white paper hats like the students wear to toss in the air, Tony?"

"Sure. It should be a lot of fun for the children. Do they drink Sima, too?"

"Not the ones who haven't yet graduated. They drink a regular lemonade, I'll make for them."

Tony turned to Lucy, "And that's what you'll drink too, Lucy, no Sima for you, you're too young. I don't like to think what an intoxicated dog might do."

Lea laughed, "I've never seen a drunken dog, have you?"

"Not yet. But I'm sure St. Lucia would rather see than be one."

In truth Sima was fairly mild. Tony exaggerated to get a rise out of Lea who of course would put down a bowlful for Lucy when they celebrated their late May Day with cousin Linnea and her family.

CHAPTER 23.

Lea was feeling somewhat encouraged about Lars who seemed more like the loyal, sweet-tempered Lantana he'd been in the past. Occasionally he visited alone and sometimes brought his children. The overt animosity he'd displayed for a while was gone.

Lea wished she could reach out to his wife and say, "Hey girl, we want to love you, too." The door seemed closed. Something must have happened to hurt this woman badly to make her so fearful of accepting love from her husband's family? Lea ached and prayed for a way to bring Lars, his wife and children closer. She wondered what it was that made his wife so defensive and prickly and hang on to her husband and children so tightly? She regretted and mourned his children had lost so much of what his old family had to give. But she accepted there was little she could do. Their love seemed to be a threat that was hard to understand.

Tony told her, "Sometimes things happen in life we can't change, Lea."

"I will never believe that, Lars will be back I'm sure of it," She stubbornly maintained. As Tony advised, she turned her efforts toward her other siblings she loved.

Tony pronounced, too, thinking of his lost Loridana, "When one door closes another one opens, I know this to be fact in my life. Don't knock on the closed door so hard, Lea, that you don't see the open one." He felt grateful he'd found Lea with whom he was crazy in love. Although she retorted, "I hate it when you're preachy," She listened.

Erik and Laura invited Lea and Tony on a shakedown cruise of their new motor sailor, planning to sail to Manchester-by-the-sea's harbor for lunch. As they sailed out of Marblehead past the Fort they circled around a fleet of doughty little Optimists on the second day of their regatta. These were one-person boats for children who were for the most part age ten or under. The children had to be up to, yet not exceed a certain weight.

Laura exclaimed, "Don't they look like a flock of white butterflies?"

Erik yelled, "Go Suzi!" as they passed one boat and the young sailor called back making a Vee sign, "Right on, Daddy!"

"Are all your children racing?" Asked Tony.

"Yep. All three. They love it, especially Suzi, she's a great little sailor," Erik responded with pride.

"Apparently they're not too young."

"Not my kids, they're born sailors, it's the Viking blood in them, huh, Lea?"

Every now and then one of the boats would capsize and Laura scream, "Oh, God!"

"They do that on purpose, Laura, for the fun and thrill of it. See how quickly they always right themselves? The kids are fine," Erik reassured his wife who did not appear to be totally convinced.

In Manchester's pretty little harbor they moored at the town landing and then walked up the street to lunch in a small cafe. Tony did not reveal that in his first twelve years he had sailed an Optimist often in Manchester Harbor. It was bittersweet to see the familiar small yacht club and the town again. It was much the same as he remembered it. Lea noticed his pensive demeanor.

"Old memories? Are you all right, Tony?"

He smiled at her and squeezed her hand. "Yeah. That was then, this is now, and Caramia, the now is fine."

Erik and Laura, although curious about the exchange, politely did not comment. They liked Tony and hoped things would work out for Lea, whatever Tony's past. She'd had a rough time with Ray, her family agreed on that. They all heartily detested him.

After a surprisingly gourmet lunch of crabmeat salad and iced coffee they set sail for Marblehead with a fair breeze under sunny skies. An ideal sailing day, it was perfect.

When her brother dropped them off at State Street wharf before sailing to his mooring at the Marblehead Yacht Club, Lea told him, "It was a lovely day and wonderful sail, thank you, Erik." Laura called out, "we loved it too, let's do it again soon."

As they walked down Front Street to the "Fisherman's Fjord," Lea called her studio, (like her uncle she had a penchant for naming things) Tony said wistfully, "I envy you, Lea, you have a wonderful family."

Lea knew he was thinking of his cousins. She knew as well, she did have a great deal to be thankful for despite many sorrows. Siri used to admonish her children, "The attitude is gratitude for all the good things you have in life and stop feeling sorry for yourself," whenever any would complain to her despite whether it was a major or minor problem.

John Peder at nine, when he had his arm in a sling from a broken collar bone, was told, "Count your blessings! Jumping off Papa's boat to the dock the way you did you could have drowned instead of just tripping and falling." He had given his mother a sour look but he knew better than to talk back. Siri ran a tight ship. She was the epitome of discipline reinforced with much love and compassion. They all knew Siri would have died for each of her children so they felt secure and loved which every child needs most.

CHAPTER 24.

The murderer frequently walked the streets of Lynn. Now in the process of being gentrified what was once referred to as the 'city of sin' was acquiring a better reputation. There now was a handsome college campus and old shoe factories and mills were being renovated into condos and office space.

He stayed in Captain Pete's Waterfront Inn on Fisherman's Beach in neighboring Swampscott. He did not go to Marblehead except on the darkest and moonless nights. Biding his time he patiently waited for the South American middle man to contact him by courier, the last person on a long chain of messengers.

Every day he took long walks on the boulevard in front of Red Rock. He traversed all the way through Swampscott and Lynn to Nahant and back amidst hundreds of joggers, baby strollers, dog walkers and roller-bladers. He was one of a crowd and blended in, careful not to swagger or strut, acting like a regular Joe, he congratulated himself. He never noticed the stares he elicited wearing a business suit near and on the beach when most were dressed casually in shorts or bathing suits.

On these long daily walks he fantasized about the enormous fortune he soon would have when the Bellini marble was retrieved and finally sold and delivered to the South American art collector. Taking the MTA in to Logan Airport he inquired of the various airlines about possible flights in and out again to South America, Brasilia was his target. He also wrote down the fares to a Caribbean country and Ibezia and Europe. He would decide later where to retire. In his supreme arrogance he never once doubted his carefully laid plans would go other than he precisely intended.

He paid Captain Pete, the Innkeeper, in advance and told him, "I'm a computer consultant from New York and I'm here to work with many firms on the North Shore. I'll be here only temporarily until my work with the various companies is completed, it may take a month."

He remained quiet and aloof, keeping to himself making no friends or acquaintances and he did not welcome overtures. No one questioned his presence or took much notice of him. For the most part the guests of the Inn were short term. He enjoyed the many fine restaurants in Lynn and Swampscott. Almost next door to Captain Pete's the Hawthorne-by-the-Sea offered fantastic over-large, dry (a whisper of vermouth) martinis in frosted balloon glasses he relished. He also investigated their version of a Bellini, it amused him to drink them.

He liked the Porthole Pub on Lynn's waterfront because of its large menu and specialty of deep fried dill pickles. Claire's Seafood Supreme was another favorite choice. He could walk to the Porthole without having to have a car. He didn't want to rent one because of all the information it was necessary to give. His seemingly flexible work schedule, coming and going to the Inn at all times of day aroused the suspicions of the Innkeeper but he kept his own counsel. Frequently he had Pete call a taxi to take him to his destination.

The murderer put in what is known in prison as easy time, walking, walking and waiting. Utterly relaxed, he slept well. He was as cold, as calculating, conscienceless, heartless and evil as ever. In his mind-set all the deaths he had been the catalyst for, one way or another, were not only worth it but essential to acquire the sculpture. The Bellini did not move him, only the hundreds of thousands perhaps millions, of dollars it represented.

Thus a killer walked free. He appeared quite normal, even somewhat dull and boring to most people. It was strange how the dogs he met walking the beach with their owners invariably shrank away from him and snarled as though they saw deep into his soul. He was totally corrupt and he was also doomed. He had made his pact with the devil long ago. He could not and would not turn back now.

(Once again Bellini turned uneasily in his grave and St. Theresa wept tears of blood.)

CHAPTER 25.

Tony and Lea walked barefoot along Swampscott's Fisherman's Beach. To Tony's skeptical amusement Lea was expounding on Astrology in which she more than half believed. "Your sign in July, Tony is Cancer the crab. It means you are a nurturer and a compassionate caretaker. I've taken advantage of this part of you and I bless you for it."

"Please, no more prayers!"

Lea giggled. "All right, I know I often bore you with my Mom's prayers but it helps me feel close to her, I loved her so much."

"Rightly so, Lea. Family is all important, I agree. My family is a mess, except for Nonna and my parents who died too young. I'm all for your devotion to the past, honestly. I respect and love you for it. I just want to be counted in, too as part of your future family." He said this rather wistfully. "I love you, Carissima, marry me?"

Tony was both intrigued and bemused by Lea's blend of earthy pragmatism and dreamy idealism to which Lea responded, "That's what Gemini's are!"

Seriously she said, "There's really a lot of truth in astrology and our stars and ancient cultures believed in it. Gemini's are ever split, on the one hand we can be down to earth and on the other, high in the clouds. Probably if a survey were taken, manic-depressives would probably turn out to be largely Gemini's!"

Tony himself was a realist. He knew exactly who he was and what motivated him. A free spirit like Lea moved him enormously. She stretched his perception of what life could be without preconceived ideas of what should be but what is. He felt a little in awe of her view of life, her values and ideas of what was important were vastly different from the women he had known yet he was open to new visions and vistas. Listening, albeit a trifle cynically to her extravagant spiel on astrology he admonished, "You'd better be grounded then, meo dolce, before you fly away completely." He teased as usual with a straight face and Lea laughed despite herself aware Tony delighted in getting a response from her, especially when she sometimes became verbally indignant.

"Geminis' need Cancers' to keep us on earth. You're quite essential to me, really my love, I'm just not ready to even consider marriage. I'm not entirely sure I even *believe* in marriage."

Tony hugged her to him and kissed her passionately and thoroughly.

He whispered in her ear, "Do you believe in this?" Lea pulled away looking around to see if anyone had noticed. "I do, yes I do, but not in public on the beach!"

(Thinking she sounded like a James Joyce heroine, "yes I said yes", she laughed.)

Coming toward them was a fully clothed man, strangely dressed for a beach walk, who stared at them. Tony did not notice but Lea felt a chill. The man made eye contact with her then quickly averted his gaze and hurried past. Lucy hid behind Tony, whining.

"What's wrong, Lea? Do I make you shudder? And what's wrong with you, Lucy?"

"Certainly not, Tony. I just felt a little chilly with the wind coming off the water."

"We've had a long beach walk, let's go get some coffee at Dale's."

Suddenly wanting the safety and security of the studio, Lea said, "Let's go home and have coffee, I made Finnish sweet bread yesterday."

Tony agreed happily. He and Lucy both loved Lea's sweet bread. Lucy had been walked on a leash and he wondered why she had pulled back and hid behind him a while back. Perhaps she, too, was averse to public displays of affection, unless directed toward her? He smiled and patted her. "I love you, too, Lucy."

At home Lea felt out of sorts. A thunder storm with crackling flashes of lightning had arrived and rain was pouring down. She'd been searching for a new subject to paint and felt frustrated. She preferred to paint in a series, a single piece never seemed to completely explore a subject. Unfortunately since the eerie, surrealistic feeling on the beach all she could think about were the multiple deaths in her life.

"I must stop brooding about it. Perhaps I could paint totally black canvases in this mood, darn it. Maybe I should continue on the watercolor abstracts I started, depicting the Psalms? I only completed Psalm 139, my favorite. However religion has deserted me lately. My church no longer seems to nourish me. I'm probably exaggerating but it seems to have become immersed in marketing techniques to attract a specific age group in their thirties and their tots."

"I'm depressed, I've got to shake this mood off," She told herself.

Tony, after coffee and sweet bread had driven to Boston to see Gitte and discuss what now was best to do in light of John Randall's suicide. His mood was also one of frustration and anger because he still did not know the whereabouts of the Bellini statue or his cousins.

After attending church one Sunday morning and nearly running down an elderly man on a bicycle as she angrily recapitulated the service, pounding on the steering wheel, Lea complained to Tony somewhat bitterly about the changes in her childhood church. (She didn't tell him how the old man had shaken his fist at her and yelled, "Watch it, Missy!" She blamed this inattention on her part on the new Pastor, also!)

Tony rarely attended his Catholic church's Mass. Impatiently, he'd said, "Give the new man a break, Lea. No doubt he's doing the best he knows how. Perhaps, like all new CEO's he wants a clean sweep? Didn't he hint at this rather candidly when he stated the older, hard working members should step aside for the newer, younger ones? Did any of them oblige him and leave in droves?" He laughed. "What exactly bothers you so much, is it change you don't like or the new Pastor?"

"No, I like the new Lutheran Pastor, Jorge Jorgensen, he's amiable and full of jokes. He perhaps fancies himself as a sort of Garrison Keillor of Prairy Home Companion on the radio. His sermons are embarrassingly full of anecdotes about his home town in the mid-west, describing his relatives sins and peccadilloes! If I were related to him I'd kill him for revealing to the whole congregation so many personal and intimate details. I suppose he is not used to our New England reserve?"

"Or to be charitable, Lea, perhaps he wants to show he shares many of the same troubles and relatives the members of the congregation have?"

"I suppose so, and I agree that's a good trait. Mostly I resent the circus-like atmosphere. I suspect he caters to the young parents of small children to build up the membership and incidentally his ego? The kids love it."

"They race up to the altar to listen to his Children's sermon and to receive candy, bribes and balloons he passes out. Tony, he is really into balloons! Of course the kids love to let them go and see them floating up to the rafters. We don't have a nursery any longer so infants and little tots banging toys and eating cheerios are noisy and present in the pews. It just is shocking to me that the church service is not reverent, quiet, and holy worship anymore. It's more like some kind of folksy club or Sunday School picnic. Yes, I really dislike this, not only because I'm not used to it but because I always felt in church one could worship, meditate and listen to the holy silence of the Holy Spirit."

She was now wound up and indignantly went on, "At the passing of the peace the children race up and down the aisles giving high fives for the hand shake! They have sung and danced and banged triangles up front at the altar like a recital! The doting, fond parents are pleased and applaud loudly. (We were brought up one did not applaud in God's house.)"

"The children are more than catered to, they are highly visible and their parents permit them to talk out loud during the liturgy. They are being sent the wrong message that taking part in church is a performance to be applauded and not their offering to the Lord." She complained vociferously to Tony who seemed amused at her fervor and furor.

"You are quite the Protestant Puritan, Lea! You should visit the large cathedrals in Europe where people wander in and out, bring in food and eat, and nurse their babies. Isn't it all still worshiping and pleasing to God?"

"And you are a pious idiot!" Lea's eye blazed. "This nonsense is not worship, it's crass commercialism and a blatant effort to entice the young and I must say, often rude parents, although they seem not a bit aware their kids disturb other people! I guess they are not rude on purpose, just used to children being catered to at all costs."

"You're such a staunch Lutheran, where will you worship in this crisis of faith?"

"It's NOT a crisis of faith, nothing can ever shake my faith. It's more a crisis of denominational poor taste. I don't think God gives a shit which church you attend as long as the intent is to sincerely worship and not teach small children to show off."

Tony said, mildly, "Does God say shit? Churches need financial backing to operate and be effective. I assume to encourage and increase the membership is one way to accomplish this?"

"I know, Tony, this feeling of complete, absolute irritation I have in church is not true worship either! I'm going to take a sabbatical and try some other services. I'll still send in and keep up my pledge. I'll go to a Mass, too. I miss what my church used to give me, Tony." Lea wailed. "Can't you understand?"

She enjoyed the early 8 a.m. service at Light House Park the Old North Congregational church held in the summer. Their woman minister called it "God's Cathedral" and to sit on the grass at the edge of the sea to worship was lovely. It was informal with people dressed in shorts and yet it was reverent and short. The babies, children and dogs present were all kept under control or taken to the other end of the park.

Lea partook of their form of communion, bread and grape juice the first Sunday of each month. In a way she missed the weekly Eucharist at the Lutheran church. Being well versed in Luther's Small Catechism she knew it didn't matter whether the symbols used were wafers or bread, wine or grape juice but the meaning behind them that was important, "in, under and over the real presence of the body and blood of Christ."

Lea decided not to rush any decision to sever her connection to the church she had been brought up in and loved all her life. When Tony told her, "You just need to become more tolerant, Lea, "she suspected that perhaps he was right and she did. However, a clubby, noisy worship service still shocked and repulsed her as well as children who ran wild.

Rebelliously she said, "You never go to church, so what do you know? To me it's appalling, your attitude of obeying the letter not the spirit of the law, by going to confession once a year and attending Mass only at Christmas and Easter!"

Tony grinned at her and Lea acknowledged it was sinful to judge others. She vowed to pray for more patience and tolerance. Tolerance had always seemed rather a patronizing kind of virtue to her, as though you were "better than" but "endured.?" What's wrong with just simply loving or loathing something full tilt? *Besides that's the way Gemini's are, passionate even when at fault,* Lea thought ruefully, *and no doubt I am, my way is not the only or correct way, forgive me, God? I certainly don't think I know it all! But neither does the new Pastor.* She added, rebelliously.

CHAPTER 26.

On a dark and completely moonless night Lea felt lonely and alone. Before her visiting cousins would arrive Tony had returned to his flat saying, "Lea, it hurts your reputation having me stay here at night unless you marry me. My leg is fine now, I can manage at my place."

"I don't care what anyone thinks," She snapped but was glad she wouldn't have to explain his live-in presence to cousin Linnea who would not have said a word but would look volumes. Lea continued to resist a definite answer to Tony's request for marriage. She thought he was probably just blowing smoke so she would continue to sleep with him. Badly hurt and burnt by her marriage to Ray she was ambivalent about making a commitment again although she loved Tony completely.

"I need more time to think it through and what it might mean to my hard won independence and career. Painting has become first to me, after Nora of course, because I've given so much of my life and fiber into being an artist."

"Can't you still be an artist and my wife as well? I can be a boat builder and a husband at the same time. Are you less talented than I, Mio dolce?"

Leaving, Tony had said, "Keep Lucy here for protection," at which Lea raised her eyebrows. "I'll be by in the morning to kiss you both awake."

Alarmed Lea awoke at 3 a.m. when Lucy barked loudly and long. It was unlike the placid animal who usually slept like two dead logs and snored. She got out of bed and peered out the tiny loft window toward the terrace. All was dark and black. All she could make out was dimly what seemed to be a moving figure. Terrified she flew down the spiral ladder and telephoned Tony, praying he would wake. On the third ring he answered as Lea stood waiting biting her lip. Her voice trembling she whispered, "Tony, please come right away!"

He threw a windbreaker on over his skivvies and ran rapidly down Gregory and Front streets to Lea, afraid the noise of his car might not be a good idea. Once there he gave Lea a quick, reassuring hug and grabbing a flashlight he searched the rock terrace where Lea said the person had been. Lucy now brave, searched with him. They could find nothing other than the usual tangle of seaweed and mussel shells under the lobster pot table. "There's no one here now, Lea, but I'm going to stay with you the rest of the night." Tony could sense Lea was distraught and upset and Lucy still occasionally growled.

Lucy knew there had been some kind of threat to Lea and someone alien had been on the terrace. Gratefully, feeling safe, Lea slept in Tony's arms until morning. She knew she needed him but more than her feisty independence she'd nurtured and valued for so many years?

In the bright, sunny morning, the water sparkling as though a careless and extravagant hand had scattered thousands of tiny diamonds, all seemed sane and normal again. Lea was almost ashamed and angry at herself for weakly calling Tony in the night.

"Tony, I'm almost burnt out with worry and stress and fear. Can't we hire our own detectives and put an end to whatever these murders are about and have some peace?" She begged, deciding to be truthful about the tension she felt and for Nora.

"I hate to have you frightened, Lea. I did hire a private detective, Donald Bell, and I paid him handsomely to work for me and solve the theft and recover the St. Theresa. Right now, if he's still alive I don't trust him or anyone any more. I'm coming back to stay with you, marry me or not, gossips be damned!" He added darkly, "The hell with the statue, I can't leave you frightened and alone. If I had it now I'd toss the damn thing in the ocean!"

He was furious. Solemnly they stared at one another closer to a future both really desired underneath all Lea's bravado. She no longer doubted he honestly loved her and wanted to marry her. Suddenly Lea grinned, "Last night, I was going to say, 'get your ass over here' but somehow I didn't think you'd find it funny."

Tony laughed dryly. "No, I sure as hell wouldn't have at three o'clock in the morning and I just might not have come," He teased.

Since Tony didn't have to work until afternoon they took Lucy to Gas House Beach off Orne Street for a swim and went in themselves for an icicle-like but refreshing dip. Letting the sun dry them they put on sweatshirts and continued on a walk. Up Gingerbread Hill, past Black Joe's pond, down to Doliber's Cove to Peach's Point.

As they strolled through the Point admiring the many large, beautiful and manicured estates a caretaker stopped them. Curtly but politely he said, "This is private property and I'm sorry no dogs are allowed. I'll have to ask you and your dog to leave."

Offended and angry, Lea whispered through clenched teeth, "Tell him who you are, you could buy and sell him!"

Ever gracious, Tony smiled at the caretaker and apologized for the intrusion. He took Lea firmly by the shoulders and turned her around.

"Lea, you might as well learn that I choose my own battles and this is not one of them. Let's go home. We'll live to fight another day, never fear." He scowled, "And cut out that nobility business, I don't like it and it's not worthy of you. I'm not an aristocrat for Chrissake! I'm a carpenter and a fisherman."

Stung and hurt by his overt disapproval of her, sarcastically Lea retorted, "Just like little Lord Jesus," keeping her expression innocent. Wanting to smack her, Tony blandly ignored her. He spoke to Lucy, "It seems, St. Lucia, Protestants don't appreciate dogs or saints like you and me," having the last word.

Lea tried hard not to but burst out laughing. Tony grinned back at her and they were friends again. They'd had many theological discussions of Lutheranism versus Catholicism often finding similarities. Tony added, "I'm also an art critic, so watch it."

The next day for Lucy's birthday Lea baked a batch of special dog biscuits cut out in bone shapes. To the mixture she added a teaspoon or two of honey from their beekeeping girls for Lucy's sweet tooth and stirred in some grated cheddar cheese.

Singing in her choir alto, "All things bright and beautiful, all creatures great and small, the dear Lord who madeth us, He made and loveth all. Happy Birthday, Loos!"

Lea tossed her the first warm one from the oven. Lucy salivated with joy.

Tony came in for lunch while she was singing, "Lucy, there's no escaping it, wherever there's food and Lea there's a grace for every occasion, especially a dog's birthday." "Naturally, who better?" Lea said blithely, hugging Lucy.

Lucy looked up at Lea adoringly, wagging her tail and her tongue hanging out. She loved Lea's home made dog biscuits so much she now disdained store bought ones forcing Lea to take time out from painting to make large batches every couple weeks.

Tony kissed Lea and patted Lucy. "You are a dog chef and a Lucy lover. I bet you could sell these at Crosby's."

"Lucy appreciates me," Lea looked at Tony with a mocking smile. To tease him she then started on the birthday prayer for Lucy, "Today is my birthday, come be my guest-"

Tony groaned and Lea laughed and did not finish it. "Tony, can I borrow your car to visit my great aunt, my godmother, Solveigh, in Rowley this afternoon? I have a strong premonition I should," She said with a little shiver.

Tony tossed her the car keys, "Sure, I have to go back to the yard anyway, I can walk."

When he returned in the late afternoon, Lea was sitting in a chair staring straight ahead into empty space. She had a forlorn demeanor looking sad and depressed.

"Why so sad? Didn't you see your Aunt Solveigh?"

"Yes, I did. Lucy and I drove to the house she lives in with her nurse, Wilma. The house is the remnant of the farm Uncle Sven sold to a developer before he died. He wanted to be sure Solveigh would have enough money to be taken care of. She's 96 and still bright as a button. She's able to pay Wilma who is kind and capable. Once she and Uncle Sven had so much, Tony! A beautiful, productive farm and livestock."

"The visit seems to have disturbed you?"

"Yes. Tony, Auntie has decided it's time to go, to die! Wilma told me she has stopped eating and drinks only a small amount of water. Wilma said, "This is her choice, to do it her way. She wants no tubes or machines.""

Lea mourned, "She's so frail."

Wilma had said firmly to Lea, "I respect your aunt's wishes and I make her as comfortable as possible. Together we wait out the time left."

215

"We did have a good visit and chat.   Aunt Solveigh loved seeing Lucy, she always loved all the farm animals and cats and dogs they had. Her mind is very sharp and I suppose I got a first hand lesson how to die with dignity and let go gracefully?" Lea seemed unconvinced.

"I know I'll be hearing soon that she's gone. I know that! I had to see her once more, I'm so glad I did. Solveigh is really a blithe spirit my mother loved and admired and chose her to be my godmother." Lea burst out, "I hate endings, I hate old age, and I hate death!" She began to weep.

"We all must embrace death as part of life, Lea. Your faith should help you to be certain there's a better future we have to believe is glorious, "Tony said sympathetically although a bit piously.

Lea sobbed. "Oh, fuck you! Shut up!"

Tony knew Lea had had her share of traumatic events. Losing her parents, the coolness of a beloved brother and having her only child Nora so far away were troubling enough but losing Sarah and Elissa and the death on her patio had taken their toll on her usually strong spirit.   He desperately wanted to comfort her and give her some solace and peace.

Opening his arms he said simply, "I love you, Lea," He wisely said no more. She went to him and he folded her into his arms, kissing her tear streaked face and mopping away her tears. Patting her back, he murmured, "It's all right, Caramia, it's all right."

Lea's securities were her family and friends and of primary importance to her. Tony was awed she'd been able to bounce back as well as she had with resilience and a stubborn spirit.

The next morning the nurse called to say Solveigh had died peacefully holding Wilma's hand at around 5 a.m. Lea sighed deeply.

"May flights of angels carry you to your rest, dear Auntie."

Another death to deal with, another funeral service to attend, would it never end? At least Solveigh had called the shots, Lea thought and that counted for a lot.

CHAPTER 27.

The report from the Boston Medical Examiner finally came in and Tony was notified because he had shown some interest in the missing Italian prisoner. The body had been recovered and identified as his cousin, Andreas. He had died by gun shot, had not drowned. Andreas frequently had been picked up and booked in Rome for street disturbances and been fingerprinted which were on record with Italy's Crime Bureau. Much time had elapsed. Tony paced back and forth in his miniscule flat trying to think logically, "Think like a horse," He muttered under his breath.

He thought he knew for certain his cousins had smashed the glass case and stolen St. Theresa. Georgio, presumably died by accident in Australia. Where was Roberto? And Bell? Tony considered himself intelligent and his cousins, although cunning and crafty, had always been stupid. *Why can't I figure out Roberto's modus operandi? He is the only one left now that Andreas is dead. While Roberto had been the cleverest of the three and the ring leader, he is still a stupido.*

Growing up in Europe Tony had learned to never underestimate the sheer power of stupidity. This had been the downfall of many intelligent people trying to combat and unravel weird plots with their brains since the actions of many criminal, unintelligent bumblers stemmed not from a logical or predictable process and were therefore difficult to profile even by step-by-step analysis. Such kidnappers and mafioso were able to accomplish their basic goals while brighter minds could not follow their simplistic yet convoluted thought patterns.

What do I have?

1. I know Roberto is greedy, avaricious and unlike Nonna or me would not desire the statue for its own sake or beauty but for the money it could bring.

2. Roberto, even as a child was transparent and obvious about his intentions.

3. What is the most stupid and obvious thing he might do to hide the sculpture from me?

Tony pondered the puzzle until his head ached. "I'm crediting much too clever maneuvers to a dumb shit! Let me think dumb. If I were Roberto (thank God I'm not) where would I hide? Not still in the states, he'd be a fool. But he is a fool? Where then? Perhaps near me? Why, if he already has the sculpture?"

Tony's mind shut down. "Jesus, I can't figure out the asshole." He almost gave up. "Roberto would be pleased to have three cousins, including me, eliminated from the prize? Did he kill them? Georgio was a lucky accident for him. Next is to be me? Did he kill Bell because he was hunting for the statue for me? Why Sarah? What I really remember about

219

Roberto is his ruthlessness. Who could profile him or how he thinks? If he is close by, he is planning to kill me, and Lea, too."

Aloud Tony said softly and grimly, "I shall have to watch my back and Lea's. Roberto is no doubt a stupid, simple psychopath but a dangerous one. He will remove any one in his way for a clear path to his goal. Dammit all! Why can't I think like a horse, really dumb, and figure out where the hell he is right now?"

Lucy might have told him. She knew she'd seen and smelled an evil man on the beach in Swampscott staring at Lea and Tony, and she had sensed someone bad had been on the terrace one night.

CHAPTER 28.

Dear Mom,

What is all that terrible stuff happening in my home town? Please let me know and keep me up to date? I am so nervous and anxious about you. That Italian man who drowned here was a relative of Tony's? I thought you said Tony was such a great guy? I am beginning to wonder about him. Obviously you have omitted a lot of details! Trust me, I'm not a child any more. Shall I come home and protect you? Say the word and send the money!

I'm kidding of course. I recently had two beautiful litters of Persian kittens, smokes and tortoise shells. All eight are healthy and first class and slated to be sold. I'll have about $900 and I can easily borrow the rest for the airfare, Rod is good friends with a banker in Sydney.

Mom, Rod wants to get married. I am ambivalent. I know how hard it was for you to bring me up on your own and you did a superb job! Look how wonderful I am. I would want a commitment to be forever and today it seems difficult for marriages to last? It is hard on children when couples break up, we both want children. So I am of two minds.

I always secretly wished I had a real father in my life. You and Grandma Siri filled the gap, and the uncles did too, I'm not complaining. I appreciate, I do. I had a magic childhood, better than most. You are the greatest mother and my role model. I love you and I love Rod. I want to be with you both, why do you have to be a continent apart?

I was sad to read of my father's death, what did he die of? He was still young? After all, I never really knew him after he remarried and had all those kids. I was about twelve? I suppose they are my half brothers and sisters? I probably will never know them either, that is rather sad? You wrote, Claire, his widow has a blossoming career in music? Does that mean women do better and go further if not tied to a man? Why couldn't she have had a singing career while she was married? (She sounds pretty weak.)

Since I never truly had a father in my life, the impact of his death is not as hard as it would be if I'd grown up with him or been close to him but he still was my father? I feel bad I never really knew him and now he's gone and I never will.

It's winter here now, not as cold of course as New England winters and rarely snow yet it can be damp and chilly and raw, quite dreary. Occasionally we get a warm day and we can swim. We take advantage of living at Grantly Beach, I really love it. It has sort of a raffish, international flavor with a concourse in the center of town where all the Thai restaurants, boutiques and shops are. Taking the ferry to work is fun. Rod and I go into Sydney together and meet again after work to come home unless we are staying in town for dinner or a concert or a Steiner lecture.

I confess, Mama dear, sometimes I get very, very homesick! Especially for you. but I do love Rod and I don't want to leave him. He is adamant he will not move to the states. We argue and discuss this ad infinitum! He is convinced interracial couples are treated badly and looked down upon in America. Despite being a young country, Australia, especially Sydney (which is more cosmopolitan than a lot of the rest of the country) exhibit a tolerant and open attitude. We are fully accepted and no one looks twice at us, except maybe to notice what a handsome couple we are! (We're like an Oreo cookie with brown eyes, Rod says.)

Please, please? Fill in all the blanks in your scenario? I'm worried about you, Mom, I truly am. All love, ever and ever, Nora XXXXOOOO

Nora added a postscript.

P.S. I'm sending you a recipe for a change! For the Aussie scones served in every tea house around Sydney. I go to a favorite one in Round Corner. Australians call them "scons", like fauns, or pawns. Am sure came originally from U.K? Delicious with raspberry preserves or strawberries. Similar to our strawberry shortcake made with biscuits. There are many milk bars and tea houses in the countryside open from one to five for tea. I sometimes skip lunch and go to one for scones. Your chubby child loves them almost too much! Rod's adoptive mother makes his favorite with stewed apricots and kiwis, thickened with honey. Whipped or clotted cream is served on the side and I heap it on! Teatime here is a lovely custom. I think nicer than America's cocktail, happy hour. People don't get drunk on tea and scones!

By the way, I performed the Butterfly piece I choreographed in Eurythmy. I did it at the Steiner Hall in Sydney. I was thrilled at the applause and that it was liked. I wish you could see me perform, Mom. Love again, Nora. More X's and O's.

Nora's letter brought a lump to Lea's throat. She thought how hard it had been to leave Ray for her baby's sake as well as her own, how much resolve it had taken. It seemed you could never entirely erase the consequences of the choices you made in life. All one could do was to go bravely forward and try to rectify youthful mistakes and impulsive decisions made so often when immature. But she could never regret having Nora. She'd done her best for her and Nora was a lovely girl. Deep in her heart she felt she knew Nora would probably never live close to her if she married Rod. The main thing was for Nora to be happy, that was all Lea had ever wanted for her.

When Nora was born Lea's mother, Siri, had said, "You'll never be happy again unless your child is happy." Nora seemed both happy and productive in her work. "This will be a new beginning for her, a whole new adventurous life in Australia with a man she loves. I must be happy for her. I have a strong will, I will myself to be happy for my little girl."

Lea went to her old battered piano and played Beethoven's "Fur Elise; meaning "for Nora." Then she began to paint a watercolor from a snapshot she'd taken of Nora playing her flute.

Sometimes life seemed a great cheat, yet Lea thought, *We have to trust it's all for our best? I really try to, God. I sure hope life is not a huge cosmic joke on us poor humans?*

CHAPTER 29.

Tony was hard at work at the boatyard building on order a special rowing dory. It was slated to be a beauty. Will approached, "this boat is coming along so fine I wouldn't mind owning it myself. How soon can you be free to go fishing? The stripers are running good."

"Right now, Will. I've finished all I can do today. We have to wait for some equipment to be delivered. I can meet you at the dock in about twenty minutes."

He went home to get his rod and reel and make a couple sandwiches to bring on the Mandy. To please Will he'd make Italian sandwiches on baguettes Will was crazy about even though Tony had told him often it was strictly an American version that Italians rarely made. Will could care less, he loved the way Tony made them, more American than Italian. Provolone cheese, prosciutto, salami, hot peppers and tomatoes were stashed in the refrigerator, he would layer and sprinkle with extra Virgin olive oil on split baguettes.

Tony found Lea painting in the studio with tears running down her cheeks. Grabbing her and kissing her on the temples, he said with concern, "Bellalea, what's wrong?"

"Oh really nothing. I just had a spell of missing Nora, and missing Sarah and Elissa, and Siri and Aunt Solveigh and feeling sorry for myself. You go on fishing and invite Julia and Will back for supper. Try to catch something." (Was there a trace of sarcasm there?) "I'll make a special Finnish dish." She brightened at the thought of cooking as that and doing crossword puzzles usually saw her through the blues. She smiled at Tony, "I'll be all right, honestly. I was also pissed my painting is not going well. It's terrible! The only thing to do is start over." To Tony's horror she ripped the large full sheet watercolor off the drafting board and viciously ripped it up in pieces. The glimpse he'd had looked lovely and promising.

"Lea," He admonished, "You're much too impulsive! You should let the work cook for awhile, set it aside and not destroy it so soon. When you look at it later you'll be better able to judge its merits objectively."

"Tony, please, please, PLEASE don't tell me what to do or how to feel! This is how I am. If you can't like me with all my flaws, warts and all, just leave!" She said coldly with vehemence.

Tony hastily retreated to the kitchen tamping down his rising, hot temper. He made the sandwiches in a total silence. He made one for Lea, too, and put a note on it, "por mea caralea e amore" and left it in the refrigerator. He sang out, "arriverdeci," and left barely missing the sneaker Lea threw after him. He grinned, cognizant high-strung, sensitive and talented people were sometimes moody, way up or way down. Tony felt confident she'd be back to her usual, sunny self when he returned.

The better part of valor, he'd learned, was to leave Lea alone when she became depressed with her work. He understood how she felt when her painting did not measure up to the mental image she'd envisioned. In this respect Lea was a perfectionist, although certainly not at house cleaning, he'd noticed. Tactfully and in fear of imminent death he'd never mentioned this. He shrugged, if she would marry him he could well afford household help for her. He preferred a lover to a maid any day in the week!

In the early afternoon Tony returned with fresh striper filets. On the spur of the moment Lea called Sylvia and Claire and invited them and the lawyers they were dating to come along for supper with Julia and Will. Claire had seemed strangely reluctant.

"I don't know them, Lea." Claire sounded uneasy and nervous.

"Nonsense, you'll love Julia and you must remember Will from school?"

"Well, yes, but not that well. He was older and I left school at sixteen. Well, okay and thanks, we'll come for the famous Finnish dinner."

Wearing a white caftan embroidered with gold thread and adorned with several pounds of gold jewelry Sylvia bounced in, looking smashing, bringing Claire, who seemed nervous, and the young men. One young lawyer, Abe, was head over heels in love with Claire. Julia and Will had already arrived and were drinking an Italian aperatif Tony mixed up in a shaker with ice. (He said it was Italian, it was really a bone dry Beefeater martini with very little vermouth, he topped each glass with a cocktail onion and a ripe olive and waved the bottle of vermouth over the shaker.) Now starting his third, Will was a bit bleary eyed, and Julia shook her head at Tony, mouthing, "no more!"

At the introductions all around, Will said easily, "Hi Claire, long time, no see." Gentleman that he was he did not indicate in any way that he and Claire had more than once tangled legs in the back seat of his car parked at Devereux Beach some years before. Claire visibly relaxed at his bland demeanor. "Weren't you a few years behind me in high school?" Will asked innocently, not betraying they'd known each other intimately. When he'd dated Claire she was fourteen and tagged as "jail bait".

Julia would not have been upset or surprised. She'd never assumed that handsome, earthy Will was a virgin when they met. She might even have been disappointed if he had been because his animal magnetism had attracted her from the start and still did. Will was now a dedicated monogamist with no intention of ever straying from the love of his life, Julia, whom he felt lucky to have. Julia smiled benignly at Claire and passing Will gave him a little pat on his butt, meaning she guessed and it was okay.

They sat around the old scarred table Lea had set with her mismatched china and odd pieces of silverware. "Someday, "she told Tony, "I'm going to have a beautiful set of Spode for twelve. In the meantime, if the hostess doesn't care, the guests usually don't," She said airily.

Tony made a mental note that she should have her Spode as soon as he could persuade her to marry him.

With a bottle or two of Pinot Noir they were relishing the fried striped bass, cut into three inch chunks, Finnish lemon-creamed potatoes, cold pickled beets and cucumbers. Dessert was to be Siri's "Fluffy Lemon Delight", a light refreshing ending for any heavy meal. (Siri had mandated it had to be made with fresh lemon juice and no packaged jello and it made all the difference.) For a first course they were served a cup of tart, icy cold aeblesuppe (apple soup) with a spoonful of sour cream, a mint leaf and a dusting of nutmeg on top.

"Sunday night we watched you, Claire, on that PBS Channel 2 program about early jazz singers. You were great, Will and I loved it and we know you have a huge singing career ahead of you. You sounded just like Lady Day when you sang, "God Bless the Child who Has His Own.""

"Billie Holiday was always a favorite of mine, "Will added, "Claire, you're as good!""

Claire replied, blushing a little at the compliments, "All thanks to Sarah, my guardian angel and now Sylvia. Sarah helped turn so many women's lives around, I hope she knows her life counted." Claire spoke humbly and sincerely.

"We all pray and wish our lives will count for good. Lea touches people's lives and hearts with her painting."

Touched, Lea hugged Julia and murmured, "So do you, just by being you." Lea had recovered from the doldrums and was now jolly and witty and as sparkling as the Frascati wine Tony served with dinner.

Tony recited his now favorite abbreviated grace, "Grazie Dio" at which Will laughed aloud and Julia kicked his shin hard under the table.

"Lea is her old self again, aren't you, Signora?" Tony beamed. Lea phonily smiled sweetly at him. She thought *do I know what my real self is?* To Tony she said, "Gemini's have more than one self, Signore Antonio, my love, so watch out."

"Ah, exclaimed Sylvia, "This is so good, Lea!" as Lea had instructed them to do, she took alternate forkfuls of fish and creamed potatoes.

"In Finland this dish is traditionally made with fried eels, lemon-creamed potatoes always accompany it. Since Tony refuses to bring me eels I had to adapt the recipe to the striped bass to suit his silly prejudice." Tony winked at her, unperturbed.

"And mine!" said Will. "Sweet Jesus, I cannot abide eels or anything I use for bait, mussels either, to eat. Might as well cook up sea worms. Lea, you never will have an eel caught from my boat."

"Europeans and Italians have been eating mussels, eel, calimari and snails cooked in wine for centuries," Tony said mildly. "I do draw the line at eel."

He frowned recalling the severe food poisoning he'd had at fifteen eating fried eels his cousins had deliberately laced with hot pepper to disguise the bitter taste of the poisonous roots and bane sprinkled over them when Maria's back was turned from her big saute pan on the stove. They added so much Nonna and Tony became very ill and a doctor was called. Tony, at that age had been too trusting and naive to notice the cousins did not eat any and just pushed their portions around on their plates. Nonna and Tony ate most of the dish and were violently sick, the doctor pronounced it food poisoning. Nonna almost died.

Maria, the cook, suspected the cousins whom she detested had tampered with the sauteed eel dish, one Nonna particularly enjoyed and had requested. Maria, as she always did, put in a great many herbs but was helpless to accuse the little devils. She had been too busy cooking and serving to eat more than a taste herself.

Uncharacteristically the cousins helped clean up after the meal disposing of the remainder of the eels so there was none for the doctor to take to the lab to test. Tony started and brought himself back to the present.

After dessert and coffee Sylvia and Claire and their dates left with profuse thanks pleading all had to work early in the morning. Will and Tony talked far into the night about local politics and town history. The town was still governed by five elected Selectmen, one at present, a woman. Will's father's family went way back to the original settlers from the islands of Jersey and Guernsey. Lea and Julia washed the dishes happily chatting over coffee in the kitchen about art and music.

Lea was delighted to discover Julia, as she had suspected was knowledgeable about the arts. She had attended the Boston Museum School of Fine Arts and had a Master's Degree from Tufts University. Julia had been a summer visitor to Marblehead, sketching at State Street Wharf where she met handsome, black-

haired and brilliantly blue-eyed Will and instantly fell
in love. He looked like a dashing pirate with a red
kerchief knotted about his head. Julia loved him for
his untutored, simple goodness his debonair
appearance concealed.

"Will is really a saint-like guy, Lea. If
opposites do attract, I've got to be the sinner!"

"You're some sinner," laughed Lea.

Julia rejoined with spirit, "I am not the
saccharine, sickly sweet person you seem to think I
am, Lea. I'm a steel magnolia! I'm from Georgia."

"I bet you are, Julia. I'm sorry, you are sweet
but certainly not sickly saccharine! So it must be yin
and yang, two halves to make a whole?"

It was after midnight when Julia and Will got
up to leave. Tony had shut and latched the Indian
shutters earlier against the drafty wind. A storm was
brewing on this moonless black night, the tide running
dead low. All evening Lucy had snoozed peacefully
under the table after enjoying her share of fish and
creamed potatoes, particularly liking the latter.
Suddenly awake as farewells were being said she raced
to the terrace door barking furiously, leaping and
scratching at the door.

Tony flicked on the flood lights he'd helped an
electrician install after Lea's last scare. Lea invariably
forgot to turn them on. Lucy with Will and Tony
rushed onto the terrace. Lea and Julia, frightened by
the sudden commotion huddled inside. The too
familiar feeling of angst and apprehension swept over
Lea. The men saw nothing alarming on the terrace yet
Tony subconsciously noted the kayak appeared to be
resting in a different position against the house, it was

now upside down.   Both men were uneasy but reassured the women, "There's nothing out here."

"Probably it was just that increasing flock of pigeons Lucy is always barking at. They roost on the roof of the nearby restaurant and lay eggs all over every neighbor's patio and deck," Tony grumbled, "They make a bloody, royal mess with their pigeon poop."

"Shouting "shoo" at them a million times a day doesn't faze them a bit. They are so bold and forever are flopping and pooping and laying eggs all over my patio, it infuriates me!" Lea said angrily.

"No doubt they are called an endangered species," Will responded sarcastically, "But with their filth they're permitted to endanger your health."

"Isn't there some humane way to solve the problem?" Julia asked quietly.

Lea and Tony groaned.   "We've been trying and trying, so far nothing works."

"Importing falcons won't help," Will offered, "They won't nest this close to the ground as they will in skyscrapers in New York which was pigeon plagued before they brought in the falcons."

"Like Rome." Tony agreed. "I think it still is. Tourists find it romantic."

"I say the pure and simple solution is to poison them, the hell with the town's stupid rules!" Will raised his voice angrily. Julia looked aghast but wisely kept still.

"I guess enough of us will have to go before the Board of Health again for permission to 'off' them. Last time they said they couldn't do anything about private property." Lea patted Julia's shoulder trying to make light of it.

The killer the pigeons had been blamed for had left earlier as did Julia and Will now saying fond good nights to Lea and Tony and Lucy.

Tony kept the Indian shutters latched. It seemed certain a big Northeast storm was brewing. The incoming tide crashed noisily against the rocks, churning spirals of white foam. The starless and moonless dark, stormy night felt ominous and foreboding.

"Lea, this would be a perfect night for the 'moon cussers' Will was telling me about tonight. In the late 1700's on moonless nights (they 'cursed' the moon when it shone bright) renegades would gather on the shore by the boulders with flashing lanterns they waved back and forth. This would lure ship Captains into thinking they were seeing lights from a port. The ships would be wrecked on the rocks and go aground. With a special 'moon cusser's" ladder which could be hooked over the side of the ship, these pirates would climb aboard and kill and loot."

"The ladders folded up into an innocent looking cane. A law was passed in 1773 outlawing these ladders and anyone seen carrying one was jailed."

"I never knew about that," Lea said, interested, "Will certainly knows a great deal about old Marblehead history."

She had gained more respect for Will as she realized anyone who could capture Julia's devotion as well as knowing so much lore and history was a more intelligent, complex person than one would at first perceive him to be under his rough and bluff persona.

She was now convinced he deliberately cultivated a Marblehead character for himself and relished playing the "townie."

CHAPTER 30.

The threatened No'easter had blown over but another one was promised soon. In Lea's kitchen Tony sang off key but loudly, snatches of operatic arias from Tosca and Aida. He was preparing Maria's Sicilian entree of fresh asparagus, slivers of prosciutto and penne pasta. It would also contain Lea's tomato sauce and be topped with grated Romano cheese.

Lea sat outdoors on the rock terrace working on a *New York Times* crossword puzzle. She was almost ashamed to admit she was addicted to solving crosswords but she knew she was and worked on everyone in sight. Nora had tried unsuccessfully to do one or two at one time. Accusingly she pouted, "You crossword people are a little *in* clique! All of you know the special clues and the answers."

"You mean 'had at' for a fight and 'planet' for a revolver and 'etui' for a needle case?" Her mother said looking innocently at Nora. However, Nora was correct. Like any other art one had to learn the attendant jargon, practice a lot and be alert for puns and jokes in the clues which were Lea's favorites.

True crossword aficionados never used a dictionary unless desperate. That was deemed cheating and spoiled the fun. The smug satisfaction when a puzzle was completed was the sole reward for doing them yet apparently it was enough for thousands of people. Lea loved working a crossword and she thought it did help one's vocabulary. At Christmas time, her sister Pat sent her a subscription for five a month, one a week. Lea could never resist doing all five as soon as they arrived in the mail. Ruefully, she remarked to Lucy who lay beside her in the late afternoon sun, "I'm a pure crossword nut, Loos, that's three letters, N-U-T." She winced at Tony's singing, it was pretty bad.

Tony set up two old rusty tray tables and covered each with a napkin. He carried out the plates of pasta, asparagus and smoked ham and uncorked a bottle of Cianti. Hastily he said, "I'll say grace." Lea's nostalgic compulsion to invoke her mother's presence by intoning all of Siri's thanksgivings at every meal bothered him a little. Also some were really lengthy! "Grazie Dio."

Lea raised her eyebrows, "Is that it?"

"That's it," Tony replied blandly yet firmly.

Tasting the pasta dish Lea exclaimed, "Delicioso! I could have served this to all my vegetarian cousins if I left out the prosciutto and used a little chicken or bacon."

"All you really needed to serve was your famous Finnish Simi, Lea."

Tony was rarely modest about the culinary skill he had learned from being underfoot in Nonna's kitchen from age twelve to sixteen when he was sent off to boarding school at Eton. Nonna's Sicilian cook,

Maria, was from the town of Gangivecchio (or old Gangi). Tony, whom she doted on, pestered her to let him help her and be the chief taster.

And so he agreed. "This dish is quite lovely and one of the meals the villages in Sicily can be proud of with or without prosciutto. They also make it with pancetta, country style bacon. What do you think of it, St. Lucia? You are the gourmet. I'm sure you would eat my boiled rubber boots if I put Lea's tomato sauce on them."

Lucy licked her chops and wagged her tail. Licking clean her empty plate she pushed it around on the rocks dangerously close to the edge. Lea grabbed it quickly before it could fall into the water because she owned little in the way of chinaware. Tony refused to use paper plates at home complaining except on a picnic they spoiled the taste of the food and were esthetically unappetizing.

Lea went in to answer the ringing telephone. It was John Peder, her brother and Gerda his wife. "LeaLea" (calling her by the childhood nickname he had for her Uncle Bill had changed to Lily, he was Jay Pee or just Jay) "How would you and Tony like to drive up to Portland and take the ferry over to Nova Scotia with us?"

"Jay, I'd love it, especially seeing both of you. Are the boys going?"

"No, they both have summer jobs, Erik at a golf course and David is washing dishes at a small restaurant. We can take the Evangeline Trail and have your favorite fried clams in Digby. We'll stop in Yarmouth and Peggy's Cove. Maybe Lea, you can make your fortune on the slot machines on the boat or in Halifax."

"Remember when we were kids and Papa gave us each the princely sum of five dollars to play the slot machines? Mama disapproved and was convinced you'd become a gambler when you won the grand total of two dollars!" He chuckled.

Lea laughed. "I certainly will try! Let me get back to you and if Tony can't come I'll go myself. I need the break." Silently she added, "and your healing presence."

John Peder and Gerda were caring, thoughtful and humorous and always lifted the spirits of everyone around them. Lee basked in the sunny aura they emitted.

Tony said there was too much work to be done at the boatyard and he couldn't go. He urged Lea to take his car for the two hour drive to Portland, leave it at Jay Pee's house and go on with them in their van. They were arguing about this, Lea insisting she could take a bus to Maine when a rotund policeman came through the terrace door.

"Your outside door was open," said Dog McDougal accusingly. "I knocked but I guess you couldn't hear me." He eyed the food enviously, "I'm really sorry to intrude on your supper." Sternly he added, "You should keep your doors locked."

"I've been assigned to ask you a few more questions about your Italian relatives, I'm sorry Lea." Dog had been a friend of John Peder. Both Lea and Tony groaned, "Not again?" The chubby, youngish policeman took out a notepad and pen.

"Where and when did you last see each one? You have three cousins, you told us? Can you give me their full names, last known addresses and occupations in Italy?"

"Occupations? Liars and thieves!"

Tony gave their names and addresses in Italy. Dog took down all the details still glancing at Lea's plate of unfinished pasta. Tony went to the kitchen and brought Dog a plateful and a glass of Frascati wine. He placed them on the lobster pot table in front of him. Dog demurred, "I really shouldn't, I'm on duty." Nevertheless he pulled the canvas deck chair closer and enthusiastically dug in.

Lea laughed. "Signore Amberetti is a talented chef, is he not?"

"He sure is!" Dog put aside his notebook to finish the plate appreciatively. Lucy expected a little left over but his plate was almost as clean as hers.

"I guess that's all for now. The FBI are closing in on the case and we expect they'll be giving us all the answers soon."

Her voce trembling a little, Lea asked, "Dog, what have you found out about the murder of my friend, Sarah Gross?"

The officer sat down again. "That's a completely separate case and appears unrelated to the murder that took place here." He looked around at the rocks. "Local police are handling the case of Ms. Gross, not the Fibbies. So far there are no clues, no fingerprints, and no witnesses. The clients she dealt with in her practice have all been interviewed more than once. I can assure you each one has an alibi for the time frame involved."

Tony remarked cynically, "*Somebody* killed Sarah."

"Yes indeed, someone did." (To himself, *and a bloody mess it was, too*) He averted his gaze from the red smear of tomato sauce on his plate.

"Look, Lea, "He addressed her gently as J.P.'s younger sister, "Our local detectives are very good and solve cases many times that the FBI can't. That's because it's helpful to personally know the local people well, their reputations, habits, past behavior and their relationships. A picture emerges of a motive and when you have that the perp is not far behind. The motive could be for revenge, money or sometimes a love triangle and usually leads us to the murderer a lot quicker than out of town cops can do." He said this with some sarcasm and native pride.

"Don't give up, Lea. I promise you we'll find who shot your friend and lock him or her up for a good long time!" He patted Lea sympathetically on the shoulder.

"Thanks for the great pasta, Mr. A. Could I have the recipe for my wife? She loves to cook." Patting his round belly he grinned, "And I love to eat." He left, Tony saw him out.

"I'll do the dishes," offered Tony magnanimously.

"Good! "Lea said, pulling down her kayak, "While it's still light Lucy and I will go for a quick paddle."

Tony could do nothing but smile weakly and pretend he really had wanted to wash all the dishes. He vowed once again to buy Lea a dishwasher as soon as she'd permit it. So far she proudly resisted letting him buy her much of anything even though she knew now he was not the poor carpenter he'd once appeared to be. It irritated him.

"Lea, why do you bristle so when I want to give you something? Didn't Siri teach you how to accept graciously as well as give?"

Lea had flushed. "I know I'm like that, Tony. I think it's because I worked so hard not to be dependent upon anyone and to paddle my own canoe. You can give me a kiss and a hug if you want so badly to give me something," When he enthusiastically complied she teased, "That's much better than mink or diamonds, especially your brand."

CHAPTER 31.

John Peder - or as he'd been called as a child, Jay Pee - telephoned again with his wife, Gerda on the other line. When he was little other children used to tease him, "Jay Pee pees!" Ever good natured he would chant back, "I pee, you pee, we all pee, so what?"

"Lealea, have you decided yet to take the ferry from Portland with us to Nova Scotia? I need to make reservations. We can take about a week and stay in B&B's. I know you love Digby fried clams. We can stop in Halifax, too. You can drive to Portland and leave Tony's car and we'll go in the van."

"I'm sorry I didn't call you back right away, Jay, as I promised. Something came up. Of course I'd love a little trip. Tony's not sure he can get away but I'll talk to him again and I promise I'll call you."

Tony insisted once more he had too much work lined up at the boatyard to leave for a whole week. He urged Lea to go and take the beetle. She said she really didn't mind taking the bus for the two hour ride. Tony was adamant he could walk everywhere he needed to go or get a lift from Will. Lea called Jay and Gerda and told them in a happy tone, "I'm on my way! I hope the Bay of Fundy won't be rough this trip. I've never been sea sick in my life so I don't expect I will be."

While in Nova Scotia Lea called Tony collect every evening.

"Yes, I miss you and Lucy. Yes, I'm having a splendid time, a really wonderful time. I love you, too. Kiss, kiss."

The Evangeline Trail and the old church they visited was as interesting as she remembered it. She learned more of the history of the Acadians. At Peggy's Cove along with seventeen tour buses from cruise ships and motorcycles and campers, they enjoyed the famous gingerbread in the restaurant. Lea was certain she'd uncovered their secret ingredient and was eager to get home and try it.

She was saddened and appalled at the mobs of tourists over-running the quaint fishing village which had a population of seventy-five or less in the off season. There was triple that number here now. People swarmed all over the light house and the rocks. She knew the tourist trade had a great deal to do with Peggy's Cove's survival and she bought things in the gift shop she didn't need or want. The necessity for fishermen to prostitute their noble profession by selling souvenirs and cheap trinkets was a deplorable reality and saddened her.

Lea called Tony from Halifax. "We visited the Titanic Cemetery today. The grave stones are laid out like the hull of a ship. It's filled with stones marking the remains of the known and unknown passengers and crew of the ill fated Titanic. A group in Halifax keeps fresh flowers and plants on the graves, it's touching to see. I was moved by one stone marked with the name of a young woman, a mother of five. Beside it was a grave stone reading, "the only child recovered."

"Many were marked 'unknown', Tony. It's tragic how many perished at sea and how few bodies were recovered and buried although there are over a hundred graves."

On the ferry on the way back from Yarmouth to Portland Lea lost the twenty-five dollars she'd allowed herself to gamble with after building it up to two hundred. John Peder was sympathetic to her chagrin and offered to stake her to another twenty-five at least. Since he had already paid for the bulk of the trip - the cabins over, the meals out and the B&B's - Lea firmly refused. He'd only permitted her to treat them to one dinner out saying, "Honey, I never get to do much for you, don't spoil my pleasure. Remember, Siri always told us we must be gracious receivers as well as givers, so don't argue any more." (*Did Tony tell him to say that?* Lea wondered, *why is everyone so hell bent on me accepting things?*)

Lea mentally added up all he'd spent and vowed she would paint a full sheet of Peggy's Cove and frame it for them as soon as she got back to her studio. Lea loved Gerda like a sister and she'd been an easy and enjoyable companion. Jay liked seeing his two favorite women get along so well and giggle together.

In Maine she reiterated her grateful thanks, kissing them both goodbye she took off in Tony's red bug. At home she and Tony had a sensuous and happy reunion and Lucy was overjoyed to see her, leaping in circles, but they'd gone to bed five minutes after Lea's return which miffed Lucy, left alone in the studio again.

While Lea was gone Tony found himself at loose ends for what to do after work. He decided to try his skill at wood carving honed by his carpentry experience. He started a large cod for over Lea's door. He planned to gold leaf it when he learned how. It was coming along nicely but Lucy felt neglected.

Tony hadn't been able to go fishing as Will had sprained an ankle and torn a ligament on the Mandy. Julia insisted he give the leg a complete rest with it propped up on pillows. Will complained loudly yet he enjoyed the tender, loving care of his nurse. Tony didn't want to impose on their time together too often so he spent hours on his wood carving at the shop after hours where Lucy was not welcome to come and roam amongst all the debris and machinery. Alone in the studio she was lonely. She chewed up one of Lea's shoes and peed in front of her easel like a retaliatory child.

Tony felt guilty about leaving her alone a lot of the days and nights and didn't have the heart to scold her. Mopping up the puddle he looked at her sternly, "Are you an art critic, now?"

The next morning Lea bundled up all her soiled laundry and took it and Lucy in Tony's car to a coin operated Laundromat. She'd never owned a washer or dryer, "I'd really give in and let Tony buy them but where could I put them in the studio?"

There was a sign on the door of the Laundry. "Closed because of a power outage. Machines are temporarily out of order. Try our other Laundromat on Humphrey Street in Swampscott, just over the Marblehead line."

Lea groaned. She decided she might as well get it over with as she had few clean clothes left to wear. She hated doing laundry, it was a royal pain. It took twenty minutes to find a parking space along the street. Holding Lucy's leash in one hand and horsing the laundry basket from the car into the shop she bumped into a man walking along the sidewalk. "Oops, sorry!" She said looking at him pleasantly as he jumped aside for her.

In a flash of recognition she knew this was the same man who had stared at her on the beach out front so coldly and ominously. He stepped up his pace, turned his head away and rapidly walked on. Lucy snarled at his heels.

Inside the laundry Lea muttered, "Even a creep has a right to walk on the sidewalk and the beach, what's the matter with me?" She tried to calm herself and the feeling of foreboding as she piled clothes into the washing machine.

That evening she didn't mention the incident to Tony. She was sure he'd tell her, "You're over imaginative," in the superior and detached manner he sometimes displayed which she loathed. She loved everything about him except his occasional cool objectivity which made her feel like an hysterical fool. But Lucy agreed with her, she had recognized the man and growled and snarled at him.

When finally through and home again Lea dismissed the encounter and got busy mixing up the Peggy's Cove gingerbread she was dying to try. She guessed it had applesauce in it that gave it the different flavor and kept it moist. Tony and Lucy loved it that evening at supper and Tony praised her for figuring out what made the dessert she'd had in Nova Scotia at Peggy's Cove so special. Lea knew it was good but she knew as well she really didn't have their secret ingredient after all.

.

Captain Pete at his waterfront inn in Swampscott was becoming increasingly suspicious of his boarder. The old phrase, "He's up to no good," kept running through his mind. The man was present too frequently to be doing any kind of serious work with computers? He decided to talk to his brother-in-law, Andy, a police Lieutenant in Swampscott and get his take on it. "Perhaps I'm over-reacting and imagining boogie men."

Pete courteously greeted his boarder on his many entrances and exits to the inn with a genial hello and a friendly nod. To this the killer responded with an unsmiling duck of his head and a terse muttered "Hello" if he bothered to acknowledge Pete at all.

He was obsessively preoccupied with his burning goal to retrieve the Bellini from its hiding place and sell it and be done with it. On moonless nights when the tide was low, which he checked by the beach out front of the inn, he bicycled on a rented bike to Marblehead to reassure himself once more that the statue was still safe.

He was extremely careful now since he'd discovered Tony with Don, an electrician friend had installed flood lights on the terrace even though Lea kept forgetting to turn them on. He didn't want to arouse the damned dog and regretted that nearly fatal mistake.

He feared keeping the statue at the inn for long as he suspected the cleaning people went through his things either innocently or being nosy. He could wait a while longer to get further instructions, he steeled himself. The statue was safer where it was, it wouldn't be much longer before he'd hear final plans on its delivery? The killer had sent his inn address on to the agent in South America. He'd received just one enigmatic message by courier, "The deal is still on and eagerly awaited. It will be finalized soon, stand by."

And so the murderer walked his days away while Lt. Andy Anderson was quietly and methodically looking into his credentials with the help of the State Police and the Boston FBI. as a suspicious person.

He told his brother-in-law, "Pete, don't worry, eventually we do run the bad guys to earth and they pay heavily for the "error of their ways." He said this facetiously but he too, smelled something was rotten. The man just didn't ring true.

"Hang in. Above all, don't ask him to leave on any excuse. It's better to have him where we can watch him." Kidding he added, "Never fear, murder will out."

Little did he realize how close to the truth he was.

CHAPTER 32.

Sunday was an unusual day for weather starting out bright and sunny.

"Red sky in the morning, sailor take warning," Will quoted as he and Tony set out very early on the Mandy to fish. Will's leg was heavily bandaged but he could hobble around now sufficiently to run the boat. In about an hour or so the seas became rough and lumpy and looked an oily, sardine gray and ominous. The sky was an eerie John Marin or Winslow Homer seascape with a sulfurous yellow cast and purple and gray edged clouds.

Will announced, "We're in for a real No'easter this time. We'd better head in pretty soon before she hits."

They returned to port having caught only a couple of cod and haddock. Tony brought his share home. It was still late morning but Lea decided to make an authentic Marblehead Fish "chowdah" with the fish Tony had caught so it could sit and meld until time to reheat for supper.

She "tried out" a scored chunk of salt pork in a large soup pot. Then she discarded the browned pork leaving only a few crisp rashers she set aside. Chopped yellow onion was sauteed in the pork fat with some unsalted butter. Potatoes were sliced thin, never diced, and added next. Barely to cover she added bottled clam juice and water to cook the potatoes until tender but not mushy. She laid the filets of cod and haddock on last and over all and poured whole milk to just cover. (Never, never would Lea even consider using canned evaporated milk as some traitors did!) Soon the chowder was at a happy, gentle simmer. The fish would poach in the milk and break up into large pieces.

Salt and pepper, Worcestershire sauce and a wee smidgen of thyme were stirred in to taste. Some overdid the thyme, ruining the chowder completely. Another dollop of unsalted butter and the stove was turned off for melding time. Voila! Done. She would reheat it on a simmer, careful not to let it boil. Maybe add some coffee cream.

Later she would heat rolls and toss together a cold salad. Chowder would be ladled over a hard tack common cracker or two in big bowls and garnished with paprika and chopped fresh chives and a chunk of butter.

For the salad she planned to mix together fresh new, barely blanched peas, diced cheddar cheese, and chopped dill pickle, stirred with her mayonnaise and plop it on some garden lettuce. Lea loved this salad combination she'd first been served when working at

Stillman Infirmary at Harvard University as a Lab technician. (It was a secret of the Stillman cook whom Lea loved and begged the recipe from. The students liked it, too, and told their doubting mothers about it until a print-out had to be done.")

When she first served this unusual medley to Tony he backed away, "Yuk! What kind of ghastly, unholy mixture is this? Road kill?" ducking Lea's upraised spatula. Soon enough he became a devotee just as much as Lucy was. Lea would make plenty.

They sat down at the old pine table in the early evening. It was too cool and unpleasant to eat outdoors on the terrace. The wind was blowing hard. It was already dark. The No'easter was ascending into full fury. Outside the surf ferociously pounded against the rocks. Sheets of rain along with vicious, gigantic waves were flooding the street making it impassable even with rubber boots. Spray burst high over the fence leading to the Fort.

It was warm and cozy inside by the wood stove in the studio. Tony and Lea were not afraid, the large craggy rocks helped protect the small house and it was exhilarating to look out and see the exciting wild surf. It was a giant symphony of timpani, drum rolls and cymbals. The wind banged against the wooden shack sounding like cannon shots. They'd not lost electricity yet but Lea knew they soon would as happened during every big storm.

"I think I should lock the Indian shutters, Lea, inside as well as outside." Tony flipped on the flood lights and began to lock the shutters more securely inside first looking out the window at the fury of the wind and water. It was terrible and yet thrilling to see

the wind and water wreaking havoc and boats tossing
to and fro, some breaking away from their moorings to
crash on the rocks near the Fort.

"What the devil?" He yelled and burst out the
terrace door. Usually urbane and calm Tony kept a
tight rein on his volatile temper but when he was angry
he exploded like Sicily's Mt. Etna. He was angry and
infuriated now seeing an intruder again on Lea's
terrace.

Lea screamed, "Tony, don't go out there!"

She watched Tony grappling with a hooded
figure in oilskins. He was trying to wrest from him a
seaweed covered object the man held close to his
chest. The two men slipped and slid on the slimy
rocks as they scuffled, sea spray breaking over their
heads as the fierce strong wind kept knocking them
down to their knees.

Lea, panic stricken, screamed over and over for
Tony to come in. "My God, please, Tony!" Lucy
whimpered by the open door trying to get to Tony as
Lea held her back. Torrents of rain flooded into the
studio. Tony struggled to his feet and managed a
heavy blow to the other man's head who was kneeling
on the rocks, trying to get up. The man lost his footing
and went sliding and crashing off the rocks into the
angry ocean below, now at full tide. The package he
held smashed and flew into a hundred pieces and with
him slid off the rock patio into the wild churning surf.
In the brief moment of flood light as it flickered and
went out, Tony had gotten a glimpse of Bell's scarred
face before he drowned below.

Lea was sobbing and pulling and yanking at
Tony who crawled on his hands and knees to the open

door. The storm was at its peak. Lucy helped, valiantly hanging on with her teeth to Tony's pants leg. Together Lea and Lucy managed to haul Tony inside the studio. He sprawled on the wet floor, gasping for breath, hands and face bleeding. Both Lea and Lucy were crying and kissing him. Lea wiped his face with a damp dish towel. Tony looked up at them and with a crooked grin he croaked, "Now will you marry me?" His blue-green eyes were dancing.

"Tony, Tony, who was that man? Was it your cousin, Roberto?"

"It was Donald Bell." He whispered. "I saw the scar on his face. The poor bastard killed Andreas and Roberto for the Bellini. It's gone now."

"But why Sarah, too?" Lea was now in tears. Tony clutched her hand and squeezed it tightly. He sat up and wiped his face on Lea's shirt. He now seemed quite recovered from his ordeal. He patted a soggy Lucy who was licking his face.

The furious No'easter and angry ocean crashed against houses and rocks destroying much in its wake, it continued raging on all night as they slept, exhausted. Front Street was flooded, lights and telephones were out of commission.

"Cara, I'll report all of this in the morning. There's nothing we can do now but go to bed, Lea." He gave her a suggestive look and grinned at her.

"I don't believe you! Is sex all you can think of when you almost died and scared me nearly to death, too? And Tony, a man just drowned? Tony!"

He said, "Well, yeah."

CHAPTER 33.

In the morning as often happened in the aftermath of a tremendous storm, the sea was deceptively calm. Lavender sea smoke spiraled, frothing and steaming. It bounced all across the now placid harbor. They were still in a power outage so Tony and Lea ate a cold breakfast of cereal and fruit and milk. Lea really missed her jump start of morning coffee.

"This is the day the Lord hath made, let us rejoice and be glad in it."

"Grazie Dio. Amen."

Spooning up her cereal mixed with apricots and walnuts, Lea said, "Tony, I still have many unanswered questions. I'm afraid you've lost the St. Theresa forever. I think it was hidden all this time in Papa's lobster pot I used as a table?"

"I reported Bell's drowning this morning while you were still asleep. They plan to grapple for the body today, I suggest you visit with Sylvia or Julia or go off and paint."

"I'm pretty strong, Tony, but I've had enough. I'll call Julia, she may like to paint outdoors with me. I'll take Lucy so she won't be in the way of the police and scuba divers. I'm so sorry you lost your grandmother's statue, Tony." Lea hugged him.

"Yes, we have and thank God it's all over. With the deaths and misery it caused it's much better no one has it. I think Gian Bellini and St. Theresa would agree. They can rest easy now. The exquisite large sculpture he did from the small marble model still exists, Lea, we can see it on our honeymoon?" The latter was asked with a pleading look Lea ignored.

Tears welling up, "Tony, why Sarah? Who killed her?"

Reluctantly Tony answered truthfully, "I think Ray met Bell in a barroom when he was drunk and hired him to threaten Sarah off because he was extremely angry about the divorce. Ray probably never intended Bell to shoot her. He'd lost you and Nora through divorce and he was afraid he would lose Claire and his other children."

"Ray was a mean drunk but not a murderer! His remorse must have eaten into him deeply to hang himself."

"We know alcoholics are often manic-depressive and self-medicate with alcohol. In a depressed state Ray could easily have decided to end all his pain."

Lea needed some vestige of an excuse for Nora's father. Tony said nothing to challenge her defense of him and did not bring up Ray's vicious attack on him and his physical abuse of Lea, Claire and little Tommy.

"Was it Ray's fault he became an alcoholic, Tony? Once he was a beautiful, graceful boy."

"Perhaps not," he said gently. Grimly he thought, *emotionally Ray stayed an egocentric teenager and never took responsibility for any of his actions.* He deemed it more charitable not to say this aloud. Ray had hurt Lea enough.

"Who nailed that dead raccoon to my door? Was it Ray?"

"No, Lea. The police received complaints about three or four similar incidents. Dog called this morning to tell us it was done by an amateur Animal Rights Group made up of zealous, self-righteous adolescents who distributed leaflets about their Raccoon Rights Club."

"These were traced to the high school's computers. The kids got information on destroyed raccoons from the Police Log in the Reporter. Police have been investigating for quite a while but while they were in the process they didn't publicly make any statements to alert the group. These ruffians also killed some raccoons themselves to nail on complainants doors!"

At Lea's look of disbelief, Tony said, "Irrational causes are often like that from abortion opponents to animal rights groups, the modus operendi being "kill to save."

"The telephones are operating this morning. Dog called to apologize for keeping it quiet and leaving you in anxiety. He said all six kids had been expelled from school and were on probation and may not be able to graduate because of their' malicious mischief.'"

"He also asked me again for my recipe for his wife. In all the fracas and storm I forgot to tell you until now."

Lea shooed away a pigeon. "I suppose a Pigeon Rights Group will be next!"

"What made that Donald Bell so twisted that he went from white to black, from doing good and enforcing the law to doing evil and breaking the law? It's incomprehensible."

Tony patted Lucy, "From what I was told while you and Lucy were still sleeping, (my two sleepy-heads) the FBI believes the deaths of his wife and infant son, I didn't know about when I hired him through John Randall, filled him with an obsessive, overwhelming grief. He had a terrible anger toward the world, to the FBI, to criminals and he blamed his personal loss on everyone. Their take on it is he became mentally and psychologically unbalanced. In his sick mind-set after he lost his family all he lived for was revenge and money. It was his way of getting even, with the FBI and the whole world."

Hesitantly, Lea said, "I'm sorry about your cousins, Tony. They were your family, after all."

Unemotionally Tony replied, "My cousins, Lea, were amoral, egomaniacal and evil men, nevertheless they attended Mass faithfully. Will that cut any ice with St. Peter? I think not but many of the mafia believe their false piety and ostentatious funerals will open heaven's doors for them."

Bob Dylan's song, "Knockin' on Heaven's Door" ran across Lea's mind.

"My cousins were intent on destroying anyone or anything they saw as a threat to their power or preeminence or anyone who stood in the way of them acquiring a fortune. Their jealousy and their cruelty began many years ago in their boyhood when they killed Nonna's pet cat and tried to kill Nonna, Vito and me several times. I feel nothing but revulsion and horror they were part of my family and relief they are gone!"

"They tried to kill our grandmother with poison, who gave them so much. They had to find a way to do it so their mothers, her daughters, wouldn't find out. I'm sure they eventually would have killed Nonna but she conveniently died first."

Lea brushed the tears from her eyes. Tony was dead serious, ever scrupulously honest and spoke with vehemence through his pain, his voice rising.

"Then they could steal the statue they knew she would never will to them. Nonna had probably already told her daughters it was to go to her beloved only son's son, me. I became the only one left in their way. Please Deo, forgive me I am glad they are all dead! Although I suppose their mothers will grieve."

With some irony Lea murmured, "Yes. Mothers are like that."

"Tony, tell me how the lawyer, John Randall figures into all of this?"

"I don't know yet the extent of his collusion with my cousins or Bell. Obviously he couldn't face the disgrace and loss and ruin of his firm as well as his professional and personal reputation so he destroyed himself. Randall's snobbery ruled all his actions. He stole valuable art to acquire status, the poor bastard!"

Lea frowned. "Lea," Tony said firmly, "You know that great art is not for sale or to give the owner status, the way it is at all the high priced auctions. It's priceless and should be revered for it's own sake and the genius who created it and on display for all of us to enjoy."

"Anyway, Carissima, the worst is over and we can get on with our lives, grazie Dio."

He changed the subject. "I noticed on your book shelves, Lea, you have Joseph Campbell's 'The Power of Myth' have you read it recently?"

Surprised not only at the abrupt change of subject she felt was too painful for Tony to continue with but at his question, she answered, "Why? I never knew you were interested in that kind of metaphysical philosophy, Tony? You're always so sure of yourself and pretty practical and contained. I also have every book Carl Jung ever wrote that I could find. I really liked his 'Man and His Symbols'. Like the Mythologist Campbell, Jung stated 'behind every myth lies a truth.'

"And Campbell advised," Tony broke in, "Follow your bliss in life, didn't he? You do that with your painting, Lea. You're my bliss!" (Lea blushed.) "I just thought perhaps if what Campbell or Jung, whom you admire, wrote applies you might resolve your big problem with your church."

"A difference in taste is not a 'big' problem to me, Tony, but like what?" Lea was interested now.

"Oh, that we all live in a myth or metaphor. If we were Hindu we'd live their beliefs, or if Jewish like Sarah and Sylvia, their beliefs."

"You mean if I can discover the right metaphor for me to live by it would be my personal solution to my, um, discomfort?" You could be right! I'm still searching. My unrest with balloons is just a symptom of something deeper, I suppose." Lea said thoughtfully.

Tony probed further. "Could the myth we live in be there is only one way to be correct and right with God? Most of us instinctively realize behind everything there is a truth and the various paths share much that is similar?" He continued, "I think the outward manifestations are themselves symbols and count for little in the grand overall scheme of things."

Tony was delving so deep Lea was a little nervous. She remained silent for a while, stung by his words and pondering. Although he spoke gently his serious demeanor demanded a thoughtful response.

At last, "Tony, I'm sure you and I are Christian probably because we were born into it, just as primitive tribes in Africa, and Buddhists and others were born into their customs and beliefs. I don't care for any beliefs to be trivialized or made superficial. I guess, to answer your unspoken question my basic 'metaphor' I was brought up in and lived by was the profound sense of awe our church always had I feel is lacking now."

Rebelliously she added, "I shall go on searching for a whole suit of clothes that will fit me!"

"You'll find it, Lea, if you haven't yet. You and I already have resolved many of the differences between my family's age old Catholicism and your ex-Priest Martin Luther's beliefs. We certainly discussed it often enough," He said with a twinkle in his eye reminding Lea of their many, long, drawn out, late night talks.

"A 'holy curiosity' is good, the Jesuits taught?" She threw out at him.

"Yes.   So did C. S.   Lewis, an Anglican; Thomas Merton, a monk; Martin Luther, a rebel, some called a rogue Priest, and the Quakers as well.   They all felt it God pleasing to question their God.   Even Jesus on the cross asked, 'My God, my God, why hast Thou forsaken me?"   Remember Doubting Thomas who pleaded, "Help me my unbelief'?   Questioning God is a form of prayer whether done in anguish or in joy."

"So Tony, behind every balloon is a truth?" She said somewhat sarcastically yet very curious as to Tony's meaning.

He laughed.   "Could be.   It's all within the limitations of each person's perception which is truth to him.   For instance, a paranoid's perception of persecution is genuinely real and truth to him whether it exists in reality or not.   Perhaps your Pastor's perception of gaining souls through enlisting small children and their parents through the use of balloons or whatever, is truth to him?"

"I remember in 'The Seven Story Mountain', Thomas Merton wrote, 'the Lutherans almost have it right!' Of course that was before he joined the Society of Jesus and became a monk. Perhaps I should 'get me to a convent'?"   Lea, quoting Shakespeare looked mischievously at Tony.

"You wouldn't make a very good nun, Lea."

"Why not?" She bristled.

"You could never keep a vow of silence, "He teased.

"Or chastity?" Lea said coldly. "Poverty I can do, could you?"

Lea's ire was short lived. "Thank you Tony, you've just done what you wanted to do, shake me up and make me think!"

Lea was impressed with Tony's keen insights and knowledge of the Bible with which Protestants rarely credited Roman Catholics. Early on Lea had fallen irrevocably in love with Tony. Now she respected him and desired his respect for her with all her heart and soul. She thought *this complex, many layered man is a marvelous piece of work, please God, let me keep him?* As she was ever honest she acknowledged this was a selfish but desperately sincere prayer.

"Tony, enough! Let's make breakfast."

"And say grace," Tony added smiling at her.

Seriously, Lea recited, "Ah, dearest Jesus, holy child, make me a bed soft, undefiled, within my heart that it may be, a quiet chamber kept for Thee."

"Not too quiet," Irrepressible Tony said softly. "Lea, isn't that a bedtime prayer?" He looked at her suspiciously as he cracked eggs for a mushroom omelet.

"It probably is, Tony, but so what? Just hush, I have to think!"

Tony smiled as he whisked four eggs together with four tablespoons of water, a cup of chopped fresh mushrooms, salt and pepper, some minced shallots and sweet red pimiento. He melted butter in the omelet pan and slid the mixture in carefully. Lea admired him tilting the pan expertly to spread the mixture and finally flipping it over and removing it with a spatula to a warmed platter. He'd taught her to use water and not milk in an omelet and stuff it with plenty of mushrooms.

"I am crazy about your omelets, Signore!"

"And I'm crazy about you, Signora." He leaned over and planted a noisy kiss on her forehead.

CHAPTER 34.

In the past there had been many young women in love with Tony or his wealth. He had been considered a great catch in Rome. Until he met Loridana, a beautiful model who was also intelligent, he'd been wary and cool. Since Nonna liked her too, after many months of a feverish courtship they set a date to marry at the Lake Como estate. Tony went first as Lori had a final fitting on her wedding dress to do and planned after that to drive in her Ferarri to join them and complete their wedding plans with Nonna's happy participation. Loridana had fallen in love with Tony's lovely grandmother. Recklessly and eagerly speeding to Tony, her love, she was killed in a head-on collision.

For ten years he mourned his first love and while dallying in short-lived affairs he remained impervious to many overtures of women eager to become Mrs. Antonio Amberetti-Scola. He buried himself in London in his work at the Tate Gallery as a Curator. Occasionally he went out with many different, attractive women, some only once or twice, especially if they came on too strong and he felt pressured.

Tony had been attracted to Lea from the first moment he met her at Fort Sewall. Leanora was not as breathtakingly beautiful as Loridana had been; a tall striking platinum blonde with maple sugar color eyes, yet he felt Lea was more talented, perhaps more intelligent and had a keener sense of humor. The paint smear on the side of her face, her tangle of red Popsicle color curls tickled him and the way St. Lucia immediately took to her drew him to her. Loridana, nevertheless, had been special to him and he felt sad when he learned Lea's first love had been disastrous without many good memories to relive.

"But Ray gave me Nora, Tony, and I wouldn't have missed her for anything."

Finally Lea agreed to marry him. With the murders behind them she was ready and wholeheartedly enthusiastic.

"We'll have so much fun, Tony! We'll be anima and animus, two halves of a whole. Love is the glue that will keep us together."

Tony raised his eyebrows in mock horror. "That's pretty flowery, even for you, Lea. I do love you, Amore, but we'll still disagree on many issues-such as art, religion, how much to feed Lucy, and who's the better cook! I shall still admire the works of Paul Klee and Pablo Picasso you're lukewarm about and you'll still see all the symbolism in Jackson Pollock I fail to uncover. Do you really think we can make it?" He said quizzically.

Lea knew Tony delighted in teasing her and getting a lively response from her. He loved to see her green eyes flash and her strawberry blonde hair almost vibrate when she became passionately angry. He smiled fondly at her, "I shall say grace the rest of my life, Leanora, my love, in gratitude for finding you. However," looking down at her tenderly, "We'll get along much better if occasionally you'll admit I'm usually right."

Playfully Lea punched him on his cheek, instead hit him in the eye as he turned his face to avoid her fist. It was a surprise to them both he would have a large black and blue shiner for their wedding day. Tony was not at all embarrassed and Lea apologized over and over. He wore his black eye insouciantly and no one dared ask about it. "Two firebrands will be united, sparks will surely fly but neither Lea or Tony will ever be bored," Will remarked to Julia, "Both have red hot tempers!"

For Lea's wedding gift surprise Tony sent Nora and Rod airline tickets they promised to keep secret. He also made arrangements for them to stay in a luxurious B&B near the Fort where the marriage vows would be exchanged. Will met Nora and Rod at Logan Airport in Boston. Tony timed their honeymoon departure for Italy the day after Nora would leave for Sydney so Lea would be too busy packing to brood.

Father Joe and Pastor Jorge were to officiate together at the wedding. They hit it off splendidly. Father Joe was heard to say to Pastor Jorge, "You Lutherans are practically Catholic except you have no Pope."

Pastor Jorgenson laughed. "No Pope, but we have Bishops, and we ordain women and my wife and I have children."

"I think I'd rather have the Pope than kids, "Replied Father Joe who taught a rowdy bunch of confirmands he managed to just barely keep in line. Yet he loved them, and they him.

Lea had made her peace with the "balloon Pastor", Tony called him. When she attended church she listened attentively to the lessons and the Gospel, read from the center of the church. She participated in the Passing of the Peace, the prayers of the church and the Eucharist. She enjoyed singing the familiar hymns, "Children of the Heavenly Father," Beethoven's "Joyful, Joyful we adore Thee" and "How Great Thou Art."

Mostly she daydreamed through the two sermons, the simplistic Children's and one for the adult congregation she had to admit were often deeper and more thoughtful than she'd given the "balloon Pastor" credit for. She valiantly ignored all the distractions and smiled sweetly and phonily when balloons (although of late this seemed to have been dropped?) or candy were distributed. Intermittently Lea visited other services, including the Temples and the Roman Catholic. She liked the Greek Orthodox in Lynn. She was still seeking the perfect worship venue even though Tony pronounced, "Such perfection is unattainable, it doesn't exist. Why don't you start your own church, 'Mother Leanora and the Lucy Brethren'?" Lea pretended she was not amused by his remarks.

Tony rarely attended Mass yet secretly Lea humbly acknowledged he was an evolved, spiritual person who lived his faith daily and didn't need as much as she the reassurance of the liturgy. Never would she admit this to him, however, scolding him instead for not going to his church. "You're just a C. and E. Christian."

"Oh? What kind is that, Signora?"

"Christmas and Easter." "I thought you meant codfish and eel," said Tony innocently, "For the fishermen in town who don't go to church Sunday mornings because they have to fish to make a living," suavely chiding her, "In order to raise their children."

They'd reached a comfortable compromise on their religious views and did not plan on having children to complicate matters. Lea announced, "Lucy is enough."

"If by some crazy miracle I should ever become pregnant we'll fight the choice of church affiliation for them, then," Airily she told Tony, tossing her head. He did not reveal his one unfulfilled wish was a son to carry on the Amberetti-Scola name. If Lea had known she would have been extra careful on birth control which she was careless about and Tony kept hoping she'd forget to take her pills one time too many.

Sister Pat, her husband and little girls flew in from California and with Sylvia's generous hospitality were staying at her palatial house on the ocean in Little's Point, Swampscott. The children loved Sylvia's swimming pool and coaxed Lucy into it. They loved Lucy who was their favorite treat of the whole trip and lavished attention on her. Lucy was staying with Sylvia, too for the duration of the wedding and then going to Julia and Will's house during the Roman honeymoon or "Bellaluna" as Tony called it.

The girls were overjoyed when Lucy obeyed their command, "Catch the cookie, Lucy!" Adeptly she'd jump up and catch dog biscuit after dog biscuit in her mouth. She was a professional at this. Tony would have been horrified if he knew just how many she ate during the little girls' visit.

Among the wedding guests were Belinda and Jackie and other old friends, Gail and Bob who delivered milk and eggs to Lea for many years from their farm in Peabody.

Dog had asked if he and his wife could come, he was eager to taste the refreshments. "I'll wear my uniform and keep watch at the Fort for nosy interlopers," He promised. Of course the noisy Jazz boat, "The Ranger", sailed by during the ceremony, rock and roll blaring over loud speakers quite drowning out Lea's "I do's."

Affectionately the sea sparkled and the sun shone down on the wedding party on Fort Sewall. Their rings had been made by a jeweler on the appropriately named Darling Street. Tony preferred a plain gold band. Lea insisted on matching rings with emerald chips, for her Gemini birthstone and Tony's sea green eyes, embedded all around the pink gold bands.

Julia had gathered a bouquet of white, wild flowers for Lea: Queen Anne's Lace, daisies and cinnamon fern. She had refused Tony's offer of white cymbidium orchids, the wild flowers were what she really loved and wanted.

All her brothers and their wives and children came, to Lea's joy. She gave Lars' wife a special hug for coming with him. Not wanting to hurt her sister or three best friends' feelings by choosing one, she told Lucy, "You're my Maid of Honor, Loos."

Will and Julia; Sylvia with Skip, her Police Lieutenant friend; Claire with her lawyer friend, Abe, were all present and beaming. Lucy stood quietly beside Lea and Will stood proudly beside Tony when Nora suddenly appeared, embraced her mother and took her place beside her. Lea's cup runneth over.

She fervently believed with the thin veil separating this world from the next that Sarah, Einar and Siri, Elizabeth Hawthorne and Tony's parents and Nonna, Elissa, Uncle Bill and Aunts' Mae and Solveigh, and Ritz, as well as Gian Bellini and St. Theresa were watching over them as they exchanged vows of fidelity and love. (Tony knew better than to ask Lea to keep obedience in the ritual.)

Lea had requested Claire sing Dean Martin's popular "That's Amore" in Italian as Tony was forever warbling it off key to her. Claire diligently studied the words phonetically and a surprised Tony grinned guessing Lea had put her up to it. Nora accompanied Claire on her flute and it was touching rendered in a slow tempo. In honor of Nonna and St. Theresa Tony had asked her to sing "Ave Maria" in Latin. Claire studied hard practicing long hours to please the couple who meant so much to her.

Lea wore her white silk pant suit (and bare feet as the ground was soggy and wet). Tony had retrieved an emerald necklace of Nonna's for Lea he'd stored in Gitte's vault in Boston, she was invited as well and Tony's former room mate at Eton, Jem, and his wife.

Tony wore an elegant, white Italian-made linen suit he had never worn in Marblehead when playing the role of fisherman and carpenter. He sported his black eye, jauntily. (He also was barefoot, it was so squishy and sodden on the grass.) Both Lea and Tony looked splendid and were radiant.

When the ceremony was almost completed, the sun disappeared abruptly and the rain poured down in torrents and buckets full, leaving all bedraggled and thoroughly drenched.

They encouraged all the guests to run fast down the street for the reception they had prepared at the studio. There they gave them all towels to mop up with and changed into blue jeans themselves. Sylvia's long, gold silk dress with miniscule mirrors sewn all over it had become a soaking wet, gold rag, so Lea lent her some jeans, too.

For the reception Tony and Lea had both cooked for days on end. Lea made the layered Finnish wedding cake and Sylvia furnished a tiny bride and groom for the traditional topper. She painted the hair on both blonde, the bride's pinkish as Tony, a Northern Italian and the "Viking Princess" (she called Lea) were blondes.

The old pine table of Einar's groaned under Beluga caviar and sour cream Tony had bought and lobster pie, oyster quiche, Tony's spinach and ricotta lasagna, salads, fruit, a seafood casserole with shrimp, fish, scallops and more lobster.

The wedding cake was layered with a Cherry Heering whipped cream icing, decorated with candied violets and slivered toasted almonds as well as Sylvia's tiny bride and groom she'd dressed in jeans and madras shirts.

BETTIE HAMILTON

It was a blessed nuptial feast. Pastor Jorge and
Father Joe enjoyed the three kinds of champagne Tony
supplied; Pommery, Veuve Cliquot, and Moet et
Chandon, and became quite merry and jolly friends
from then on.

At the reception, Will took Lea and Tony aside
and addressed them seriously, "Hey! If all else fails
you guys can always open a restaurant. I'll even give
you my special Marblehead Salt Fish Dinner recipe I
don't usually part with," in a magnanimous tone he
added "and the red flannel hash, too."

Julia winked at Lea who turned her head away
to hide a broad grin and pretended a sneeze to cover
her strangled laughter. Tony frowned at her severely
and poked her side with his elbow which further broke
her up. She and Julia dissolved into helpless guffaws
while Will looked bewildered. Annoyed but still
smiling, Tony murmured suavely in a low voice to
Lea, *"Ah, Signora, is my beautiful bride going to be a
big problem?"* Lea smiled back sweetly, *"You got it,
Signore."*

So it came to pass, the limitless ocean became
the ultimate destiny for many, swallowing up the
cousins, Roberto, Georgio and Andreas as well as
Donald Bell. Two others were tragic suicides, Ray
Larson and John Randall whose lives and deaths were
complete and miserable failures. One innocent victim,
Sarah, was lost in this world to her friends who loved
her yet she had turned many young women's lives
around for good. Sarah's and Elissa's lives were
blessings to Lea as well as to others.

The sea continued eternally to be itself and ever shall, at times enraged and sometimes smoothly benign. The ever changing, ever enthralling, ever enchanting, implacable, inscrutable ocean Lea loved.

THE END-FINITO

BETTIE HAMILTON

INDEX TO RECIPES

TONY AND LEA'S FINNISH AND ITALIAN CUISINE
(with a little help from their friends, relatives and chief taster-Lucy.)

APPETIZERS
Tony's Antipasto
Lea's Artichokes stuffed with Blue Cheese (SEE VEGETABLES)
Gerda's Apple and Brie in Puff Pastry
Lea's Basic Clam, Crab and Variations Dip
Tony's Smoked Bluefish Pate (SEE FISH)
Lea's Spiced Pecans (SEE DESSERTS)
Lea's Red Pepper Jelly Atop Cream Cheese, Brie or Havarti (SEE SAUCES ETC.)
Tony's Clam Pizza
Tony's Grilled Figs Wrapped in Prosciutto (smoked ham or use smoked salmon)
Aunt Solveigh's Pickled Herring (SEE FISH)
Lea's Oyster (or Lobster) Quiche
Tony's Grilled Shrimp in Prosciutto

BREADS, CAKES AND COOKIES
Gerda's Apple Cider Sugar Cookies
Lea's Applesauce Gingerbread
Tony's Apricot-Pistachio Biscotti
Lucy's Dog Biscuits
Aunt Mae's Blueberry Cake
Siri's Finnish Sweet Bread (coffee cake)
Lea's Akvavit Sorbet to serve with cakes and cookies
Sarah's Perfect Popovers
Sylvia's Mother's Raspberry Cheese Cake with Lavender
Lea's Finnish Wedding Cake with Cherry Heering Icing
Finnish May Day Crullers with Sima
Julia's Joe Frogger Cookies
Siri's Pineapple Upside-Down Cake
Grandmother Eleanora's Finnish Spinach Pancakes
Nora's Aussie Cream Scones with Raspberry Preserves

DESSERTS
Uncle Bill's Snow Apple Pie (Fameuse Apples)
Aunt Solveigh's Brownie Cashew Pie
Siri's Caramel Custard
Lea's Spiced Pecans
Lea's Christmas Caramels
Siri's Fluffy Lemon Delight
Lea's Pastry for Two-crust Pie-9"
Lea's Akvavit Sorbet (SEE BREADS, CAKES, COOKIES)
Lea's Strawberry Pie

ENTREES

Lea's Boston Baked Beans

Lea's Cold Poached Chicken with Herbs (SEE SALAD AND SANDWICHES)

Siri's Finnish Baked Chicken with Almonds, Grapes and Havarti Cheese

Tony's Italian Grilled chicken with Lemons and Olives

Scandinavian Fricadeller (meat loaf, or meat balls)

Ray's Cheapie Meat Loaf with Tomato Soup

Tony's Mushroom Omelet

Maria's Sicilian Pasta with Asparagus and Prosciutto (or Panetta-bacon)

Lea's Baked Stuffed Peppers with Sirloin and Pine nuts

Any Fish: Baked, Broiled, Grilled or Poached in Lea's Style (See FISH)

FISH

(Cod, Bluefish, Striped Bass, Flounder, Herring, Salmon)

Will's Baked Bluefish

Tony's Grilled Bluefish

Bluefish Pate

Einar's Cold Striped Bass (Gravadlax) with Tuna Sauce

Will's Codfish Cakes

Julia and Will's Salt Cod Dinner and Red Flannel Hash

Will's Fried Flounder with New England Original Tartar Sauce

Lea's Baked Stuffed Haddock or Shrimp

Lea's Cold Poached Salmon

Solveigh's Pickled Herring (see APPETIZERS)

Tony's Grilled Shrimp in Prosciutto

SOUPS AND CHOWDERS
Gerda's Chilled Apple Soup (Aeblesuppe)
Lea's Marblehead Clam Chowder
Tony's Mediterranean Clam Chowder
Lea's Marblehead Fish Chowder
Tony's Pasta E Fagioli (Pasta and Beans)
Lea's Seafood Chowder
Tony's Sicilian Seafood Stew
SALADS
Tony's Antipasto (SEE APPETIZERS)
Sarah's Avocado, Bacon and Orange Salad
Lea's Poached Chicken Salad
Tony's Italian Salad
Lobster Salad
Lea's Pea, Pickle and Cheese Salad (Tony called aka "Roadkill Salad"
Siri's Potato Salad
Tomato Salad with Basil, Oil, Pepper
Cold Poached Chicken Platter

SANDWICHES
Lea's BLT's
Lea's Cold Poached Chicken Salad (SEE ENTREES AND SALAD)
Lea's Lobster Salad Rolls (SEE SEAFOOD)
Maria's Fig and Prosciutto Sandwiches
Tony's Americanized Italian Submarine
Peanut Butter and Jelly Sandwich
Fluffernutter (Peanut Butter and Marshmallow Fluff)
Fish Sandwich, Made with Any Cooked Fish Filet and Tartar Sauce

SALADS
Tony's Antipasto (SEE APPETIZERS)
Sarah's Avocado, Bacon and Orange Salad
Lea's Cold Poached Chicken Salad (SEE ENTREES)
or Platter
Tony's Italian Salad
Lobster Salad (SEE SEAFOOD)
Lea's Pea, Cheese and Pickle Salad (AKA ROADKILL)
Native Sliced Tomatoes with Basil, Olive Oil and Ground Black Pepper

SOUPS AND CHOWDERS
Gerda's Cold Apple Soup (Aeblesuppe)
Lea's Marblehead Clam Chowder
Tony's Mediterranean Clam Chowder
Lea's Marblehead Fish Chowder
Tony's Pasta E Fagioli (In parts of Italy this is considered a thick soup.)
Tony's Sicilian Seafood Stew
Lea's New England Seafood Chowder

SAUCES, MAYONNAISE, RED PEPPER JELLY, PEPPER RELISH
Aioli Garlic Mayonnaise
Lea's Mayonnaise
Tony's Hot Sauce for Cold Seafood
Lemon-Thyme Butter for Grilling (SEE SEAFOOD)
Lea's Sour Cream-Dill Sauce
Will's Original New England Tartar Sauce
Einar's Tuna Sauce for Gravadlax (SEE FISH)
Lea's Tomato Sauce (For Pasta and Entrees)
Lea's Pepper Relish
Lea's Red Pepper Jelly

BETTIE HAMILTON

SEAFOOD
Tony's Clam Pizza (SEE APPETIZERS)
Tony's White Clam Sauce on Linguini
Finnish Fried Eel with Lemon Creamed Potatoes
Lobster, (Boiled, Baked Stuffed, Broiled, Salad, Grilled, Rolls)
Tony's Lobster Tetrazzini
Lea's Scalloped Oysters
Claire's Marblehead Seafood Casserole
Tony's Shrimp Cacciatori
Lea's Baked Stuffed Shrimp Casserole
Tony's Grilled Shrimp in Prosciutto (or Pancetta) (SEE APPETIZERS)

VEGETABLES AND VEGETARIAN DISHES
Lea's Artichokes Stuffed with Blue Cheese
Finnish Cold Pickled Beets, and Pickled Cucumbers
Tony's Pasta E Fagioli (Chili-type entree or thick soup) (SEE SOUPS)
Linnea's Cauliflower Mornay
Tony's Vegetable Lasagne (Spinach, Tomato, Cheese)
Lea's Ratatouille
Siri's Finnish Spinach Pancakes (SEE BREADS AND CAKES)
Lea's Mushroom Stuffed Peppers
Native Ripe Tomatoes with Basil, Oil, Black Pepper (SEE SALADS)
Aunt Mae's Garden Thinnings, (The First Baby Peas, Baby Carrots and Baby Potatoes)

WINES CHAMPAGNES
Bolla Soave Asti Spumonte
Cabernet Moet et Chandon
Chablis Pommery
Chianti Veuve Cliquot
Frascati
New BeaujolaisPinot Noir BEER: Danish Tuborg
Valpocella Classico Pinot GrigioFinnish Sima (SEE BREADS) APPETIZERS
TONY'S ANTIPASTO (Arrange in sections on a platter, fasten rolls with toothpicks)
(MARINADE: olive oil, vinegar, salt, pepper, garlic, sugar, wine, mustard mixed together.
Marinated green beans
Marinated artichoke hearts
Marinated mushrooms
Hot red peppers
Anchovies rolled up with a caper inside
Green and black olives
Rolled slices provolone cheese
Sardines, garnished with paper thin slices of onion and lemon
Rolled up Prosciutto slices
Cubes of Genoa salami
Quartered hard cooked eggs
Smoked salmon rolls
Cantaloupe balls
Watermelon shoestring pickle slices or whole Cornichons

Plate or separate with parsley or watercress. Some or all of above serves 10 to 12 for a cocktail party. Sparingly sprinkle food with Virgin olive oil and red wine vinegar or an Italian vinaigrette. Serve with bread sticks or quartered slices of Italian bread spread with unsalted, sweet butter, warmed in the oven.

(Tony's version of antipasto was ever welcomed, always disappeared fast.)

LEA'S ARTICHOKES STUFFED WITH BLUE CHEESE (SEE VEGETABLES)
GERDA'S APPLE AND BRIE IN PUFF PASTRY

1 sheet prepared puff pastry
1 8 oz. Brie (Camembert or Havarti Cheese optional)
1 egg beaten with 1 T. water
2 T. sweet butter
2 T. sweet butter
1 small Jonathan apple, peeled, thin sliced
2 T. brown sugar
Sprinkles of cinnamon and nutmeg

Saute apple in butter until soft. Sprinkle with brown sugar, cinnamon and nutmeg. Roll pastry 10" X 10" into an oblong. Chill cheese first for 15 minutes in freezer. Mound apples on top of partially frozen cheese. Wrap in pastry. Seal with egg wash. Seam side down place on ungreased cookie sheet. Bake 350, 10 minutes until puffed and brown. Cool. Cut in small diagonal wedges, serves about 8 to 10.

LEA'S BASIC CLAM OR CRAB DIP

8 oz. cream cheese with chives (or plain cheese, add 2
T. chopped chives or shallots)
1 T. mayonnaise or sour cream
1 tsp. white wine Worcestershire Sauce
Garlic powder, and horseradish to taste
Salt and pepper, dash Tabasco Sauce

Mix or pulse in blender until smooth. Into base
stir 8 oz. drained, chopped clams or 1 cup crabmeat.
(May use tuna fish or any cooked fish, adding 1 tsp dill
weed.) Serve hot or cold, may zap in microwave to
heat. Accompany with rusk or any crackers. Lea liked
small Wheat thins. Serves about 12.

VARIATIONS:

1. To base add 1/2 lb mashed liverwurst and 1 tsp.
   deli mustard. Pulse smooth. Serve cold
   accompanied by pumpernikel bread rounds or
   quarters.
2. To base add 2 ripe, peeled mashed avocados, 1
   seeded medium tomato, pinch chili powder, 2
   T. fresh lime or lemon juice, dash of Tabasco
   Sauce. Serve cold with crackers.
3. To base add 1 can Deviled Ham, 1/2 cup
   chopped watermelon pickle, 1 tsp mustard.
   Serve cold with crackers or potato chips.

4. Place base into one bowl. In second bowl place stirred red pepper jelly. Guests spoon some of each on crackers or melba toast.
5. Blend 8 oz. jar marinated artichoke hearts (drained) into base, and 1/2 cup Parmesan cheese. Pulse smooth or leave chunky. Serve hot or cold with crackers.
6. Into base stir 1/2 lb chopped fresh sauteed mushrooms and 1/2 cup chopped cashew nuts. Serve hot with sturdy rusk.
7. Into base stir 1 pt. lightly sauteed fresh oysters with a dribble lemon juice. Serve hot.
8. For Oyster Mousse, blend ingredients until smooth, chill. Serve cold with crackers.
9. Or add a tin of smoked oysters (or smoked salmon) to base, stir in whole or puree smooth. Serve hot or cold.
10. Stir into base 3/4 cup shredded or slivered cooked roast beef, corned beef, tongue, turkey or chicken, a dash of mustard and Tabasco Sauce. Serve cold.
11. Three cheese spread. (Type found in restaurants) To base add sharp shredded cheddar cheese, and some grated Parmesan or Romano cheese. Serve cold.
12. 1 bowl Lea's Red Pepper Jelly, 1 bowl base (Put jelly on base on each cracker) (SEE SAUCES for Red Pepper Jelly recipe)

TONY'S CLAM PIZZA

1 large thin pizza crust (may use Lea's piecrust recipe (SEE DESSERTS)

1 pint chopped fresh clams
1 T. olive oil
2 minced Jalapeno peppers
2 cloves minced garlic
3/4 cup Alfredo Sauce (OR a simple white sauce SEE SAUCES)
1 1/2 cups Mozzarella cheese for topping with
1 T. Parmesan cheese and
1 T. each chopped basil and oregano

Mix all ingredients together. Pour into pie shell. Sprinkle cheese topping over. Bake 400, 10 minutes. Cool slightly, cut in wedges. Serves 6. Serve with Danish beer, Tuborg. (This is a white instead of the traditional red pizza, delights clam lovers)

AUNT SOLVEIGH'S PICKLED HERRING

3 or 4 salted herring packed in brine
Milk
Water
2/3 cup red wine vinegar
1/3 cup sugar
2 tsp. ground allspice
2 medium sliced onions
1/4 cup red wine or sherry

Wash herring thoroughly in cold running water. Place in deep bowl and cover with equal amounts of milk and water. Let stand overnight. Drain. Cut off heads, trim dark edge of neck. Filet herring, do not remove skin. Trim bottoms and sides of each herring filet to remove fins, cut off top fin. Cut filets crosswise in 1/2" strips, set aside small tail ends.

Combine vinegar, 1 cup water, sugar and allspice, bring to a boil. Cool. In a wide mouth jar or a bowl place a layer of tail pieces. Cover with sliced onions. Repeat, alternating layers. Pour marinade over herring and onion. Cover tightly. Let stand 2 or 3 days before serving. At serving time sprinkle wine or sherry on fish after first draining off the marinade. Serve with Scandinavian Flatbread which although it resembles cardboard, is delicious when buttered. Place herring and onion on pieces of flat bread for an appetizer.

(There are literally dozens of methods to prepare pickled herring. Lea's family were loyal to Lea's Godmother Solveigh's way and naturally considered it the best.)

LEA'S OYSTER (OR LOBSTER) QUICHE

1 9" unbaked pie shell (SEE DESSERTS)
1 pt. raw oysters (or large pieces of cooked lobster meat)
1/8 cup of oyster liquor
1 T. butter
1/3 cup finely minced onion
3 slightly beaten eggs

2 cups cream
1/2 cup grated Swiss cheese
Dash Tabasco Sauce or cayenne pepper, salt and nutmeg.

Saute onion briefly in butter. Mix eggs, cream, cheese and seasonings together. Add onion and oysters and stir. Pour into pie shell. Sprinkle top with more nutmeg. Bake 10 minutes at 450. Lower temperature to 325, bake about 20 more minutes or until custard sets. Insert silver knife to test. Serve warm in wedges with a sprig of parsley, dill or basil and wedge of lemon for garnish. Serves approximately 6 to 8. (Oyster lovers find this as nice as scalloped oysters. Lea made it for her father who loved oysters. Einar claimed every Finn was partial to fish and seafood.)

TONY'S GRILLED SHRIMP WRAPPED IN PROSCIUTTO

8 jumbo cleaned raw shrimp, tails on (Or 4 halved large figs)
1/2 lb. Prosciutto (or Pancetta (bacon) slices, halved
Virgin olive oil

Wrap each shrimp in the smoked ham slices, rub lightly with olive oil. Grill on each side until shrimp pink, and ham crispy. Serve with a cold, spicy "hot" sauce or Lea's mayonnaise. (SEE SAUCES) For two apiece, serves 4.
Everyone seems to love a hot appetizer.

Variation: Tony also wraps half a fresh fig in Prosciutto or Pancetta and grills for an appetizer. Sometimes he wraps raw oysters in pancetta and grills. Lea named these "Romans on horseback." Why? Who knows. May substitute American or Canadian bacon.

BREADS, CAKES AND COOKIES
GERDA'S APPLE CIDER SUGAR COOKIES

1 cup soft butter
3 cups confectioners sugar
2 T. apple cider
1/2 cup Macoun or Macintosh apples, chopped fine
1 cup pecans, chopped fine
2 -1/4 cups flour
1 tsp each baking powder and baking soda
3/4 tsp salt

Cream butter with 2 cups sugar until fluffy. Beat in cider, apples, pecans and salt. Add flour, baking powder and soda. Mix well. Cover dough and chill overnight. Let stand at room temperature until just pliable and form into 3/4" balls. Place on lightly greased and floured baking sheet, 1 "apart. Flatten slightly with back of spoon to make small discs. Bake 375 12 to 15 minutes until bottom is pale gold, test one. Roll cookies in remaining confectioners sugar in a shallow dish as they come out of oven. Cool on a rack and roll in sugar again. Store in air tight container with a chunk of unpeeled apple in it. Makes about 60 more or less depending upon size. Very fragile, best small.

LEA'S APPLESAUCE GINGERBREAD

1 cup butter
1 cup brown sugar
1/2 cup molasses
2 large eggs
1 cup homemade applesauce
(OR variation: 1 cup blueberries and dribble of orange juice instead)
2 cups flour
2 tsp baking powder
2 tsp baking soda
2 T. grated fresh ginger or 2 tsp ground ginger
1 tsp each cinnamon and nutmeg
sugar to sprinkle on top before baking

Grease and flour a 9" X 13" pan. Melt butter, pour into bowl, beat in brown sugar and molasses, add eggs one at a time and beat. Stir in applesauce. Sift dry ingredients together, stir into applesauce mixture. Beat well. Pour into baking dish and sprinkle with sugar. Bake 350 for 35 minutes or until silver knife inserted in center comes out clean. Cool 5 minutes in pan then turn out and cool completely or serve warm. Cut in squares and top with sweetened whipped cream flavored with almond and vanilla, (or vanilla ice cream.) Not quite Peggy's Cove, but close.) Makes 24 small or 16 large squares.

TONY'S APRICOT-PISTACHIO BISCOTTI

1-1/3 cups all purpose flour
1 tsp baking powder
1/4 tsp salt
4 T. sweet butter
3/4 cup plus 1 T. sugar
2 tsp vanilla
1 tsp almond flavoring
2 eggs
1 cup; unsalted pistachio nuts
1/2 cup chopped dried apricots (fluffed up in hot water and drained.)

Preheat oven to 350. Line baking sheet with foil, shiny side up. Sift flour, baking powder and salt. Beat butter, eggs, sugar and flavorings together until well blended. Stir in nuts and apricots. (Of course may substitute chopped pecans, walnuts, or macadamia nuts, pistachio are traditional) Gradually beat in flour mixture.

Turn dough out on a floured surface and divide in half. Flour hands. Shape each half into a log 12" long and 2" wide. Place logs on baking sheet 3" apart. Bake 20 to 25 minutes at 350 until tops are golden and feel firm. Place baking sheet on a rack and let cool for 10 minutes. Lower oven temperature to 300. With a wide spatula transfer logs to a cutting board and slice diagonally into 1" slices. Set biscotti, cut side down on baking sheet, bake 300 for 10 minutes. Turn over, bake 10 more minutes, to a pale gold. Cool on rack. Store in airtight tin. Should be fairly hard to dunk in coffee or wine. Will keep for 2 to 3 weeks. ("Mine won't," boasted Tony shamelessly, "They'll all be eaten up by the second day.")

LUCY'S DOG BISCUITS

3-1/2 cups flour
2 cups whole wheat flour
1 cup rye flour
1 cup cornmeal
2 cups bulgar
1/2 cup dry milk
2 tsp salt
1 pkg dry yeast
1/4 cup warm water
3 cups chicken broth
3 T. butter
1 egg beaten with 1 tsp water
OPTIONAL - Add some, about 6 T. of YOUR dog's favorite foods. Lucy liked =
2 T. honey
4 T. grated hard cheese

Mix first 7 ingredients together. Dissolve yeast in warm water and add. Add chicken broth just until dough forms. Roll out on floured board 1/4 to 1/2" thick. Use a large commercial dog biscuit for a template and cut out bone shapes. Place on greased baking sheet and brush with an egg and water glaze. Bake at 300 for 45 minutes. Turn biscuits over and leave to harden in cold oven overnight or several hours.

(Lucy found these so delectable and made them look so tempting Lea and Tony could not resist a trial. Lea gagged and made a horrible face. Tony said, "They're not bad, really, let's serve them at our next party?" Lea said, "Tony, what a horrible thought! Unless we invite just dogs? We could have a birthday party for Lucy."

AUNT MAE'S MELT- IN- YOUR- MOUTH BLUEBERRY CAKE

1-1/2 cups flour
1 tsp baking powder
1/2 tsp salt
2 large eggs, separated
1/4 cup butter
1 cup sugar
2/3 cup whole milk
1/2 tsp each vanilla and almond flavoring
1-3/4 cup floured blueberries

Sift flour, baking powder and salt together three times! Beat egg whites stiff and set aside. Cream butter with sugar, add egg yolks. Alternately beat flour mixture and milk into butter mixture. Fold in flavorings. Gently fold in beaten egg whites. Last, fold in the lightly floured fruit. (Sometimes Aunt Mae used fresh peaches, blackberries or raspberries, in season) Spoon into greased and floured Bundt pan, a tube pan, or 9" X 9" pan. Sprinkle top with sugar. Bake at 350 for 40 to 45 minutes until tests done with a toothpick or silver knife inserted. While hot, sprinkle on more sugar. Cool in pan 5 minutes. Remove. Makes 16 pieces. (Devour a feather light and lovely blueberry cake!)

(TIP: Separating the eggs, folding in beaten whites is the secret. May apply this to almost any cake recipe to improve the texture and lightness.)

SIRI'S FINNISH SWEET BREAD (Coffee cake)

1 1/4 cups milk TOPPING
1 PKG dry yeast dissolved in2 tsp ground cinnamon
1/4 cup warm water2 T. sugar
(Hot liquid will kill yeast)1/2 cup chopped almonds3/4 cup sugar
6-1/4 cups sifted all purpose flour
1/2 cup soft butter
1/4 tsp salt
3 egg yolks
3 tsp ground cardamon

CAKE: Scald milk and cool to lukewarm. (Do not use it hot) Dissolve yeast in luke warm water. Add to warm milk with 1 T. sugar. Beat in 3 cups flour. Reserve remaining flour for kneading. Cover, let rise until double in bulk, about 1 or 1-1/2 hours. Turn dough onto a floured board and knead and knead and punch down and knead with floured hands until smooth and elastic. Place in a greased bowl, turning dough around to grease all sides. Cover once more and let rise a 2nd time until double in bulk. (Perhaps another hour) Divide risen dough to make two cakes. Divide again each half into three pieces. Roll each piece into a strip 16" long. Pinch three pieces together at end and braid.

(This part is fun,) Pinch ends together. Place cakes on ungreased baking sheet. Cover and let rise for a third time until double, perhaps 45 minutes. Preheat oven to 375.

TOPPING: Combine sugar, cinnamon and nuts. Brush with milk, sprinkle on topping and bake 25 to 30 minutes. Each cake makes 5 or 6 servings, may freeze one.

(While Lea waits through three risings, starting in early morning, she takes Lucy for a walk or a paddle in Katie, the kayak. Or she paints. You could also chat on telephone? TIP: Despite the necessary pauses for rising it is a relatively easy cake to make and finished result LOOKS complicated. "Yeast coffee cake is always better than a quick bread," Siri told her daughters, Lea and Pat. "Just find something else to do while it's rising.")

With cake and cookies Lea often served a simple sorbet-

LEA'S AKVAVIT SORBET

2-1/2 cups Akvavit (or Vodka)
1-1/3 cup sugar
1 cup fresh lime or lemon juice
1/2 cup water

Process all in blender or beat smooth. Pour into 2 refrigerator trays and freeze. Makes one quart. (Lea does not own an ice cream maker, If you lucky ducks do? by all means use it!) A scoop of sorbet on a glass plate with a cookie is a pretty and refreshing and light dessert with which to close a heavy meal.

TONY'S GARLIC BREAD (SEE SOUPS AND CHOWDERS)
SARAH'S PERFECT POPOVERS

2 eggs
1 cup whole milk
1 T. melted butter
1 cup all purpose flour
1/4 tsp salt

Preheat oven to 450. Beat eggs until light. Add next 4 ingredients until just blended. (30 seconds in electric beater!) Batter should be like heavy cream. If necessary add more milk. Pour into muffin tins or custard cups about 2/3 full. Bake 20 minutes, WITHOUT OPENING OVEN DOOR reduce heat to 350 and bake 20 more minutes. Makes 8 to 12.

(TIP: Sarah's popovers are "perfect" because they are crisp on the outside and tender and moist inside. Her secret is she does NOT OVER BEAT the batter and she does not open oven door when baking. She also tests one before she removes them from oven to be sure are thoroughly baked. She told admiring Lea, "They are really super simple to make, IF you follow my directions!")

SYLVIA'S MOTHER'S RASPBERRY CHEESE CAKE

CRUST:

1-3/4 cups graham cracker crumbs
1/2 cup sugar
1/4 cup chopped nuts
1 tsp cinnamon
1/2 cup butter

Combine ingredients and press into 8" spring form pan, on bottom and up the sides. (Or purchase ready made graham cracker pie crust.)

FILLING:

3 eggs
16 oz cream cheese (2- 8 oz. pkgs)
1 cup sugar
2 tsp vanilla
dash salt
3 cups sour cream
(Optional: 1 tsp crumbled fresh lavender. The secret ingredient!)

Mix eggs, soft cream cheese, sugar, vanilla, salt and sour cream until smooth. Stir in lavender. Pour into crust lined pan. Bake 325 for 45 minutes or until firm (will still wiggle a bit.) Remove and cool, spread cooled topping on cooled cake.

TOPPING:

1 10 oz. pkg. frozen raspberries (or fresh sweetened raspberries)
1 T. cornstarch

Heat raspberries and corn starch until thick. Cool. (TIP: Important to spread on top of cheesecake AFTER BOTH CAKE AND TOPPING HAVE COOLED.) Refrigerate and chill several hours before serving. Serves 12. Garnish with fresh raspberries and mint leaves dusted with confectioners sugar in a ring around cheese cake.

May vary fruit toppings, use frozen or sweetened fresh strawberries, blackberries, cherries or canned crushed pineapple. Overlap slices of banana, kiwi or sweetened fresh or canned peaches. This was one of the few things Sylvia knew how to cook, but it was a winner!

LEA'S FINNISH WEDDING CAKE WITH CHERRY HEERING ICING

1 cup butter
1 cup sugar
4 eggs, separated
1 tsp almond flavoring, 1 tsp vanilla flavoring
1 cup blanched almonds, ground fine
1 cup sifted flour
1/2 tsp baking powder
1 cup whipped heavy cream flavored with Cherry Heering liqueur (Or Grand Marnier)

Preheat oven 350. Cream sugar and butter together. Beat in egg yolks one at a time, beat well after each addition. Stir in ground almonds and flavorings. Sift flour and baking powder together and gradually stir into batter. Beat egg whites stiff, fold into batter. Bake in 3 - 8" buttered and floured cake pans until golden, approximately 30 minutes. Cool 5 minutes before removing from pans.

Whip heavy cream, add 1 tsp almond flavor. Slowly fold in 2 oz liqueur of choice. Spread whipped cream between cooled cakes and cover sides and top. (TIP: DO AT LAST MINUTE or cream will fall. Can have it whipped and ready in refrigerator.)

Decorate wedding cake with slivered almonds, candied violets and a miniature bride and groom. In Iceland this cake is made with strawberry jam spread on cake layers and plain whipped cream on top and the sides. You can vary by using apricot or raspberry preserves or jam. (Finns prefer it jamless)

Lea made her own wedding cake, a family custom in Scandinavian countries. Who could do it better than the bride-to-be who presumably had been taught well by her mother?

This is a beautiful cake that it is not over sweet. It must be eaten at the wedding feast and not brought home in stupid little boxes as it is much too delectable when fresh to allow it to stale. Cherry preserves or jam can be used if desire a pronounced (along with the cherry liqueur) strong cherry-almond flavor. Lea preferred it to be more subtle so used only the Cherry Heering and almond for flavoring as Siri, her mother, and Eleanora, Siri's mother had done before her.

A few years later for Claire and Abe's wedding Lea made it with the orange flavored Grand Marnier and stirred 2 T. orange marmalade into the whipped cream icing because Abe said he preferred orange to cherry flavor. Candied orange peel decorated the cake instead of violets. Abe loved it and Claire did as well, mostly because Lea had made it especially for them.

FINNISH MAY DAY CRULLERS AND SIMA

CRULLERS:

3 eggs
5 T. sugar
1-3/4 cup sifted flour
1 cup heavy cream
Confectioners sugar
Fat or vegetable oil for deep frying

Beat eggs with sugar until thick. Stir in flour and cream alternately. Beat until smooth. Heat frying oil or fat to 380. (TIP: Test with a bit of dough, if hot enough dough will rise to the surface. If not hot enough crullers will soak up the taste of grease.)

Spoon batter into a pastry tube, squeeze a circle in a crisscross stream the size of a doughnut. (Making a sort of figure 8.) Fry on each side until browned, about 2 or 3 minutes. Drain on paper towels and sprinkle with confectioners sugar. Serve crullers hot with "Sima" (TIP: Easily make a pastry tube from foil or waxed paper rolled into a cornucopia. Fold one end

BETTIE HAMILTON

under to keep batter in and cut other end off to squeeze
batter through into hot fat.)

FINNISH SIMA, THE MAY DAY DRINK

1 lemon
4 quarts water
2-1/8 cups sugar
2 cups lt. brown sugar
1 12 oz. can beer
1/4 tsp dry yeast
Raisins

Pare off yellow rind of lemon and reserve. Peel
off white part and discard. Slice lemon, remove seeds.
In a large kettle (or an enamel bucket) combine water,
2 cups each of sugars, lemon slices and the lemon peel.
Bring to a boil. Remove and add beer. Cool mixture
to lukewarm. Dissolve yeast into 1/2 cup of the warm,
not hot, mixture and stir into the brew. Cover tightly.
Let stand overnight at room temperature. Strain Sima.
Prepare four 1 quart bottles, rinsing with boiling water
to sterilize. Place 1/2 tsp. sugar and 3 or 4 raisins in
each bottle. Fill with Sima and cap bottles. Store in a
cool place. When the raisins rise to the surface the
Sima is ready. Chill to serve. Makes one gallon.

(May Day, the first day of May, is a traditional
Finnish holiday. Schools and businesses and
municipal offices are closed for the day. Students put
on their traditional white caps showing they have
graduated from high school or university or are at
present a student. There is general rejoicing with great

dancing, singing and drinking of Sima with crullers. Sima is a slightly acidic, refreshing kind of lemonade with a little kick to it. One would have to drink a great deal of it to become intoxicated although the younger students enjoy pretending they are to shock their elders. The latter are mostly amused as they had done the same in their young student days. Finns put great store on education even to making a holiday to honor students.)

JULIA'S JOE FROGGER COOKIES

1/2 cup butter
1/3 cup brown sugar
1 slightly beaten egg
1/2 cup molasses
1/4 cup rum (or more to taste)
2 cups flour
1/2 tsp salt
2 tsp ground ginger
1/2 tsp cinnamon
1 tsp baking soda

Cream first two ingredients together. Add egg, molasses and rum. Sift together and add last five ingredients. Drop by large soup or serving spoon onto buttered and floured cookie sheet. Bake 10 minutes at 375. Makes 25 to 30 large Joe Froggers. Wrap individually and store in a covered tin. May freeze.

(Tony and Lea often walked Lucy up Gingerbread Hill, past Black Joe's Pond and Tavern. Joseph Brown, an African American, was a respected

Revolutionary War Hero. He and his wife were famed for their outsized, rum flavored cookies served in the tavern to dunk in ale, and also sold individually.

One can only surmise the name came from the many frogs in the pond beside their tavern and his name, Joe? Joe Froggers are an old, Marblehead tradition, still made and enjoyed today by 'headers. They were always great big, round cookies not at all frog shaped. It is only conjecture and highly debatable that in those days "froggers" was a slang term for any large item as some said early writers referred to anything or person oversized as a "frogger." Then again some think Joe caught frogs in the adjacent pond to cook up their legs for the tavern menu and he might have been nicknamed "Joe Frogger"?

When his wife made huge molasses cookies, perhaps because it was easier than cutting out a lot of small ones, they were dubbed Joe Froggers and still are to this day and no one really knows why. In any case Joe Froggers are a large, wonderfully tasty, rather hard cookie to take on a fishing trip or a picnic. They are even better and softer when you double the rum, old timers say. They claim the cookies got harder when thrifty Joe made his wife cut back on the amount of rum she put in them. Will made sure Julia put plenty of rum in the batter. There are many recipes claiming to be the original one but all are similar- molasses, brown sugar, ginger and rum being the essential ingredients. Will said, "It's the ratio of rum to the rest of the stuff that's important, Julia, so don't be stingy." He'd add more when her back was turned to insure an authentic Joe Frogger.)

SIRI'S PINEAPPLE UPSIDE DOWN CAKE

1 box of white or yellow cake mix (or a simple home made white cake)
1 cup brown sugar
Pecans
Maraschino cherries
1 large and 1 small can sliced pineapple rings

In a heavy fry pan or skillet melt butter and spread brown sugar over it evenly. Sprinkle with pecans. Lay pineapple rings close together with a cherry in center of each ring. Cover with the cake batter, use some of pineapple juice for the liquid called for in the cake mix. Bake 400 for 35 minutes until top (which will be the bottom!) is crusty and brown. Invert the pan and turn out on serving plate immediately with the pineapple now on the top. Serve with whipped cream or ice cream. Serves 6 happy guests who recall their mothers used to bake this when they were kids. One of Lea's guests insisted his mother served it with the pineapple on the BOTTOM and that was why it was called upside down cake! (No one agreed with that version but didn't want to say out loud his Mom was one dumb lady.) Very easy cake to make, nostalgia makes it taste great, too.

Variations: Make with 2 cups cut up sweetened rhubarb, or fresh inverted peach halves, apple slices (sugared), fresh whole, pitted sweet cherries or fresh strawberries. Try it with sweetened blueberries, raspberries, blackberries or all three. (Then it's called a JUMBLEBERRY CAKE.)

Whichever fruit used, the romance and the challenge lies in turning it out upside down in one piece.

SIRI'S FINNISH SPINACH PANCAKES

(This plain batter may also be used for waffles with blueberries, strawberries or lingonberries folded into the batter.)

1 cup milk
1 tsp salt
1/8 tsp nutmeg
1 cup flour
2 T. melted butter
2 eggs
1 tsp sugar
1/2 lb fresh spinach, blanched and chopped or 1 thawed pkg frozen chopped spinach drained
Butter to cook in

Season milk with salt and nutmeg. Sift flour in a little at a time, beat constantly. Stir in melted butter. (IMPORTANT TIP: Let stand for one hour.) Beat eggs with sugar and stir into batter. Add spinach. Prepare and cook pancakes as usual in hot buttered saute pan. Make small and thin and cook them through. In Finland they are served with lingonberries. Choose any berry you prefer.

(A fine luncheon entree with a salad, these were a favorite of Lea's bud Sarah. Every time Lea

made them she thought fondly of Sarah who called
them "The spinach-in-my-teeth pancakes.")

NORA'S AUSSIE CREAM SCONES WITH
RASPBERRY PRESERVES

2 cups flour
4 tsp baking powder
2 tsp sugar
1/8 tsp salt
4 T. butter
2 eggs
1/2 cup cream
Raspberry jam

Sift together flour, baking powder and salt.
Work in butter with fingertips (or a fork if squeamish)
Break 2 eggs iln separate bowl, reserve some white for
topping. Beat eggs with cream, add to flour mixture.
Turn out on floured board and knead lightly 1/2
minute. Pat and roll into an oblong 3/4" thick.
Cut into diamond shapes with diagonal cuts of sharp
knife. Brush with reserved egg white diluted with 1
tsp water. Sprinkle with sugar. Bake 450 for 15
minutes. (TIP: Dough should be firm but soft.) Makes
12.
Remove hot scones, split and butter
immediately. Cover one half with raspberry preserves
or jam and some sweetened, whipped heavy cream.
Place other half over this.
Cover with whipped cream and drop a dollop
of jam on top. May use fresh raspberries in season.

("Scons" as the Aussies call them (like fauns, or lawns) not "scones" (as in moans or tones) are definitely NOT diet food, Nora discovered after gaining several pounds when making "scons" her lunch at a teahouse or milk bar in the mistaken idea she wasn't eating much.)

DESSERTS

UNCLE BILL'S SNOW APPLE PIE (FAMEUSE)
(An apple variety that came down from Canada to New England)

Pastry for two crust pie
Peeled and sliced Snow Apples enough to fill bottom crust heaping high. (TIP: will shrink in baking. Hard apples such as Cortland, Northern Spy, Baldwin, Granny Smith all good pie apples. Macs, a delicious eating apple and their kin are too soft and mush up in baking.)
1-1/2 cups sugar, to taste
1 tsp nutmeg
1 T. cinnamon
Dribble cider (or apple juice)
1 tsp lemon juice
1 4 oz. stick butter

Mix sugar, nutmeg, cinnamon together. Pour over apple slices heaped in bottom crust. Dot with half the butter and dribble in lemon and juice. Fit top crust over apples. Pinch edges to seal. Slash in steam vents. Sprinkle the top with more sugar, nutmeg and cinnamon. Thickly dot with remaining butter. Bake at 400 10 minutes to set crust and avoid sogginess. Reduce to 325 bake 30 or plus minutes until pie golden and juices are coming up, apples are fork tender but not mushy. Serves 6. Bill ate pie with breakfast.

(When a child, Lea would climb into Uncle Bill's hammock under the Snow Apple tree and read his Western Adventure magazines while munching on the small, pink fleshed

Snow apples she reached out to pick with one hand, holding the magazine with the other.)

AUNT SOLVEIGH'S BROWNIE CASHEW PIE

1 cup unsalted cashew nuts (may substitute pecans)
1 unbaked 9" pie shell
2 oz unsweetened baking chocolate
1 T. butter
8 oz (1/2 bottle) dark corn syrup, Karo.
3 well beaten eggs
1/8 tsp salt
1 tsp vanilla flavoring

Sprinkle nuts in pie shell. Melt chocolate and butter together on low. Combine corn syrup, eggs, salt and vanilla, mix well. Pour over the nuts. Bake 450 10 minutes to set crust. Reduce to 350, bake 30 minutes more or until knife comes out clean inserted in center. French vanilla homemade ice cream goes very well with Brownie Pie.

(This was Nora's birthday pie, all the family eschewed birthday cakes in favor of a favorite pie)

SIRI'S CARAMEL CUSTARD

1 pint heavy cream
8 egg yolks or 4 whole eggs
1/4 cup brown sugar
1/4 tsp salt

Scald heavy cream in a double boiler. Beat eggs, brown sugar and salt smooth. Add cream slowly to egg mixture. Bake in a shallow heat proof pan or individual custard cups in water bath until custard set, about 30 minutes at 350. After chilling custard sprinkle 1/4 cup brown sugar over top, run under broiler to glaze. Rechill to make glaze crackly.

(Siri never knew this was called Creme Brulee and was of French origin. All the Scandinavian countries made it and considered it theirs. You had to be her sick child and an invalid who needed to be coaxed to take sustenance in order to be the recipient of Siri's caramel custard! She did not take lightly using a pint of heavy cream and 8 egg yolks and discarding the whites! But she loved her children and they were worth it.)

LEA'S SPICED PECANS

1 lb raw pecans
1/2 tsp garlic powder
1/3 cup (5 T.) melted butter
1/2 tsp Tabasco Sauce

1 T. Worcestershire Sauce
1 tsp salt
1/4 tsp white pepper

Mix last six ingredients together and pour over pecans spread out on a baking sheet. Set oven at 300. Set timer, turn and stir nuts every five minutes for four times.

(TIP: Be careful not to scorch!) Cool. Store in covered containers. May use as gifts or as an appetizer. They are not the usual sweet, spiced pecans.)

LEA'S CHRISTMAS CARAMELS

1 cup butter
1 lb brown sugar (2-1/2 cups)
1 cup light corn syrup Karo, about 1/2 bottle
1 15 oz can sweetened condensed milk (NOT evaporated)
1 tsp vanilla or rum flavoring
chopped nuts, if desired

Melt butter in heavy 3-quart skillet. Add sugar and salt and stir. Add corn syrup. Mix well. Over medium heat gradually add milk. STIR AND STIR AND STIR! Cook to firm ball stage. (Test by dropping a little into a glass of cold water and form ball with fingers.) Cook and stir about 20 minutes. Remove and stir in flavoring. Pour (should go thickly) into a buttered 9" X 9" X 2" brownie pan. Cool and cut into squares. Wrap in squares of waxed paper (or red and green foil) twisting ends. Store in covered tin.

(TIP: Wrapping is the hardest part, most tedious of all. If possible con another to do it!) Most important- be sure to cook to the firm ball stage; undercooked will be runny, overcooked rock hard.)

Nora asked for Lea's recipes for Christmas Caramels and Spiced Pecans to make for gifts for special occasions. Since Lea habitually was short of ready cash yet loved giving gifts she made caramels and pecans, placed them in pretty jars or boxes with a ribbon tied around them. Nora, who was also often short of money wanted to carry on this tradition in Australia for her friends.

She wrote, "Please, please send recipes! I remember how the recipients over the years loved getting these goodies and even hinted for them. I know all your friends preferred them to store bought presents."

Making these treats was a labor of love on Lea's part and not truly as inexpensive to make as Nora thought.

SIRI'S FLUFFY LEMON DELIGHT

5 eggs, separated
1/2 cup sugar
2 T. unflavored gelatin (Knox)
1/4 cup ice water
Juice from 3 fresh lemons, and the grated rind
1 thin sliced seeded lemon

Beat yolks with sugar until thick and lemon colored. Soften gelatin in water for 5 minutes, heat over hot water stirring until dissolved in double boiler. Add gelatin to lemon juice and rind. Stir this mixture into the egg mixture. Beat egg whites to firm peaks. Fold into lemon mixture. Pour into 1 quart pretty glass bowl over thin sliced lemon slices.

Chill in refrigerator until set. (A perfect ending for any hearty or heavy meal, a kind of lemon floating island.)

LEA'S PASTRY FOR TWO-CRUST 9' PIES

2-1/2 cups sifted all purpose flour
1 tsp baking powder
2 tsp vanilla
2 eggs
1 cup butter
1/2 cup sugar

Sift flour and baking powder together. Make a well in center, place sugar, vanilla and eggs in it. From the sides mix in a little flour until it forms a thick, creamy paste. Cut butter into small pieces and place on top. Knead gently until smooth. Divide into two balls, wrap in Saran and refrigerate.

When ready to assemble a pie roll balls out for two crusts. May cut one in strips for a lattice top crust. To top pie the Scandinavian and German way is to sprinkle sugar, cinnamon and nutmeg over it and dot with butter. (The rest of the world brushes top with milk which to Lea always looked naked.)

BETTIE HAMILTON

LEA'S AKAVIT SORBET (SEE BREADS, CAKES, COOKIES)

To accompany cakes or cookies.

LEA'S STRAWBERRY PIE

Pastry for 9" 2 crust pie
5 cups sliced fresh strawberries
3/4 cup sugar
2-1/2 T. cornstarch

Gently mix strawberries, sugar and cornstarch together. Pour into bottom crust in pie plate. Roll out remaining dough and cut into strips. Weave a lattice top, pinch and seal edges. Sprinkle on sugar, nutmeg and cinnamon and dot with butter. Bake 425 for 20 minutes. Reduce oven to 375, bake an additional 25 minutes or until golden and juices coming up. Serves 6. Serve each piece with a blob of whipped cream or ice cream with a whole fresh strawberry with cap, on top. (Or may serve whipped cream or ice cream in a separate bowl with several whole capped strawberries on top.) Serves 6. (Einar and the children with Siri abstaining. "I bake 'em, I don't eat "em", she avowed to be sure there was enough to go around.

(The twins always asked for this pie on their mutual birthday. Pat and Lea opted for Brownie Pie, John Peder changed his order every year, from Lemon Meringue to Uncle Bill's Snow Apple Pie or Brownie

314

or Strawberry Pies. When he blew out his candles on the lemon pie and plastered the meringue all over the dining room wall his mother told him, ("No more lemon meringue pie for you!")

(TIP: It is difficult to put birthday candles on some pies, so Siri finally bought a single fat token candle and placed it beside the pie to be blown out by the birthday child. She wanted no more meringue stuck to the dining room wallpaper!)

ENTREES

LEA'S BOSTON BAKED BEANS

3 kinds of beans (pea, kidney and soldier beans)
1 cup each, soaked overnight
Chunk salt pork
1 whole yellow onion
3/4 cup each of molasses, cider and water to make 2 cups liquid, mixed
1/2 cup brown sugar
3 T. prepared mustard
Dash Worcestershire Sauce, salt and pepper and maple syrup to glaze top

Score salt pork, place in bottom of bean pot. Rinse and blow off peels of soaked beans. Reserve a little of liquid to add to molasses, cider and water mixture. Bury a large, scored onion in the beans in in pot and pour liquid over, adding more when necessary. Cook, covered in low 275 oven for about two hours until beans are tender, not mushy. Remove cover, pour a dollop of genuine maple syrup over beans and glaze in 350 oven for about five minutes.

Serve with warmed brown bread, Lea's pepper relish, mustard and catsup to taste. Frankforts boiled just until skins burst are a traditional accompaniment in New England although some prefer a slice of baked ham or fried fish cakes with the beans or a hamburger patty or steak. This is the staple Saturday night supper for New Englanders (where baked beans are known as "the musical fruit".) Cole slaw is served as the vegetable, making an easy meal to put together. Serves 6 to 8.

COLE SLAW

Chop 1/2 cabbage, 2 carrots and 1 onion. Mix with mayonnaise thinned with lemon juice.
Season with celery seed and salt and pepper. May double.

LEA'S POACHED CHICKEN WITH HERBS

2 boned and skinned chicken breasts
1/2 bottle white wine and juice of 1 lemon
Fresh herbs, such as listed below or your choice, 3 garlic cloves

Place chicken in skillet on top of stove in wine and lemon juice. Add water to cover. Add to liquid, 1 or 2 Bay Leaves, (remove at end) mint leaves, sprigs of fresh dill and basil, tarragon, rosemary, garlic cloves, salt and pepper. Simmer low until tender, basting occasionally, uncovered. Drain off marinade and chill chicken. Slice to serve for a cold supper with sliced tomatoes, cucumbers and green pepper rings on a platter. May cut poached chicken with bits of herbs clinging to it into chunks for chicken salad. Also the herbed, cooked chicken can be used for chicken a la King, with mushrooms and green and red peppers in a cream sauce. Use pre-poached, herbed chicken whenever cooked chicken is called for in a recipe. Serves 4 to 6.

FINNISH BAKED CHICKEN WITH ALMONDS, GRAPES AND HAVARTI CHEESE

4 skinned, boned chicken breasts
Minced garlic, salt and hot red pepper flakes
3 T. butter, softened
1 2-1/4 oz package slivered almonds
1-1/2 cups seedless green grapes
1-1/2 cups milk
1 T. cornstarch
8 oz. Havarti cheese

Mash together garlic, salt, red pepper and butter and spread on chicken. Brown in butter on both sides Saute almonds in drippings. Sprinkle over chicken. Bake 350 for 40 to 45 minutes. Turn off oven, and arrange green grapes over chicken and keep warm in oven while making sauce from the last three ingredients. Stir cornstarch into milk, add cheese gradually in small pieces over low heat until melted.

Cook, stirring until thick. Pour over chicken and grapes. Serve with brown rice. Serves 4.

(This was much beloved by Nora, who called it "Hot Grapes" when little. She asked for the recipe to make it for Rod who was properly impressed. She wrote, "Now Rod thinks I can really cook, ha ha!" (TIP: Since the cheese sauce is mild and bland, the cayenne or red pepper flakes pep it up, may add more to taste if desire.)

TONY'S ITALIAN GRILLED CHICKEN WITH OLIVES AND LEMONS
2 quartered 3-lb chickens (or whole Cornish Game Hens)

2 thin sliced lemons
12 (YES, 12!) cloves smashed or minced garlic
1 cup Virgin olive oil
1/2 cup brandy, cognac or apple jack
salt and pepper, sprinkle of capers
1 cup black or Nicoise olives
1/2 cup Spanish or green olives

Marinate chicken overnight, or all day, in lemons, garlic, oil, brandy and salt and pepper. Keep refrigerated, occasionally turn. Remove chicken and grilll luntil juices run clear when piercing thick part of a thigh. Bring marinade to a boil and simmer with olives five minutes. (Health TIP: Safest way is to discard first marinade, make another and simmer with olives.) Serve on a platter with the olive mixture and capers spooned over chicken pieces.

(At first Lea frowned at the combination of olives with chicken and what seemed an exorbitant amount of garlic, which she found mellowed in cooking. She became an immediate convert and to his smug satisfaction appropriated Tony's recipe for her own earning their friends enthusiastic praise. Lea blandly took the credit to Tony's amusement but he said nothing. It tickled him.)

SCANDINAVIAN FRICADELLER (for meat loaf or meat balls)

1/2 lb each pork, veal, beef, ground fine
1/2 cup flour
1 egg
1 small grated onion
1 tsp grated lemon rind
1 tsp nutmeg
Salt and pepper
1/2 cup club soda (or ice water is next best)
4 T. butter
Scant 3/4 cup light cream for gravy

Combine meat, flour, egg, onion, lemon rind, salt, pepper and nutmeg. Blend lightly, do NOT over handle. Stir in club soda. (TIP: It makes the meat loaf or meatballs light and fluffy and fly-away.) Shape into a loaf, place in buttered loaf pan, Bake 350 for 45 minutes, test for doneness, red color gone. Or shape into small meat balls and brown in butter, top of stove, on all sides, lower heat, cook 20 minutes until done.
CREAM GRAVY

To the juices add cream, stirring, bring to a boil for traditional Scandinavian cream gravy. Makes 20 small meatballs for an appetizer kept hot with cream gravy in chafing dish. Meat loaf serves 6 to 8. May use combination of ground meats you prefer. This is the authentic, well-known Finnish, Swedish or Danish recipe for meat balls.

RAY'S CHEAPIE MEAT LOAF WITH TOMATO SOUP

3 or 4 slices of day old bread marked down in price, or stale frankfort rolls
1/2 cup milk
2 lbs inexpensive ground beef, (hamburger)
1 egg or 2 T. mayonnaise
1 large yellow onion, chopped
1/2 tsp garlic powder, salt and pepper
Dash Worcestershire Sauce

Soak bread in milk and squeeze out. Mix all together with your hands lightly. Press into a greased loaf pan. Top with pieces of salt pork or slice of bacon. Sprinkle with paprika to help browning. Let stand for 10 minutes. Bake in a pan of water at 350 for 45 minutes to an hour. Remove from oven, pour fat off into sink. Return to oven covered with one undiluted can of store brand tomato soup, let it heat a few minutes. Don't waste any, rinse can out with a little water! Serve with a quick cooking packaged rice or a baked potato that can go in oven with the meat loaf. Use the cheapest canned vegetable to accompany meal, such as canned beets or peas and carrots.

(Lea includes this recipe as some women out there might be saving the grocery money to make their escape as she did and because, actually, it's not half bad. However, Fricadeller is the best, any day in the week.)

TONY'S MUSHROOM OMELET

4 eggs
salt and pepper
4 T. water
1 cup fresh chopped mushrooms
Minced scallion and pimiento to taste
(Optional: 1/4 cup any grated cheese)
Butter to cook

Whisk all ingredients together and stir in mushrooms. Slide into melted butter in omelet pan, cook and flip over to platter. Serves 2. Double recipe for 4. Serve with raisin toast or English muffins and marmalade. Adding cheese is a good option but Tony preferred mushrooms to dominate.

Lea also liked his PROSCIUTTO AND CHEESE OMELET

Substitute smoked ham slices for mushrooms, lay cheese slice over it and fold omelet as usual. (TIP: Use water instead of milk for a better omelet. In ham and cheese, use large slices and do not chop up ham or cheese.)

MARIA'S SICILIAN PASTA WITH ASPARAGUS AND PROSCIUTTO

1 lb asparagus, trimmed, cut into 1" pieces
1/4 cup Virgin olive oil
4 T. butter
4 thin sliced scallions
1/4 lb prosciutto, cut into matchsticks
3 T. tomato sauce, or 2 fresh chopped seeded tomatoes
1 lb pasta (penne, angel hair, twists, elbow, linguini or spaghetti) your choice
3/4 lb grated Parmesan cheese

Cook asparagus in boilling salted and sugared water for two minutes or until just tender, drain and reserve. Heat oil and butter together. Cook scallions in it over medium, three minutes. Stir in ham, tomato and salt and pepper. Simmer five minutes, stir occasionally. Remove from stove and stir in asparagus.

Cook pasta in large pot of salted water until al dente, about six minutes. Remove and reserve one cup of water. Drain pasta. Add to the tomato mixture. Thin saauce with pasta water a little at a time. Season. Sprinkle with Parmesan cheese.

(TIP: Of course Maria's pasta was always cooked al dente with a bite to it. Tony liked his a little more cooked but never told Maria who doted on him and taught him to cook so well. Sometimes Maria made this dish with fresh broccoli florets. Lea found the colors and textures in this dish artistically appealing, a feast for the eyes as well as the belly.)

Maria made another dish with 2 cups of heavy cream, peas, prosciutto or panetta and 2 lbs of cheese tortelloni. The simmered cream, 2 T. flour and 2 T. butter sauce was cooked until thick, then poured over cooked tortelloni. Julienned strips of smoked meat and cup of blanched peas were stirred into it and all covered with grated cheese and more julienne strips of meat. (May omit for vegetarians) Bake 375 for 20 minutes Tony's favorites were from Maria, Nonna's Sicilian cook who thriftily combined pasta, vegetables and a little smoked meat, prosciutto or pancetta, with a sauce and cheese into delicious casseroles.

LEA'S BAKED STUFFED SIRLOIN PEPPERS WITH PINE NUTS

1 each of large red, green and yellow peppers
1/4 cup pine nuts
1 cup garlic and cheese croutons
1-1/2 lbs chopped sirloin
1 egg
1/2 lb sauteed fresh mushrooms
Salt and pepper, dash red pepper flakes
Grated Romano cheese to top
Can V-8, or tomato juice or red wine

Seed peppers, core and halve lengthwise. Parboil a few minutes, not too long. Mix all ingredients together with a light hand and stuff the pepper halves loosely. Sprinkle Romano cheese over them. Place in baking dish, pour can of V-8 or tomato juice around them or some red wine to keep from

BETTIE HAMILTON

sticking to pan. Cover dish with foil. Bake 350 about
25 minutes. Test for doneness, best when a bit rare.
Uncover to brown the tops. Serve two halves of
different colored peppers on beds of chopped,.
buttered spinach. Spoon some of remaining liquid
over. May serve with rice and Lea's tomato sauce in
separate bowls. Serves three, or if serve one half
apiece, six! (Stuff four peppers for 4 or 8. Red, yellow
and two green.)

ANY FISH BAKED, BROILED, GRILLED OR POACHED, LEA'S STYLE

Lea's way is to first squeeze fresh lemon juice
over skinned boned fish fillet. Coat with mayonnaise
and sprinkle with garlic and chopped fresh herbs: dill,
parsley, basil, tarragon and rosemary. Add buttered
crumbs and a dusting of paprika. If baking may baste
with a little liquid in pan, such as white wine, orange,
apple or tomato juice. Cook fish by any method until
just flakes with a fork and is not dry. Salmon is nice
poached in wine and herbs and served hot or chilled
with sour cream. Fish and seafood are also excellent
entrees.

FISH

Cod, Haddock, Halibut, Bluefish, Striped Bass,
Flounder, Salmon- baked broiled, grilled or poached.

WILL'S BAKED BLUEFISH

Fresh caught bluefish fillets, sprinkled with lemon juice
1/2 cup Italian Salad Dressing (or oil and vinegar dressing=2/3 to 1/3, seasonings)
1 cup hot water
Bread crumbs made from Italian bread
Season with basil, oregano, paprika (or Cayenne) and salt and pepper

Soak fish in milk for a half hour. Spread fillets in ungreased 8" X 10" pan Mix salad dressing with hot water, pour over fish. Cover with bread crumbs tossed in some melted butter. Bake 350, for 25 to 30 minutes, until flakes with a fork. Serve with thin lemon slices, parsley and a cold sauce of your choice. (SEE SAUCES)

Bluefish has been much maligned because of it's oiliness and strong flavor. When fresh caught, skinned and cleaned while still on the boat, it is delicious. Those who believe they dislike bluefish perhaps never tasted it fresh caught and cleaned promptly. Can also be broiled or grilled. Sprinkle wine or lemon juice on it before broiling or grilling, add some garlic powder and salt and pepper and dribble olive oil over it. Always give a milk soak before cooking. If Bluefish is treated correctly will reward with a delicate flavor. Smoked bluefish makes an elegant pate for an hors d'oeuvre. A favorite on Cape Cod and Cape Ann. Serve with crackers and drinks.

BETTIE HAMILTON

SMOKED BLUEFISH PATE

1 lb smoked bluefish fillets
8 oz cream cheese
1/4 cup butter
2 T. Cognac
3 T. minced onion
1/2 tsp Worcestershire Saauce
2 T. fresh lemon juice
salt, fresh ground black pepper
optional= toasted walnuts

Follow directions on smoker to smoke fish. Puree bluefish, cream cheese, butter and Cognac in food processor. Add onion, sauce and lemon juice. Pulse until combined.

Season with salt and pepper. Pack into serving dish, sprinkle with nuts. Keep refrigerated. Makes 4 cups pate.

GRILLED BLUEFISH A LA TONY

1-1/2 to 2 lb bluefish fillets
Milk
Lemon juice
Virgin olive oil
Salt and pepper, paprika

Soak fish in milk, half hour. This cuts strong, oily flavor. Squeeze lemon juice and dribble olive oil over all. Salt and pepper. Place on grill, sprinkle paprika to help browning. Grill until light brown, fish flakes with fork, is still moist. Serve with Lea's or Tony's chilled tomato sauce on the side.

(A simple way to prepare fresh bluefish, but still one of the best.)

GRAVADLAX (EINAR'S COLD STRIPED BASS WITH TUNA SAUCE)

1 whole, cleaned striped bass
1 cup white wine, (Soave, Chablis)
1 qt water
1 chopped onion
Juice of 1 lemon or lime
1 Bayleaf
Dill sprigs, parsley, chopped celery stalk
5 pepper corns
1 tsp salt
2 T. sugar
2 T. cider vinegar
Garnish with dill and lemon slices

Rinse fish and pat dry. Wrap in cheesecloth, or a porous dish cloth. Place in large shallow baking pan. Combine remaining ingredients and ring to a boil. Reduce heat, simmer 15 minutes. Pour over the fish. Cover all with foil. Bake 350 for 20 to 25 minutes. Remove fish whole and place on a platter. Chill at least 3 hours in refrigerator covered. To serve remove cheesecloth and lay fish on a bed of dill with lemon quarters surrounding it. Serve with tuna sauce on side. An entree or an appetizer when served on Finnish flat

bread with a dab of sauce. May refrigerate in the marinade over night for a more intense curing before baking, Discard marinade after baking and chilling before placing on plate to serve. Serves 6 to 8. This cured cold cured bass goes well with hot lemon creamed potatoes, and corn on the cob.

TUNA SAUCE (SEE SAUCES)
WILL'S CODFISH CAKES

2 cups dried salt codfish
2 cups hot mashed potatoes
1 T. butter
1/4 cup milk
1/2 tsp baking powder
Dash black ground pepper

Soak dried cod for 2 hours in cold water or overnight in refrigerator. Drain. Cover with fresh cold water, simmer on low until fish tender. Drain, chop fine. Mix milk, butter, baking powder and pepper thoroughly with mashed potatoes. Add codfish and mix well. Shape into flat cakes or balls and fry in butter on both sides until browned. May use fresh codfish, poached in water and wine, half and half, until tender. It is not only easier, Julia thought, but a little better! (Old fashioned "Townies" like Will believe salt cod has more flavor, they relish these fish cakes with baked beans on a Saturday night.) Makes 10 to 12, depending upon size. (Cover and refrigerate unused portion for another meal.)

JULIA AND WILL'S MARBLEHEAD SALT COD DINNER AND RED FLANNEL HASH

1 lb dried salt cod (1/2 lb per person)
1/2 lb salt pork
1 peeled, boiled potato per person (2 or 3 extra for the red flannel hash)
1 or 2 small onions per person (1 or 2 extra for the red flannel hash)
2 or 3 boiled beets per person, (2 or 3 extra for the red flannel hash)

Soak fish in cold water to cover overnight. Boil desired amount of onions, beets, potatoes in separate pots. Dice salt pork and "try out"(fry) until pieces are crisp. Drain on paper towel. Drain fish, cover again with water and bring to a boil. Turn heat down and simmer for 12 to 15 minutes until tender. Drain fish again Place fish, beets, potatoes and onions on each plate, keeping separate. Serve pork rashers in a side dish on table. The accustomed procedure is each diner mashes all his food together and sprinkles it with pork rashers. No 'header has ever been seen keeping or eating the ingredients separately. It is against the rules.

(Julia says, "This is bloody horrible!" Will says, "Nonsense, this is a dish fit for a king!")

RED FLANNEL HASH (how to use the leftovers)

Mash all leftovers together. (Of course you cooked extra to have enough for the hash?) If necessary add an egg to bind it all together. Place in a fry pan and saute in butter on both sides until brown and crisp on outside for the next morning's breakfast served with a poached egg on top. Make one big or several small rounds of the hash as you prefer or fancy dictates. (Or give it to your dog, Lucy really likes it a lot.)

WILL'S FRIED FLOUNDER AND ORIGINAL NEW ENGLAND TARTAR SAUCE

6 small flounder fillets, cut in serving size pieces
1 well beaten egg
1 cup flour or dry bread crumbs or corn meal
1/3 cup butter
Dill, salt and pepper

Salt and pepper flounder, dip into beaten egg, then in crumbs or flour. Repeat. Heat butter in skillet. Fry flounder until golden brown on each side. Garnish with lemon quarters and dill sprigs. Serve with original tartar sauce.

NEW ENGLAND ORIGINAL TARTAR SAUCE (SEE SAUCES)

The original cooked tartar sauce is served at fried clam, fried oyster and fried fish bars and shacks from Marblehead to Maine. Will keep for a week in refrigerator. May double recipe to have tartar sauce on hand to use.

(Or make a quick cold tartar sauce mixing together 1 cup mayonnaise, 4 fine chopped Cornichon pickles and 1 fine chopped shallot. Add 1 T. drained capers, 1/4 cup mustard and 1 tsp lemon juice. Makes 1 cup. Is close to the original and easier to make.)

LEA'S BAKED STUFFED HADDOCK OR SHRIMP

2 lbs haddock or halibut fillets (plan 1/2 lb per person)
1 sleeve Ritz crackers
1 lemon
1/4 cup melted butter
2 oz tomalley or small tin of lobster paste

Make a stuffing of ingredients above mixed well together. May coarsely crumble the crackers by hand. Lay fish on top of stuffing in a buttered baking pan. Squeeze lemon juice over the fish and sprinkle with paprika. Bake 350 about 30 minutes, until fish is fork tender. Before baking dribble a small amount of wine around fish and stuffing, to keep from drying out. Garnish with lemon slices and dill sprigs. Serves 4.

BAKED STUFFED SHRIMP

2 lbs shrimp, layer with stuffing. Serves 4. 350, 30 minutes, test shrimp.

POACHED SALMON

One of Tony and Lucy's favorites was Lea's poached fresh salmon simmered in wine, water, bay leaves and peppercorns. She chilled it whole sprinkled with capers and served it cold on a bed of fresh dill surrounded by lemon wedges, black olives and mounds of sour cream-dill sauce. (SEE SAUCES)

SOLVEIGH'S PICKLED HERRING
(SEE APPETIZERS)

SEAFOOD
TONY'S CLAM PIZZA (SEE APPETIZERS)
TONY'S WHITE CLAM SAUCE ON LINGUINI

1 cup clam broth, or bottled clam juice
1 stick butter
1/2 cup Virgin olive oil
4 cloves garlic, minced
1 cup chopped flat Italian parsley
2 cups chopped clams or whole small cherrystone clams
1/4 cup Chablis, or any white wine

Melt butter, add garlic and parsley. Add clams and broth. (TIP: Heat just until hot, clams toughen if overcooked.) Cook linguini, drain, serve clam sauce over it, sprinkled with Parmesan cheese. (A great meal if all you've eaten all day is peanut butter sandwiches!)

FINNISH FRIED EEL WITH LEMON CREAMED POTATOES

3 large eels (or use 3" chunks of bass or haddock)
1-1/2 cups flour
2 beaten eggs
1-1/2 cups dry bread crumbs
1/2 cup butter and olive oil

Skin eels. Cut skin around head, peel back slowly with a pair of pliers. Remove intestines and cut off head. Cut eel into 3" pieces, wash and dry. Sprinkle with salt, let stand one hour. Rinse with cold water, pat completely dry. Roll in the flour, next in beaten egg and last in bread crumbs. Melt butter and oil in skillet. Fry eel 10 minutes each side until golden brown. Stir occasionally. Serves 4 to 6 with lemon potatoes.

LEMON CREAMED POTATOES

6 medium potatoes, peeled and diced
1/4 cup melted butter and 1/4 cup flour
2 cups milk
2 T. grated lemon rind

1/2 tsp white pepper, and 1 tsp salt
2 or 3 T. parsley, chopped fine

(Alas, if no eel substitute chunks of white fish)
Cook potatoes until tender. Drain, keep hot. Melt
butter, add flour, stir in milk gradually. Stir in salt,
pepper and lemon rind. Pour over potatoes. Surround
potatoes with fried eel, sprinkle parsley over all Serves
4 to 6. (An old traditional Scandinavian dish. Lea had
to substitute striped bass for eel because not only was
Tony prejudiced against eel, most of her guests
secretly were as well. Eel is in truth sweet and
delicious.)

LOBSTER (boiled, baked stuffed, broiled or in a
salad)
(Chicken lobster are 1 lb to 1-1/4 lbs. Selects are 1-3/8
and up. Lea and Tony preferred chicken lobster for
tenderness.)

TO BOIL

Bring a large pot of salted water to a boil. (If at
the beach, sea water.) Remove rubber bands from the
claws. Grasp each lobster by the back of the body and
plunge into boiling water. (They have no nervous
system and do NOT scream as some like to say when
they hit the boiling water.) When comes to a boil again
start timing. Two chicken lobsters take about 12 to 15
minutes. Will be a bright red. For larger lobsters, plan
on 20 to 25 minutes. (TIP: Do not crowd pot, cook
only 2 or 3 at a time, or use two or more big pots for a
crowd.) Remove with tongs and drain in sink. Serve

hot or cold with melted butter mixed with lemon juice for dipping or mayonnaise and lemon juice.

TO EAT

Break off claws and tail and set aside. Remove the green tomalley (liver) and the coral (roe) from the body. This makes a delicious tidbit when mixed with a little mayo and spread on a cracker. Discard the poisonous "lady" from the body. If you are patient you can pick morsels of meat from the body, and can roll out the meat in the small legs with a rolling pin. (Lea never let Tony see her extravagantly throw the whole body away while he painstakingly picked out every last bit of lobster meat.) Claws and tail are the best. Grasping tail by the back, force it inwards with your hands to crack the shell. Use a nutcracker to crack claws and tail. With practice one gets good at removing whole pieces.

Serve hot or chill to serve cold or in a dish such as salad mixed with a small amount of chopped celery and mayonnaise served in a frankfort roll or on Bibb lettuce. Cooked lobster meat is used in many dishes such as Newburgh or Ravioli or Tetrazinni. Allow at least one lobster per person.

BROILED OR BAKED STUFFED LOBSTER

Boil an extra lobster for the stuffing. Cut raw lobster down center of body. Remove claws and boil separately with the extra lobster, 12 to 15 minutes. Reserve. Mix tomalley, coral and extra lobster meat with Ritz cracker crumbs and 1/2 stick melted butter. Fill the cavity with the stuffing. (Before stuffing remove body pieces and tentacles and the "lady." May add a few raw shrimp or scallops to the stuffing if desire.) Sprinkle stuffing with a touch of sherry or lemon juice or wine for moistness and paprika. Bake at 350 about 20 minutes or broil on HI about 20 minutes until lightly browned.

To serve reassemble lobster with cracked cooked claws beside body. (TIP: Lea covers stuffing with foil for first 8 to 10 minutes so will not be dried out, removes foil to brown top of stuffing.) Place lemon wedges and container of melted butter next to lobster.

GRILLED LOBSTER WITH LEMON-THYME BUTTER

Plunge a knife between each lobsters eyes (ouch?) and cut in half. Brush with lemon-thyme butter. Grill 4 or 5 minutes a side until bright red and flesh opaque. Serve with the remaining lemon-thyme butter. Grill corn on cob with husks on at same time. A cold pasta salad goes well, too.

LEMON-THYME BUTTER

1/2 cup melted butter
3 or 4 minced garlic cloves
2 T. chopped fresh thyme (TIP: If cannot find, substitute basil, tarragon, rosemary, mint, dill or chives, or your favorite herb, fresh not dried.)
1/2 cup lemon juice, dash of salt
Tomalley or roe from cleaned body of lobster

Melt butter, mix all together and serve hot with lobster, fish or vegetables such as asparagus, cauliflower, broccoli or brussel sprouts, a change from Hollandaise sauce.

Will got a great many lobster in his string of traps. His buoys were patriotic- red, white and blue. Each lobsterman has his own identifying colors on his buoys that mark where the traps are sitting on the ocean floor for unsuspecting lobster to enter the one-way door. When he didn't sell them all they cooked them up and ate them until they were heartily sick of lobster! Julia made lobster pie, lobster salad, lobster rolls and simple hot boiled lobster. Tony gave them his recipe for lobster Tetrazinni, Will hated to admit he enjoyed this Italian way to use lobster but he did as it was different and tasty.

TONY'S LOBSTER TETRAZINNI

(TIP: Good made with left over cooked turkey or chicken, instead.)

1/2 lb spaghetti (or another pasta) cut into 2" lengths (may use wide noodles)
1 cup heavy cream
4 T. butter
1 cup fresh, sliced mushrooms
2 T. flour
1 cup chicken broth
1 cup Parmesan cheese
2 tsp ground black pepper
1/2 tsp garlic powder
1/2 cup white wine (or dry sherry)
3 cups cooked lobster meat
2 T. chopped fresh flat Italian parsley (TIP: stronger flavor than the curly parsley)

Butter a 3 qt. casserole. Cook and drain pasta of your choice. Heat cream, set aside. Saute mushrooms in butter. Into this blend flour, chicken broth and 3/4 cup Parmesan cheese. Stir until thick and smooth. Season to taste with salt, pepper and garlic. Remove from heat. Gradually blend in the hot cream and wine. Pour half the sauce over the pasta and toss together. Stir cubed large pieces of lobster into the remaining sauce, pour over and toss again. Sprinkle 1/4 cup Parmesan cheese and parsley on top. Bake uncovered at 325 for 20 minutes. Serves 4 to 6.

LEA'S SCALLOPED OYSTERS

(To start with let us pronounce it correctly, i.e.= scallops as in wallop or trollop or fall up and never scallops as in well or shell or tell. A small thing but important to those on the seacoast who fish for scallops and can be touchy about this!)

1 pt fresh shucked oysters
16 Ritz crackers
1/2 cup butter
2 cups cream
1/4 cup oyster liquor
Sherry or white wine
Salt and pepper

Butter a 2 qt casserole. Crush 4 crackers coarsely by hand, place on bottom. Place 1/3 oysters over this, season with salt and pepper, dot with butter. Continue to layer 2 more times, top with last 4 crackers, salt, pepper, butter. Over all pour cream and oyster liquor and sherry to taste, a good dribble. Let stand 2 hours in refrigerator to absorb liquid. Bake 350 40 to 45 minutes until oyster when tested is cooked, top puffy and lightly golden brown. May scallop scallops (are you saying it right?) same way. Lea tried out many oyster recipes on Einar, he liked them all. Most of all he liked oysters raw on the half shell with lemon and a hot sauce.

(Siri would scold him when he'd wink and say to her, "Oysters put lead in my pencil, Siri!" Flustered and flushed, she would respond, "Hush, Einar, not in front of the children!" Einar loved to tease Siri as

Tony did Lea. "Where did you think they came from, Siri?")

CLAIRE'S MARBLEHEAD SEAFOOD CASSEROLE

1/2 lb shrimp
1/2 lb scallops
1/4 lb tomalley (or tin lobster paste)
1/2 lb lobster meat (cooked)
2 sleeves Ritz crackers, crushed (1 small box)
1/3 cup coffee cream or Half and Half
1 stick melted butter
Dash Tabasco Sauce, dash sherry or wine

Mix cracker crumbs with butter. Alternate layers of mixed seafood with 2/3 cup crumbs in buttered casserole, or individual ramekins. Pour cream over to cover. Bake at 325 for about 30 minutes. (TIP: Test a shrimp and scallop for doneness. If cannot find tomalley buy a lobster cull at fish market and scrape out the tomalley and roe and cooked meat from it to use.) Serves 4 to 6. (A "cull" is missing one or both claws.)

Claire's Mom had been a friend of Chet Damon who owned McClain's Fish Market. He was also a fine cook and famous for this recipe. Alas, McClain's is gone, an antique shop in its place). (TIP: Please remember to pronounce "scallop" correctly or you will drive all fishermen bananas!) Interestingly enough, the Porthole Pub in Lynn serves a similar casserole called "Claire's Seafood Supreme." These gals are two different Claires but their namesake dish is supreme, although each a little different. For a crowd on New Year's Eve, double the recipe and serve in patty shells or on toast points.

LOBSTER PIE =Julia used up excess lobster in a pie, omitting shrimp and scallops, using 1-1/2 lbs lobster meat adding a good slug of sherry, cover with crumbs, bake.

TONY'S SHRIMP CACCIATORE

1/2 lb raw cleaned shrimp
28 oz can or equivalent fresh tomatoes, chopped
1 chopped small green pepper
1 chopped yellow onion
2 or 3 chopped celery stalks
1/2 lb fresh mushrooms
1 tsp sugar
1/2 cup red wine, dash Worcestershire sauce
Fresh basil leaves, flat parsley, garlic powder, salt and pepper to taste

Mix all together, pour over shrimp. Bake 350 uncovered for 40 minutes or until a shrimp tests done and pink and celery and pepper tender. Serve over rice or angel hair pasta or noodles. Sprinkle with Parmesan or Romano cheese. Tony sometimes served this over a large, split baked potato. Also can be made with raw chicken breasts, 1-1/2 to 2 lbs, cut in large pieces. (Lucy could eat Tony's Shrimp or Chicken Cacciatore until the cows (or raccoons) came home.)

TONY'S GRILLED SHRIMP WRAPPED IN PROSCIUTTO (SEE APPETIZERS)

SOUPS AND CHOWDERS

GERDA'S COLD APPLE SOUP (AEBLESUPPE)

1-1/2 lbs tart apples (Ingrid Marie, Granny Smith, Rhode Island Greening)
2-1/2 quarts water
1 Cinnamon stick or 1 tsp ground cinnamon
1 lemon rind, cut into strips
1/4 cup corn starch
1/2 cup water
1/4 cup sugar
1/2 cup white wine
6 whole zwieback rusks
Whipped cream

Quarter and core apples. Do not peel. Place in deep soup pot and add 1-1/2 quarts of water, cinnamon and lemon rind. Cook on low until apples very soft. Do not drain. Remove cinnamon stick. Puree in blender or force through a food mill or sieve. Add remaining quart of water. Blend cornstarch in 1/2 cup water to smooth paste. Stir into soup. Cook over low heat until thick and smooth, stirring constantly. Add sugar to taste and white wine. Chill well. Serve cold over crushed or whole zwieback rusks in bowls. Serves 6. (TIP: This soup should have the consistency of heavy cream and be a little tart. A blob of whipped

342

SEA SMOKE

cream and a dusting of nutmeg tops each bowlful.
May serve it hot but Danes prefer it icy cold.)

LEA'S MARBLEHEAD CLAM CHOWDER

1 quart fresh, raw shelled clams (chop if large)
Bottled clam juice and water
2 thin sliced onions
4 cups thin sliced (not diced) potatoes
1-1/2 chunk scored salt pork
3 T. butter
salt and pepper
4 cups scalded milk

Fry out salt pork, saving out a few rashers.
Cook onion in fat and butter until tender. Add 4 cups
sliced potatoes and 2 cups boiling water, cook until
just tender not mushy. Add about 2 cups clam juice.
Add 4 cups scalded milk. Season to taste with salt and
pepper. Simmer together. Last add clams, simmer 4
or 5 minutes longer and don't over cook the clams. If
wish to thicken stir in some broken hard tack or
common crackers. (not flour!) Turn heat off to allow
chowder to meld. At serving time reheat at a gentle
simmer, do not boil. Serves 6. Pour over a common
cracker in bowls sprinkled with chives, paprika, a few
pork rashers and dab of butter. (TIP: Authentic New
England clam chowder is not thick or creamy as so
many restaurants serve it. There are otherwise
excellent restaurants who thicken a New England Clam
Chowder so that the spoon can stand straight up in it as
though in library paste! It should be PACKED FULL

OF tender clams, thin sliced onion and potatoes in a thin, milky broth to be the real "Clam chowdah" with more filling than broth.

TONY'S MEDITERRANEAN CLAM CHOWDER

2 pints chopped fresh raw clams, large quahogs (or smaller cherrystones, whole)
4 T. sweet butter
2 cups fine chopped onion
1 cup chopped celery
5 cups chicken broth
1 bay leaf
Dashes Worcestershire and Tabasco sauces
4 minced garlic cloves
2 lbs chopped Italian peeled tomatoes (fresh or canned)
1 cup chopped Italian flat parsley
2 medium boiling potatoes, peeled and diced
1/2 cup red wine
salt and pepper
Shredded Mozzarella cheese

Melt butter in large soup pot. Add onions and celery, cook covered over low heat until tender, approximately 25 minutes. Stir in red wine, chicken broth and all remaining ingredients except clams and cheese. Partially cover, simmer 30 minutes or until potatoes are tender, not mushy. Before serving add clams and simmer only 1 or 2 minutes to heat through and not toughen. (TIP: Clams are temperamental Prima Donnas, if overcooked will resemble chewy pieces of elastic but are lovely and tender when cooked correctly.)

Top each bowl with cheese, run under broiler briefly to melt and string. On the dining table provide bottles of Tabasco Hot sauce, rum and dry sherry. Each diner adds any or all to his/her taste.

This tomato based clam chowder or soup is similar to Florida's conch chowder, favoring added sherry, and Bermuda clam chowder where added rum is favored, or the New York Saloon or Manhattan clam chowder who add Tabasco Sauce. (Rhode Island clam chowder contains both tomatoes and milk. The rest of New England serves a milk based chowder. Purists are aghast at adding tomatoes to a clam chowder, but if you think of it as a clam soup, it is really delicious.) Serves 6 with warmed garlic bread.

GARLIC BREAD

Cut diagonal slices (not all the way through) into long loaf of French or Italian bread. Mash 2 cloves minced garlic with 2 T. butter. Spread in each gash. Wrap in foil, warm in low oven.

LEA'S MARBLEHEAD FISH CHOWDER

4 lbs cod, cusk, or haddock fillets (a firm white fish is best)
2 cups fish stock or bottled clam juice
2 thin sliced yellow onions
4 cups thin sliced potatoes (dice if you must, sliced are traditional)
Chunk of scored salt pork (Save some crisp rashers to top chowder)
2 cups boiling water
4 cups scalded milk
salt, pepper, butter

"Try out" salt pork. (Old time term meaning "fry".) Remove, saving pork rashers=crisp pieces of pork.) Cook onion in the pork fat and butter until tender. Add scalded milk, may use part cream if prefer, and season with salt and pepper to taste. Turn stove to simmer. Lay the fish fillets on top of the potatoes in the milk and allow the fish to poach. It will break up into large pieces as it cooks. Test for doneness, flakes with fork.

May turn off and allow flavors to meld, reheat later on a gentle simmer.

New England Fish chowder, like clam chowder, contains a thin milk broth stuffed to bursting with fish, onion and potatoes. If wish it thicker stir in and dissolve a couple hard tack or "common" crackers (not flour) and use cream instead of milk. Ladle filling into bowls, pour broth over and garnish with chives, paprika, dab of butter and pork rashers. (TIP: Lea pleads, "Please, never ever use canned evaporated milk and call it a Marblehead chowder.") Serves 6.

TONY'S PASTA E FAGIOLI (pasta and beans)

2 T. Virgin olive oil
1 chopped red onion
2 cloves minced garlic
1 bunch celery leaves, chopped
40 oz. fresh shell beans or 2-20 oz cans of cannelini beans, drained and rinsed
4 cups tomato sauce
1 cup ditali (small tubular pasta)
1/4 cup chopped fresh flat Italian parsley
salt and pepper

Heat oil in ovenproof casserole, cook onions over medium 10 minutes, Add garlic and celery leaves, cook and stir 1 more minute. Add beans and tomato sauce, bring to a boil. Simmer 25 minutes until thick. Cook pasta in a large pot of salted water al dente, about 6 minutes. Drain and add to bean mixture. Add salt, pepper and parsley. Spoon into soup bowls, serve with grated cheese on top. (This is as close as Italians get to American Texas Chili, and some consider it a thick soup)

BETTIE HAMILTON

TONY'S SICILIAN SEA FOOD STEW

To Tony's Mediterranean Clam Chowder use only 1/2 pt raw clams, add 1/2 lb. scallops, 1 lb. crabmeat, 1 lb skinned fillet haddock or cod, 1 lb shelled shrimp. May use in shells (scrubbed) a mixture of 1 lb soft shell clams, cherrystones, and oysters Simmer 30 minutes or until shells open and fish and scallops are cooked. Pour over chunk of Italian bread in soup bowls. Serves 6 to 8. Sprinkle with Romano cheese. Thin with more red wine if too thick. This stew is similar to a Bouillabaisse.

LEA'S SEAFOOD CHOWDER

Made like her Fish Chowder, adding when fish is added, 1/2 lb each raw clams, shrimp, scallops, oysters and lobster meat and cutting down on amount of fish to make 4 lbs in all of seafood. Simmer until scallops and shrimp are tender, 5 to 8 minutes. Serves 6. Tony and Lea had a lively contest between his tomato based Mediterranean chowders and soups and her milk based New England chowders. Their friends refused to vote on a winner but enjoyed being asked to supper to try each type. They loved them all as well as Tony and Lea and would not, dared not choose one cook over the other!

SALADS

Tony's Antipasto (SEE APPETIZERS)
Sarah's Avocado, Bacon and Orange Salad

1 large ripe avocado, squeeze lemon juice on to keep from discoloring
3 slices crumbled crisp bacon
2 or 3 sliced shallots
Juice of 1 lemon, (for avocado and dressing)
1 small tin mandarin oranges, or fresh sliced oranges, halved
Leaf of Bibb lettuce, never iceberg!

Dressing: 1/4 Balsamic vinegar, 3/4 Virgin olive oil, 1 T. lemon juice, 2 minced garlic cloves, salt and pepper blended together and shaken well.
Line salad bowl or individual ones with lettuce. Toss all the ingredients lightly together. Pour dressing over all and toss again.
(Sarah created this salad as both she and Lea were enamored of avocado) Serves 2.

LEA'S COLD POACHED CHICKEN SALAD

2 cups cubed chicken, poached in wine and herbs and chilled
1/2 cup toasted pecan halves
1/2 cup fine chopped celery
1/4 cup slivered ripe olives

DRESSING: 1/2 cup whipped heavy cream, 1/2 cup mayonnaise, 1/2 tsp mustard, 1 tsp drained capers, salt and pepper. Stir all together.

Cut poached chicken (SEE ENTREES) into chunks or dice after chilling. Whip cream until almost stiff, stir other ingredients (save chicken) into cream. Fold in celery, ripe olives and pecans gently. Last, fold in chicken dice or chunks. Pile salad on lettuce leaves and sprinkle with drained capers. May use chicken salad in sandwiches. Serves 4.

TONY'S ITALIAN SALAD

1 cup diced blanched zucchini
1 cup lightly cooked asparagus cut into 2" pieces
1 cup blanched petite peas

Garnish: rolled up anchovies with a caper in each, interspersed with ripe olives.

DRESSING: 1/2 cup mayonnaise, juice of 1 lemon, 1/4 tsp mustard., salt and pepper

Combine vegetables. Thin mayonnaise with lemon juice, stir in mustard. Fold vegetables into the dressing. Spoon onto lettuce leaves on a flat platter. Place garnish around edges. Serves 4 to 6 as a side dish.

(Tony's rebuttal to Lea's pea, pickle and cheese salad. Neither would admit the other was superior but they liked them both, maintaining their own version the best, of course.)

LOBSTER SALAD

Lettuce
1-1/2 cups cooked lobster meat in chunks, chilled
1/4 cup chopped celery
Lea's home made Mayonnaise

Fold lobster and celery into mayonnaise and pile onto lettuce. For lobster rolls warm buttered, split frankfort rolls in oven. Line with lettuce leaves (to prevent sogginess) and pile lobster salad into rolls. Serve with potato chips and pickles. Serves 2.

LEA'S PEA, PICKLE AND CHEESE STILLMAN SALAD (aka ROAD KILL)

1 cup blanched baby peas
4 oz. cubed Cheddar cheese
1 chopped dill or sour pickle
Mix all together with mayonnaise and plop onto a lettuce leaf. Serves 2.

(Stillman Infirmary was part of Harvard University where Lea worked temporarily in the summer when attending Montserrat College of Art.)

SIRI'S POTATO SALAD

4 boiled potatoes
1/4 cup chopped celery
1/4 cup blanched baby peas
1 large chopped onion
1 small green pepper, seeded and chopped, or half a large one
2 T. pimiento
1/4 cup chopped green or ripe olives
1 T. vinegar, salt and pepper, 1/2 tsp mustard
Enough mayonnaise to bind

Boil potatoes, skins on until tender. Cool and peel. Sprinkle with vinegar. Slice or chop potatoes in large pieces. Add and fold in other ingredients using just enough mayonnaise mixed with mustard, salt and pepper to hold it all together. May add minced herbs, parsley, dill or tarragon to mayonnaise mixture. Sprinkle with paprika and chopped chives. Cover and keep refrigerated until serving time. Serves 4.

(Lea assumed everyone knew how to make Potato Salad and was astonished when people asked for Siri's recipe. A good potato salad is dependent upon a good mayonnaise. It is easy to make your own fresh.)

TOMATO SALAD, BASIL, OIL AND GROUND BLACK PEPPER

Thick ripe slices of native tomatoes, one per person, lightly salted
Fresh basil leaves, torn and inserted between slices of tomato.
A dribble of Virgin olive oil
Fresh ground black pepper
     This platter is probably the simplest and best salad course of any.

SUMMER COLD POACHED CHICKEN PLATTER
Slice cold poached chicken. (SEE ENTREES)

     Arrange a platter with lettuce leaves and place chicken, tomatoes dressed as above, a mound of pickled beets, a mound of pickled cucumbers (SEE VEGETABLES) and devilled halves of hard boiled eggs, 1/2 per person. Serve Lea's mayonnaise (or the whipped cream dressing in the chicken salad) on the side. Stuff eggs with mashed yolks, minced anchovies and pepper.
     Keep each ingredient in a separate row on platter. Tony and Lea enjoyed this on a hot and humid night for their cold supper, and so did Lucy. Hot biscuits go well with it.

BETTIE HAMILTON

SANDWICHES

LEA'S BLT 'S

Toasted, buttered sourdough bread, 2 per sandwich
Crisp fried bacon, 2 per sandwich
Fresh native tomato slices. 2 or 3 per sandwich
Leaf Lettuce, Mayonnaise spread over ingredients.
Layer on toast and top with 2nd piece. This is a summertime staple that everyone surely knows how to make? What makes Lea's special is the freshness of the ingredients and the fact that they are put together with homemade mayonnaise Simple things are usually superior.

LEA'S CHICKEN SALAD SANDWICHES (SEE SALADS)

LEA'S LOBSTER ROLLS (SEE SEAFOOD)

MARIA'S FIG AND PROSCIUTTO SANDWICHES (TONY'S FAVORITE)

Fresh figs, one per sandwich
2 slices prosciutto smoked ham, each sandwich
Virgin olive oil
Watercress or shredded lettuce
Italian or French bread, 2 slices per sandwich, buttered

Place fig, spread out, prosciutto, watercress and a dribble of oil on a slice of Italian or French bread. Butter second slice and cover, cut in halves.

TONY'S AMERICANIZED ITALIAN SANDWICH

6" Baguettes, sliced the long way, 1 per person
Virgin olive oil
1 or 2 slices Prosciutto per sandwich
1 or 2 slices Mortadella per sandwich
1 or 2 slices Genoa Salami per sandwich
1 or 2 slices Provolone cheese per sandwich
1 or 2 slices tomato per sandwich
1 or 2 sliced roasted red peppers per sandwich (or red pepper flakes)
Shredded lettuce

Sprinkle olive oil on baguette half. Line with lettuce. Layer the remaining ingredients. Sprinkle on a little more oil. Cover with other half of baguette also lined with lettuce. (Tony vowed to avoid soggy sandwiches at all costs) Cut in half. Wrap tight.
(Will's favorite to take on fishing trips on the Mandy. Tony told him repeatedly he'd never find one in Italy as he'd made it up. Will said he did not plan on going to Italy anyway.)

PEANUT BUTTER AND GRAPE JELLY OR PEANUT BUTTER AND MARSHMALLOW FLUFF

Peanut butter
Jelly or jam of choice, grape is preferred
Marshmallow Fluff
Soft white bread

Spread one piece of bread with peanut butter for each sandwich and the other slice with jelly. For a "Fluffernutter"- peanut butter and marshmallow fluff. Press together, halve.
(This is a universal favorite of children all over the world and many adults-Lea and Tony included!)

RED PEPPER JELLY AND CREAM CHEESE SANDWICH (SEE SAUCES FOR JELLY) LEA'S TUNA FISH SANDWICH

1 can solid white albacore tuna packed in oil (less flavor when in water)
Olives chopped
Celery chopped
Green pepper chopped
l small Cornichon pickle chopped
Lea's mayonnaise

Flake (drained of oil) tuna, chop remaining ingredients. Mix with mayonnaise and spread on lettuce lined whole wheat bread. Cover with other slice. Serves 2, may double amounts for more.

(Sylvia told Lea she'd had many a sad tuna fish sandwich eating out at lunch time as she usually did from the office. "But Lea, yours are the best, no one makes them like you do!" This amused Lea as what could be simpler than a tuna fish sandwich?)

SAUCES, MAYONNAISE, RED PEPPER JELLY, PEPPER RELISH

Roast turkey cries for cranberry sauce, lobster needs drawn butter with lemon juice, fried fish, oysters and shrimp are lost without a tartar sauce, it seems most dishes are enhanced by a good sauce.

AIOLI GARLIC SAUCE

8 peeled garlic cloves (Garlic will bring down your cholesterol and blood pressure!)
2 egg yolks
salt and pepper
Juice of 1 lemon
1 tsp. mustard
1-1/2 cups Virgin olive oil

Puree or mash garlic. Whisk yolks and add with lemon juice, salt and pepper.

Blend or process into a paste. Pour oil in slowly in a steady stream while mixing. Process until a thick, shiny, firm sauce. Chill. Store in refrigerator up to 2 weeks. Excellent for fish or seafood. Makes about 2 cups.

BETTIE HAMILTON

TONY'S HOT TOMATO SAUCE FOR COLD SEAFOOD

1/2 jar very hot tomato salsa
1 tsp lemon juice
1 T. horseradish
1 tsp Tabasco sauce
4 or 5 minced anchovies
garlic powder

Mix all together, chill well. Excellent with iced, jumbo shrimp for those who enjoy a red hot sauce. (Place shrimp on a glass plate over a glass bowl filled with ice. As the ice melts the shrimp will not sink into the ice water. Tony showed Lea this little serving tip who batted her eyelashes at him and said "Thank you very much, Antonio, you are so smart!" Shrimp cocktail was a favorite of Lea's and she personally liked the sauce very hot and pungent. If you like it milder, substitute tomato catsup for salsa.)

LEMON-THYME BUTTER FOR GRILLING
(SEE SEAFOOD)

LEA'S SOUR CREAM DILL SAUCE

1 large cucumber, peeled, seeded and finely chopped
3/4 cup sour cream
1/8 tsp sugar
1 T. mayonnaise
4 minced dill weed sprigs
salt and pepper, a few capers

Drain cucumber and pat dry. Fold gently into sour cream mixture with dill, sugar, mayonnaise and salt and pepper. Sprinkle capers and more dill on top. Chill. Makes about 1 cup. Use with any fish or shellfish, or as a cocktail sauce for cold cooked shrimp, this is a typical Finnish sauce.

WILL'S COOKED ORIGINAL NEW ENGLAND TARTAR SAUCE
(Use with fried fish, fried clams and fried oysters)

1 T. butter
1 T. flour
1/2 cup milk
1/3 cup mayonnaise
1 tsp vinegar
4 T. chopped dill or sour Cornichon pickle (your choice)
1 T. chopped onion

Melt butter, blend in flour and stir in milk to make a white sauce. Cook on low, stir constantly until thick and smooth. Remove from heat and stir in mayonnaise, vinegar, pickle and onion. Blend well. Chill covered. Makes about 1 cup. Keeps in refrigerator a week. May double recipe if wish to have on hand. This is original cooked tartar sauce served at Fried Clam, Fried Oyster, Fried Fish stands from Marblehead to Maine.

SEE FISH for a quicker, cold tartar sauce under "WILL'S FRIED FLOUNDER"

EINAR'S TUNA SAUCE FOR GRADVADLAX
(SEE FISH)

LEA'S TOMATO SAUCE
(For pasta and entrees)

12 chopped fresh native tomatoes (or large can Italian Roma Tomatoes)
2 minced garlic cloves plus to taste
1 chopped green or red sweet pepper
1 chopped large yellow onion
6 chopped fresh mushrooms (or small can, drained)
Dash sugar (cuts acidity of tomato)
1 bay leaf
Dash Tabasco sauce
Dash Worcestershire Sauce
Salt and pepper

Combine all ingredients. Simmer until thick and vegetables tender.

(This is a fine sauce to add 1 lb shrimp to. Bake uncovered about 10 minutes. Test a shrimp.

Remove bay leaf, and serve over any type of pasta. Serves 4.)

LEA'S SWEET RED PEPPER JELLY
(serve with cream cheese base or Havarti as an appetizer- guests put a spoonful of each on a cracker.)

6 large red sweet peppers
1 lemon
1/2 cup red wine vinegar
1-1/2 cups sugar
1 pkg pectin or Certo (follow directions on bottle)
If want it hotter add 1/2 tsp Tabasco sauce.

      Deseed and chop peppers. Cover with water. Boil 5 minutes. Drain thoroughly. Add quartered deseeded lemon and the vinegar. Pour in water to cover. Cook 30 minutes. Add sugar, boil 10 more minutes. remove lemon. Stir in pectin or certo. Pour into 4 sterilized with boiling water 6 oz jars. Store in refrigerator. (Also use for a cream cheese and red pepper jelly sandwich. This is different! Only a few people love it with all their hearts, special people like Tony, who also loved fig and Prosciutto smoked ham sandwiches.)

LEA'S PEPPER RELISH
(for baked beans or hot dogs or hamburgers)

24 peppers, half red, half green, seeded
12 chopped yellow onions
1 qt. mild cider vinegar
2 cups sugar
3 T/ salt
1 T. mustard seed
1 T. celery seed

Place peppers and onions in cooking pan, cover with boiling water and drain. Cover again with fresh cold water. Bring to boiling point and drain. Add remaining ingredients. Cook 10 minutes. Taste, adjust salt or sugar. Pour into sterilized (with boiling water) jars, makes 6 pints. May freeze. (Lea got this recipe from Aunt Mae from the farm and it is the best pepper relish anywhere.)

LEA'S HOMEMADE MAYONNAISE
(Makes 1-1/2 cups. Keeps 2 weeks in refrigerator with no preservatives.)

Juice of 1 large lemon
1/2 tsp. dry mustard
1/2 tsp salt
1 egg
1 cup Virgin olive oil

Place first 4 ingredients in blender or processor, add 1/4 cup of oil. Beat on low. Uncover. Pour in 3/4 cup of oil gradually in a steady stream while beating. Should thicken immediately. Pulse a few times if all oil not incorporated.

(Lea used to make this by hand before Tony bought her a hand-held, small blender. If do it by hand prepare to beat and beat and beat some more! Well worth the effort as no preservatives and fresh taste is far superior to the best of commercial brands. With right appliance it is a snap to make quickly in less than 5 minutes.)

CHILI-MUSTARD SAUCE
(Great for grilled bluefish.)

Before grilling 2 lbs bluefish fillets, 5 minutes each side- place Jalopeno pepper on grill while coals still flaming. Turn pepper to lightly brown all sides. Cool, stem seed and mince. Combine pepper with 1/2 cup prepared mustard, 1 tsp chili powder, tsp olive oil, salt and pepper. Brush sauce on bluefish and grill. (Or broil) Serves 4.

HORSERADISH SAUCE

Einar served a variety of these sauces with Gradvadlax or any fish hot or cold. This one is good with cold, poached salmon in particular.

1 cup sour cream
3 or more T. horseradish
1 tsp sugar

1/8 tsp salt.

Combine all ingredients and chill well. Just before serving stir in 2 T. fresh minced dill weed.

MUSTARD SAUCE
(Combine all and blend. Refrigerate 2 hours. Whisk with fork before serving with Gravadlax, salmon or other cold fish. Good with mussels.)

9 T. Virgin olive oil
3 T. white vinegar
2-1/2 T. prepared mustard
3/4 tsp salt
1/4 tsp pepper
1/4 tsp sugar
1/8 tsp ground cardamon seeds.

VEGETABLES AND VEGETARIAN DISHES
LEA'S ARTICHOKES STUFFED WITH BLUE CHEESE

6 cooked artichoke bottoms (cook in salted water, remove choke and discard outer leaves and top half. When a leaf comes away easily they are done.) Also can be purchased in jars.
2 or 3 oz crumbled Danish blue cheese or Gorgonzola
3 heaping T. fresh bread crumbs (pull soft white bread with a fork)
3 T. melted sweet butter

Rinse cooked or canned artichokes in cold water, set 4 aside. Cut remaining 2 into cubes. Blend and process with crumbled cheese until smooth, season with ground black pepper. Spoon mixture into 4 artichoke bottoms, shaping puree into a mound or dome and place in buttered baking dish. In another bowl mix bread crumbs and half the melted butter together. Sprinkle over tops and drizzle with remaining butter. Bake in 400 oven for 15 to 20 minutes or until golden brown and fork tender. 2 per person make a lunch entree with a salad and cup of soup or chowder first. Also an appetizer for 4; and when carefully halved for 8. May serve any sauce separately with them, Lea's tomato sauce is good. (TIP: Bake with a little liquid in pan to keep from sticking and drying out. Test after 10 minutes.)

FINNISH COLD PICKLED BEETS

24 medium beets
1 cup sugar
3 cups white vinegar
2 bay leaves
1 pc fresh or processed horseradish, if desired

Scrub beets well, cook in boiling salted and sugared water until tender. (TIP: A little sugar in water when cooking corn on the cob, fresh peas and other vegetables brings out their sweetness.) At the same time boil together sugar, bay leaves and vinegar. Drain beets and slip skins off when warm. Slice or leave whole if small. Place in boiling vinegar mixture.

Bring to boil again and boil 1 minute. Place in sterilized jars or a bowl with cover. (TIP: A bit of horseradish helps preserve their flavor) Serves 4 to 6, assuming each has 4 to 6 beets as his/her vegetable serving, less as a side dish. In the Scandinavian countries pickled beets and pickled cucumbers are common and served with most meals as a side dish.

FINNISH COLD PICKLED CUCUMBERS

2 medium seedless cucumbers (unwaxed)
1/2 cup white vinegar
2 T. water
1/4 tsp salt
1/8 tsp white pepper
3 T. sugar
3 T. minced dill and/or flat chopped parsley

Combine all ingredients except cucumbers. Wash and dry. Do not peel unless waxed. Slice as thin and transparent as possible! Pour dressing over cucumbers in bowl and refrigerate 3 hours before serving. Drain to serve. As a side dish about 6 servings.

TONY'S PASTA E FAGIOLI
(pasta and beans- SEE SOUPS AND CHOWDERS)

LINNEA'S CAULIFLOWER MORNAY

1 whole cauliflower, about 1 lb when trimmed
2 T. butter
1/4 cup all purpose flour
2 cups milk
1 tsp. fresh grated nutmeg (or pinch dried), salt and pepper
1/3 cup heavy cream
1 cup shredded cheese (Gruyere, Cheddar or Swiss)
2 egg yolks

Remove outer leaves, break into large florets. Cover with cold salted and sugared water and bring to a boil. Reduce heat, simmer for 10 minutes or until cooked but still firm. Drain. Refresh in cold water, drain again. Make the cheese sauce. Melt butter, stir in flour and cook on low for 3 minutes. Remove from stove and gradually stir in cold milk. Return to stove and while stirring bring to a boil. Add nutmeg, salt and pepper. Stir in heavy cream. Remove and add 3/4 cup cheese with egg yolks. Cover with a damp cloth or Saran wrap. Brush baking dish with butter. Pour thin layer of sauce in bottom and arrange cauliflower florets on sauce. Pour remaining sauce over so coats florets. Sprinkle with remaining cheese, pepper and nutmeg. Bake 15 minutes at 350 or until golden brown. (TIP: If use a mild cheese, such as Swiss, add a little mustard to sauce to bring out the flavors. Gruyere and Cheddar are strong enough.

(Vegetarian cousin, Linnea had given Lea this delicious recipe many years before and Lea wanted to surprise her with it on her visit.)

TONY'S VEGETABLE LASAGNE
(Spinach, Tomato and Cheese)

9 Lasagne noodles (1- 8 oz. pkg.) cooked, rinsed and drained
10 large Italian plum tomatoes, thin sliced
1 lb fresh spinach, stemmed, washed, coarsely chopped (OR 2 pkgs frozen chopped spinach, squeezed of water when thawed)
2 T. Virgin olive oil
2 or 3 cloves minced garlic
1/3 cup each minced-onion celery, green or black olives, green or red sweet pepper, flat Italian parsley or fennel- mix all together, place in a small bowl and add salt and pepper, oregano and basil (leaves or dried) to taste. Stir to mix.
1 cup shredded Mozzarella, 1 cup grated Parmesan, 1 cup Ricotta cheeses.

Spread al dente cooked lasagne noodles on a clean dish towel. Butter 10" long baking dish. Overlap 3 noodles on bottom. Layer tomato slices sprinkled with some of garlic, celery, olives, parsley, green pepper, oregano, basil salt and pepper mixture. Next lay spinach over tomatoes, sprinkle with olive oil. Layer next with Ricotta cheese. Over that layer with Mozzarella and 1/2 Parmesan cheeses. Continue layering until pasta, (3 at a time) are used up, ending with pasta noodles. Drizzle oil on this top layer and sprinkle with remaining half of Parmesan cheese.

Bake 450 15 minutes or until bubbling. Cool slightly, slice and serve.

(TIP: Delectable meatless vegetable Lasagne. Use canned, whole Italian plum tomatoes if cannot get fresh. IF desired add a layer of 1 lb cooked, scrambled chopped hamburg OR cooked scrambled sausage meat over tomato layers.)

FINNISH SPINACH PANCAKES
(SEE BREADS AND CAKES)

LEA'S STUFFED PEPPERS WITH MUSHROOMS AND CHEESE

3 or 4 sweet peppers, red, yellow, green, mixed or one color
1/2 lb fresh sauteed mushrooms
2-1/2 cups fresh bread crumbs =(butter slices bread, pull into crumbs with a fork) Reserve 1/2 cup crumbs for topping
Garlic, salt, pepper, basil and nutmeg to taste
1 egg
1/2 cup grated cheese (any kind)
and 1/4 cup for topping
2 mashed up fresh tomatoes in pieces with juice

Parboil peppers, cut in halves lengthwise. Mix remaining ingredients together and stuff peppers. Reserve topping. Drizzle a little olive oil on top of reserved crumbs and cheese placed on each pepper half. Put a little tomato sauce in baking pan. Bake 350

for 30 minutes or until browned on top. Serves 6 to 8.
Serve with LEA'S TOMATO SAUCE and rice. SEE

SAUCES. Lea also bakes=

STUFFED PEPPERS WITH SIRLOIN AND PINE
NUTS (SEE ENTREES)

LEA'S RATATOUILLE

(Use only fresh vegetables)
1 diced yellow onion
1/3 cup olive oil for cooking
4 peeled, seeded and chopped tomatoes
1 seeded, sweet red pepper, cut into strips or a julienne.
HERBS: Bay leaf, parsley, basil and thyme, tied
together. At end, remove and discard.
2 zucchini or summer squash cut into strips
2 cloves minced garlic
2 baby eggplants, drained, seeded, cut into strips
Salt and pepper to taste

Saute onion in a little of olive oil until soft.
Add tomato and garlic, cook 15 minutes. Saute red
pepper in some oil in separate skillet 2 or 3 minutes.
Strain peppers, add a little oil to tomato mixture with
peppers. Place securely tied herb bouquet in center of
mix. (Before serving discard!) Saute eggplant and
zucchini in oil 3 or 4 minutes. Drain oil. Add to
tomato mixture. Season with salt and pepper to taste.

Pour in an oven proof casserole. Bake 350 for 30 minutes. (TIP: Ratatouille is a tasty fresh vegetable dish hot and a tasty side dish served cold which is how Tony liked it, as a condiment on its second day of melding in refrigerator.) Makes about 4 cups.

TONY'S ITALIAN SPINACH PIE

3 lbs fresh spinach leaves, cleaned and stemmed OR
2 pkgs frozen spinach, squeezed of water when thawed
6 T. minced onion
6 T. grated Parmesan cheese
6 T. cream
1 beaten egg
5 T. melted butter
2 minced garlic cloves, salt and pepper
1/2 to 3/4 cup Ritz cracker crumbs mixed with 1 T. butter

Cook fresh spinach in salted, sugared water until tender. If using frozen thawed use in recipe as is. Add and mix together remaining ingredients, reserving crumbs and 1 T. butter for top. Place all in a large buttered pie plate or shallow baking dish. Sprinkle with the buttered crumbs. Mound up in center. Bake at 350 until golden, about 25 minutes. Serves 4 to 6. Cut in wedges to serve, can be a luncheon entree or a side vegetable dish. (Lucy was particularly fond of spinach (and everything else.) (TIP: when knife inserted in center of pie comes out clean, and top is puffed the pie is done.)

BETTIE HAMILTON

NATIVE FRESH SLICED TOMATOES WITH BASIL, OIL AND GROUND BLACK PEPPER (SEE SALADS)

AUNT MAE'S GARDEN THINNINGS = the first new peas, baby carrots and potatoes)

Equal amounts of the very first peas, marble-size potatoes with the skin on, dug from the side of a potato hill, and baby carrots no longer than your little finger. Shell peas and scrub carrots and potatoes. Cook separately in 3 skillets of boiling salted and sugared water. Drain. Toss all together in a large mixing bowl with salt and pepper and a big dollop of sweet butter. Amounts depend upon number of diners.

(TIP: Keep potatoes and carrots whole. Thin out your vegetable garden early on in order to serve this wonderful, fresh vegetable dish. Cannot be surpassed for simplicity of assembly, all you need is a vegetable garden! You won't find these little jewels in the store. Gild the lily with a sprinkle of chopped parsley or fresh, chopped chives over pat of butter on top. Almost any dish can be vegetarian by omitting meat, adding cheese.)

###

ABOUT THE AUTHOR

Award winning artist, Bettie Hamilton, lives on Marblehead Harbor, Mass. with her husband Jack, and dog, Lucy."